C000121660

© Frank T. Morgan. Bermuda, B.O.T., 2018. All rights reserved.
www.morganpublishers.com

For Kara

May we come and go like swallows.

Thanking (in alphabetical order) Shane D. Snow: visionary and friend; Jane Alexander (who took in this stray book); Claire, Gary, Ellen, Alan, Anna, Dana, Betsy, Steve, Ladd, Ruby, Linea & J.D. (who took in this stray hack); **Lola** for sharing her friends and for *being* a friend; the good doctor Grant Farquhar, M.D., who sees through this brittle, crazy glass; Christopher Patton, Esq.: peerless attorney & brother; Benjamin Blum, Esq.: peerless attorney & friend; **to my Patrons Alia, Janelle & Debra:** *artis amici habere debent*—the arts must have friends; poet & seer DeAnna Morgan (*Holding the Sun*); to my father, who loved *Mutiny on the Bounty* and *Men Against The Sea*); to Deen, my first cover-to-cover reader; to Jared, with love (*Noro lim, Asfaloth!*); more follow…

Foreword

DOCTOR Stewart Henry Scott lived in Scotland.

In 1838, when Victoria was being crowned Queen of England, Doctor Scott was keeping a little practice in Bread Street, Edinburgh, with the help of his younger associate Albert Grey.

Now if you've read *The Chronicles of Narnia* (and I highly recommend you do) then you know that tall, exotic queens tend to be tricky and dangerous. Victoria stood five foot and she was about as exotic as a cucumber, so of course she made an excellent monarch. She ruled for sixty-three and a half years, and most people agree that her reign was comparatively peaceful and prosperous.[1]

Doctor Scott was comparatively peaceful and prosperous too—mostly because at the distinguished age of fifty-five[2] the doctor wasn't married, and he didn't have any children. So when he wasn't keeping his practice in Bread Street, Doctor Scott amused himself by reading books about ancient history, and he would take long holidays tramping all over Scotland and Ireland, poking his bald head and his long nose and his wiry mutton-chop whiskers into ancient tombs and crumbling castles.

Doctor Scott wanted to know how people ever came to live in a place so far-removed as Scotland. Scotland is beautiful, but rugged and wild, and in bygone days the people who lived there were rugged and wild too. He learned about times, centuries ago, when Scotland's charming capital was little more than a grim fortress perched on the edge of a lawless frontier; when the noblemen all carried hidden daggers and old-fashioned pistols, and they plotted and schemed and fought in brave duels and cowardly ambushes.

---

[1] Unless you happened to be a soldier or a chimney-sweep.

[2] Life expectancy was dismal in the early 1800s. Less than 45 years for British men.

The Borderlands between England and Scotland were even more perilous. Sometimes the English knights would invade Scotland leaving fire and destruction where they passed, and sometimes the Scottish lords would go pillaging and plundering in England. A good number of Bordermen made their living as soldiers of fortune, fighting for anyone who paid them and changing sides whenever they pleased. The Scots called these outlaws "reivers"[3] or "lost men." The reivers' unceasing banditry made it particularly dangerous to travel in the Borders.

So it happened, long ago, that the reivers found a champion in the notorious Sir Francis Stewart, fifth Earl of Bothwell. Francis was the favorite nephew of Mary Queen of Scots, and he was as handsome and as charming and as daring as a man could be. But there was a streak of pure madness in Sir Francis. His madness infected all his schemes (and proved his ruin, in the end).

There are enough stories about the wild earl to fill a dozen books, yet the strangest tale of Francis Stewart was never told—not until doctor Stewart Henry Scott of Edinburgh happened upon an ancient, leather-bound book in a crumbling wooden chest in Hermitage Castle, Roxburghshire, on the evening of April 7, 1838.

Writing in his diary Doctor Scott would later recall that he pulled a heavy, grayish tome more than eight inches thick out of a much-decayed wooden box. He said the pages were of vellum,[4] badly stained and smelling like a leg of mutton that has been left out overnight in a warm pantry.

Doctor Scott was not a superstitious man, and he certainly didn't believe in anything so unscientific as ghosts. But as the last gleam of blood-red sunset faded from the western rim of the moors, and as the rising wind began to make a trembling cry through the gaps in the castle's ruined keep, then the doctor began to hope (rather unscientifically) that ghosts didn't believe in *him*.

The book was so worn by time and decay that Doctor Scott could only make out a few words in the flicker of his little lantern. But before he left the ruin (rather briskly) Doctor Scott saw the title page was written in bold, even letters which read:

---

[3] Raiders

[4] Parchment made from sheepskin or calfskin, scraped thin.

The LAST WILL and TESTAMENT of

The Pirate John Blackjohn

*Transcribed and rendered in **Modern English** by **Dr. Stewart Henry Scott, M.D.***

*Edited for **today's reader** by **F. T. Morgan, Esq.***

Introduction

From the letters of Doctor Stewart Henry Scott—

The Sign of the Buck and Crown
Newcastleton, Roxburghshire – April 7, 1838

Albert:

I'm terribly excited. I've found an old book, hidden (it would seem) in the inner wall of the castle keep at Hermitage here in Roxburghshire.[5] I got into Newcastleton on Thursday and I meant to chase a rumor about an ancient burial-howe while my little holiday lasts, but then I met a shepherd who told me the lords of Buckley[6] made some attempt to restore Hermitage years ago when Sir Walter was retoured,[7] and I simply *had* to go and have a look at it. I think the workmen must have disturbed the crevice where the book was lying. I spotted a brick of a lighter shade than the others and it proved to be a sort of tile, two feet broad and a couple of inches thick. A little rotted chest lay behind it (which immediately fell apart), but the book inside was admirably well-preserved given the length of time it must have lain there in the cold and damp.

The book is full eight inches thick and I have only just begun to decipher the first page. It seems to be written in old-fashioned Scots. From the title it purports to be a "Last Will and Testament," though what else it may contain I cannot guess. I'm all a-twitter (as you can imagine) and I want to begin transcribing it immediately. I'll send my work back to you by post so long as I am in Roxburghshire. The accommodations here are dreadful of course (might as well be sleeping in Hermitage) but *cuivis dolori remedium patientia est.*[8]

---

[5] The former county of Roxburghshire was located in the Scottish borders, roughly fifty miles south of Edinburgh.

[6] Buccleuch

[7] A nobleman is "retoured" when he officially receives his predecessor's lands and title.

[8] Latin: *Patience cures all suffering*

I'll have to run to catch the post. More follows, whether that's agreeable to you or not.

Yours.

—*S.H.S.*

The Sign of the Buck and Crown
Newcastleton, Roxburghshire – April 25, 1838

Albert:

Please find herein my first batch of transcription from this extraordinary book, *The Last Will and Testament of the Pirate John Blackjohn*. I wanted to send this sooner. Foul chance and foul weather have conspired to keep the post stuck at Hawick and me abed[9] at the Buck. I've got a fit of coughing for which there is no remedy save white pine syrup with a generous admixture of English courage.

In between coughs I'm completely engrossed in *John Blackjohn*. I've been steaming the book like an oyster. A good hour suspended over a hot kettle and the vellum becomes flexible such that I can pull the leaves apart and blot them with alcohol. Then I coat them with mineral oil and leave it out to dry with matchsticks and bits of wool keeping the pages apart. Nearly a quarter of the book has come free this way. I'm deciphering the script as quickly as bad light permits. (And now I've coughed the candle out!)

You'll see it reads nothing like a will. For convenience I'm putting it down it in modern English, as I fear neither you nor I can read *ye olde braid Scots*[10] comfortably. I shall badly need your help to keep my notes in order. I remain—

Yours.

—*S.H.S.*

---

[9] In bed
[10] The old broad Scots, *i.e.*, the old northern variety of early modern English.

— Here begins Doctor Scott's transcription —

Prologue

To my dear nephew Charlie—

This must seem strange to you, Charlie: your uncle James writing to you in a book like this. You're a big strong boy now, and someday when you're grown you'll learn that you are my only heir, the last of our line.

I am sick, Charlie. I cling to life like an oak leaf clings to a snowy branch. This is my LAST WILL AND TESTAMENT.

All my money is gone. Silver and gold have I none; only a weary curse. And here's a dead man's counsel for you: face the dragon sword in hand and you'll die a hero's death. Or you may run from the dragon for a while, but the dragon will find you, my boy. The dragon will find you at the last.

I can feel him now. Gnawing at the root of the tree.

I lost my father when I was just a boy. I was about ten years old when they brought him home across the winter fields, slung over his horse like a barley sack. He'd gone out reiving[11] against Bewcastle in the Westmarch,[12] but all Kenneth McKenna ever got for his love of English cattle was a pike-thrust between the ribs and a young widow at home with three boys to feed. Our quarrel with the English was ancient when the house of Scott still held the Border and my father was just a boy running barefoot along the Tweed. My father and my uncle Andrew farmed a little freehold near Buckley[13] in Roxburghshire until the day my father rode against the English under the banner of Sir William Scott.

All my father ever knew was how to farm and how to fight. Someday you'll learn, Charlie, that a man is just a glass which traps his fiery soul inside. When the man withers, then his restless soul gets eager to slip its strange mooring, and wander free among the stars.

---

[11] Raiding
[12] Northern England
[13] Buccleuch. Pronounce *BUCK-lew*

This is a story about a girl—and you must save her, Charlie, for I cannot.
Read this, I beg you!
My soul is ready to embark.

CHAPTER 1

Nota Bene[14]—The ink changes here. The handwriting is similar, but not the same. I think the first page was a sort of preamble added to the beginning of the book at a later date. It begins:

When I was sixteen I saw a girl in the woods. I was hiding there.

Peter was gone and John was sick again, so uncle Andrew sent me to the fields to guard the barley from the crows. But I thought bird-scaring was child's work and I was angry. Then some fighting men of the Kerrs rode by with their spurs all tinkling and they laughed and called me 'brae wee mannie'[15] for so terrifying the hoodies,[16] and I was ashamed. So I slipped into the friendly cover of the woods.

That was eight days after my older brother Peter went to fight the English for Sir Francis Stewart our lord. Francis and his knights were leading an army of reivers[17] over the borders to bring fire and vengeance to the cowards of Northumbria. Peter was eighteen and a man now. He was to ride in the earl's train and guard the army's stores. (Little enough of that.) It was early April and food was scarce, but the earl's men would soon be rich with plunder. They'd butcher fat English cattle and come back heavy with gold.

It was a fine sight when Peter rode off. The fighting men of Selkirk and Haick[18] and the nearby glens all gathered in our little churchyard in Buckley, and our priest, Father Lara, blessed them with the sign of the cross (for Buckley kept the old faith).[19] They gave Peter the bright tartan[20] of Clan Scott

---

[14] Latin: *note well*
[15] Scots: *Brave little man*
[16] Scots: *crows*
[17] Scots: *Raiders*
[18] Present-day Hawick
[19] Roman Catholicism

to carry on an ash pole, and then all the fighting men raised the Scott battle-cry—*A Bellendaine!*[21] —and Peter (riding Jenny, our old mare) waved the pole in the air and joined in.

I hardly knew him he looked so fierce—with my father's sword by his side and that wild note on his lips. But Jenny had no saddle; just an old blanket tied on with a rope, and Peter clung to her with his knees. My mother cried as they rode away, but I don't think Peter knew it, for he never once looked back.

There was always something unwell about Peter—not about his body, but about his soul. I felt it even though I worshipped him. He could be so kind sometimes, and then so terribly cruel. It showed in his face, which was narrow and sharp. His eyes were like knife-slits; so light blue they were nearly white, and when he got angry (and he often did) then his eyes got narrower still and his whole face went hard and flat like a snake. I was afraid of him.

Inside the woods the new leaves were beginning to open. The elms were still bare, but I liked them just the same. They stretched their twisted arms up into the gray sky while the rain ran down their trunks in silvery threads. I was nearly wet through.

So was the girl. She was tall and slender, with dirty bare feet. She stared at me like a startled fawn and for a moment all the world was quiet. I was caught by her strange eyes.

Her eyes are blue, I thought.

Then she was gone, and it seemed as if the birds suddenly started up singing again.

The girl simply vanished. One moment she stood under the oak tree—lips parted as if she were about to say something—and the next moment I was alone. It gave me an odd feeling inside. I stood there a moment, pondering.

Then I turned and plunged deeper into the forest, making for the hermitage of Friar Kol.

---

[20] Plaid fabric. The pattern could sometimes denote a particular house or clan.

[21] Scots: *To Bellendaine!* Located northwest of Hawick, Bellendaine (Bellenden) was a customary Clan Scott gathering place in times of war.

Friar Kollam Keeli lived in an odd little hut in the middle of Ettrick Forest. I wanted to talk to him because I knew the girl was a fairy, and I thought brother Kol (being a man of Éireann[22]) ought to know about such things. Friar Kol came to Alba[23] from Éireann when he was a young monk "to repay Alba," Kol said, "for sending us holy Saint Padraig[24] in olden times."

Kol had been a novitiate[25] at the famous abbey on Iona, but Father Lara called him the Irish Heretic and said he'd strayed from the true path in many respects, "foremost in his forehead." Irish monks persisted in shaving the front half of their heads rather than shaving their hair in a circle around the top, "as our Savior instructed." This, Lara said, was the practice of Kol's heathen forefathers, the druids, who worshipped the demoness Dana in oak groves at midsummer instead of praying to the blessed Virgin in cloisters, as they ought.

For my part I thought it was a silly argument, at least as far as Friar Kol was concerned. Kol hadn't any hair to shave, unless it were within an inch of his ears. He was very nearly bald. Kol liked to say God himself had decided where his tonsure[26] ought to be. He quite made up for it with so much hair everywhere else: blanketing his thick forearms, spilling out at the neck of his cassock, springing from his chin in wiry black curls. Uncle Andrew once fought the Irish pirates in Cumbria and he said the men of Éireann were red-faced and red-haired and blue-eyed and vicious as dogs. But Friar Kol was the blackest and the kindliest man I knew. His beard was black. His bushy eyebrows were black. His eyes were black and bright as jet.[27] And from the tips of his toes to the crown of his shiny head, Friar Kol was black with soot, for he was a charcoal-burner by trade.

The leaves of years lay thick on the forest floor. Weird shapes of trees left bare by winter faded into the crowded distance. And still the rain filtered down from the low gray sky. I pressed forward in dizzy starts and turns,

---

[22] Ireland. Pronounce *EH-rin*.

[23] The largest of the British Isles, including England, Scotland and Wales.

[24] Patrick

[25] Novitiatcy is one of the early stages in joining a monastic order.

[26] The shaved area of monk's head. Wearing the tonsure was a common practice of clerics during the Middle Ages.

[27] Black semi-precious stone

crawling under trunks, scraping through brambles, stumbling over the rotting bones of trees.

At length and by good fortune I struck upon a faint path that led to Friar Kol's cottage—little more than an easier track among the trees, with the wet mould lying deep on it. I started to run, brim-full of my news about the fairy.

Deep in the wood the trees hid a rocky hollow. The glen's northern face was steep and overhanging, carved out by some ancient stream run dry. In the shelter of this outcropping there grew an enormous elm, so close to the cliff that the rocks bit into its gnarled trunk. Buttressed between the tree and the cliff sagged Friar Kol's little hermitage, like an old man propped up between a staff and a stone wall.

Nearer the hermitage a change came over the woodland. The trees, which had been so dense and grasping before, grew farther and farther apart. Now they reached their arms toward the sky in a comfortable way. The clinging undergrowth disappeared altogether. Ferns lifted their feathery heads above the rotting leaves. Rocks poked stubbornly out of the mould. And tiny yellow flowers (which the rocks had secretly been guarding) winked suddenly from a hundred cracks and crevices.

The whole forest seemed to stretch itself and breathe easy, and I was so caught up in the scene that before I knew it I had walked straight into a perilous fairy's ring of red-capped toadstools, where I was likely to fall under some enchantment.

No sooner had my foot touched the ground inside the ring when suddenly the sun broke through the clouds and turned every drop on every twig into a diamond. The sun touched the rocks and the toadstools. It touched the ferns and the leaves and the raindrops. At last it came to rest on a little bald friar, all covered in soot. He was smiling and leaning on a shovel.

"James McKenna!" he said.

The mouldy track had grown into a well-beaten path. With one last turn around a big ash-tree, the path dropped down into the glen. Beside it were the charcoal pits where Kol set logs on fire, then buried them and left them to smoulder in the airless soil. Heavy baskets of charcoal stood in a neat row. Friar Kol would take these to the village for coin or barter.

With his charcoal and with his garden, with the charity of his friends—and with the grace of God, Friar Kol kept body and soul together and rose each morning to hear the birds sing Lauds. He was whole.

Kol put down his shovel and wiped his forehead. I broke into a run.

"I saw a fairy!" I panted.

Kol grinned.

"Now that's strange," he said. "There's a girl inside my house says she saw a dirty, freckle-face boy standing in the woods, all wet and crying."

(I had been crying.)

"I was *not* crying!" I said angrily.

"Of course not, of course not," Kol put his thick arm around my shoulders. "You know girls." He lowered his voice conspiratorially. "Half mad. Something to do with the moon. Come inside!"

Inside was another world.

Kol's floor was bare clay, so hard-packed from years of wear that it was shiny and smooth as a cathedral. There weren't any rooms; only a loft raised on log pillars. Kol's ceiling was a neat dome of willow branches expertly woven together. Kol cut them when they were green, oiled them, and then covered them in pitch like a basket.

Fascinating things were everywhere. Bottles and flasks. Bunches of herbs. Horn lanterns. Tools and instruments of a thousand mysterious purposes. Hides. Ropes. A rusty sword wrapped in leather. And, in a special corner of its own lying open on a rough-hewn lectern: Kol's magnificent bible.

The bible was richly illuminated; more fit for a cathedral than for a hermit's cell. Kol had illustrated it himself, from Genesis all the way to Maccabaeus, when he was a young monk at the abbey of Iona.

Innocent that I was, I never wondered why a hermit would have a book that might have graced an archbishop's pulpit.[28] Every page was a rainbow. Scaly green dragons transformed themselves into letters, then into knot-work, then back into dragons again. Knights and men-at-arms marched against the Saracens. Wild Tartars charged on shaggy ponies, shooting arrows and screaming war-cries.

---

[28] Books were hand-copied and extremely valuable before printing became common.

And of course there were scenes from the holy book itself. Prophets and apostles; battles and miracles. Kol's feminine subjects (mother Eve, for instance, or the fastidious Bathsheba) showed the most painstaking skill with the brush. I wondered if the young Friar Kol might have appreciated the female form a bit more than a churchman ought.

But the brilliant scenes eased the dull winter hours when Kol taught my brothers and me to read, scratching words onto a rawhide screen with bits of charcoal. Kol's bible was Latin, of course, and we never learned much in it. But Kol used the square letters to fashion new words in Scots, and we took to that more quickly. John could always best Peter and me at spelling. He said he wanted to be a priest like Friar Kol someday.

John spent the most time with Kol because John was often sick. His crooked body was too weak for the plough. John halted on his right leg, and he mostly got around on a crutch. His arm was bent and would not go straight and his nose went somewhat slantwise across his wry face. But if the children ever made fun of John, then they made it from a considerable distance. Peter was savage when he was angry.

At the back of Kol's house stood a comfortable hearth. In front of the hearth sat my fairy.

My heart sank.

She was just a poor farm girl of maybe fifteen. She was sitting on Kol's three-legged stool, eating oat porridge out of a clay pot. Then I remembered Peter and the Kerrs and the crows and the endless rain, and I very nearly cried again.

Kol swept in behind me.

"I give you," he said grandly, "mistress Diana O'Neil, my countrywoman." He turned smartly and made a low bow to the barefoot girl on the stool.

"At present Diana is a guest of the good farmer Sowter, who lives hard by. But today she graces my humble cell, where I am a prisoner in Christ Jesus—"

"Amen!" the girl interrupted.

"—where I am—" Friar Kol trailed off, losing his thread. He coughed. "Will you have some porridge, my boy?"

17

"No, if you please!" I returned haughtily. "I think *she* needs it more than me." I knew who she was now. Old Sowter's bastard niece; come from County Kildare to make herself useful on his farm.

The girl looked stricken. Her white face went red and there were tears in her eyes, but I was so angry at her for not being a fairy and for catching me crying in the woods that I felt no pity.

Kol shot me a stern look. "She needs it indeed," he said quietly. "Thank you, James."

The girl turned away from us. In the dim light I could see a blue bruise running down her delicate cheek. There was dried blood at the tip of her ear. Then I tried hard not to feel sorry, because it wasn't fair that *I* should feel guilty when I was the one who'd been wronged.

Kol studied us both a moment.

Then, "Come, my children!" he said brightly. "One sermon I'll give you—or a hymn—and then it's off with ye both. I've prayers to say for the soul of Wicked Wat,[29] and—my faith!—where he is now he'll be needing them."

We both brightened at that. Kol's 'sermons' ranged from long discourses on the ways of ducks to strange tales about the ancient Irish heroes before holy Patrick came and turned them all into saints.

"Preach a sermon about fairies," I demanded. "And giants."

"Very well," Kol sighed. He took a stool for himself and sat down by the hearth.

"Long ago," Kol began, "before our Savior ever walked in Galilee, the fairies came to Éireann from Avalon—the Apple Isle. They were led by Dana, daughter of the queen of Avalon. In Éireann the fairies found a simple fishing people without wagons or swords or books or anything of the sort.

"Worse yet—" Kol scowled ominously—"the fisher people were slaves to the terrible Firbolg. (Those are your giants, James.) The Firbolg kept the fisher people like cattle, for work and for slaughter."

"The Firbolg *ate* them?"

---

[29] Sir Walter Scott of Branxholme and Buccleuch (1495 - 1552). Known as "wicked Wat," Sir Walter was a notorious border reiver with a deep hatred for the English. In 1552 he was set upon and stabbed to death on High Street in Edinburgh by members of rival clan Kerr, with whom Clan Scott was feuding.

"They ate them indeed!" Kol said warmly. "But Dana and her followers fought a tremendous battle with the giants and drove them into the wastelands. After that there was peace. Dana chose some from among the fisher people to learn her arts, and from then on they were called the *Tuatha Dé Danann*[30]—the People of Dana. Dana loved Éireann. She and her people watched over it, and the island was like a garden until the coming of the Gaels.

"And who are the Gaels?"

"*I* am a Gael," Kol replied, "for one. The Gaels were a fierce and a warlike people. They came from the East in ancient times—some from the coasts of Belgae and Gaul,[31] and some from as far away as Spain. At first they were only traders, or pirates raiding the coasts. But as the years went by the Gaels pushed and deeper into Éireann. Soon they were bringing women and children, horses and cattle, scythes and plows.

"And the Gaels brought swords!" Kol growled, looking up at me so fiercely from under his bushy eyebrows that I jumped. "Gaels fought Gaels. The war was endless. Many of Dana's people were slaughtered."

"Didn't the fairies have swords?" I asked. "You said they drove away the giants."

Kol laughed. "You can't kill a giant with a sword, James," he said. "Imagine stabbing a rock!" He chuckled and wiped his eyes. "They drove out the Firbolg, yes, but Dana and her people didn't fight with swords. They had strange weapons."

Kol got up and prodded the fire with one end of a log.

"Dana comes when this world is in grave danger," he continued. "Sometimes she takes the form of a white doe that no man can catch. Sometimes she passes through the woodlands like the wind, riding on a mighty stag. Dana guards the wild places, and she teaches her secret songs to those who can hear."

I glanced over at Diana O'Neil. She was leaning forward on her stool with a look of rapt attention.

Kol resumed his seat.

---

[30] Irish: *People of the Goddess Dana*
[31] Modern-day France

"The Tuatha Dé Danann held back the Gaels," he said. "Or they did at first, anyway. But Dana knew the fight would never end. Every spring brought more people from the east. The fisher folk were doubtful allies. Some stayed true to Dana, but most became enamored of the Gaels: of their fierceness and cunning and of their swords and golden ornaments. The Gaels worshipped Lú,[32] the Shining One, and they prized valor above all. They would rather die a warrior's death than live to be bent by sickness and age."

Kol sat silent a moment, staring into the fire.

"A noble race, the Gaels," he said reflectively. "Bloody, yes. But it's a bloody world. They were born to war, and war was all they ever knew."

He scraped his stool nearer the hearth. "Be that as it may," he said, "Dana would not fight on. She gathered up her people and as many of the fisher folk as remained true to her, and all at once they vanished and left Éireann forever. Where they went none can tell, but people said she took them all to Fairyland, to live with her in bliss. The green isle weeps for Dana now, but Dana will never return."

Kol sighed. He got up and stretched his calloused hands over the fire. I stole another furtive look at Diana. She was watching Friar Kol, waiting for him to go on.

"And the People of Dana?" I ventured. "What *could* they do? With no swords, I mean?"

"Oh, the Tuatha Dé Danann had strange gifts," Kol replied. "Sometimes they could take the forms of swans or salmon. Their songs could call down the hail—lightning, even. Avalon had many friends and alliances then, but that was long ago."

"So has anyone ever really *seen* a fairy?" (I was getting skeptical.)

"Why, yes!" Kol exclaimed. He strode purposefully across the room. "Of course! People most certainly have. In fact, when I was a young monk at Iona—"

Kol stopped in front of his beautiful bible. His hand rested affectionately on the margin, where Saint Michael with a flaming sword was serenely impaling a writhing green dragon.

---

[32] The Celtic god Lugh (or Lú) was associated with the sun. Some scholars find similarity between Lugh and the Greek god Apollo.

"—while I was laboring on this very book I happened to meet a pirate who—"

"You met a *pirate*?" I interrupted.

"Aye. That I did."

"Didn't pirates plunder that abbey? And carry off its treasures? And— and kill the monks and everyone?"

"They did!" Kol returned cheerfully. "Several times. But the last great sacking was centuries ago, and this particular pirate wasn't such a bad sort. He and his mates on the brig *Otter* had disrupted a good deal of shipping (mostly Dutch), and they'd sent a fair number of innocent men to the cold black bottom of the sea. But the pirate was quite sorry for it. He said he wanted me to say prayers for his soul (me hardly more than a boy!) and he went on confessing and apologizing like it was *me* he'd sunk off the Dogger Bank in a March gale."

Kol came back to the hearth.

"Wasn't the pirate's fault," Kol went on. "Not entirely, anyway. Son of a poor farmer. Big lad. Family couldn't feed him, so he goes to sea when he's just twelve. Falls in with a wild crew—"

Kol stopped short and looked at the door. We could hear footsteps outside.

Without a knock the door burst open. In stomped uncle Andrew, red-faced and dripping with a muddy black staff in his hand. I jumped to my feet in terror. Fairies, pirates, enchanted isles—all vanished. In their place: grim old uncle Andrew, with his eyes scowling deep in his craggy head. The sun was setting. I'd forgotten the barley.

I cringed, eyeing his staff.

But uncle Andrew smiled.

"Up, lad!" he said. "Peter's come home."

CHAPTER 2

Peter was home, but he wasn't the same.

It was evening. We all knew the raid had gone badly, but Peter wouldn't talk about it. John said he came home walking. His bare feet were tied up in rags, and he was alone.

Peter sat on the floor, staring vacantly into the fire. Every few moments he would tug at a dirty bandage wrapped around his right hand. John sat down beside him, and then uncle Andrew and my mother came near.

Peter looked around at us. He smiled strangely as he slowly unwound the cloth from his hand. In the firelight we could see an ugly black 'H'—cracked and bloody at the edges—burned deep into Peter's palm.

Mother screamed. Peter only laughed.

"H for *heretic*," he said.

A week went by. Then another. It was early May, and still Peter wouldn't talk to me. He wouldn't even fight—that was what irked me most. I knew he was ignoring me because he'd been on a raid and he was a man now.

One morning I tried to draw him out, though I knew I'd get a beating for it.

"Where's Jenny, Peter?" I taunted. "Where's our horse, Sir Peter? Will *you* pull the plow, Sir Peter?"

I braced myself for a thrashing. The old Peter would have blackened both my eyes for half so much. But Peter only winced and pressed his burned hand as if it hurt him.

Uncle Andrew was listening. Without a word he went over to the hearth and laid his big hand gently on Peter's shoulder.

Peter didn't stir.

Then with a sudden start he turned and looked up at uncle Andrew, blinking. Their eyes met for a moment. Then Peter got slowly to his feet, and they went out together.

I was burning with shame. Uncle Andrew wasn't a gentle man. I knew he and and Peter understood each other because they had both seen battle: uncle Andrew in Arran and Peter in Northumbria. They were fighters. I was just a boy. Peter didn't want to be my brother any more.

With my eyes on the ground, I trudged out to the fields behind them.

At midday uncle Andrew and Peter went home. I was hungry and I ought to have gone home too, but I was ashamed to face them after what I'd said that morning. So when uncle Andrew put his mattock down I lingered behind. The moment their backs were to the hedge I bolted for the friendly woods.

The forest was a cathedral. Trees made a vaulted arch overhead, bluebells a living carpet under foot. Then the rain stopped, and suddenly every bird in every tree was singing like a choir.

Down in a misty hollow, a fairy ring grew around an oak tree. In the tree perched a handsome pink-and-gray bullfinch. He was busy cracking seeds in his short bill, but he stopped to watch me as I passed. Suddenly I felt very cross and very hungry.

"Damn fat bird!" I muttered. "Him eating while I starve!"

The bullfinch cocked his head as if he heard. He fixed me with one shiny black eye, said *chirp chirp*, and then he went back to cracking seeds in a satisfied way.

I growled at him. The bullfinch hadn't learned to fear men, but *I* would teach him. I bent down, picked up a rock, and launched it at the bird.

My rock took the bullfinch square in the middle of his folded wing. He dropped onto the mossy ground and lay there fluttering and panting. I stood over him with my hands on my hips and a cruel smile on my face.

A twig snapped behind me. I spun around.

Dirty, ragged Diana O'Neil sprang out from behind a fallen pine (where she'd evidently been hiding). With a cry of grief she ran to the bullfinch. Dropping to her her knees beside it she gently picked up the wounded bird.

"*Really?*" I asked loftily. "You're going to blubber over *that*? It's just a dirty bird!"

Diana didn't seem to hear. She was rocking from side to side, whispering to the bullfinch. Between her fingers I could see the delicate pinkish feathers open and close as its tiny breast heaved.

Diana shut her eyes. She began to murmur a sort of song. I couldn't understand the words, but her voice was urgent and pleading. It gave me an uneasy feeling inside. I was starting to be ashamed of what I'd done, so I decided to interrupt her.

"Shut up!" I jeered. "Stop wailing. It's bound to die and *I'm* not sorry. It's just a finch anyway."

Diana was on her feet. Her blue eyes burned with pure hate.

"Wicked boy!"

Quicker than a breath Diana pulled back her dainty fist. Then she punched me square on the nose.

Peter never hit so hard. I fell backward into the leaves with silvery sparks wriggling in front of my eyes. Blood streamed from my nose, dripping off my chin and blackening my shirt. Diana was back on the ground again. Her song was different now: more comforting and more sad. The pink feathers opened once, then gently closed again. The little bird was dead.

Diana set the bullfinch tenderly on a green pillow of moss that lay hidden between the roots of the oak tree. She got up. Tears were running down her cheeks. I touched my nose and instantly regretted it. It was broken. Diana looked down at me without a trace of pity. Then she stepped over the fairy ring and reached out toward my bleeding face.

I cringed backward. Diana only took a step nearer and cupped her hand (not very gently) over my nose. I yelped from the pain but she held firm. She spoke some words which I didn't understand and then she took her hand away.

"You're a wicked boy."

She turned on her heel.

"And an idiot!" she called over her shoulder.

The white mist closed around her. I was alone again, like the first time.

Strange to say, no sooner had Diana touched my face than my nose suddenly left off bleeding. The pounding in my head began to fade. After a minute or two I had to laugh in spite of myself: the pain was gone and my nose (when I finally got up the courage to touch it) felt straight and ordinary again.

A different pain set in. It sat in the bottom of my stomach like a stone.

Wicked boy, I thought.

Peter was a man. Uncle Andrew was a man. I was just a wicked boy, playing at boys' games.

I got up slowly and started for home. Storm clouds were gathering. The forest looked gray and ordinary again.

It began to rain.

CHAPTER 3

From the letters of Doctor Stewart Henry Scott—

Branxholme Castle, Roxburghshire

May 1, 1838

Dear Albert:

You're probably wondering where I've run off to. (And, no, I'm not stranded in the Orkneys again; things are going swimmingly, in fact.) I'm proud to report that I've come up in the world, Albert Grey! And you thought I was just a humble Bread Street sawbones?[33] Nothing of the sort! Allow me to inform you that in this, the sixth decade of my life, I am finally rubbing elbows with nobility! I am the guest of no less person than young Sir Walter Montagu Douglas-Scott, fifth duke of Buckley.

Granted, Sir Walter doesn't *know* I'm his guest, but that's no matter. The young duke lives in London, mostly. His steward, a Mr. William Fitzhugh, has let me into his ancestral castle at Branxholme (that's about an hour's brisk walk from Hawick.) Fitzhugh says His Grace hardly ever visits his northern estates. The old stronghouse mostly stands empty now, ghostly sheets and blankets draped over all the furniture. Apparently Sir Walter was here a good deal last April when they were making alterations. Fitzhugh said he wanted the place to look more 'baronial,' but you can't turn a sow's ear into a silk purse, as they say in Fife. This is a tough, useful old house. It was built to hold the Middle March against the English, not to hold garden parties with croquet and cucumber sandwiches.

---

[33] Doctor

Branxholme is gloomy inside; not overly spacious. The windows are deep-set and narrow. They look out warily, it seems to me, as if they were still afraid of arrows. Fitzhugh has lent me a garret at the top of the ancient tower (the oldest part of the building) but it's considerably more cheerful than the haunted rooms in the main house. My garret at least looks occupied. I have a window looking down on the Tiviot[34] (just a narrow burn[35] here) and there's a meadow on the other side where I mean to poke about for arrowheads and such.

But for the present I'm determined to keep to my garret and work on transcribing more of this old book I found at Hermitage: *The Last Will and Testament of the Pirate John Blackjohn.* I've got about half the pages unstuck now and I'm eager to read them. I confess I haven't told Mr. Fitzhugh precisely what I'm about. It occurred to me that *John Blackjohn* belongs (strictly speaking) to young Sir Walter, as I found the book in Sir Walter's own Hermitage Castle where I was (strictly speaking) a trespasser.

So I told Fitzhugh I'm an amateur historian on holiday (which is perfectly true) and I gave him an old Roman denarius which I happened to have in my valise (he loves old coins). When he heard I was a doctor of course he had a half-dozen aches to tell me about (people always do). I said the best remedy for rheumatism is trout fishing, which treatment I offered to administer personally at first light tomorrow. So Fitzhugh has gone to see about the tackle and in the morning we mean to angle at a little ruined weir in the burn. Fitzhugh is very protective of this particular pool; says it's a good one and not even the gamekeeper knows about it.

You'll laugh, Albert, but I think we ought to make a copy of my work for safekeeping. I know, I know. *It's not the holy grail*, you were going to say. But what if it *is*? What if it's an important historical discovery, I mean? It would certainly be my first.

So humor me, and there's a good fellow. Kindly deliver every batch of transcription, so soon as you receive it, to Mr. Constantine at the scrivener's in Cowgate. Constantine copies tolerably well, and I'm not at all convinced the

---

[34] Modern-day Teviot
[35] Creek

man can read. If he can't, then so much the better: our patients won't hear I've gone off chasing fairies.

I have, sir, the honor to be, &c.

—SHS

CHAPTER 4

Doctor Scott's transcription—

Nota Bene—the next page is badly stained and unreadable. The only words I can make out are Peter, June, 1593, *and* Green Lady. *The other side has some kind of drawing on It. Looks like a woman's head surrounded by flowers (though it could just as well be a plate of bacon and spinach). I'll have to simply move on to the next page. James McKenna continues:*

Summer came, and the days were endless. It got so warm that Peter and I could sleep in the hayloft over Jenny's empty stable. Peter was more like himself now, although he was still oddly silent. Often he would sit up late into the night, staring into the fire and rubbing his scarred hand.

There came a June morning when I set out for Friar's Kol's hermitage with John and a basket of eggs. Mother and uncle Andrew were gone to market in Haick and wouldn't be back all day. Peter had slipped away on business of his own.

John and I left the cottage together and we'd just crossed the cabbage patch when all at once we noticed Peter standing in the lane a little way off. He wasn't alone. Two proud gray horses paced in front of him. On their backs, two proud gray soldiers looked down at Peter. One of them spoke. We couldn't hear what he said but Peter's face looked solemn. I wondered if he knew them from the Northumbria raid, and I was trying to get a better look at their harness when suddenly they both turned and thundered off. Then the fragrant green arms of the forest took us in and I forgot all about Peter in the blush of the midsummer morning.

"We need to be on our guard," I announced.

We were halfway to Friar Kol's hermitage. I was walking slowly so John could keep up with me on his crutch.

"On our guard?" John puffed. "Why?"

"It's this path here," I said, scuffling my feet on it. "This path is enchanted."

"*This* path? The path to Kol's?"

"Oh, certainly!" I nodded hard. "After Kol's, this path goes on to Jerusalem. Or—or to Fairyland. You cross over an enchanted stream and suddenly—*pop!*—" I waggled my fingers mysteriously. John laughed.

"I'm not popping off to Fairyland," he said serenely. "*I'm* going to Melrose to be a priest."

"Bravo, my boy!"

We stopped short.

I shaded my eyes and peered through the leaves. Someone was rustling around nearby.

"Bravo—oof!—my boy. Noble ambition."

Friar Kol clumped out from behind an elderberry shrub. He had a clutch of yellow flowers in each hand. Muddy roots trailed down his cassock. Kol grinned.

"*Pax vobiscum, filii mei.*[36] What errand brings you to the Lord's garden this fair morning?"

"We came to hear a story!" I said.

"We came to read and pray," John said. "And to bring you these eggs. What are those flowers for, brother Kol?"

Kol gasped in mock surprise.

"You really don't *know*?" he cried. "Why, tonight is Saint John's Night, isn't it? Surely I'm gathering Saint John's flower while the dew lasts!"

We stared at him, uncomprehending.

"My dear boys!" Kol exclaimed. "Hasn't my superior in Christ, the good Father Lara, taught you about the perils of Saint John's Night? Hasn't Father Lara told you about the evil things that creep out at sundown?"

We shook our heads.

"What *has* he taught you, then?"

---

[36] Peace be unto you, my sons.

"Er—he taught us not to dance," I ventured, "and not to tumble with girls in the haymow."

Kol dropped the flowers and clasped his hands in exaggerated horror.

"Quick, my sons!" he cried. "Into the hermitage! Father Lara has left you defenseless. But no matter. I've got a remedy. Gather up those flowers, will you James? There's a good lad. Briskly now!"

John and I were sitting on a log bench outside Friar Kol's cottage. A little stone furnace stood in the dooryard with a fire burning in it. Kol set a pot over the fire. White steam and a clean, fresh smell poured out.

Kol scowled at us through the steam.

"Tonight," he said ominously, "is Saint John's Night. Tonight evil things roam the earth, until the sun of Saint John's Day rises."

John shivered. I smirked and wondered if Kol was serious.

Kol stirred the pot with a twig. "Tonight the witches will gather to their black masses," he went on. "The spirits of the unhallowed dead will rise from their graves to haunt the living. Tonight the werewolves will prowl the wild woods and fells."

He fit a copper hood over the pot. A bent tube stuck out of it like a funnel.

"Therefore—"

Kol sat down on the bench beside us.

"Therefore I went out at dawn to gather Saint John's flower." He held up a blossom. The little yellow crown glowed in his rough hand like a jewel.

"You see?" said Kol. "It looks just like the sun. Saint John's flower reminds evil things that the sun will surely rise again, once the short midsummer night is over."

Kol got up and went back to the furnace. Taking off the copper hood, he shook a few drops into a tiny bottle. It flashed green in the sunlight.

"Oh, you like it?" Kol asked, noticing our interest. He held the green bottle up to the light. "My brother Maewyn gave me this," he said. "It's called a fairy glass."

"Is there a *fairy* in it?" I almost screamed.

Kol laughed and shook his head.

"No fairy in this one," he said. "I use it to hold the spirit of Saint John's flower. Just a drop here—"

Kol wet the tip of his finger and made a cross-shaped smudge on his forehead.

"—and I'm safe! No evil will touch me."

"Now me! Now me!" (John and I were on our feet, both shouting at once.) Kol laughed and slapped his knee.

"Easy there, *filii mei*," he said. "Of course I made enough for you both! Who but Friar Kol watches over these lost McKennas? Come inside! We'll do your letters while the pot boils."

We followed him into the cottage.

I couldn't keep my mind on spelling—not after hearing Friar Kol talk about Saint John's Night. Kol must have seen me squirming. "That'll do, my son," he called, looking up from John's slate. "God's green earth has lessons to teach you. Go wander! But come back before sundown. You still need a drop of Saint John's flower."

"I'll be back in a minute!"

I flew out the door.

Northward the forest gave way to open heaths above the Rankle Burn. Oaks ceded to evergreens. The air was heavy with the scent of pine.

I stopped to watch a honeybee hard at work on a foxglove. Big clumps of pollen clung to her velvety sides. She turned around inside the flower and stared at me with every facet of her round black eyes. Then she took flight and went shooting off to the northeast.

I followed in hot pursuit.

She'll take me to the hive, I thought. I chased the bee up the rising ground.

The day was warm. I was sweaty and winded, but still the restless bee shot from left to right. She led me up one last, burning climb, and then we topped the ridge. The forest lay spread out below me like a carpet with the silvery thread of the Rankle Burn running through it.

The bee landed on a fat thistle (as if that were what she'd been looking for all along) and buried her head in its purple crown. I bent over, wheezing.

I stood up again.

I was looking straight into the mossy face of an ancient standing stone.

The stone towered over me like a giant in Friar Kol's stories. I turned around. I was in the center of a smooth green circle, about fifty yards across, guarded by eight standing stones.

I scurried out quickly. Stone circles were even more perilous than fairy rings! These had to be the ancient stones on Tursahan Knowe.[37] I'd heard of them, but this was the first time I'd ever seen them. I looked cautiously in.

Did it have a roof once? I wondered. *Was it a fairy castle?*

The circle was ringed with smaller stones which lay half-buried in the grass. No heather grew inside, and the springy turf was as smooth as a bowling-green. Only the lone purple thistle stood out like a sentry in the middle.

Gathering my courage, I tiptoed back into the circle.

I looked up at the standing stone. It was weathered and cracked. Sparrows had built a nest in it. One of their little fledglings hopped in the grass. He ruffled his feathers and chirped angrily about being left to fend for himself.

I laughed.

"Fairies!" I said. "Looks like a sparrow to me." Feeling wiser (and slightly disappointed) I sank down on the turf with my back against the cool surface of the stone. Monstrous clouds drifted across the sun. I closed my eyes with a sigh.

I was just beginning to dream in a casual way when I heard a shrill chirp. I opened one eye.

The little sparrow was hopping on the turf beside my knee. He looked up at me with what I thought was an anxious expression (for a bird).

I dug into my pocket and threw him some crumbs of an oat cake. The bird looked down at the crumbs. He hopped twice, and then with an expectant chirp he went back to staring at me again.

"Ungrateful sparrow!" I muttered, closing my eyes.

---

[37] Knoll

33

I opened them with a yelp. The little sparrow was on my stomach! He fluttered his wings and chirped insistently.

"Go away!" I shouted, waving him off.

The bird flew a few feet, but then he stopped. He hopped in a circle and came toward me again with a commanding *Chirp!*

I was wide awake now, and on my feet. No sparrow had ever behaved like this! I edged closer to the fledgling. It flew a short distance, turned, and called to me again.

Thus we went—the bird leading and I following—over the jagged rim of the stone circle, down the slope, and into the first clump of fir trees that grew there.

No sooner had my sleeve brushed a tree than the sparrow gave a triumphant *chirp* and took flight. Wobbling in the air he half-flew, half-hopped, up the slope and all the way back to his post at the foot of the standing stone.

"Cheeky bird!" I growled. The spiteful little thing wanted to be king of the circle! I was just about to march back inside when a sudden uneasiness made me hesitate. Was there a note of warning in the sparrow's song?

"Oh, you're a fool!" I said aloud, but I turned back just the same. Crawling underneath the first friendly tree I dropped full-length onto the fragrant carpet of needles.

I laid my head on my arms. The drooping boughs closed over me like a curtain.

I was drifting in and out of a restless dream. Something about Peter chasing a bullfinch. I shouted at him to stop, but he wouldn't, and then there was a blinding flash and I sat up abruptly and scratched my head on the tree.

I shivered.

Why is it so dark?

A chilly wind was blowing down from the north and all the stars were blazing in a clear sky.

Where did the day go?

I crawled out from under my tree and peered dazedly about. Above the hills a faint white halo showed where the moon was about to rise. Beneath it I saw a reddish glow that shone out, faded, then shone out again. Then a happy thought occurred to me:

It's Midsummer's Night!

(I started to run.)

They must have lit a bone-fire[38] up on the knowe! I'm missing all the fun!

I jogged up the slope as quick as I dared in the shifty moonlight.

Then I stopped.

I dropped down into the grass, trembling and holding my breath.

The stone circle was lit up red. Where the thistle had been, a roaring fire sent trails of sparks into the sky. The standing stones cast black shadows that danced across the heather. I stared openmouthed. The air was full of laughter and strange voices.

Inside the circle, a weird assembly were gathered.

---

[38] Bonfire

CHAPTER 5

From the letters of Doctor Stewart Henry Scott—

Branxholme Castle, Roxburghshire

May 14, 1838

Dear Albert,

Please find enclosed another pile of transcription from this most surprising book, *The Last Will and Testament of the Pirate John Blackjohn.* Nothing in it about piracy so far, but I've got bigger news: Sir Walter Douglas-Scott, the young duke of Buckley, has returned to these his ancestral lands— *and has graced me with an audience!* (Didn't I tell you I'd come up in the world?) The young duke stopped over yesterday night with his solicitor[39] (a Southerner[40] name of Radan) and he was gone again to Edinburgh before ten this morning. I don't think the ancient seat of clan Scott interests him much. The duke has the cut of Kensington. He's dropped every trace of the Scottish brogue Fitzhugh said he had as a child. Fitzhugh uncovered the furniture for him and worked up a considerable fire in the drafty old library. (I doubt the house has seen such a blaze this century.) It's a fine old specimen of a hearth— wide as a church door with the Scott coat of arms hanging over it in chilly bronze: the stag *trippant*[41] with the motto *Amo*[42] underneath. The chimney doesn't draw quite so well as one would hope (I think it has rooks nesting in it), and we were obliged to sit on one side so as to be out of the intermittent

---

[39] Attorney

[40] *i.e.,* an Englishman, probably a Londoner.

[41] Prancing

[42] Latin: *I love*

smoke. Sir Walter looked bored and said little. I suppose a solicitor and an old duffer like me must have been poor company for him. After dinner His Grace ate pecan tart and talked airily about his doctor in London (who is quite renowned, apparently) while Mr. Radan drank coffee and gnawed at his fingers like he had a case of bad nerves. He's a tall man, Radan. Long, narrow face. Unhealthy yellowish complexion.

I reckon Sir Walter thought me a harmless old eccentric. He seemed to rather like the idea of keeping an antiquarian at Branxholme; gives the old house an ancestral air. I thought it best to show him *John Blackjohn* right away and explain how I found it at Hermitage. Sir Walter was mildly surprised I'd managed to spot a hidden cache at dusk, but as for the book itself he wasn't much interested. Mr. Radan was all a-quiver, though. He wanted to know where I'd found it, what part of the keep, where I entered the estate, etc., etc. (his mind reeling with Trover and Conversion, no doubt.)

But Sir Walter said I may keep the book for as long as it takes to transcribe, and to that end I mean to stay here at Branxholme for the time being. The duke didn't mention my leaving and I'm sure Fitzhugh will give me some hint when the generosity of the house is exhausted. We're thick as thieves, Fitzhugh and I. He really is a fine old fellow. He talks about pheasant-shooting in the fall as if I'll still be here.

John Blackjohn sits on my little escritoire all ruffled out like a grouse, matchsticks and woolen bits everywhere. I've got about a third of the pages separated and oiled now, but the bottom two thirds are an entirely different matter. These last pages aren't stuck together by age and damp: they have a curious copper device pinned over them. I suppose I'd call it a sort of seal. I'd got down the spine a few inches when the book opened onto a large plate—about a quarter-inch thick—with four copper pins drilled through it. It has an image like a woman's face surrounded by water lilies. There's another plate of similar shape and design mounted on the back cover. The better part of the book is compressed between the two seals, but I dare not break the pins for fear this brittle old parchment will disintegrate all at once. There's an opening in the lily-woman's mouth that hints at a keyhole, but no key have I found.

I'll forge ahead anyway. I've more than enough work to do with the pages I've freed already and as to seals, I shall cross that bridge if ever I come to it. I remain faithfully yours, &c.

—SHS

P.S.—If Mrs. Haig comes around complaining of double-vision or convulsions or numbness or anything of the sort, just send her off with a solution of 1 part white pine syrup to 4 parts honey (with a bit of laudanum in it). That should fend her off for a day or two.

CHAPTER 6

Doctor Scott's transcription—

I can't remember, but John said I looked like I'd seen the devil.

John said I staggered in a little past sunrise, scratched and bleeding, sticks in my hair, shouting *Lead us not into temptation!* over and over again, and then I collapsed face-down onto our only table and would not speak nor stir no matter how he and Peter slapped my cheeks and rubbed my hands. Peter threw cold water on my face but I just lay there like a sack, so John and Peter debated what to do with me.

"Run get Father Lara," said John. Peter rushed off, and then after a minute he came rushing back again.

"No one's seen Lara since yesterday," he panted. "But here's Friar Kol. He's coming."

A donkey brayed outside. Friar Kol came puffing up to the door as fast as he could drag Iohannes Calvinus,[43] his old jack.[44] He shoved through the door and bent over me, putting his ear to my chest. Peter and John waited breathlessly.

"I think he'll be alright," Kol said at last, standing up. "He's breathing easy and he's got a steady pulse." He fumbled his hand along my spine.

"Doesn't appear broken."

Kol took out a needle and jabbed me in the foot. I gasped and jerked my leg. Kol clucked gravely.

"Been up on the heath, I'd say."

"How d'you know?" Peter demanded.

---

[43] John Calvin
[44] Male donkey

"He's got cotton-grass in his ear. Easy! Don't crowd him! I think he's coming round."

My eyes fluttered open. I turned over and sat up.

"Lead us not into tempta—"

"That'll do, my son, that'll do," Kol interrupted. "Rest easy. No temptation here."

I stared at Kol like I'd never seen him before. My glance fell on the little green vial he held in his hand.

"Green Lady!" I choked.

"What's that?" Friar Kol asked sharply.

"Green lady. He said call the green lady. Need a—need a strong house. To keep her in."

Kol's face went white.

"Who?" he demand. "Who said to call the green lady?"

I sank back on the table and closed my eyes.

"Father Lara."

CHAPTER 7

Friar Kol stayed the whole afternoon and evening. Mother and uncle Andrew came home from Haick and by that time they'd got me off the table and back in my right mind.

Kol and uncle Andrew sat on the split log bench outside and talked about crops and weather while the long summer twilight lingered in the sky. Then Kol said he'd a mind to teach me the *Ave Maria* (I'd never learned it past *fructus ventris tui*) and uncle Andrew said he wasn't one to stand in the way of God's work, so Kol went to look for me while uncle Andrew swung his long legs over the back hedge and vanished like the earth had swallowed him up.

Friar Kol found me in the little hayloft above the empty stable. I watched the dome of Kol's bald head come up the ladder, followed by Kol himself. He settled into the straw next to me with his usual '*pax tecum*' and his usual grin. We sat quietly a moment while the stars came out in the east.

"Well, now—" Kol said at length. "And what have *you* been at, my boy? Why, you never so much as came back for your drop of Saint John's flower!" Kol's voice was cheerful but he had a worried look in his eyes. I hung my head.

"I'm sorry, brother Kol."

Kol reached into his cassock. "Here," he said. He held out a thin leather strand with something green hanging from it. I took it respectfully. Kol's little fairy glass glowed faintly in the twilight.

"Don't ever take that off!" Kol said sternly.

"I won't, brother Kol."

"Good lad!" Kol smiled. "Now what's this about Father Lara and a green lady?"

I wrinkled my forehead, trying to remember.

"Come on now!" Kol prodded me with his elbow. "You've been up on Tursahan Knowe—that's plain enough. Did you—er—you didn't see our worthy Father Lara up *there*, now did you?"

41

I nodded.

"So you *did* see him up there?"

I nodded.

Kol scowled. "And what was my superior in Christ doing up on the knowe, on a Midsummer's Night?"

"Well—" I squirmed.

"Well *what?*"

"Well at first he was just speaking."

"And then?"

"And then he was more—more like shouting, and then after that—" I hesitated.

"Go on," said Friar Kol.

"And after that he was dancing around a fire singing *Kissy-me please Betsy, hey! Kissy-me please Betsy, hey!*[45] over and over again."

I looked down at my knees, blushing a little. Kol didn't smile. "I don't think that's what he was singing," he said, "but suppose you start at the beginning?"

So I told Friar Kol how the bee had led me into a great circle of standing stones, and how I'd almost fallen asleep inside before a little sparrow led me out again. ("That was lucky," said Kol. "Very lucky.")

"—and when I woke up under the fir tree it was already dark. Then I saw a red light on the hilltop so I climbed back up to the circle to look, but there were—" I hesitated.

"There were what?"

"There were strange—" I searched for the word—"strange *people* inside."

"What sort of people?" Kol demanded.

"Witches."

"You— You think you saw *witches?*"

"I *did* see witches," I insisted. "Some of them were old and crooked and ugly, but—but some of them were young and beautiful too, and some had black hair and some had coppery hair and some had golden hair—"

"Women?"

---

[45] Latin: *Quis similis bestiae*

42

"All women. Except for Father Lara. There was a big fire right in the middle of the circle—that's where the light was coming from—and the women were dancing and singing and making a ruckus. I wanted to get a closer look so I crept up behind a rock and I was almost near enough to touch it, and then—"

"And then what?"

I shivered. "And then it wasn't a rock any more. All at once the rock seemed to unfold itself and there was this—this black—*feathery* thing standing between me and the fire."

"Merciful heaven!" Kol gave my shoulder a squeeze. "What do you think it was, James?"

I shook my head. "I don't know. It was something like a woman and—and something like a bird. It was as tall as me. It walked like a heron. Long, careful steps. And it was making a noise. A sort of—croaking noise."

I shuddered.

"So what did you do?" Kol asked.

"I just got down on the ground. I was too scared to run. The bird-woman went croaking away into the shadows and then I heard one of the young witches talking to an old witch just in front of me. *Our father which wert in heaven*, she said, *unhallowed be thy name*."

"God save us!" Kol gasped, crossing himself.

"Yes, but the old witch says *Oh, give that a rest!* she says. *You're as bad as Lara.*

"*Pardon, Mother*, says the young witch. *It's my first Sabbath.*

"The old witch looks her up and down. *Yesss*, she says all slow and thoughtful. *Yes, you're very pretty. Our brother Lara has a keen eye.*

"*Oh yes!* the girl says all proud, *I was the bride of spring*—and then I knew who she was, brother Kol. She was Nessa Blair from Clearburn Loch."

"Was she indeed?" Kol rejoined. "I'm very sorry to hear that."

"I knew some of the others, too. Mother Glynis from Gamesly[46] was there, and Ilsa and Ina Glendywyn. Jenny Crosar was th—"

"Ahem—yes!" Friar Kol interrupted. "That'll do, James. I know the enemy of our souls has been busy amongst us. Now tell me what you heard about the green lady!"

---

[46] Gamescleuch

"Right. Well then Nessa Blair asked if they were going to raise the green lady, and the old woman (I don't know who she was) she said *The Black Stag bids it.*

"*Black who?* Nessa asks, *D'you mean brother Lara?* The old woman just laughs. *Wait and see, daughter*, she says, *Wait and see*, and then she picked up a tambour and went prancing off—"

I stopped for breath. Friar Kol patted my shoulder encouragingly.

"Well when I heard *that* I almost fainted for fright because I thought the Black Stag was the Devil and he was coming to the stone circle that night. Then I heard footsteps in the grass behind me. So I lay flat on the ground scarcely breathing and Father Lara walked by so close I could have reached out and touched him."

"But he didn't see you?"

I shook my head. "He walked right past me. He went inside the circle and the women all gathered round him making a great hurly-burly and fuss. They started dancing and Father Lara danced first with Nessa Blair, and then he danced with Mother Glynis, and then he stood up on a barrel and raised his hand and suddenly they all went so quiet I could hear the fire crackling. When he spoke he sounded just like he does at mass."

"Did he? And what did he say?"

"He said, er—" I rubbed my eyes. "Near as I can remember he said *Maidens*—er— *Maidens, mothers*—"

"Crones?" Kol ventured.

"Crones! That was it, brother Kol! *Maidens, mothers, crones*, he says, *I bid you welcome to this our Midsummer Sabbath. Discordia vobiscum*, and the women answered *Et quoque tecum* all together.

"*We await the coming of our captain*, says Lara, *the Right Horrible Black Stag. The Black Stag will lead us in the mystery of the Midsummer Sabbath. Even now he is coming up the glen from Gamesly Tower. Let us make ready to receive him!*

"Then father Lara got down off the barrel. He took a drum and started beating on it all measured and slow, and the whole crowd of women started chanting at once and it was terrible to hear. I pressed my hands over my ears and lay there shaking because I thought the Devil was coming. Presently I heard the crush of grass and the jingle of spurs. In a blink they were all quiet."

"Someone came?"

I nodded. "Someone came into the circle from the south side. I heard the women murmur in a prayerlike sort of way and someone said *Oh!* and then he spoke and I was so surprised when I heard him that I almost stood up to look. He didn't sound like the devil at all, brother Kol. He sounded like a lordly young gentleman, all cheery and good-mannered. He said *Bless me, Father, for I have sinned.* Then he laughed, but none of the women made a sound. I was so curious I got up on my elbows and raised my head. When I saw him he looked like the gladdest, handsomest young lord in the whole world. The women were all kneeling around him with their eyes on the ground, but the young lord was sitting on the barrel as easy as you please with his fine hat on his knee and his dark hair falling over his shoulders. He wore a blue coat trimmed with gold fit for a king and he carried a magnificent sword in a silver scabbard. Father Lara said something to him and the two of them clasped hands. Then the young lord stood up again.

"*I am much obliged to you, Sisters,* he said, *for your song. But if we want the Green Lady to come to our Sabbath we'll need some big strong lads to fetch her. And we'll need a strong house to keep her in.*"

I stopped and looked down at my collar. Kol's fairy glass seemed to glow with a faint light of its own. Kol noticed my glance.

"He had a fairy glass?" Kol asked.

I nodded.

"I thought it was yours, brother."

Kol shook head. "Go on," he said.

"So then Father Lara brought out a monstrous bronze cauldron and he set it over the coals at the edge of the fire. It was so big he could barely lift it in both arms, and it was covered with tracings like leaves and vines and strange creatures all woven together. Lara poured out a wineskin into the cauldron and then he said *Do you have you the crook, my lord?*

"*I do,* says the young gentleman, and then he reached into his coat and pulled out a curved blade as long as my forearm.

Father Lara took it from him all worshipful and he said, er, he said something like *pull creaky*, er, *pull creaky deformities*[47]—something like that. Then he cut through what looked like a bunch of mistletoe with the stems all tied together and he shook a few drops of sap into the cauldron. It seemed at once the fire burned low and left off crackling. Everything was dark and still and I could hear the night wind whispering among the stones.

"Then the young gentleman—I swear to you, brother—the young gentleman took the curved knife from Father Lara and he cut himself with it; cut himself deep on the middle finger. I saw his blood drip off the knife into the cauldron. Father Lara ran to him with a handkerchief but the gentleman only laughed and put his finger to his mouth. He said *Sisters, we wait for moonrise.*

"After that they were all quiet—the young gentleman, the women, Father Lara standing by the cauldron. The sky was bright with stars. Even with the fire dying I could see the plumes on the gentleman's hat nodding in the breeze. The moon is at the full, you know?"

"I know," Kol grunted.

"Right. So for a moment there was that halo where the moon was about to come up, and then the moon peeked out over the hills and the Sisters all said *Ah!* like they tasted honey. I was on my feet by then, peering in between the rocks. I looked up and—I swear it, brother Kol—milk was coming out of the moon."

Stunned silence from Kol.

Then, "*What?*" Kol stared at me like I'd lost my mind. "*Milk?*" he barked. "Speak up, lad! I don't follow you."

"It's true, brother Kol!" I insisted. "The moonlight turned into milk! I mean it *was* milk. It poured straight down into the cauldron. Filled it right to the top. The young gentleman got up to look, but he had to jump back quick because milk was already spilling out over the sides. The gentleman laughed and said *Though my sins be as scarlet, apparently*, and then I heard the fire sizzle where the milk touched it.

"Milk?" Kol sounded unconvinced.

"Aye! Milk!"

"Are you *sure* it was milk?"

---

[47] Latin: *pulchritudo deformitas*

"I'm sure! I could smell it. There was a big cloud of steam rose up in the moonlight and milk was just gushing over the sides. The women stayed on their knees crying *Oh!* and *Ah!* and their skirts were soaked. Father Lara was sloshing around waving his arms like he'd gone mad. The young gentleman's boots were wet but he sat down on the barrel again like it was nothing while the pool just grew and grew until it filled up the circle."

"Did it ever *stop*?"

I nodded. "It stopped when it got all the way around the standing stones."

"And what made it stop?" Kol demanded.

I scratched my neck thoughtfully. "I—I don't know. Suddenly it just wasn't overflowing any more. Like a tap got turned off. All at once the cauldron was quiet on top. Just the moon's face shining on it." I glanced up. Friar Kol was thumbing his rosary with the same worried expression. I couldn't tell whether he believed me or whether he thought I was making it up, so I forged ahead.

"Then the standing stones—" I said, "they—well it was rather like the bird-woman, you know?"

"I *don't* know," Kol returned. "Tell me what happened to the standing stones."

"Well they started to crack and—and they started to—change."

"Change *how*?"

"Just a little at first. Little pebbles started to crumble off around the bottom. And then longer cracks went running up the sides—faster and faster—all the way to the top. Soon great big pieces were breaking off, splashing down into the pool. The moon shone off the milk so bright. It was like daytime in the circle. The stones were beginning to look like—like—"

"Like what, James?"

"It—" I shook my head. "You're not going to believe me, brother Kol." Kol squeezed my shoulder.

"Did they look like giant men?" he asked quietly.

I stared at him wide-eyed.

"Ye-es!" I returned wonderingly. "They looked like giant men! How did you—"

"Ah!" said Kol. "I thought so."

"I couldn't tell what they were at first. It was only a rough shape. Giant heads on top of giant shoulders. But then arms and hands and feet grew out of the stone. I was watching the one nearest me. His face was only flat at the beginning, but then little chips started to rain out and I could see hollow black eyes and a wide lumpy nose and a big ugly mouth with teeth like flagstones. All at once he broke free from the stone—or else the stone crumbled away from him—and he started to move. He took a clumsy step and turned his head this way and that. Oh, I was witless! What an awful grinding noise his neck made, brother! He let out a groan like a church door and stretched himself all over—"

I shuddered and pressed my knuckles to my eyes.

"My legs might've been tree stumps. I couldn't run away. And then all eight giants started to stumble and stretch and bellow and scratch themselves at once and the circle turned into a regular bog of mud and milk. The young gentleman stood up on the barrel and shouted and waved his arms but he only came as high as a giant's waist.

"*Bolg-men!* he was shouting. *Bolg-men! The Black Stag commands you!*

"No-o!" Kol gasped. "Did he really try to command them?"

I nodded solemnly.

"*Did* he command them?"

I shook my head. "Not at first. At first the giants just stood there looking at him, so the gentleman says *The crook, brother Lara! Quick!* and Lara hands him the blade. The gentleman holds the blade high over his head and he shouts *Behold! The corran ag bearradh! The pruning-hook of Esus!*"

"My faith!" Kol muttered, crossing himself again.

"And one of giants said—"

"It *spoke?*"

"Aye."

"The giant *spoke?* Are you certain, James?"

"Oh yes!" I returned. "The biggest one. Oh, his voice was horrible! Like if an ox could speak. *I SMELL BLOOD*, says he. He was weaving his huge head from side to side, sniffing the air.

"*Yes, yes*, says the young gentleman, all impatient. *That's fairy blood. With this crook I slew the priest of Dana.* And then the gentleman, he—"

48

"Wait!" Kol interrupted. "*Fairy* blood, James?"

"That's right," I nodded. "He said *I slew the priest of*—Dana? Danu? It sounded like Dana."

Kol was silent.

Then, "Go on," he said thickly.

"So the young gentleman, he drops the blade *slap* into the milk, then *Come!* he shouts at the giant, *Drink up!*

"The giant looks at him with his head on one side like he was thinking about it. He'd a greedy face on him, brother, eyeing all that dirty milk. Then all at once he goes *thud!* right down on his hands and knees and he was just about to dive his ugly face in when *Stop!* screams the Black Stag."

"Did he stop?"

"Aye, the big devil! He rumbled and showed his teeth like a dog, but he just froze there on all fours. *You know the law, bolg-man,* says the Black Stag like he was pleased with himself. *Blood for blood. Brother Lara? Bring us the corran!* So Lara fished the blade out of the mire. But the Black Stag just threw it *clang!* against the giant's knee.

"*Cut away!* says the Black Stag. *Cut away every one of you, and then come! Join our sisters! We'll have a hunt tonight. Cut away, I say, and drink!*

"Well the giants were all creaking and grunting and shuffling around like they couldn't make up their minds. Finally the biggest one picked the blade up out of the milk (it was like a quill-knife to him, brother) and he closed his craggy hand over it. It made a nasty scraping noise when he jerked it out. Big drops of black blood ran off his hand and fell into the pool. He gave an angry grunt and handed the blade to another giant. And strange to say, brother Kol, I don't think the blade was curved any more."

"What?" Kol asked sharply. "What d'you mean the blade wasn't curved any more?"

"I don't know," I shrugged. "Maybe it was only the moonlight. But I could have sworn, brother: suddenly the blade wasn't curved like a pruning hook. I think the giant must have bent it out straight. It looked just like the point on a pike. Or a spear."

Kol cleared his throat violently.

"Go on."

"Well, so the giants passed the blade around. Every giant spilled some blood in the pool and the dirty milk went white again. After the last giant had cut himself then the Black Stag coughed into his handkerchief in a satisfied sort of way. He didn't say a word; he just took off his hat and waved it at the pool. And then oh! what a riot, brother! You never saw such drinking and singing and bellowing and beating on drums. I shouldn't wonder they heard it in Holyrood! Giants, women, Father Lara—they all went at it like pigs at a trough. The Black Stag tried to keep his manners but soon even *he* had his head in the cauldron, milk all down the front of him and his fine lace collar soaking wet. They were all shouting and staggering around. Finally when the cauldron was empty and the circle was nothing but mud again, then the Black Stag set the barrel back on end and he stood up on it.

"*Bolg-men!* he shouts. *Bolg-men, your wage is paid! Kneel ye now, swine! Kneel and swear faith to the blade!*

"The giants bellowed and wagged their heads and stomped around like an earthquake, but at last every one of them got down on his knees. They roared out something like—like *Tha sinn a— Tha sinn a*—something something—*corran ag Esus*. I can't remember, but it went like that. Then *Up, Bolg-men!* screams the Black Stag all fierce and wild. He had the blade in one hand and his fairy glass in the other. *Up, bolg-men!* he shouts. *Up, Sisters! The green lady is coming to our Sabbath. With this blade we'll knock on her door, and in this glass we'll keep her. These isles will be ours, aye! and more anon!*

"Then the giants raised such an awful roar that it shook the ground and I had to cover my ears again. The Black Stag gave a whistle and a great black warhorse came thundering into the circle. Such a fine horse, brother Kol! Fifteen hands high and sleek and shiny like jet. The Black Stag swung up into the saddle and swept out his sword. *The hunt!* he shouts, and he wheels the stallion around, fetlocks in the air. But then I—then I saw someone.

I stopped.

"Come!" Kol snapped, losing patience. "What d'you mean *I saw someone*? You saw rather a lot of creatures, so you say!"

"No, I saw someone *different*," I returned sullenly. "It was a girl."

"Oh, God grant me patience!" Kol groaned. From the gloom came the nervous click-clicking of his rosary beads.

"Not like the *others*," I said hurriedly. "This girl was standing outside the circle like I was. And she sort of—sort of sparkled. Like dew on a spiderweb."

"Go on," said Kol. There was something strange in his voice.

"I don't know why I didn't notice her before. She was dressed in white as bright as the moon; standing there watching the lot of them like she'd been there all along. And then she did a strange thing, brother Kol: all of a sudden she raised both her arms up to the sky and clapped her hands together, and she sort of half-sang something. It sounded like *beod solus ahn*, high and clear in a girl's voice, only it sent a shock all over me. At once it seemed like the moonlight came out of the stone circle and filled her up instead. She was shining like a lantern, brother! I could see the tips of her hair all silvery. The circle went quiet. They all just stood there and blinked at her like sheep."

"*All* of them?" Kol growled. "Even this—this 'Black Stag' of yours?"

The Black Stag? No, he had his back to her. He wheeled his horse around, and when he saw her he screamed *Ban-sìthe! Ban-sìthe!* like he'd lost his mind. Then he dug his spurs in and charged. His sword was pointed at her heart. I thought she was going to die, brother Kol. And then I—I—"

"Then you *what*?"

"Then I threw a rock at him."

Kol gasped.

"You threw a *rock* at him, James? Whatever *for*? And where did you get a rock from just then?"

"I don't know!" I cried, "I don't know! I'd just been down on the ground, and then I got up again and suddenly there was this perfect rock like an apple in my hand. It was yellowish like an apple too. I must have picked it up somehow. Anyway, I threw it at him as hard as I could and it caught him square on the ear. His fine hat flew off and his sword just missed the girl."

"O-oh!" Kol groaned. "This is bad. This is awful. Why, why did you do it, James?"

I hugged my knees into my chest, remembering.

"I don't know," I said at length. "She was all alone."

Kol's rosary beads were click-clicking again.

"Then the girl did another strange thing," I went on. "She stretched her arms straight out in front of her and there was a terrible light in her hands.

51

White rays, see?" (I demonstrated.) "Shooting out between her fingers. Like she was holding onto a star. It burned my eyes just to look at it. The Black Stag was cursing and fighting to bring his horse around again, but then the girl opened her hands. There was a mighty flash and a chime like a bell—only so sharp I could feel it in my teeth. I think everyone went blind. The Black Stag fell off his horse with a *thud*. The women were all shouting, and—"

"And the giants?" Kol interrupted. "What about the giants?"

"The giants? Oh, they turned back into standing stones, I think."

"*Really*, James? Back into stones?"

I nodded vigorously.

"Yes, they must have. It was darker with the milk gone, but I'm sure of it, brother Kol. When I could see again there were eight stone pillars in the moonlight just like before.

"And what about the Black Stag?"

"Oh *he* was no stone. He got back on his horse and went chasing after me instead. They all did."

"After *you*, James? Why?"

"Well—" I hesitated. "Well I—I tried to cut him with his blade, you see."

"With his—" Kol gasped. Then he was silent. It was too dark to read his face. I imagined he was furious at me.

"Well I *had* to," I said defensively. "He meant to kill the girl. Father Lara was two steps away from me, stumbling around with the blade in his hand like he'd gone daft. In a wink I snatched it from him and I went after the Black Stag with it. I didn't manage to *cut* him, brother! I missed him by a yard. But Father Lara howled *The corran! The corran!* and they all took after me like a pack of hounds. I went running down the slope and through the glen, the whole company of them behind me. Black Stag. Witches. Lara. I must have fallen fifty times. I went over the rocks and through the brambles—"

"The blade!" Kol hissed. "Where's the blade now?"

"How should *I* know?" I retorted. "I dropped the cursed thing before I jumped in the Rankle Burn. I couldn't very well swim holding onto it, now could I? Once I got across the burn they left off chasing me. I think Father Lara has the blade."

"How do you know?"

"Because when I got to the other side he was shouting *the corran the corran*, only now he sounded happy about it." I shivered and rubbed my palms against my knees. "That blade was strange," I said. "I was glad to get rid of it. It left this black stain on my hands and I can't get rid of it, and I can't—"

I yawned.

"—can't remember how I got home—"

I fell silent. We sat together in the dark while the sky filled up with stars. Friar Kol neither moved nor spoke.

I heard a choking sob.

"Brother Kol?"

Kol sobbed again, then he bowed his head down to his knees and wept like a child.

"My brother!" Kol cried. "My brother Maewyn is dead! They have killed him!"

CHAPTER 8

From the letters of Doctor Stewart Henry Scott—

Albert:

I meant to post this from Hawick[48] three days ago but the strangest thing has happened: I've quit Branxholme (escaped it, you might say) and I think the young duke of Buckley is hunting for me. Or his solicitor is, at any rate. I haven't gone mad, Albert; I'll simply have to tell you how it happened: it was round about seven in the evening, Fitzhugh's day off. We were down at the *Queen's Head* in Hawick. Fitzhugh was playing his concertina and we were singing *Twa Bonnie Maidens*, merry as larks. We got as far as *the nicht is dark and the redcoat is gane* when suddenly an eerie kind of dread came over me— a sort of premonition; like I'd mislaid a watch or left a stable door open or somesuch thing. The uncanny feeling grew on me until (to my own great surprise) I broke it off mid-refrain and told Fitzhugh I was unwell. Of course the good old fellow was quite concerned. *You're the doctor*, says he. *Tell me what you need me to do.* I said *Get me back to Branxholme and don't spare the horse.* He was awfully worried and I felt wretched for scaring him like that, but I was in a panic. I couldn't stop thinking about my book—about *John Blackjohn*, that is—sitting in my garret with the door unlocked and all the windows open.

So I jumped into Fitzhugh's gig.[49] Fitzhugh tried to persuade the old mare to pace. The old mare pinned her ears back and gave him a sulky trot.

---

[48] Pronounce *HOY-ick*
[49] A light two-wheeled carriage.

Fitzhugh whipped the reins and glanced at me with a worried look. I gnawed my fingers and silently cursed the mare and the mud and every bump in the road.

At last we turned into the gravel drive. I vaulted over the side without waiting for the gig to stop and rushed upstairs. To my profound relief, there lay *John Blackjohn*: precisely where I'd left it on the little escritoire.

Wheels crunched on the drive below. Not the gig. Something heavy. I heard a carriage door slam. Then a creaky voice like a bagpipe. Radan was back! I don't know why, Albert, but the solicitor's voice made my flesh crawl. I heard him say *Where's the doctor?* Fitzhugh replied something with the word 'unwell' in it. *No matter!* squawked Radan, *I must see him at once!*

I heard footsteps coming toward the servants' door.

I did a foolish thing, Albert, and I think I'm going to regret it. I snatched my mackintosh[50] off the chair and threw it over the writing table, then I frantically scooped everything into it—*John Blackjohn*, pens, scrapers, blotters, matchsticks, woolen bits, scraps of paper, mineral spirits, everything. Then I grabbed my valise without bothering to close it and I fled down the tower stairs. I knew there was no escape. I knew I'd run into Fitzhugh on the stairs. But I ran just the same.

Halfway down I heard Fitzhugh coming up. I stopped short: despairing; making up some speech for Radan (*Here's your book, sir! Just fetching it for you, sir!*) Upon my life, Albert, I don't know why I assumed Radan would want to take *John Blackjohn*, but assume it I did. I was picturing his yellow-stained fingers; the smug delight on his deathlike face.

I should mention that the tower at Branxholme is an old rectangular *tour-de-guette*: five stories high with a big chimney that serves every room. It was nearly dark inside except for where the twilight showed through the distrustful little windows, one window on every landing. I stood beside the window and listened to the steady *scrape-scrape* of Fitzhugh's boots, getting nearer.

All at once I noticed a big iron plate set in the wall. I must have passed it by a hundred times without seeing it before. It was about chest-high; just a blacker square against the gloom. I saw it jutted out slightly from the wall and quite aimlessly I hooked my thumb into the gap. Then I jumped backwards

---

[50] An early rubberized raincoat.

with a start. The whole plate had swung out silently toward me. Behind it a pair of sooty iron hinges extended from a black opening. An entrance! Made for a chimney-sweep, no doubt. A boy, probably.

That the entrance was probably made for a boy was my chief impression, Albert, when I plunged through it headfirst with my valise in my teeth.

It was dark as a coal-mine inside. I turned slantways and wriggled in up to my waist. *Ye gods!* I thought, *I'm already stuck!* My hand fell on a heavy iron bar set into the stone. Then another. I seized them and wrenched my legs through. In a twinkling I was perched on the sweep's ladder with my back against the wall and about an inch of soot on my head. I had just enough presence of mind to drag my mackintosh inside and close the plate before Fitzhugh rounded the corner.

Fitzhugh stopped. I held my breath. The rung creaked faintly under my weight. A few trembling heartbeats, and then the labored *scrape-scrape* started up again. I breathed out slowly as his footsteps faded into the tower.

Now that I had a moment to gather my wits, I could see the complete absurdity of my situation: I was trapped inside a chimney! I must either climb down and be buried in an ash-pile centuries in the making, or else yell for them to come drag me out like a rascally Father Christmas.

I tested the next rung higher. *Is that soot,* I wondered, *or is that rust?* (I was considering the twenty feet of blackness underneath me.) I thought of crying out for help.

Then I thought of Radan.

Up you go! I said to myself, *Up you go, old fellow!* With my free hand trembling and my back pressed against the wall I slowly started to climb.

Oh! to be younger and thinner! I muttered. *I'll find out about the rooks, at any rate.*

Sounds came dully through the stone. Fitzhugh rushing downstairs. Muffled voices below. Then Radan. He sounded furious but I couldn't make out the words.

Next time I see him, I said to myself, *I'll be in shackles before a magistrate.*

Feeling bold and desperate I climbed two rungs, then I opened my teeth. My valise slid down to my hand in a shower of soot. The air was dank and foul. I choked back a cough.

If anyone lights a fire, I thought, *I shall suffocate.*

I made another climb. Nine rungs. Ten rungs. Then I dropped my head back and saw a glorious sight: the flue was coming to an end! One blessed star had managed to shoot a beam under the big old-fashioned chimney cowl. No chimney-pot here. The iron ladder went right up to the top and there was just room enough for me to scramble out.

I'd got my valise, mackintosh, and one leg out, when in a flash it occurred to me that it was *very* late in the evening and I was *very* much on the roof of Branxholme Castle.

I shivered.

Only a faint blue streak showed where the sun had set. Around me: a shadowy mountain-range of peaks and gables. Broken slates. Wet moss. Forgotten pipes and gutters lying wherever the workmen had abandoned them. Here and there impressive stands of weeds grew out from between the slates. It was only a short drop from the chimney, but in the dying light the tower roof looked steep and slippery as a glacier.

Out of the bog and into the briar! I muttered.

But there was nothing for it, so I wrapped up *John Blackjohn* again (doing a better job this time) and I tied it crossways over my chest. I buckled my valise and jostled it from hand to hand, considering.

At length (and with a sigh) I put the handle back in my teeth. It tasted of soot.

Need my hands free, I muttered.

With my heart in my throat, I dropped onto the tower roof.

Shouting in the courtyard. I lay flat. Fitzhugh's bull's-eye lantern came bobbing along the garden side. I was up too high for him to see. Plucking up my courage I crawled down the roof on all fours and peered cautiously over the raingutter. Another drop to reach the housetop, and a proper drop this time! I'd have to hang full-length from the gutter and let myself fall onto the slates below. I got down on my stomach and wriggled my legs out over the edge. I took a deep breath.

This will make for a fascinating obituary. Shame I won't get to read it.

My feet hit the roof and instantly flew out from under me. The slates were loose! I was sliding fast, clawing frantically on either side, the epicenter of my own little avalanche of tiles.

By some miracle I caught hold of a patch of weeds, and (God bless our tough old Scottish weeds!) they were rooted much better than the slates. I came to a stop with my ankles hanging over the abyss. One broken slate went whizzing off into the darkness.

I cringed. *What if it should hit Fitzhugh?*

The idea sickened me. Poor old Fitzhugh!—worried and looking for me. I lay there with bleeding fingers; breathless, shivering, thoroughly angry with myself.

You fool! I thought, *you could have just given him the wretched old book!*

Radan was braying in the garden, drawn to my broken slate, apparently. I sat up and started counting on my fingers.

Trespass to land,

Trespass to chattels,

Larceny,

Conversion,

Property damage, a bill for my lodging—

I was on my feet again, loping across the roof like an ape. The bull's-eye played dimly about the eaves. I dived over one of the little dormers and crouched behind it, panting like a fox. I tried the window. Locked! In a blink I was off again, making for the next dormer.

Then I saw something.

Not something inviting, Albert, but something familiar at least: a black iron plate standing hard and square against the main house chimney. The plate was open. I could feel thin eddies of smoke trailing out.

Fiat lux![51] I muttered. *Hence the draught in the library.*

I gingerly put my hand inside. The brick was cold. I had a fleeting vision of myself forever entombed inside some pipe, but I put that out of my mind. Grimly I stuck my valise back in my teeth.

---

[51] Latin: *Let there be light*

58

They won't even smell my corpse, I muttered as I wormed through the opening. *Smoke'll dry me out like a codfish.*

I knew where I was going now. The main chimney ends in the library: a wider flue rising from a hearth big enough to play ninepins in. I began climbing down into the utter blackness.

Then a brittle old rung broke and I lost my grip, fell a few feet, and caught myself, trembling and wishing the wall were tighter against my back. I reached down one shaky foot but there was nothing to put it on.

Steady, old boy! I told myself. *Mustn't panic now!*

I had an overpowering urge to scream out. I sucked in a breath, and then I noticed the air had gotten fresher. I looked down. Wonder of wonders!—there was the faintest ghost of a light under my feet. The library.

Pulling myself together for the final throw I groped downward with my foot. My toe found the next rung. I inched my weight onto it, expecting every moment it would break. But the iron held firm. A step down. The broken rung was jabbing into my stomach now.

Almost there!

The ladder ended. I dropped softly into the hearth. There was the blessed, damp old library (looking rather odd from this angle.) The light I'd seen in the chimney was coming from a single candle burning on the whist table.

I'm ashamed to say it, Albert, but I was so relieved to get out of the ancient piping that I felt positively giddy and not at all sorry for my foolishness. *They'll think I'm a wizard*, I almost chuckled. *They'll think I vanished into thin air.*

Then I looked down at my coat and trousers. I was caked in soot from head to toe. Little black showers came off my clothes when I moved.

Wizard! I thought. *They'll see my tracks all over the carpet.* I brushed myself off as quietly as I could and then I took off my shoes.

Footsteps in the corridor! My heart sank. Then Radan's voice.

"Well, damn it, man," he was saying, "the doctor hasn't got wings! If he wasn't in his room, then either, *unus*, you're lying, or, *duo*, he snuck by you on the stairs somehow. Your eyes are failing, I believe."

"And why would the doctor sneak by me?" Fitzhugh sounded angry. "He was going after his medicine-bag. I told you he's unwell, sir."

"Unwell, hey? Was that what he said? Your accomplice seems pretty spry to me! Climbs tower then disappears. Did he ever really go upstairs, I wonder?"

"I heard him close his door."

"Nor are your ears what they once were," Radan growled. "This is *your* fault, master Fitzhugh. *You* let him escape."

"This isn't an asylum, sir!" Fitzhugh returned hotly. "His Lordship was happy to entertain Doctor Scott not two days ago! Beg your pardon—you still haven't told me why you're looking for him."

Radan made some reply, but I didn't hear it. I'd already slipped out the servants' door shoes in hand, taking care to close it softly behind me. I fled down the corridor and into the dark kitchen.

The servants' door opened.

I held my breath. For a moment I saw Fitzhugh's head framed against the candlelight. He looked up and down the corridor and then he closed the door.

I breathed a sigh and tiptoed past the massive iron stove. Comforting *click-click* of dying embers within. Back kitchen door.

Rosemary bramble.

Garden fence—

Gone! Sweet enfolding darkness. Sweet free air of a spring night.

And so, Albert, to make a long story longer: I'm in desperate need of ten pounds, and there's a good fellow. I meant to cash a note, but *alas!*—I spent half the day tramping cross-country to Jedburgh, keeping clear of the roads. I forded the Tiviot above Branxholme under a lovely crescent moon and then I struck out eastward across the meadows. I marched as straight a course as I could all through the night and morning, floundering through every bog and burn, making twenty miles out of fifteen. About midday I saw the ruined tower of Jedburgh Abbey rising above the trees. By the time I set foot on High Street I was so spent that I made straight for Greyfriars' in the hope that I might lie under some friendly shrub like a common beggar. To that end I was limping past the Relief Church, and I think I must have made an awfully pitiful sight because the ladies of the Temperance Society sallied out when they saw me and seized me forthwith. They bore me off to the Strangers & Orphans Lodge where they deposited me in a wash-house with three copper kettles and a cake of yellow soap so caustic you could have tanned an oxhide with it. They've taken away my clothes to be washed (or maybe burned) and left me with a dressing-gown and a mighty stack of religious tracts. In light of the foregoing, kindly post a bearer's note in the amount of ten pounds to *The Black Bull Inn*, Jedburgh, care of Mr. Christie or his agent, drawn upon the account of Stewart H. Scott, M.D., Edinburgh, etc., etc.

In the meantime I'm comfortably installed here with the strangers and orphans. It's really as good as the inn, Albert. The Society will give you a clean bed gratis and a copy of, *e.g.*, *Six Sermons on the Nature, Occasions, Signs, Evils, and Remedy of Intemperance*, from the pen of Lyman Beecher, D.D. (Boston Yankee), foreword by John Edgar, D.D. (Irishman)—a dubious tract if I ever saw one. I've no choice but to stay here and pen some explanation for Fitzhugh, as I have no clothes. Once I'm dressed I'll get back to deciphering *The Last Will and Testament of the Pirate John Blackjohn*. No treasure map so far, but you'll be the first to know. My latest transcription follows. I remain, Sir—

Yours, etc.

—*SHS*

CHAPTER 9

Doctor Scott's transcription—

The other time Diana caught me crying in the woods was when Peter went away to be a soldier.

It happened in July. One morning two men-at-arms rode up to our cottage at first light—big men on big gray horses. One of them was leading a saddled mare. They found Peter outside splashing water on his head out of a wooden bucket. He went white as death when they called him "yeoman McKenna" and handed him a dirty strip of tartan with the seal of the Crichton castle guard stamped on it in red wax.

Uncle Andrew and my mother came outside. One of the soldiers gave my mother a purse and told her Peter was chosen to bear arms for the earl Sir Francis Stewart, "on account of the courage he showed in Northumbria." The soldier said we would see Peter again on Saint Barnabas' Day and at Epiphany.

Uncle Andrew looked solemn. My mother clutched the purse and cried. I thought Peter should have been happy but he only stared at the ground. By sunrise he was gone—on a better horse this time. Like before, he never once looked back.

Uncle Andrew said Peter had saved our farm. Three bad years and the barley was almost gone. We'd been living on milk and cabbages, and now the cow was drying up. Uncle Andrew said we might have sold our freehold—and what then? Like as not we'd have been tenants on the same land we'd owned, and we'd have starved anyway.

Oh! how I envied Peter, watching him go! Peter was a man—a *fighting* man. To serve the earl. To wear armor—carry a *sword!* To win fame in battle. To never touch a plow again. What bliss!

Coughing and wiping my eyes, I ran straight for the forest.

I was in the hollow behind old Sowter's farm, sitting on a fallen tree. Diana must have climbed up beside me. I never heard her come. All at once I looked up and there was a young girl with a narrow, serious face and piercing blue eyes looking at me.

I knew there was no use in pretending.

"Peter's gone away," I sobbed. "He's gone to Crichton and we shall hardly see him again."

Diana didn't answer; she just picked up my hand and squeezed it until my shoulders stopped shaking.

"Come," she said, "I want to show you something."

An ugly shout made us both jump.

Diana! Slattern!

It was farmer Sowter's voice, just beyond the hollow.

"Diana!" Sowter screamed, "Bastard, willst hide all day? Will the whore's daughter eat the bread of the laborer? I've an ox-whip to give thee, love."

Diana squeezed my hand harder. I could feel her shaking.

"Come!" Sowter screamed. Four ravens in a birch tree heard him and rose noisily above the forest. "A-*ha*!" Sowter crowed, "thou'rt betrayed of thine own black cousins!" I heard him blundering off toward the tree. Diana turned to me with a wry smile. I saw her cheek was bruised and purple again.

"He tried to touch me," she whispered. "You'd best be going."

"No," I snarled, "I'd best be murdering him and feeding his warm guts to the birds!" I slid off the tree but Diana caught my sleeve.

I turned around. She was laughing quietly.

"You can murder him later," she said. "Hurry! There's someone I want you to meet."

Diana moved fast, scarcely leaving footprints. Old Sowter's cursing was swallowed up in the trees. I jogged and panted along behind her. We were headed south on the game trail that followed the Rankle Burn. The day was getting hot. I struggled to keep up. Diana glided effortlessly on, humming a monotonous little tune to herself.

I stopped.

Diana turned around. "What is it?" she asked.

"That's strange!" I mused.

"*What's* strange?"

"Strange I've never seen that ford before." I squinted and shaded my eyes.

Diana smiled.

"That's where we're going."

To our left a faint track split off the game trail and turned directly into the burn. Across the burn the track climbed up a ferny brae[52] and disappeared among the trees.

"Where *are* we?" I asked wonderingly.

Diana smiled. She picked up her skirts and stepped into the burn.

"Is that Priest Sike? It doesn't seem as if we've come that far."

Diana laughed.

"We're almost there."

I splashed into the stream behind her.

"It looks much nicer on the other side," I remarked.

A kind of golden haze seemed to brood over the opposite bank. The reeds were overhung with meadowsweet and somehow the trees looked greener than ordinary. Diana picked her way across the chattering rocks, her bare feet hardly touching the water. We brushed through the reeds at the water's edge. Two ancient willows arched over the track like a church door. I passed between them with a solemn sort of feeling. Together we trudged up the slope.

The track became a path. Then whitewashed stones appeared on either side as if someone had been watching for travelers in the dark. Here was a fallen tree chopped through; there was a little causeway of branches laid across a bog. "This is wonderful!" I exclaimed. "How have I never been here before?"

"Shhh!" Diana hissed. Stillness like a cathedral hung over the woods. The birds seemed to twitter in hushed voices.

We walked through a living arch where two holly trees twined their branches.

I stopped, spellbound.

---

52 Brow, (*i.e.*, slope)

The trees abruptly ended. We were standing on a smooth-cut lawn like a bowl speckled with yellow celandine. Beyond it, a still green pond lay glistening in the sunlight.

"What *is* this place?" I breathed.

"This is the Lilylock," said Diana.

"What's a lilylock?"

"Not *A* lilylock—"

Diana was walking toward the pond.

"—*The* Lilylock."

I followed her to the water's edge. Lily pads covered the pond like an emerald carpet. Every pad had a white lily flower, and every flower had a little yellow sunburst in the middle. Enormous blue dragonflies darted everywhere. My foot crunched the gravel rim and instantly a thousand frogs croaked at once and jumped into the pond. I shouted *Oh!* and tripped backward. Diana laughed.

"I guess she knows we're here."

"*Who* knows?"

"Someone I want you to meet."

"Is she a frog?" I growled.

Diana ignored me. She was looking at the pond and singing one of her strange songs, almost in a whisper. It sounded beautiful in a wild sort of way.

"Is that song from Éireann?" I asked.

Diana only closed her eyes. Her lips were moving but I couldn't hear the words. I sat down on the gravelly bank. The sun was hot. The dragonflies were making an endless drowsy whir and the whole place seemed safe and restful.

My head was just beginning to nod when all at once I noticed Diana had stopped singing.

I opened my eyes.

Blinked.

Blinked again.

I jumped up with a yelp. The lily pads had whisked aside like a curtain. I could see the little ripples the breeze made on the naked water.

"Diana! Did you see—"

There was a long, dark something in the water. At first I thought it was Diana's reflection—

No. Not a reflection. I leaned over the pond. Something solid was floating just below the surface. The sunlight played across it in little golden ripples.

I squawked and skipped backward. "Oh, she's drowned!" I wailed. "She's drowned!"

A woman's face stared up at us with open, glassy eyes. Her limbs were suffused in a filmy green gown. One white hand hung motionless by her side. Only her mossy hair stirred slightly.

The corpse smiled.

I shrank back in horror.

The mossy hair came together as her white forehead lifted. She looked at me through the water.

"G—God save me!" I gibbered.

One hand broke through the surface, water running down it. She beckoned me to come. I clutched Kol's fairy glass against my heart. My knees buckled.

The last thing I heard before I fainted was Diana laughing.

CHAPTER 10

I opened my eyes.

I was lying on my back in the greenest room you can imagine.

I raised my head, blinking stupidly. The low vaulted ceiling above me was inlaid with magnificent tracings in green—vines and branches, leaves and tendrils, climbing down to the windows as if they were alive. Deep window casements. Rippled green glass set in a latticework like willow branches. The walls were hung with green tapestries. I was stretched out on a sea-green couch with my head propped up on a velvety green cushion.

I flopped back again with a start. The dead lady from the pond was standing over me, watching me with calm green eyes.

"Wh-what—"

I coughed up pond water. Diana snickered.

"You fainted and fell in," she said.

I sat up quickly, reddening.

"I—I thought she was dead!" I was gaping at the lady like an idiot. Her hair and her shimmering green gown were completely dry. She spoke, and her voice was low and musical.

"Welcome, sir," the green lady said, "What brings you to the Lilylock?"

No one had ever called me 'sir' before. I could only stammer and look at my feet, so Diana had to answer for me.

"This is James," she said. "*I* brought him here."

The green lady studied my face.

"Has he come to murder me?" she asked serenely.

Diana's mouth fell open.

"No indeed!"

"But his hands are stained with fairy blood," said the green lady. "Also, he reeks of giant."

I looked down at my hands. My palms still carried faint brown smudges.

"It—that came off the blade," I said. "I grabbed it from Father Lar—"

Diana interrupted me.

"A Black Stag has risen."

"Truly?" asked the green lady. Her delicate eyebrows lifted slightly. Diana nodded.

"A Black Stag woke the firbolg on the knowe. It's you they want, my lady. They'll come for you again when the moon—"

"Why did you bring *him* here?" the green lady asked pointedly. Now it was Diana who looked down at her feet with a troubled face.

"I— He saved someone," she said quietly. "He hit the Black Stag with a rock."

"Ah," said the green lady, "then he's as good as dead." She studied my face again. "Did you kill a priest, sir," she asked, "a gray-robed mortal with eyes the color of a raven?"

"God's sake no!" I cried, crossing myself and kissing Kol's fairy glass by mistake. "I only know two priests in the whole world. One is Friar Kol, and the other one was dancing with the giants."

The green lady shook her head slightly. She turned to Diana. "I see the priest Maewyn's death," she said, "by the hand of a young mortal very like to this one."

"No, my lady," I put in, "the Black Stag—*he* said he killed a priest. I heard him tell the giants so."

The green lady looked me over again. "Strange," she said with a sigh. "But I suppose he doesn't have the mark of a killer of men. A killer of birds, maybe. If he hit a Black Stag with a rock then there's not much *I* can do for him. Come, mortal," she beckoned, "sit beside my window."

"What will the Black Stag *do* to me?" I quavered, getting up. "Will he put a curse on me?"

The green lady laughed merrily.

"No," she said, "but he'll be very angry. I think his head must have hurt terribly."

The lady led us down a short flight of steps. Then a carved stone archway opened into a cozy sort of apse. Three cushioned chairs were arranged beside a low table. Behind the table stood a tall window, green like church glass.

The green lady motioned me toward a chair. I sat down.

I bounced back up again.

A fish swam past the window.

The fish turned, flipped its tail, and glided past the window again. A brown trout.

With a pounding heart I inched nearer. I looked up. There lay the surface of the pond above my head, dancing needles of sunlight piecing down into the water. A big speckled pike swam up from below the windowsill, and the brown trout flipped its tail and retreated into the wavy shadows.

I rubbed my eyes in disbelief.

Silvery schools of minnows were roaming through the lilies. Petulant brown turtles nosed upward and downward between the glittering surface and the gray mud. The space just outside the window was clear of weeds and neat and orderly as a kitchen garden. Water plants I could not name grew in even rows, white pebble borders in between. Diana and the green lady had already taken chairs.

Still gaping at the window I slowly sat down, thoroughly convinced I was dreaming.

I realized the green lady had been asking me my surname.

"I—I was christened James McKenna, my lady," I answered dazedly.

"Tell me, Seumas MacCionaodha—" the green lady smoothed her gown over her knees— "how did your hands come to get those stains?"

I rubbed my palms together, wondering where to begin.

"I—I took a blade from Father Lara," I said. "The giants—they all cut their hands with it. It was covered in blood, and—"

"Giants?" the green lady interrupted. "Giants are made of the stuff of the earth. Giant blood comes off easy enough. *You've* got fairy blood on your hands, mortal boy. Fairy blood will never wash away."

I studied my palms.

"They called it the—the 'Crook of Esus,' I think it was." I looked up. "Who is Esus, my lady?"

"Esus," the green lady replied, "is the immortal forester, the guardian of the woodlands. He tends the trees and all the things beneath them.

"He is my master," she added. "I obey his Word."

"Is Esus an angel?" I asked wonderingly.

The green lady laughed. "If you like," she said. "There are many makers and doers in the earth of which mortals know nothing. I, for one. I am Farahain-air-an-Lili. I keep the Lilylock and the forest around it. You may call me 'Lily,' for short."

"They were calling you Green Lady," I said. "The Black Stag—I think he meant to—to put you in a little green bottle." I glanced up at her bashfully. Lily's face was serious. She was divinely beautiful, I thought, though not in a human way. Her gown made a watery swirl about her limbs as she got up and stood before the window.

"What else did they say?" she demanded.

"Well—er—the Black Stag said *These isles will be ours*, but it sounded like he needed *you* for that. What do you think he meant, my lady?"

Lily was gazing out the window with her hands clasped behind her slender waist. "He meant these isles," she said quietly, almost to herself. "Alba, Éireann— He needs me, or else he can't take them. He knows the Crook of Esus can work a powerful enchantment on me."

"How so, my lady?"

"Power in the blood—"

Lily turned on her heel and looked at us crossly. "Giants are of this world," she said. "Fairies are of the Other. You say the pruning-hook of Esus is stained with blood of both worlds? The one who sheds the blood is the one who has the power and Word of Esus."

"What does the 'Word of Esus' mean?"

"It means the Black Stag can command me."

I bit my lip thoughtfully, trying hard to understand.

"And what will he command you to *do*?"

Lily turned back to the window. The pike was still prowling outside, staring down at us with a defiant expression. Lily clasped her hands behind her again.

"I have many gifts," she said, "that a selfish man might covet. To me is given power over rivers and streams; to make them overflow their banks, or to bring up hidden treasures from their depths. I can bear a man dry-shod across the flood. I can wake the ancient creatures that lie sleeping in the deep lochs—"

Lily sighed.

"I'm sure he has some wicked scheme in mind for me.

"He's a fool," she added, leaving the window and taking her chair again. "Murdered Dana's priest, did he say? An awful curse will haunt the priest-slayer! Dana is a huntress, you know. She'll cut the stag's heart out at last."

Diana pressed her hands together with a wretched expression. "What can we *do*, Lady Farahain?" she asked despairingly. "The Black Stag saw me by moonlight. James knocked him off his horse—"

"Can Esus help us?" I suggested. "It's *his* pruning-hook, after all."

Lily smiled and shook her head. "I cannot summon Esus," she said. "It is the law. We *shiori*—immortals—we are not changeable like men."

Lily fell silent. Diana sat with her chin in her hands and a worried look on her face. High above us a cloud had covered up the sun. The window went gray. Lily's house was plunged into darkness.

At last she spoke.

"I see only one choice," Lily said. "This boy must take me prisoner before the Black Stag can do. That is why he came with a fairy glass."

"I b-beg your pardon?" Diana sounded like she was choking.

Lily shook her head gravely, sending little waves down her hair.

"It is a desperate chance," she said. "Once I enter the fairy glass my gifts will become this—" She looked at me (a bit distastefully, I thought)

"—become this boy's to use. We'll have to hope *he* doesn't put me to some foolish purpose. But we shall see."

Diana looked bewildered. "But—but James doesn't have the Crook of Esus," she said. "And if James didn't kill the priest, can he command you to enter the fairy glass?"

"He cannot command me," Lily replied, "but I can enter of my own free choice."

Diana shot me an uneasy glance.

"But—"

"Blood of this world," said Lily, "and blood of the Other. James has both. I shall simply have to grant him the Word of Esus—at least so far as *I* am concerned—and I'll have to do it quick, before the Black Stag comes with the *corran* and takes me himself."

She heaved a regretful sigh.

"He'll hardly know what to do with me, at any rate."

"But I haven't *got* any giant's blood," I protested, looking down at my hands again.

"You've got enough of it under your fingernails," Lily returned tartly, "to paint a door with."

I blushed furiously.

"We are poor farmers, my lady. We do not know gentle ways."

Lily laughed, but not unkindly. "Don't be troubled," she said. "*I* know your substance better than you do yourself. A king is made of the same stuff as a beggar. It is by deeds and not by birth that mortals differ one from another.

"You're more than half a fool," Lily continued serenely, "and many hard lessons wait. But I see you've got a kind heart. It is because of that kind heart that I dare hazard myself to your—" (her face betrayed a faint grimace)

"—your keeping."

Lily drew her chair nearer the table.

"When you need my help," she said, "simply touch the fairy glass and call my name: Farahain. Or just 'Lily' will do—but beware!" she said, "When one soul departs, another soul will enter—take care it is not your own! And, mortal boy, if you set me to work evil," (Lily's eyes were like needles) "then with evil you will be repaid. It is the law.

She turned to the low wooden table.

"Now we begin!"

A shallow basin of water was on the table. The basin was rough and unadorned; carved from one gray stone. A water lily floated in the middle with its golden crown in full bloom. Lily gently nudged the lily to one side.

"Give me the giant blood."

Reddening, I took out my quill knife and pared off the end of my dirty thumbnail. I dropped the paring on the table with an embarrassed squirm. Lily bent low over the basin. She pursed her rose-petal lips and blew softly, making tiny ripples in the water. Then she picked up the nail paring and dropped it in.

"Wash your hands."

I plunged my hands into the water and rubbed my palms together.

"That will do," Lily said. She stood up, trembling slightly as she reached out and took Kol's fairy glass, which was still hanging from the leather strand around my neck. She closed her perfect hand over it. I sat there blinking up at her like a calf on a rope. I could feel the slight tug of her grip on the strand.

"Take a deep breath, then close your mouth."

"Why—"

Everything vanished.

Lady, basin, table, window—gone. Cold water surged into my mouth. I choked. Water filled my lungs.

Crushing darkness. I thrashed and struggled. My hands plunged into freezing mud.

I'm dying, I thought.

My finger caught the leather strand.

'*Lily.*'

Blackness.

I was lying on my back again. This time Diana was on top of me.

Diana's mouth was pressed over mine. She pulled back her shoulders and heaved a blast of air down my throat. My chest rose and my lungs wrenched inside like they were going to tear open. I tried to suck in, but nothing came. Diana took another breath. Her cold lips closed over mine and strands of wet hair fell across my eyes. Another wrenching blast, and then she drove my belly in hard with both hands. Air and water exploded out of my mouth. I gulped in a huge breath. Then I turned my head and vomited. I lay there gasping and shivering while the giant wooly clouds of summer marched serenely across the sky.

I felt for Kol's fairy glass.

"Did Li—"

I coughed up water again.

"Did Lily save me?"

"*I* saved you!" Diana snapped. "*You* were swimming down instead of up! I pulled you out by your hair. Why didn't you close your ugly mouth like Lady Farahain said?"

"I—I was going to ask her why."

73

"*Why?*" Diana fairly spat. "You wanted to ask an Immortal *why?* I thought you were dead! It was all I could do to drag—" (tears were running fast down her cheek) "—drag your fat carcass out of the pond. Wish I hadn't! Look at my feet—all cut up from the gravel. I must have breathed into you a hundred times. Well are we *quite* satisfied now, my lord? Now that we—"

I already had my arms around Diana.

"—now that we know *why?*"

I squeezed her shoulders together and kissed her wet cheek furiously until the color returned.

"I'm sorry," I whispered. "Diana, I'm so sorry."

We got up on our feet. Diana limped across the lawn toward the forest path. The Lilylock lay green and untroubled behind us.

As we passed through the holly arch, clouds covered up the sun. An east wind came from the sea bringing something wild with it. It gave me a sudden pent-up feeling.

I wish the wind would carry ME away, I thought.

To Jerusalem—or maybe to the Apple Isle, to hear the fairies sing.

Diana's feet were bare and muddy on the path. She walked with her eyes on the ground. I thought of vile old Sowter waiting for her back at the farm.

"Who are—"

(The words came before I realized I was saying them out loud.)

"Who are you, Diana?"

Diana kept walking.

"I am Diana O'Neil," she said, as if she'd been expecting the question.

CHAPTER 11

From the letters of Doctor Stewart Henry Scott—

Kelso, Roxburghshire
May 21, 1838

Dear Albert:

A terrible thing happened: Fitzhugh's been sacked! I'm entirely to blame. It was only by a lucky chance I ran into him, poor fellow. I found him in Jedburgh at nine o'clock in the morning outside the post-carriage house in Market Place, sitting on a trunk full of all his possessions in the world. Radan only gave him twenty-four hours to pack his things. He left Branxholme Friday afternoon. (I vanished up the chimney on Thursday).

I expected he'd be furious at me, but Fitzhugh only said *I'm glad you're well,* and *I was sure the fairies must have spirited you away.*

"You weren't dismissed on *my* account, were you?" I asked him.

"Aye, that I was," Fitzhugh said despondently. "Mister Radan gave me the boot, the acka soothern[53] rat! I was looking for you half the night," says Fitzhugh, "and I told Mr. Radan, *Maybe the doctor's fainted. Maybe he's lying insensible somewhere.* But Radan, he stomps off to his room without a word. He waits until just after I'd served him breakfast next morning and then—"

Fitzhugh blew his nose into his handkerchief.

"—and then he shows me the door."

"No!" I gasped.

"Aye."

Fitzhugh coughed and wiped his eyes.

---

[53] Geordie: *crazy southern*

"Bloody well knew where the door *was*. I *kept* that door five-and-twenty years. 'T was I who drove all the way to Warkton to see the old duke buried. 'T was I who carried the young duke's fishing-tackle when he came from Eton on holiday—"

Fitzhugh blew his nose again.

"But *why*?" I cried. "Fitzhugh, I'm so sorry! What was his reason?"

"Oh, something barmy," Fitzhugh growled. "He said we were in a 'conspiracy,' you and I, but he wouldn't say why he so much as cared you'd gone."

Fitzhugh slid off the trunk and pretended to fiddle with the buckles.

"Bloody quarter-century in service," he muttered. "Gave the best years of me life to the house of Buckley. Then one day *snap!* Lunker[54] I never laid eyes on marches in; says *His Gryce no LONG-uh requize yuh SUHvices*—"

I laughed in spite of myself.

"But where will you *go*?" I asked. I felt utterly wretched about it, Albert. I said "Do you have any family?"

"Aye," says he, "me widowed sister in Sooth-Berwick.[55] She's all the family I've got and I meant to make Kelso before Sunday, but now they tell me Her Majesty's bloody post aren't running and I'll have to stay two more nights in the bloody Black Bull Inn—"

"Why, my dear fellow!" I interrupted, "I'm going to Berwick myself (probably). But to Kelso for sure. We'll hire a hack and go together![56] Or we'll find a carter bound that way. There's no need to fear the Bull—ha ha! Besides," (I put my arm around his big shoulders) "I owe you supper and a rather long explanation. I'm a vagabond myself now."

Fitzhugh brightened. "Well," he said thoughtfully, "if Berwick suits you—"

"It might!" I said warmly. "Truly it might. I wasn't certain where I'd be going to next, but maybe here's the answer. And you, my friend—five-and-twenty years in service, did you say? You're in desperate need of a holiday, laddie! Doctor's orders!"

---

[54] Londoner

[55] Berwick-upon-Tweed, Northumberland. Pronounce *BEAR-ick.*

[56] Hackney coach.

So, Albert, to make another long story longer: I'm in desperate need of a fresh ten pounds, and there's an *especially* good fellow! If you'd be so kind as to send a note to Berwick-Upon-Tweed: payable...order of...drawn upon...so forth. Me, I'm Berwick-bound with a butler, a book, and just two shirts to my name (one of which is out at the elbows and stuffed inside my mackintosh.)

Please find herewith another installment of *John Blackjohn*. You *are* sending these to Constantine's, I hope? We need a copy for safety's sake. I confess I'm growing rather fond of the boy, James. Seems like a good sort.

I remain, &c.

—*SHS*

CHAPTER 12

Two Sundays went by and I didn't see Diana. With Peter gone, all the haymaking fell to uncle Andrew and me. It was the second mowing. Uncle Andrew said with any luck we might get a third. Ordinarily Peter would have mowed alongside uncle Andrew while I raked, but now I had to wade through the waist-high meadow with Peter's heavy scythe in my hands and swing and swing while my shoulders burned and the sweat ran into my eyes.

Uncle Andrew mowed like a pendulum. The grass fell in neat little waves at his feet while I staggered and tried to keep up. Now and again I'd get too far behind and then uncle Andrew would pretend our scythes were dull and we'd stop to whet them. But once I'd caught my breath again he'd start to get impatient. *Don't like the looks o' that sky*, uncle Andrew would say, squinting up at some imaginary cloud. *Devil wants to make it rain on the hay.*

Strange to say, I only thought about lady Lily once. It was on Sunday. I was inside Buckley kirk,[57] nodding along to the familiar drone of Father Lara saying mass.

> *...ex hac altáris participatióne sacrosánctum,*

I yawned and looked up at the bright windows.

> *Sánguinem sumpsérimus, omni benedictióne—*

---

[57] Church

My eyes wandered across the glowing panes. I knew each one by heart. Cain and Abel. Moses and Pharoah. Mary and Joseph kneeling by the manger, just like they'd done a thousand weary masses before.

There was Jesus in his usual corner. He was bending over a sort of couch where a yellow-haired girl lay waiting to be raised from the dead. She had a sour look on her face, like a mopey dandelion. Jesus reached out to her with an open hand.

Then I remembered another hand—a white hand, breaking through the surface of a still green pond.

I looked down at my shirt. A little bump showed where Friar Kol's fairy glass hung against my chest.

Did I really see a woman in a pond? I wondered, *Or was that something I dreamed?*

That evening I was restless. *It's only more mowing tomorrow*, I thought.

Crickets were beginning to sing outside. I climbed up into the hayloft above the stable and looked out across the valley. Night shadows were spilling down from the heath, flooding all the little hills and coombs.

A big black crow landed on the roof. She yelled *Crawk!* and gave me a knowing look. Then she flapped off again.

"Where are you going so late?" I shouted after her.

The evening star came out in the east. Then more stars. It was a warm night. Across the hollow candlelight showed through Sowter's open window. Up by the heath I saw a flicker like a campfire winking out of a glen.

Who's up there? I wondered.

Highwaymen? Poachers?

I stretched out on my stomach.

Maybe it's Queen Maev.[58] I smiled and propped my chin up on my hands. The light blinked redder now in the gathering dark.

I sat up with a jolt.

Maybe it's the Kerrs!

I scurried down the ladder. *That* explained it! The Kerrs were out, and up to no good! Cattle thieving. Horse thieving. We *had* a horse now—an old

---

[58] The fairy queen Mab of legend

gelding dozing in Jenny's stable. He nickered drowsily as I slipped across the lane.

I crouched in the shadows beside the hedge. The ancient brambles grew so dense they could have stopped a rabbit, but I knew a way under. Peter and I used to crawl through it playing Knights and Reivers.

Bare dirt stood out in the gloom. I dived in.

When did it get so small?

I wriggled out on the other side, scratched and bleeding. Brushing myself off, I skirted the cabbage field and ducked into the forest.

I found the path along the Rankle Burn—just a ghostly ribbon under the trees. The mysterious campfire was hidden now. I thought I'd seen it in the glen between Creag Hill and Cacra. Crossing the burn above the little weir,[59] I made for the open fell.

I'll sneak up on the Kerrs, I thought, *and see what they're getting up to.*

The fell was steeper than I remembered. There was nothing like a path. Thick furze and heather blocked my way. My legs ached. The slope went up and up.

Clouds covered the moon and it got quite dark. I was tripping over rocks now. I climbed and I climbed, and it felt like I was standing still. At last I turned around, hoping some light from the village would show how far I'd come.

Nothing.

Buckley was keeping quiet and dark somewhere down the valley. I rubbed my eyes and squinted into the murky distance.

Was that a light?

I thought I'd seen a faint gleam shine out, then gone again.

Could be mother Ebber snuffing out a candle.

There was a happy thought! If it really *was* a light from the village, then I'd climbed more than high enough. I struck out across the hillside, trying to walk a level path in the stumbling dark.

---

[59] Dam

The slope bent inward, then a black rift showed where a stream cut the hill from top to bottom. The ground dropped off sharply. I stopped short. Somewhere below I could hear the chatter of water over rocks.

I hesitated.

Then with a heavy sigh I got on my hands and knees and started edging down into the blackness. *The Kerrs will find me dead with a broken neck*, I said to myself.

Blind darkness closed over me. I had my right hand in front of my face, fending off branches. Then the branches stopped and my feet touched loose dirt. I skittered sideways down a gravely slope. Icy water went over my foot. I hopped back with a yelp, then I clapped my hand over my mouth.

Idiot! Now they've heard you!

I crouched beside the stream, trying not to breathe so loudly. But the minutes crawled by and there was no sound but the water on the rocks and the wind in the willows.

If anything I've come too high.

I got up cautiously and started to pick my way downhill, following the silver-gray ribbon of water.

Two big boulders loomed up black in front of me. The brook squeezed between them like a rabbit and disappeared. I edged to the left with my hand on the stone, feeling for a way around.

I froze.

Then I dropped down beside the boulder, shivering.

A ghostly light was filtering through the ravine. Not from where I thought the campfire was; it seemed to come from high up above, and it grew and grew until the tangled willows stood out hard and black against it. Now I could see the fluttery willow leaves. The leaves seemed to pass along a fluttery kind of song—faint; reedy; like a piper at the very edge of hearing.

One is sorrow,
Two is mirth—

I know that song!

I was running back up the glen.

Three's a wedding,
Four's a death—

Silly rhyme! Mother taught me. Tell your fortune by crows. Count the crows on a fence.

Yellow fingers of light groped through the mist. The web of branches blocked my way. I charged straight into the stream.

Five's, a blessing,
Six, hell—

Now I was wet up to my waist. The light was so strong I couldn't tell rocks from water. I shaded my eyes and tried to run.

I tripped and fell.

Staggered up.

Ran.

Fell again.

—Seven, the devil's own self.

The song ended on a flourish of the pipe, and the singer answered with a silvery laugh. It was a woman's voice. She took up the tune again, only this time the words were different:

One's a lady,
Two's a blade,
Three were brothers,
Four's a maid,
Five were his wounds,
Six, a hag,
Seven—His Worship, the Black Stag!

The sides of the ravine closed in. Now a crag cut it off—all but the narrow gap that let the stream through. Light was shining through the cleft like a golden keyhole in the blackness around it. As from a distance I heard my own voice singing:

One's a lady, two's a blade—

I wedged myself sideways in the gap. The stream swirled over my knees.

Three were brothers, four—

I scraped in deeper. The gap was so tight I couldn't breathe. I dimly felt the pent-up stream rising above my waist.

Five were his wounds, six—

My shoulder was bleeding. I lunged my arm through the gap and clawed desperately at the stone.

—a hag!

My shirt tore wide open and I broke free. I stumbled out into the light.

Peter was there.

CHAPTER 13

From the letters of Doctor Stewart Henry Scott—

Berwick-Upon-Tweed, Northumberland

May 23, 1838

Albert:

I've seen a ghost.

I'm in earnest, Albert: I've seen a ghost. I suppose from a medical perspective this raises the question of whether or not I am losing my wits. I remember my old father quaked and babbled toward the end; said he saw a whole regiment of angels and imps gathered around his bed (that was after we took away his bottle). The angels, said he, were playing sweetest music on their silvery harps—bidding his soul welcome to heaven—while the devils were trumpeting his sins and claiming his soul for hell. *Help me, sir!* he cried, *Send those sooty fellows away!* (for he didn't know who I was.) He was writhing and twisting the sheets in his hands. I was only a student at the College[60] but I did what I could for him—gave him a dose of laudanum and told him to be still. He lay back and rolled up his eyes in the most ghastly way until only the whites were showing, and he went on raving about angels and devils—but softer now.

He closed his eyes when the first rooster crowed. I pronounced him dead at half-past five, just as the sky began to show gray along the horizon.

Thus died my father on a January night. But I might be a worse case, Albert: *I* was haunted in broad daylight. It was on Old Bridge, in fact, coming into Berwick. Fitzhugh and I were crossing over in a cooper's cart bound for

---

[60] Probably the Royal College of Surgeons, Edinburgh

his sister's house in Ravensdowne. We'd got out of Kelso early enough, but the post coach stopped at Coldstream to change horses and neither the coachman nor the hostler[61] seemed particularly eager to see the job done (the pair of them were eating cold pie and drinking ale in the common-room). Fitzhugh reckoned if we hoped to call on his sister before midnight then we'd better find a driver on a more pressing errand than mere delivery of Her Majesty's mails.

We happened on a cooper's in Duke Street, where as luck would have it the cooper's man was just then setting out for Berwick with a cartload of barrels and an old brown mare.

Fitzhugh saw me eyeing them.

"Cart looks heavy, Doctor," he cautioned, reading my thoughts.

"That it does," I agreed. "Cart looks heavy; mare looks fifty."

"Aye," said Fitzhugh.

I put on my spectacles and took out my watch.

"Was the girl bringing out pie?"

"Aye," said Fitzhugh.

I squinted at the watch. "Seems the hostler's gone and married the coachman's cousin," I remarked.

"Aye."

"Was that *The Lass of Swansea Town* they're singing?

"Aye!" Fitzhugh growled. "All verses."

I was digging around in my pocket. "Maybe a slow ride is better than no ride," I ventured. "You haven't got two shillings, have you?"

Fitzhugh grimaced.

"Ho there!" I shouted at the driver. "Good day to you, my friend!"

The massive clock on Town Hall was chiming six in the afternoon when we rolled across Old Bridge into Berwick. Neither Fitzhugh nor I could see over the load of barrels in front, so we watched the scenes of the high-road slowly disclose themselves behind. I was swinging my legs off the back of the cart like a boy in church. Fitzhugh sat behind me with his briar-root[62] in his

---

[61] A groom or stableman who looks after horses. Commonly spelled and pronounced "ostler" in England.

[62] Pipe

teeth. You remember how narrow the venerable bridge is, Albert? Two carts can hardly pass in opposite directions, but the low parapet curves out over each pillar, making little alcoves where a person can stand back from the traffic. One by one these nooks unfolded to our view—some vacant, some occupied by idlers who stood gaping at the passers-by or casting with rods into the tide.

I looked up from the water.

I was staring straight into the face of a young man.

He looked about twenty-five—standing so near me that (ignoring metaphysical concerns) I could have reached out and touched him. I stared at him, and he stared back at me with such sad, imploring eyes that I felt a sudden impulse to ask him what was the matter. And he was strangely dressed, Albert! Have you ever seen a great-kilt of days gone by? His was homespun, I swear it. His kilt went well below his knee, and he had a sort of tartan on crossways over his shoulder. He wore the brimmed Monmouth cap of a sailor—light blue— and upon my life I think it was dyed in woad![63]

His short beard was dark and reddish—a bit pointed at the chin—and his gray eyes had a kind of dead emptiness in their expression. They called to mind the first cadaver I ever worked on at the College. (Young bricklayer, I think he was. Cudgel-dent in the back of his skull. They said he cheated at cards. So the bricklayer was consecrated to Science and the cudgel's owner was retired to Old Tolbooth to swing for it.[64] *Why am I stretched upon this unholy table?* the bricklayer's eyes seemed to plead. *Why are you sawing apart my ribs?*)

Forgive me, Albert. I had a few good seconds to look at him there in the alcove (the old mare was practically asleep). The young man stared at me so fixedly that I blurted out *I beg your pardon, sir?* before I could recollect myself.

"Eh—what?" said Fitzhugh drowsily. His pipe had gone out and he was dozing.

The young man opened his mouth as if to speak.

Fitzhugh sat up.

"Doctor?"

---

[63] The plant *isatis tinctoria*. Woad was the main source of blue dye in the British Isles before indigo became common in the 1700s.
[64] Awaiting execution

The young man disappeared.

I tore off my spectacles and rubbed my eyes.

"Did—did you see that fellow?" I cried. "Did you see that fellow standing there?"

"Nay." Fitzhugh stretched his legs and yawned. "What's that?" called the cooper's man. He craned his neck over the barrels. "The fisher, hey? Caught him a shad, did he?"

I gaped at the empty parapet where lately a man had stood.

"Had a fit at the *Queens Head*," I muttered to myself. "Climbed up a chimney. Got taken in by a charity. Now a young gent vanishes—"

"You're counting on your fingers again," Fitzhugh interrupted.

I looked up quickly. It occurred to me, Albert, that in the event I'd really lost my wits I would still need a bed that night.

"Am I?" I laughed. "I beg your pardons, gentlemen. I—I thought I saw a boy climbing on the rail. Trick of the light. Sorry I roused you, Fitzhugh, though there's not much harm done: we're nearly there."

"Right glad about that!" Fitzhugh groaned. He turned stiffly in the straw. "Bloody awful road. Howay man!" he shouted to the driver. "You haven't got a rug up there or anything, have ye?"

"Nay, milord," the cooper's man sniggered, "but you can ask the footman!" He pretended to curtsey. Fitzhugh grumbled something profane and went hunting for his tobacco. I pulled my legs in and stared down at the road.

The man didn't cast a shadow! I thought to myself. *If there's a lunatic asylum in Berwick, I think I'd rather not see it.*

So, my dear Albert, permit me to inform you that: *unus,* I'm now lodged at the home of one Elizabeth McRoy, Ravensdowne, Berwick-Upon-Tweed; and, *duo,* you're the only soul who knows I've quite possibly lost my mind. Fitzhugh has taken a rod and gone out to soothe his aching heart in his accustomed way. (He went back to Old Bridge, in fact. Says the fishing's good there.) Me, I've invaded Mrs. McRoy's back parlor, where I'm transcribing this enigmatic book again. If I see any more ghosts I'll be drawing up a Last Will and Testament of my own. Please find my latest efforts herewith.

Yours, &c.

—SHS

Postscriptum: There ought to be a bottle of turpentine behind the big hall clock. Kindly leave it there, and thank ye. Malcolm should be coming around to clean it (if he hasn't already). That clock was my grandfather's and I'd hate to see it come apart. *Tempus fugit*, lad. *Tempus fugit.*

CHAPTER 14

Doctor Scott's transcription—

He was there, Charlie my boy!

I limped out of the stream, wet up to my ears.

I gasped.

Rubbed my eyes.

The little clearing by the brook was lit up like a ballroom. Pipes were piping. Drums were drumming. Gorgeous couples were dancing. The trees were all hung with silver lamps. There must have been a hundred men and women—lords and ladies, from the look of them. A mighty log fire was sending up such an inferno you couldn't come within twenty feet of it, and there in the middle of it all stood your uncle Peter stony-faced beside a sort of woodland throne, a glittering cup in his hands.

On the throne beside him sat a lordly young gentleman in a plumed hat. The gentleman laughed, and his voice was so merry that the whole company laughed with him. He took the cup from Peter and hoisted it above his head.

"This island!" he shouted.

"And more!" the company roared back to him.

The gentleman handed the cup back to Peter, then he beckoned to me. His face was both proud and friendly. I thought I'd never seen a finer-looking person in all my life.

"And who but young James?" the gentleman cried, "brother to brave Peter McKenna. Welcome, James! Come near!" He waved his gloved hand toward the revelers. "Tonight our court is in the greenwood."

I gaped at him like I'd lost my wits.

The gentleman laughed again. "Here's a proud Scot!" he said. "Unbowed even before royalty." (He winked at Peter.) "But I'll do *him* the honor."

The young gentleman stood up. Instantly the music stopped. The hiss and snap of the fire rang out in the sudden stillness. Every head turned to look at us. The gentleman swept off his plumed hat. His chestnut curls fell across the short beard on his cheeks as he made me a low bow.

"For your brother's courage!" he said fervently, "and for the memory of your father, who spilt his blood in my sire's cause—I am Francis, Earl of Bothwell, at your service."

The lords and ladies murmured in admiration. I quickly dropped to my knees.

"I—forgive me, Your Majesty," I croaked, finding my voice.

Sir Francis laughed. "Up, lad!" he said in a kindly voice. "One kneels to a king. *I'm* not a king." He turned to the company. "Yet."

Franciscus Rex! Franciscus Rex! they all shouted at once.

The earl waved them off carelessly. "Pah!" he said. "Come to my bower, yeoman James. I've a word to say in your ear." He turned back to the company. "What? No dance?" he cried. "Is dancing anathema[65] in the Middle March? I hadn't heard so!"

The ruckus resumed in an instant. With a dazed faced I followed Francis to where a high couch was set under a silk canopy. Peter marched behind us silent and stiff, as if he hadn't seen me. I thought Peter looked magnificent in his steel-plate brigandine with the prancing stag over his heart.

Francis took the couch. He pointed me to a footstool next to it.

I looked down at the velvet cushion. Then at the mud caked on my clothes.

"My lord?"

"Sit, lad!" Francis barked.

I sat down abruptly. The couch was so high and the stool was so low that I was staring at the middle button on the earl's coat. Francis took the cup from Peter and drank deeply.

"These wastes are perilous!" he intoned, wiping his mouth with his cuff. "These wild heaths and fells. The baron's sword, the bishop's crosier[66]—they

---

[65] Formally denounced by the pope or church

90

account for little outside of settled lands. Your brother—" he paused and looked down at me significantly—"tells me that on Saint John's Night *you* came upon—shall we say—strange creatures?"

I looked up at Peter, astonished. I'd never told him anything about Saint John's Night; only Friar Kol.

Peter stared straight ahead and said nothing.

"My lord?" I faltered.

"Tell me what you saw!"

"I—I think I saw g—giants, my lord," I stammered. "But it must have been a dream," I added quickly. "I fell asleep under a fir tree."

The earl laughed uproariously.

"Giants?" he gasped, wiping his eyes. "Giants like the pagan heroes slew? *That* must have been a wonder! Pray, what were your giants doing, James mac Cumhaill?"[67]

I blushed and tried to think. The lights and noise were muddling my senses.

"I—I've forgotten," I said. "I don't recall they did *anything*, my lord."

"Ah?" The earl gave an arch smile.

"I'm sure it was a dream, my lord."

Francis laughed. "Come, lad!" he said, warmly, "you needn't be ashamed. I know whence comes this fancy. You've been listening to that daft Irish hermit, haven't you? What's his name—Padraig?"

"Kollam, my lord."

"Kollam. Yes. I have it from yeoman Peter he taught you your letters, eh? A good work that! But I daresay he's gone a bit moony out there in the forest all alone. I'd wager a silver pound it was *he* told you there were giants, when all *you* saw was a circle of old stones in the moonlight."

"Yes, my lord," I said humbly. I looked up at Peter again.

This seemed to irritate the earl.

"I'm addressing you, boy!" he snarled. I jumped and turned back to him. The clearing went silent again. The earl's face was cold and menacing.

---

[66] An ornate staff bearing the crucifix, symbol of the bishop's office.

[67] Francis alludes to Fionn mac Cumhaill (Finn MacCool), hero of Irish and Scottish legend.

Then he broke into a smile. "Don't tremble, lad," Francis laughed. "Gentle manners aren't learned behind a plow, nor—"

He raised his voice to the company—

"Nor are they learned by *rustics*."

Everyone laughed. I sank my head between my shoulders and stared at the ground. *Now* I knew why Peter wouldn't look at me. It was because he was ashamed of me. Peter was a soldier in the earl's guard, and I was just a rude plowboy. I'd embarrassed him in front of our lord—blundering in where I didn't belong; getting mud on the cushion.

Tears sprang up in my eyes.

Francis burbled on. He seemed to be talking about the fate of Scotland, though I scarcely heard him.

"—but there is none can mend the faults and fortunes of this land," (the earl was saying) "Not even if His Highness prince James were married and— Sweet Jesu!" Francis left off abruptly. "Is that some sort of charm you've got on?" He pointed at my chest. I stiffened and looked down at my torn shirt. Kol's fairy glass was casting a long green smear across my bare skin.

"Ha!" said Francis, leaning over me. "There's the hermit's work, if I ever saw it! Charms may cause strange dreams in the nighttime. Let me see that, boy!" He plucked the fairy glass off my chest with a triumphant look. But I was only thinking about how I'd embarrassed Peter. I couldn't stand it any longer.

"I'm sorry, Peter!" I wailed, jumping up and grabbing Peter's sleeve. The fairy glass jerked out of the earl's fingers. "Stop that!" Francis screamed, but I didn't hear him.

"I didn't mean to come here, Peter!"

I sidled around him, trying to look him in the face.

"Sit, you cur!" Francis shouted.

Then Peter moved.

Peter cocked his head to one side.

He leaned his head farther.

Farther.

Even farther.

I froze in utter horror. Now Peter's ear was pressed flat against his shoulder. His neck bent outward in a hideous way like it was broken. Then in one jerk Peter whipped his face around to mine.

My skin crawled.

Two lidless circles. The bonfire's flames were mirrored in them.

Peter's eyes were black and shiny like a crow's.

"Peter!" I screamed. I tripped over the footstool.

Peter loomed above me, arms outstretched like wings. I lay on my back gibbering. His cheeks stretched as his jaw dropped open.

And open.

And now his chin was touching his throat. I looked up into a yawning, toothless mouth; long black tongue hanging down.

I covered my face.

"*Sguir!*" barked a commanding voice. An angry hiss answered.

Trembling, I uncovered my eyes.

The clearing was transformed.

Now the fire burned low and red. The silver lamps were gone. Smoky torches sputtered here and there among the trees, and in their fitful light an unearthly mob were gathered.

I gagged. There was a stench like a henhouse. A vile thing—half bird, half woman—backed away from me, croaking.

One's a lay-lady! it gurgled, weaving its grotesque head from side to side. *Two's a blade!* Sullenly it made as if to peck at a smallish creature capering around us—face like a man, antlers like a buck, coarse brown hair all over.

I staggered to my feet and turned around.

Witches were bickering by the fireside, milling around a huge steaming cauldron where now and again a witch would lean over and breathe in its fumes. Nearer the ground strange faces came and went in the firelight. Sharp faces like foxes and stoats. Wide-lipped like hares. Slant-eyed like cats. Next to my knee a goblin-man was piping on a bone flute. Then the crowd parted and an ugly troll lumbered through, tongue lolling down his warty chin, claws almost touching the ground.

Wolf-men fought over an ox carcass. Huge bats wheeled overhead. The wild company made such a din of flutes and drums and grunts and squeals and shouts and curses that I wondered why Buckley village wasn't scrambling out of bed and to arms.

In the midst of it, Sir Francis Stewart, earl of Bothwell, sat calmly on a fallen tree and drank out of a clay mug.

"Ah—yes," he remarked. "So in a different light, as it were—"

He set the cup down next to him.

"—we bid you welcome to the court of the woodland king, His Majesty the Right Horrible Black Stag—myself." The earl made a slight bow where he sat.

"Where's Peter?" I choked.

"Safe abed at Crichton—or how should *I* know?" the earl returned testily. "Am I my own sergeant?" He heaved a sigh. "You see," he explained, "your presence was required here tonight, at the Midsummer session of our court. And our good brother Lara—" he glanced over his shoulder—"advises me that by the laws of our, er, *society*, it was necessary that you come of your own free will and not by way of compulsion."

Lara appeared out of the shadows like a ghost. His black cowl hung low over his face, but I knew that nose from a thousand Sunday masses.

"Brother Lara was afraid you wouldn't come, given the unusual—ah— *countenance* of our proceedings. Therefore—" (Francis stood up and put on his hat)—"by our arts we cast a different light on it, and we commanded our—"

He shuddered with disgust, though he tried to hide it.

"—commanded our sister to take the form of young Peter McKenna standing guard at my side. We knew that seeing him would give you courage to approach—and here you are!" the earl finished brightly. He elbowed Father Lara. "Let's get on with it, shall we?" Francis turned to me. "We require that fairy glass," he announced. Reaching inside his coat he took out a long blade like a dagger with no hilt. The blade looked ancient, but it's edge was newly sharpened and it glittered coppery-red in the firelight. Francis held it out to Lara.

"I'd sooner not stain my coat," he said.

"The boy must betray the nymph of his own free will too," Lara creaked.

Francis heaved another weary sigh. "Oh, very well," he said. "James, my lad? How would you like to join my guard as well? Serve alongside your brother, eh?"

My heart jumped.

"I should want nothing better in the whole *world*!" I cried, clasping my hands together. "My lord, I would serve you to my last breath!"

"You would," Francis nodded matter-of-factly. "Well, then—the glass, if you please?" He held out his hand. I eagerly pulled the leather string over my head and handed the fairy glass to him.

"Marvelous!" said Francis. "Now let's—"

"He must speak the Words of Purchase," Lara interrupted.

"Quite right!" said Francis. "I'd forgotten about that. Er—"

"*Do tibi phialum.*"

"Right!" said Francis. "*Do tibi phialum.* Repeat that, lad."

"My lord?"

"Just do your best," the earl said patiently.

"*Do tibi phialum,*" I repeated.

"Excellent!" Francis turned the fairy glass over in his fingers. "Now let's see who's inside! Touch the glass and call her forth. We'll meet our new courtière." The earl's voice was calm, but I could see his hand was trembling.

I reached out and touched the fairy glass, happy to be of use.

"Lily!" I called proudly.

A green light sprang up so suddenly that I had to shade my eyes—a wholesome, watery glow that overpowered the sullen bonfire. The wild company broke out in panic. Goblins scampered for the trees; witches threw cloaks over their faces. The light rippled for a moment, and then Lily was standing in front of us exactly as I'd seen her in the Lilylock. Her green gown flowed down to her bare feet. Tight around her neck she wore a collar like snail shells strung on marsh grass.

Lily looked at Francis. She nodded.

"He *is* impressively stupid," she said, as if answering the earl's thought. "It's some comfort to me that he will be dead soon."

"Indeed!" Francis returned cheerfully. "Green Lady, this boy just transferred your service to me, and I require your help."

Lily bowed.

"Say on, sir."

"Ahem—yes—my privy council—" Francis waved at the knot of witches by the cauldron—"advise me that Anne of Denmark, our queen-to-be, is about to set sail from Copenhagen to meet her royal betrothed."

"Yes," Lily nodded. "Your cousin James, the king."

"That's right!" said Francis. "My beloved cousin James. Long may he reign! He means to wed the fair princess of Denmark. It would make a noble match. A long line of kings might come from their union."

Lily bowed slightly.

"*Ergo*, nymph," (Francis slid off the tree) "I command that you shall raise two storms upon the North Sea."

"*Two* storms?"

"Aye! Two. The first will delay Anne's departure such that my cousin James—fearing treachery—shall go scampering off to fetch her."

Lily nodded. "And the other storm?"

"Will drown them both on their way back."

"Ah!" said Lily.

"Right!" Francis rejoined. "The throne of Scotland must have a king, after all. When the king who's on it now is *dead*, I mean. And then other thrones, and more thrones after that—" He stared off dreamily.

"Very well," said Lily. "And what of this boy? What of the banshee girl?"

"With your encouragement," Francis said earnestly, "I think the girl could be persuaded to join my cause. And I'll take care of the boy right now. Kneel, lad—" he turned to me—"and I'll give you your orders."

Something about the earl's tone made me uneasy, but I knelt obediently on the ground in front of him. Francis set the blade on the fallen tree and Lara helped him out of his coat. "I almost wish he *could* serve alongside his brother," Francis remarked, weighing the blade in his hand. "I'm curious whether he could learn one thing before he dies. But *that's* not to be."

The earl stood over me. Gripping the blade near the base he drew back his elbow in a practiced way and aimed the glittering point at my throat.

It felt like I was waking from a dream.

"No-o!" I cried.

I was backing away from him on my knees.

"No, my lord!"

"Hold still, hold still," Francis chuckled. "Or would you prefer I just hack at you?"

"Lily!" I screamed. "Help me, Lily!"

Francis stopped. He lowered his arm, utter disbelief on his face.

"Th—the *nymph*?" he sputtered. "She can't *help* you, boy! You just gave—I mean—you spoke the words—oh, hang it!" He aimed the blade at me again.

"I've never seen a *hound* so stupid!" he said, entirely to himself.

Lily sighed.

Francis looked up at her sharply. "*What*?" he demanded. There was a trace of uneasiness in his voice.

Lily daintily cupped her hand over her nose.

"Oh," she murmured, "I wish I *could* just drown the wretched king!" Lily pointed at the steaming cauldron by the fire.

"*Stoth.*"

The cauldron exploded.

Metal shards buzzed through the trees. The stench was beyond words. It blinded me and burned in my throat like cinders. I choked and couldn't breathe. The earl fainted outright. The only thing I could see was Kol's fairy glass, making a blurry green circle on the ground. I grabbed it and scrambled backward, groveling in the dirt to escape the fumes. The clearing was a riot of screaming and snarling. I got trampled and kicked. Something monstrously heavy stepped on my head and crushed my face into the mud. Retching, I wormed into the stream and furiously rubbed icy water in my eyes. I sucked in a breath.

I saw Peter.

Not Peter the bird-woman; not Peter the soldier—Peter my brother. Dear, ordinary Peter, just like I'd seen him ten thousand times before. His image seemed to waver in the foul air before my eyes.

Peter's clothes were filthy. There was an iron collar around his neck. He was sitting in straw with his knees pulled up against his chest. His head was down and his bony shoulders were shaking.

Then the vision was gone.

A fresher wind flowed down from the heath and carried off the stench. The wild commotion had already died away. Then the moon broke through the clouds, and I was sitting alone in the chattering stream with Kol's fairy glass in my hand. Its light was gone now. The glass lay in my palm like a little black stone.

"Peter?" I called. "Can you hear me, Peter?"

CHAPTER 15

Nota Bene—The next page fell apart when I tried to separate it. I fit the scraps together as best I could, but all I could make out was hill, ahead, midnight *and* Kol, *as well as the phrase 'heard something behind me.' From the following it would seem James McKenna fled the haunted glen and made for the hermit friar's cottage. James continues:*

"Let me in, brother Kol!"

I thumped softly on Kol's door, still watching over my shoulder.

The forest was dark and quiet. Kol's windows were shuttered, but I could smell smoke coming out of his chimney.

I heard a faint rustle.

"Let me in!" I beat on the door with my fist. "Let me in, quick! There's something out here!"

The bar scraped back. A crack of light appeared around the doorframe. I was surprised to see half of Diana O'Neil's face peer out. She opened the door a foot and I squeezed past her. "What are you *doing* here?" I panted as Diana lowered the bar. "It's past midnight! Sowter's out looking for you."

"Oh, farmer Sowter doesn't care for our little glen—"

Friar Kol's voice came from overhead, along with bumping and rummaging sounds. The ladder creaked. Kol stepped down carefully from the loft with a bundle tucked under his arm.

"He won't come after *dark*, at any rate—"

Kol set the bundle on the table.

"One time," (Kol chuckled), "when good Sowter came this way he stepped in a badger hole and turned his ankle, and another time he walked under that larch tree up the brae and a whole flock of pigeons anointed him at once. Not a one of them missed! Oh, how he used our dear Lord's name!"

Kol laughed and covered his ears.

"I expected the earth would swallow him up. Now he thinks the forest is haunted or something."

"Maybe it is." I collapsed onto the stool by the hearth.

"What's that?"

Kol hurried over.

"What happened to your shirt?" he demanded.

"I—I'm not sure. You should bar the windows."

"I *did* bar the windows." Kol pulled up a stool and sat down. He eyed me narrowly.

"Why are you shivering, James?"

"Some—things were chasing me," I said. "I think they stopped at the big ash tree; I hope so, anyway."

"What things?"

I swallowed.

"Bad things."

Kol clucked and shook his head. "You've still got my fairy glass," he observed. "*That's* not a bad thing."

"Let's hope not." (I touched the glass.) "Lily?" I called timidly. "Are you there, Lily?"

"Who—"

Green light filled the cottage. Kol jumped.

"Good heavens!"

Lily was standing beside us. She glared at me. She looked like she was about to say something, but then she noticed Friar Kol.

"Kollam!" Lily cried, suddenly beaming. "My dear Kollam, wherever have you *been*? I've missed you. The Lilylock misses you."

Even in Lily's wavering light I could see Friar Kol blush. He bowed (making his shiny head glow green). "Forgive me, my lady," Kol answered.

"I've longed to speak with you. The woods are grown perilous. I am honored to receive you for the first time in my—"

Kol glanced around his cluttered room. He winced slightly.

"You might've asked me to come!" Lily interrupted tartly. "You might've told the bullfinch. Here I've waited seven whole summers, and now it's this *boy*—" (she spat the word) "—this *boy* who summons me."

Kol bowed very low.

"Now I understand," he said. "Diana told me you bound yourself to this lad, and that of your own free will. That was brave!" (There was a catch in Kol's voice.) "That was very brave!"

Diana stepped up and dropped a neat curtsey. "I saw your light on Cacra, Lady Farahain," she said. "Is something wrong?"

"Oh, *that*?" Lily replied archly. "That was just the boy, summoning me to the revels of the Black Stag and his minions. Oh—and he tried to give me up," Lily whirled on me, "in exchange for a shiny coat, like his brother wore."

She was trembling with outrage.

"But it was our *earl*!" I wailed. "And he was so fine and handsome! He told me I could serve him and be with Peter again—"

"His 'earl' tried to murder him," Lily retorted. "And good riddance, I'd have said! It wounds me I had to save him."

Kol looked at me gravely. "James, this is serious," he said. "Surely you didn't *know* he was a Black Stag?"

I hung my head.

"Oh, I believe he *did* know," Lily seethed. "*The Right Horrible Black Stag*, I think he called himself. Does that sound familiar, James?"

"I'd already forgotten about that!" I blubbered. "I was only thinking how I wanted to get away from the farm and be a soldier with Peter."

"*Roost* with Peter?" Lily laughed mockingly. "His brother was just a filthy bancorra, it turned out."

"I'm sorry," I choked. "I'll go back home if you like." I started to get up, but Kol laid his hand on my shoulder.

"There, there—" Kol said kindly—"good heavens! Summoned by a Black Stag? It's a miracle you're alive! We shouldn't waste our miracles. Rest a while. There's no harm done—yet. Let's think, why don't we?"

I sank back down on the stool. Diana, Kol and Lily ranged themselves around the fire. Lily sat directly on the floor with her arms around her knees. I couldn't tell whether any part of her was touching the ground. She was near and at the same time distant, like a thing reflected on water.

Kol stared into the embers a moment. Suddenly he laughed.

"The world is simple when you're young," Kol said. "Growing up— well—the more you learn, the less you know. One learns backwards, so to speak. I've spent the better part of my life trying to reclaim the things God gave to my heart when I was small."

Lily looked up at him and smiled. "One good man almost makes the breed worth saving," she said. "It's a pity this one has no child."

Kol got a sudden fit of coughing. "I only meant—" he said awkwardly— "that I don't think James is *entirely* to blame. He doesn't know yet how Bad is often dressed up as Beautiful. All his life James has been taught that those who happen to be handsome on the outside are handsome on the inside too."

I thought they were talking about me like I wasn't there, and it made me cross and defensive.

"Everyone knows ugly people are bad as well!" I said hotly (for so I believed).[68] Lily scowled at me.

"Your brother John—is *he* bad, then?"

"John? No, he—"

I stopped. I'd never thought of that before. Next to Kol, John was the best person I knew. I was so used to seeing him that it never occurred to me there was anything ugly about him.

"Well, John—"

"Ahem!" Kol interrupted me. "James? I think we'd best take counsel of lady Farahain at present. We'll need her help if we want to see another sunrise. Why don't you tell us what happened just now? In the woods, I mean?"

I shuddered and looked at the door.

"Something followed me here."

"What?" Kol demanded.

---

[68] This sort of prejudice was common in the middle ages and persisted even in the Renaissance (*e.g.*, Shakespeare's *Richard*, though I'm certain Shakespeare himself knew better).

"I don't know. *Two* somethings, maybe."

Diana nodded. "I think evil creatures are gathering around your glen, brother Kollam. Something's fouled the Rankle Burn."

"I was just *in* the Rankle Burn," I retorted. "It didn't *smell* any different."

"It's changed," Diana said firmly. "I don't hear its voice any more."

"Nor I," said Lily.

"I walked your fence," said Diana, "and I sang my song—the song that lingers—but it was no use. Something else is working here. I don't think your fence will—"

"You have a *fence*?" I put in. "I've never seen any fence!"

"Er—yes—" Kol hesitated. "Not wattles or—or pickets or any of that sort of thing. My fence is more like—a blessing, if you will, over the forest all around."

Kol got up and threw a lump of charcoal on the fire.

"This is a place of peace," he said. "Only peaceful souls can come here—thus far."

"So what followed you, James?" Diana asked worriedly.

"*Sowter* followed me, at first." I snickered in spite of myself. "I was coming down from Cacra and I heard twigs break, so I skipped into the burn and then someone came stumping along with a lantern. When he got to me I saw it was Sowter. So I hid in the osiers[69] and let him go by, and after that I got off the path. I meant to come here straight through the woods but it was pitch-dark and I got all turned around, and then I heard a noise in the brush and I couldn't tell what it was. *It's nothing but a badger*, I said to myself. But it gave me a crawly feeling inside, brother Kol. So I took off running. And then I tripped and fell. So I just lay there and listened for a while. At first everything was still. *It WAS just a badger*, I told myself—and then I heard it again—closer this time—and I heard another noise, too, like a scratching and a rustling. Something made a bark like a fox makes, only there was a nasty sort of—sort of *chatter* in it—"

Diana stiffened and sat up. She watched me intently.

"—like it was laughing at me. I was awfully scared! My head was so muddled I didn't know which way was Kol's and I could hear the two things

---

[69] Small riverine willows

103

crawling through the leaves, getting closer and closer. I was about to scream for help (I don't know who'd have heard me), but then I saw the fairy ring."

Diana smiled.

"Fairy *what*?" Kol asked.

"The fairy ring! You know—that ring of toadstools? The red ones? When I saw them I knew I was on top of the brae. So I jumped into the fairy ring (I can't say why I did it) and at once the rustling stopped. I saw the old ash tree in the moonlight a little way off and I thought it looked so safe, and—and rather homelike, you know? So I jumped out of the fairy ring and ran for it like the devil was after me, but the two things came right up behind. They weren't bothering to hide anymore. Chattering and laughing. It was horrible! My insides felt like ice, and then—" (I shuddered all over)—"and then something brushed the back of my neck. Oh, I went out of my wits! It grabbed my ankle. I could feel claws—"

I spun around and looked at the door again.

"It's alright," Kol said gently. "We're safe now."

I shook my head. "Well it grabbed me," I said, "and I fell on my hands and knees. I couldn't run any more. I just waited for them to jump on me. But a minute went by and everything was quiet. Just wind in the branches. When I dared to look up, there was the ash tree standing over me."

"Another miracle!" Kol muttered.

"So I got up and made a run for your door. Is the ash part of your fence, brother Kol?"

"She's the watchtower on my fence," Kol smiled.

"When your 'fence' fails," Lily said curtly, "that ash won't stop them."

"I can hear the ash," said Diana. "I can't hear anything else."

For a moment no one spoke. The little cottage was hot and stifling with the shutters up. We sat and watched the white charcoal flame wavering in the hearth. I was imagining all the dreadful creatures I'd seen—gathering in the dark outside; surrounding us. In a moment they'd burst through the door—

A horrible, trapped feeling came over me. I started to tremble.

Kol broke the silence.

"Well I guess you'll have to raise the old stream, Lily," Kol said with perfect calmness. "I'd hate to see you do it. It would mean the end of the hermitage, but—"

"Ko-ollam!" Lily cried reproachfully. "Your home! We can't!"

Kol's merry laugh made me jump.

"And what's my home," he said, "really? A pile of sticks and mud! Am I a stork? I'm ashamed I even—" Kol sighed. "Still," he said, "it *has* been dear to me."

Lily smiled (a trifle bashfully, I thought, though I might have imagined it).

"Perhaps you could make *another* home, Kollam," she said quietly.

"Well that's settled, then!" Friar Kol got up. "The Lord giveth, the Lord taketh away—"

There was a noise outside. Kol froze.

"That— Was that—?"

We heard a rattle like gravel raining down. The ceiling creaked overhead.

"Holy Patrick, they're on top of us!" Kol snatched his bundle off the table. "Everyone into the loft!" he shouted. "Quick! Lily, raise the stream!"

"I *wish* you could command me," Lily said evenly, "but as the boy still breathes—"

"Right. Right." Kol was already up in the loft. "James! Tell Lily to raise the stream!"

"Gossakes raise the stream!" I squawked. I fairly shoved Diana up the ladder in front of me. Lily flew to the door and pressed her ear against it. She darted back at once.

"Look out, Kollam!"

A massive blow drove the door into the bar. The doorframe groaned. Dust and splinters rained across the floor. There was a rushing noise outside and the shutters started to rattle.

"They're breaking down the door!" I wailed. I was cowering behind Kol's pickled herring barrel with the reek of it in my nose. Friar Kol slapped his forehead. "My bible!" he cried. "We can't get to Doonbridge without it!"

"Can't get to *where*?"

Kol jumped out of the loft. He scooped his bible off the wooden lectern where it lay open, its pages gleaming faintly in Lily's light. The roar outside was like a hurricane. The loft swayed sickeningly.

Lily stood below, staring serenely into the fire.

Another heavy blow. The doorframe fell in pieces. A wide crack opened down the latch side and a long face poked in—half man, half wolf. In all my life I'd never seen anything so profane as the wolf-man's evil, drooling snout inside Kol's holy hermitage.

"Get out!" I screamed.

A nasty, chattering laugh answered.

"Courage, lad," said Kol from the darkness to my left. "Wait for Lily to raise the stream."

"Raise the burn?" I squeaked. "The burn's a mile awa—"

Kol chuckled knowingly.

"Rankle Burn's not the only stream hereabouts."

The bar splintered and the door fell in. A shaggy black mass filled the opening. Sharp faces poked in around it. Lily glanced over her shoulder at them. She turned back to the fire.

"*Bòc*," Lily said.

The shaggy black thing was swimming.

A wall of water flung it inside. The fire spluttered, and then all I could see was Lily standing in the middle of her own green radiance. She wavered like church glass. I looked down. Water was rising to my waist.

Then to my chest. Lily flickered and vanished as the air suddenly went stale.

"Hold onto the ceiling!" Kol sounded like he was inside a drum. I fumbled above my head and found a ham on an iron hook. The water was around my neck now. I squeezed my nose against the ceiling and gasped for air.

"Take a breath!" Kol ordered.

The flood closed over my head.

Through the freezing blackness I heard Lily's voice come clear and unchanged.

Cuir bun-os-cionn, she said.

There was a tremendous pull. The hook jerked out of my grip, but I caught the ham and clung to it with all my strength. Something shoved me from behind.

I landed on the ceiling.

Kol's roof was upside-down, spinning away on the flood like a runaway coracle.[70] In the sudden moonlight I saw a rushing river where the glen had been. The old elm rolled in deep water beside us, its naked roots splayed out in the air. Treetops bent and groaned on either side.

"Drown, devils!" I shrieked.

The torrent carried us on. We were almost to the Rankle Burn: a silvery ribbon in the moonlight. Kol and Diana lay in a heap along with Kol's dripping leather bag. We crested a black wave.

Then another.

Another.

Then the flood spewed us out into the Rankle Burn. I couldn't see Lily but her voice came clear as before. *Bòc*, she said, and the Rankle Burn swelled up to meet us, flooding the marshes and drowning the bottoms until only the topmost willow-plumes waved like feathers above the foam.

We bobbed slower now, turning lazily in the current. The Rankle Burn was ten times as high as in April and running fast to meet the Ettrick Water.

We passed Buckley village. Shouting and the blink of torches rose from the bank—dogs and geese making an awful racket; the old deacon was clanging away on the kirk bell (swinging from the bellrope, by the sound of it). But we drifted by, and soon the clamor faded into the shadowy moonlight.

It got very still.

We huddled together shivering—Kol, Diana and I. No one spoke.

Then a wavering green glow appeared over the side and Lily came up out of the water—not swimming but walking, like she was coming up a flight of stairs. She stepped lightly out into our strange boat.

"My bible!" Kol spluttered. "James, tell Lily to dry out the bag!"

"Dry the b-bag, Lily," I chattered.

"If you p-please," I added.

---

[70] A small round boat, traditionally constructed from branches and animal hide. Coracles are notoriously tricky to steer.

"My lady," I added.

"*Seac.*"

Everything was dry.

My hair was dry. My clothes were dry. The six inches of water that were sloshing around our feet instantly vanished. I was entirely warm and the cool night air was pleasant.

Diana stopped shivering and uncurled herself. She sat down and started to tie up her long dark hair. Kol unrolled the neck of the leather bag and took out his heavy bible. He held it up to Lily, examining the pages by her light.

"It's not hurt." Lily smiled.

Kol looked her in the face.

"I've missed you so," he said.

We were silent again, listening to the gurgle of rising water that followed us down the banks. Lily sat behind Diana. She gently undid the simple knot Diana had made of her hair and with immortal-swift fingers she wove up the dark strands into two lovely braids, swept back from Diana's temples and joined together behind.

Kol broke the stillness.

"I'm sorry, James, if I have to bring up something unpleasant, but I suppose for our safety it's best I know." He turned to Lily. "Lady Farahain, why was it James couldn't surrender you to the Black Stag when—alas!—he clearly meant to? Did the earl not have the crook of Esus?"

Lily nodded.

"He had it."

"Was it not—?"

There was a hopeful light in Kol's eyes. But Lily smiled sadly and shook her head.

"It *was* stained with his blood, Kollam," she whispered.

Kol bent his head.

"Then why—"

Lily ran her fingers through Diana's hair. She lifted her face to Friar Kol. I saw tears in her eyes, glittering in the light she shed.

"The Black Stag didn't kill your brother," Lily said softly. "Peter McKenna did."

I don't know how long I slept.

I woke from ugly dreams under a flat gray sky. I was curled up on my side. Every joint ached.

I sat up.

I cringed. Sickening drumbeat in my head.

Kol's wicker roof rocked gently. Kol was sitting next to me with his bible open across his knees. Diana stood effortlessly on the swaying floor. She stared into the distance and softly sang.

"What—"

My throat was like wood.

"What happened?" I mumbled.

Then I remembered.

I lay back down and curled up on my side again. "I want to go home," I said. "I want my mother."

"I know."

Kol didn't look up.

"You can't."

What part was a dream? I remembered Lily saying something horrible, and then I went mad.

Was I screaming at her?

Kol tried to calm me, but I shoved him and he almost went into the water. Then he knocked my feet out from under me and Diana pinned my arms back. How could Diana *be* that strong? Her wrists were so thin but her grip was like a vise.

Did Kol have his knee on my neck?

They forced a copper flask between my teeth. A taste like death. Peaceful, crushing weight inside my mind. An ugly thought I was trying to hide—

Peter.

I was too sick to cry.

"Where's Lily?" I croaked.

"Gone!" Kol said bitterly. "You sent her away! You told her in the name of Esus to leave us and never to return. And she was glad to! Twice she saved your life—and mine." Kol dropped his head between his hands.

"She was my friend."

I clutched the fairy glass and covered my face with my arm.

"I wish I were dead."

"I wish Maewyn were alive," said Kol. "Wishing won't bring him back."

Charlie, my boy: I'm speaking to you now. Your uncle James is speaking to you while the life ebbs out of me. I became a man that day, Charlie.

I put away childish things.

Kol's shoulders heaved while his tears dropped on the open page and made the ink run. Diana stood like a stone, all but the wisps of hair that escaped her braids. I looked left.

I looked right.

I turned around and looked behind me, but nothing did I see—only water, water everywhere. Green swells stretched to the horizon. We were at sea beyond the sight of land.

The sky began to turn dark. Gray-white clouds streamed toward us, driven on by the coming storm. Friar Kol put his sleeve to his eyes and closed the bible. He sat with his head bowed, speaking softly. I heard some of the words.

—*Yea, though I walk through the valley of the shadow of death I shall fear no evil, for thou art with me...*

CHAPTER 16

The worst thing about that storm was the witches riding in sieves.

Nessa Blair from Clearburn was there again. I fancied Nessa once when we were children. We were learning our catechism from the deacon at Buckley kirk, squirming on the hard wooden pews, the boys ranged on one side, the girls on the other. I was forever looking across the aisle at her. The sun slanting through the window of the little side chapel lit her white-edged Sunday bonnet like a halo while her rose-petal lips mouthed the *credo in unum deum.*

The deacon noticed my errant gaze. He called me 'little Saracen'[71] and gave me a vicious rap on the knuckles with a long candle snuffer. But Nessa came up to me as we were walking home and she took my bruised hand in hers and held it all the way to the bridge while I blushed like a bonfire and wondered if the joy of the saints in heaven could compare to my bliss. All that week I thought about Nessa and it felt like Sunday would never come, but when I saw her again she was holding another boy's hand, Willum Dail's, and oh! the misery! I knew Nessa preferred him because he was the tallest boy in the parish and he had straight black hair, while mine was nothing but red tangles and my face was speckled all over like a frog. So I pulled on my ugly farm cap even though it was warm, and I looked down at my feet that I might not see them lingering in the apse before they took their seats.

The deacon caught sight of me.

Remove thy barley-bag, boy, he snarled. *Thou'rt in the Lord's house and not the barn.*

Then he called me 'little Covenanter'[72] while all the boys and girls laughed. Nessa laughed as loud as the rest of them, and I blushed for her afresh and knew that I would never love again.

---

[71] Muslim
[72] Protestant

Nessa was bareheaded herself now, her hair blown back and all matted with seaweed. She sat sprawled in a great sieve like a washtub with her dripping legs and feet sticking out over the side and she was rowing with a broom. How she didn't sink I can't say. She came within arm's length of our roof, digging in her broom and spinning round and round. Her empty eyes stared ahead unseeing and she laughed and called out in a crazed voice like someone who hadn't slept for days. There must have been twenty witches with her—some standing up in their sieves and some sitting; some paddling with brooms and some holding out their cloaks to catch the wind like a sail. I saw one enormous sieve with two witches stuffed in it, rowing at cross-purposes to each other: the one forward and the other back. It made no difference. They were driven on by some force unseen. The wind and the witches shrieked together. The gray waves rose up to a great height, and the witches in their sieves—and we on our roof—crested every peak and sounded every valley, and somehow we did not sink.

Black Stag! Black Stag! the witches cried, and they took up a mad song, terrible in that storm:

There were three brothers in bonnie Scotland
In bonnie Scotland livèd they
And they cuist kevels themsells amang[73]
Wha should gae rob upon the salt sea[74]

There were many more words, but their voices were stripped away by the wind. I saw a wave hit a witch with such a slap that she toppled over and the speckled bottom of her sieve bobbed in the water like a turtle, but then it righted itself and up she came, dripping and singing and seeming unaware she'd been head-downward like a duck. Friar Kol had stuffed his precious bible into the front of his cassock where it stuck out from his chest like a brick, and now he was using the leather bag to bail out the roof. I was bailing frantically with my cap, but it was plain we couldn't stay afloat much longer.

Farahain! I screamed. *Lily!*

---

[73] And they cast lots among themselves
[74] Who should go rob upon the salt sea

Only the wind answered.

A wave broke sideways and swamped us up to our knees. The roof creaked miserably as we lumbered up another crest. We dropped into the trough, and I felt it sink under my feet.

Kol stopped bailing and started to pray. He clasped his hands together.

"Our father who art in—"

"Ow!" I yelped. "Damn it all!"

I was looking down on Kol's face. "Help!" I squawked.

"Fish on!" called an unfamiliar voice.

I was dangling from the prow of a ship.

Bucking through the waves, a brig's wooden bowsprit had lunged out of the spray and speared my shirt. I swung from one armpit while a ruddy, bearded sailor leaned on the rail and laughed like his sides would burst.

"Fish on!" he called again.

In a blink I had my my arms and legs wrapped around the pole. I clung desperately while the ship tossed me and the sailors gathered to the rail and laughed. Carefully I wriggled out of my shirt—first my arm, then my head, then my other arm; then, bare-chested, I inched backward toward the prow, leaving my torn shirt flying from the bowsprit like a dirty flag.

A pair of rough hands dragged me in. I lay gasping on the deck. Friar Kol had already come aboard. He was hustling down the open hatch with his arms locked around his bible. Diana stood close by. She had her elbow hooked through the shrouds and she was talking to a sailor.

I got up unsteadily.

The deck creaked behind me. I turned around.

A heavy hand thumped me on the back so hard I lost my balance and fell down again.

I raised my head.

I was squinting up into the face of a big man in a wide Spanish hat. He had a big black beard, forked in the middle and tied off at the ends with black ribbon. The man reached out a massive paw and pulled me to my feet.

"Welcome aboard!" he bellowed. "Does your father have any money?"

"S-sir?" I gurgled.

"You're my hostage!" the big man shouted over the wind. "Your kinfolk'll have to pay to get you back. Has your da' got any money, I say?"

"My fa— My father's dead, sir!" I shouted back.

The big man dragged me off the foredeck and into the lee of the windlass.

"Any of your uncles got money?"

I shook my head.

"A cousin?" he suggested.

"We are poor farmers, sir." I gawked at him like I was dreaming. The big man sighed and looked crestfallen. "Might 'a guessed," he said gloomily. "A hundred leagues from Edinburgh in naught but a coracle."

He brightened.

"You'll be my galley slave, then! Can you cook?"

"I can cook oat porridge, sir."

The big man frowned and thumbed the gold chain on his neck with a worried expression. "I don't see how I can keep you, boy," he said. "We are not a nunnery, taking in orphans out here on the North Sea. I'd hate to toss ye back into the brine—" (he squinted over the rail) "—but every man must earn his berth or the old boat can't carry him."

"B-but—" I looked out at the angry waves. The gray peaks were tipped with white foam and the witches were bobbing around the ship and shrieking in mad chorus.

"Aye, the witches!" the big man said, answering my gaze. "Been seeing more o' them these days. Always come with a gale. They scare off shipping. Hardly a prize to be taken in these waters anymore."

I turned back to him. "I could earn my board as a sailor," I said earnestly.

The big man roared with laughter.

"I like you, boy!" he said, wiping his eyes. "It would pain me, slightly, to throw you overboard. How about that monk? Come from a rich abbey, does he? Maybe *he* could ransom you. Who is he?"

"That's Friar Ko—Friar Kollam Keeli," I corrected myself.

The big man stopped laughing abruptly. He stared at me openmouthed.

"*Who* d'ye say?" he asked thickly.

"Friar Kollam Keeli," I repeated. "From Buckley in Roxburgh-shire. But he was born in Éireann."

The big man pounced on me. I squealed with fright. He scooped me up in his burly arms and swung me around like a sack.

"Don't throw me in!" I wailed. "Please, sir! Don't throw me in!"

Laughing, the big man dropped me on deck, pulling my hair and slapping my cheeks with irrepressible delight. "Welcome aboard the *Otter*, boy!" he roared. "I am Captain John Blackjohn—"

The big man swept off his hat and bowed.

"—the pirate."

CHAPTER 17

From the letters of Doctor Stewart Henry Scott—

The King's Arms, Berwick-Upon-Tweed

May 29, 1838

Dear Albert,

I've seen my ghost again, Albert, and what's worse: I've seen the solicitor Radan, and a police constable with him.

I much preferred the ghost.

Mr. Radan offered to reinstate Fitzhugh at Branxholme Castle, but it's me he's angling for; me and my book—the *duke's* book, I really should say (though a fortnight ago I'd have sworn Sir Walter Douglas-Scott didn't so much as care if it existed).

I'll explain myself: it happened thus: I was comfortably installed in Mrs. McRoy's back parlour. I'd just finished transcribing James McKenna's story up to the page where he comes aboard the *Otter*. You might recall, Albert, that about two-thirds of this mysterious book are sealed between matching copper plates. They've got a woman's wreathed face cast in them and a sort of keyhole in her mouth. These plates I must somehow remove—that or give up on James McKenna, pirates and all.

Thus on Friday afternoon, May 25th, I went to the locksmith's on Bridge Street to ask the man how I might get the seals off without destroying the aged parchment in between.

It was four o'clock and threatening rain when I left Elizabeth McRoy's. Black clouds were gathering over the town, tinged now and then with summer lightning. I had *John Blackjohn* inside my valise, wrapped up in an old leather hunting-shirt with leather strands tied around it to keep off the damp.

"It's an antique diary," I told the locksmith as I undid the strands. "It's of no value, but I'd like to see what the rest of it has to say."

"I've got every burglar's tool in trade—" says the locksmith. (He had a jeweler's loupe on and he was peering one-eyed into the copper woman's mouth.) "—But none will serve," says he. He turns to the plate in the middle of the book. "No, these are no proper locks," he says, "They're just holes. There's no mortice nor tumbler nor nothing. If something fits, then it's got to look a bit like a skull with two horns—that's the shape of it inside."

I thanked the man and walked back to Ravensdowne. A few scattered drops were beginning to stain the cobbles.

When I came in sight of Mrs. McRoy's I got an uneasy feeling. Elizabeth's door stood open and a heavy black carriage like a hearse was stationed in front. Crossing over Ravensdowne I saw it was an ugly new police van (the pride of the bailiwick, I'm sure) with a callow young constable leaning on the box. He couldn't see me as he had his back to the traces and the monstrous van was blocking his view of the street. So I crept up behind it and peeked around the splasher. Through Elizabeth's front door I saw another constable standing in the coat-room.

My heart sank. I could hear Radan's reedy voice inside.

"Yes, yes—*Doctor* Scott," Radan said condescendingly. "Where is he?"

"He's just gone out," Fitzhugh answered from somewhere past the coat-rack. "I don't know when he'll be back."

"Oh, *don't* you? Pray, where was Doctor Scott *going*, then?"

Fitzhugh made a contemptuous kind of snort. "I'm no lawyer," I heard him say, "but I don't see a warrant in *your* hand, Mr. Radan!"

The other constable was a slender, redheaded fellow with a drooping straw-colored mustache. I saw him take off his tall hat and begin to work the brim in a nervous circle between his hands. "I'm right sorry, Mr. Fitzhugh," he said. "I've never known the magistrate to issue a writ so quick. This-here solicitor" (he hooked his thumb at Radan) "spoke with His Honor privily in chambers only just this morning half past nine, and by eleven here they were—

" the constable held up a clutch of papers—"signed and sealed. Our bench isn't known for such, er, promptness."

The constable eyed Radan suspiciously.

"You have your warrants," Radan snapped, "now enforce them! Make this servant tell you where his accomplice is hiding!"

The constable glared at Radan. "These warrants give me leave to look around," he growled. "They don't say I must ask questions.

"And you a solicitor!" he added disdainfully.

Mrs. McRoy poked her blue bonnet out the parlour door. "You'll certainly *not* look around," she trilled, "until I've tidied up a bit and put the kettle on! No one said we'd be having visitors."

Radan threw up his hands. "Oh for God's sake!" he groaned. "Fitzhugh, *do* make an end of this farce! Where is the doctor?" The constable sighed and said "Yes, we may as well have it, Mr. Fitzhugh. I don't reckon the honorable solicitor will let up until he's found, and he's got to be near about."

Fitzhugh looked terribly perplexed. He shifted from one foot to the other, but before he could open his mouth I trotted briskly up the steps. "Here I am, gentlemen!" I called. "Doctor's here! What seems to be the trouble?"

"Ah-*ha*!" Radan crowed. "The 'trouble,' Doctor, seems to be that *you're* going to prison!"

"Now just a minute, just a minute—" the constable interrupted—"that isn't necessarily so! I'm terribly sorry, sir," he said apologetically. "I've never detained a man of a learned profession before, nor so respectable-looking a gentleman as yourself. But just this morning the Magistrate's Court issued a warrant for the search of these premises, together with—*hem!*—together with a warrant for your arrest, sir," (the constable looked embarrassed) "upon charges of—"

He held the documents up to his face and squinted at them.

"—upon charges of—grand larceny, conversion—er—trespass to land, and—er—trespass to chattels," he finished, looking up again.

"Trespass to *chattels*?"

"It says you knocked a slate off the Duke of Buckley's roof."

I tried not to smile.

"But *grand larceny*?" I pursued. "What treasure could I have stolen from the duke?"

"It says you took an old book, sir."

"Yes! This book!" I opened my valise. "*There* it is!" Radan gloated. He clapped one hand on my chest and stuck his other hand inside my bag. I made no resistance. Radan pulled out a heavy square parcel tied up in thick brown paper. He started plucking at the twine with his long, yellow fingers.

"Hands off!" the constable barked.

Radan's face fell.

"Hands off! That's evidence!"

Radan lowered the parcel. He glared at the constable with undisguised hatred. The constable met his gaze. "You can entangle me in your *personal* affairs, Solicitor," he said evenly, "but *I* can enforce the law. These are *my* warrants." (He shook the papers in Radan's face.) "This is *my* inquest. This book is *my* evidence. And this book will remain in *my* safekeeping until it's properly indexed and submitted at the doctor's eventual—*ahem!*—"

He shot me another embarrassed look.

"—at the doctor's eventual—trial.

"And I wouldn't hold my breath 'til then," the constable added with a wink. "Hizzonor's dockets are a bit crowded at the moment. You understand, Mr. Radan. The law's delay and all that."

Radan looked like he wanted to spit. He hesitated while his little ferret eyes darted back and forth between the constable in the doorway and the brown paper parcel in his hands.

"I've *two* pairs of handcuffs, sir," the constable observed coolly, reaching inside his coat pocket. "At the moment you seem to be hindering the court's inquiry."

Radan handed him the parcel with a sinister smile.

"Mind you keep it dry now." His voice was almost a whisper. "There's going to be a storm."

"But gentlemen!" I interjected, "Sir Walter lent me that book upon the clearest of terms: that I might study and transcribe it. I'm a humble scholar of antiquities. Of *course* I'll give it back when the job's done! I told His Lordship so not a fortnight ago in his very own library at Branxholme."

"His Lordship agreed to no such thing!" Radan snapped.

"I'm afraid I don't understand you."

"His Lordship never gave you leave to remove the book from his estate," Radan said archly, "and if you're calling the Duke of Buckley a liar, then your next charge will be for slander."

"Now, now—" the constable interrupted soothingly—"I'm sure it's all just a misunderstanding and soon to be sorted out. But we can't sort it out here, in Mrs. McRoy's cloakroom, now can we? And we're letting in the street smell! Mrs. McRoy? I beg your pardon, ma'am. We'll be off." He turned to me. "Doctor," he said, "I'm afraid you must come along, though I think this whole thing is ridiculous. This book wouldn't amount to grand larceny if it were made of gold, and," he weighed it demonstratively in his hand, "I don't reckon it is."

And so, my dear Albert, I, Stewart Henry Scott, M.D., heretofore respectable doctor; I who once treated the Duke of Cumberland after he grabbed the hot barrel of a fowling-piece (Have I told you that story? 'Twenty times,' you'll say)—I tell you that I was bundled into a dank police wagon while Mrs. McRoy wept and tried to cram handkerchiefs and sugared biscuits through the window-bars (though she might have handed them in at the door, as the constable didn't even bother to lock it), and every house on the street poked out a head to gawk at me in my shame.

It was positively thrilling!

Fitzhugh insisted on coming with us and giving his 'statement,' as he was present when I spoke to the young Duke and could corroborate. The constable promised to 'take something down.' He offered his arm to help Fitzhugh up onto the box.

"Now, now, my good man!"

Radan sidled himself in between the two of them. His yellow smile was an inch away from Fitzhugh's nose.

"Now, now, Fitzhugh!" said Radan, "there's no need to get mixed up in this barmy doctor's troubles! Has *that* ever brought you anything but grief? And besides—" (He seemed to be making a pitiable effort to sound jolly.) "—And besides, I've good news for you! I'd nearly forgotten: Sir Walter sends his most cordial regards, and he informs you that you are hereby reinstated as Steward of Branxholme Castle. Congratulations, Fitzhugh! Now if you'll just step back inside we can discuss the terms of— Fitzhugh?"

Fitzhugh elbowed Radan out of the way and sat down beside the constable without a word. The constable called *Getup!* and shook the reins. The massive van creaked and started to roll.

Through the back window bars I could see Radan lingering in the street behind—head down, hands in his pockets—as if he were considering something. Then, like a man resolved, he turned up his collars and strode off through the gathering rain.

A smothering gray fog set in as the carriage rolled slowly up Ravensdowne. Ghostly carts and wagons materialized, then dissolved into the mist. The young constable shouted something from the tailboard. Getting a '*Yes—do*' from the box he jumped off and disappeared around the corner of Woolmarket.

The afternoon grew darker. *We could use streetlamps!* I muttered, but as it wasn't yet six I could only sit and watch the dark posts vanish into the fog. It promised to be a summer storm and a good one. Lightning flashed as we passed the barracks, bound (I assumed) for the courthouse on Wallace Green.

The carriage slowed. I couldn't see ahead of us, but I knew we were facing the parade ground, and, just beyond it, the graveyard of Trinity Church.

I expected the constable would turn left and skirt the parade ground. Instead there came a furious squeal of brakes and the carriage stopped so abruptly that I pitched off the bench and went sprawling onto the floor. *Ho there!* the constable shouted from the box. Through the wall I heard faint creaking and the slap of reins as some unseen cart jostled out of the constable's way.

My heart froze.

"What the dev—?"

Blue sparks sizzled between the window bars.

There was a taste like copper. For a split second I had an awful presentiment of dread, and then with a deafening *CRACK* a bolt of lightning clove the air like the sword of the Almighty. White fire danced on every scrap of iron. The horses screamed and the van lunged forward. I rolled back under the bench. The door swung open, and I saw the muddy strip of parade ground go spinning past. The horses were wild with terror. I knew we were about to come up against the churchyard wall. I closed my eyes and braced for the crash.

But suddenly the van swung hard left. We careened madly, right-side wheels off the ground. Then the wheels touched down again and we crunched to a stop.

I heard the horses panting and snorting outside. There was a sickening stench of burnt hair.

Cautiously I stuck my head out the door.

"Constable?" I called. "Have you got the brake?"

No answer.

I jumped out. Fitzhugh was sitting alone on the box, his eyes staring straight ahead. My first dreadful thought was he'd been struck by lightning.

"Fitzhugh!" I screamed. "Fitzhugh, are you alright?"

He stirred.

"Did you— Did you see that man there?"

"What man? No!" I clambered up onto the box and fumbled for Fitzhugh's pulse.

"Y-young man standing right in our way—"

"Hm—yes?—terrible fright! Can you breathe, Fitzhugh? Are you burned?"

"Turned the horses—"

"What?"

"He turned the horses! Just before we— He raised his hand—"

"*Who* raised his hand?"

"The young man."

"*What* young man? Where is he?"

"He—he disappeared!" Fitzhugh turned to me with a dazed look. "I think I'm struck by lightning, Doctor! Oh! the hiss in my ears!"

"I think you're *not* struck by lightning," I returned, "though you're a trifle singed. No—no, you're right as rain, old boy. Pulse like a pendulum! Where's the constable?"

"D-dead, I think," Fitzhugh choked. "His hat caught fire and he—fell off."

We both turned around.

A dark, crumpled shape lay unmoving on the muddy ground.

I jumped off the box and ran to the body. At a glance I knew the constable was gone. His chin was wrenched past his shoulder and there was a sickly-sweet stench of burnt hair. A trickle of smoke rose from his charred scalp and curled up into the falling rain. His tall hat lay blasted open beside him.

"Poor fellow!"

I stooped down and closed his staring eyes.

"The lightning must've found that copper badge on his hat. We'd best leave the body where it lies, Fitzhugh, and send for the coroner."

"Perhaps—"

Fitzhugh kicked at the gravel doubtfully.

"Perhaps *what?*"

"I don't know," Fitzhugh retuned. "It just seems rather—disrespectful, you know, just leaving him in the rain like this—"

Fitzhugh took off his hat.

"Well I dare not pull his coat off," I said fretfully. "Hasn't the van maybe—maybe got a rug or something we could cover him with?"

Fitzhugh went back and searched the box.

"Nay!" he called.

I chewed my fingers.

"We could—maybe pull the van over top o' him?" I suggested.

Fitzhugh scowled.

"Keep the rain off, I suppose."

"Alright then," I sighed. "You take the reins and I'll take the brown mare by the halter. I wonder if the pair will back—"

The pair *wouldn't* back; not without considerable pushing and shouting from Fitzhugh and considerable head-jerking and hoof-dragging on the part of the horses. Our first attempt overshot the body, and I'm ashamed to say the brown mare trod the constable's lifeless hand into the mud before I could bring her forward again. At last we got the back wheels on either side of the body and the horses unhitched and tethered to a lamppost.

"Who'll take down your statement now, Fitzhugh?" I asked mournfully. We were walking back to the van to fetch my valise.

"Oh, *I'll* take his statement, doctor!"

We both looked up.

Radan was sitting up on the box, covering us with a double-barreled pistol. He smiled and cocked both hammers with a deliberate *click, click*.

"On your knees, Doctor! Hands behind your head!"

"Radan, for God's sake—"

"Fitzhugh?" Radan barked. "Fetch the key to the late constable's lockbox—I believe it's hanging from the ring on his belt. *QUICK*-ly!" he lilted contemptuously.

I knelt in the cold mud, keeping an eye on the pistol. Radan's hand was shaking violently. I was afraid he was going to fire by accident. Fitzhugh ducked under the van. I heard the cuffs jingle as he fumbled about the dead constable's waist. Presently he stood up, key in hand. Radan slid over to one side of the bench.

"Open the strongbox!"

A heavy, ironbound chest was bolted to the carriage frame behind the footboard. Fitzhugh turned the key in lock.

"Put the book in the bag!" Radan tossed Fitzhugh a little oilcloth satchel, but Fitzhugh only smirked at Radan defiantly.

"Doctor?" Fitzhugh asked.

"It's alright, my friend," I said gently. "Give him what he wants."

Fitzhugh sighed. Opening the strongbox he took out the paper-bound parcel and put it in the satchel. Radan snatched it up with his left hand, keeping the pistol on us with his right. Forked lightning flashed out to sea. A few seconds later there came the shuddering broadside of thunder.

"On your knees!" Radan ordered.

Fitzhugh knelt in the mud beside me. I felt his big shoulder press against mine.

"Now give me the tooth!"

We stared at him.

"B—beg'r *pardon*?" I sputtered. (I thought I'd misheard him.)

"The tooth!" Radan screamed. "Give me the tooth, you redneck[75] fool! Where's the tooth that opens the copper lady's mouth? Answer before you die!" His skull-like face wore a crazed look. I winced at how the pistol weaved about in his hand.

"Mr. Radan," I said sincerely, "I haven't the faintest idea what you mean. The only teeth in my possession," (I tried not to smile) "are those I carry in my head. But come now!" I said warmly, "You're unwell! Your hand trembles awfully. This silly matter of the book has upset your nerves; I can see that. You've nothing to fear from Sir Walter's faithful steward and his friend the old doctor. I beg you! Lay down that gun and let me take your pulse. This rain will be the death of you."

At the word *death* Radan looked down at me. He smiled, and his smile made my flesh crawl. He meant to do us harm, Albert, independent of any other purpose he might have had. I think Radan hated us for what goodness there *was* in us. Oh we're not angels, Fitzhugh and me! Amiable rogues we are, to be sure. Yet Radan is the sort of man who would snuff out any light if he could, from the noonday sun to the candle's little flame.

Lightning flashed. Radan was muttering to himself, counting.

"One.

"Two.

"Three—"

"Mr. Radan, enough!" I said sternly. "You *must* see how absurd this is! The barracks are a stone's throw from here. If you fire that gun the whole garrison will come scrambling out!"

Lightning flashed.

"One," Radan counted.

"Two.

"Three.

"Four.

"Five—" Radan's voice rose to a scream.

"Six!"

Thunder broke the instant Radan pulled the trigger.

---

[75] Scottish Protestant

125

I must say, Albert, he shot like a novice—hooked the muzzle left and downward, as a right-handed man will do. The recoil nearly drove the hammers into his head. (Would it had!) A hot, stinging shower suffused my right shoulder and arm. Fitzhugh (never at a loss) was back on his feet with an agility that belied his gray hairs. His fist made a dull, packing sound against Radan's face. Radan fell off the box, choking on his own blood. Fitzhugh loomed over him. Radan wormed backward on the muddy ground, the smoking pistol in one hand and the oilcloth satchel in the other.

I got up in considerable pain, white sparks wriggling before my eyes. Radan had his back against the churchyard wall. Blood streamed from his shattered nose, blackening his shirtfront. He raised the pistol. The evil mouths of its twin barrels were six inches from Fitzhugh's head. I cringed as I heard the creak of Radan's finger on the back trigger.

Fliuch, said a gentle voice behind me.

Snap! went the hammer.

No flash. The pistol didn't fire.

Then a semi-transparent young man in a sailor's cap stepped politely in between us. He faced Radan with a calm, somewhat detached expression.

Radan's mouth fell open.

Radan looked up at the young man's head.

He looked down at the young man's stomach. For an instant our eyes met through the filmy buckle of the young man's wide leather belt.

The pistol dropped out of Radan's shaking hand. With a strangled yelp he scrambled over the wall like a cat (satchel still in hand) and in a twinkling he was gone among the gravestones.

"Doctor!"

Fitzhugh ran back to me.

"Stewart!"

"I'm alright! I'm alright!" I answered quickly. "That—*ha ha!*—that idiot had his pistol loaded with birdshot!" I laughed even though it hurt. "He's peppered me like a grouse, but I'll pull through. Let's see if our gho—"

I looked up at the visitor.

"Let's see if our spectral friend has anything to say on *this* occasion."

So we waited, Albert. I tell you, as I live and breathe, we stood there with a ghost and waited while the thunder growled and the rain went drip-dripping through the elm leaves. The apparition neither moved nor spoke; he simply watched us with a glassy, unblinking stare. I tried to get a better look at him but his gauzy face was all muddled with the wings of a plaster angel on the other side of the wall. At length (not wanting him to vanish, but with the pain growing in my shoulder) I stirred and I was just about to speak, and then the ghost nodded faintly as if he understood. He knit up his brows and pursed his lips in a childish way, like a schoolboy trying to remember his lesson. At last I heard a voice, low and mild, clear as a choir bell and yet seeming to come, not from him, but from far, far away—

Iona.

We waited.

The ghost said nothing. He just stood inhumanly still and looked at us.

"Ah—will that be *all* then, sir?" I finally ventured. I was clutching my wounded shoulder and shuffling from foot to foot. A hot, aching fever was setting in.

Iona, the ghost repeated.

Then he was gone. I was staring at a churchyard wall in a gray evening rain.

I sank down on the muddy ground with my back against the carriage wheel. "Take me home, Fitzhugh," I said weakly. "Let's get this lead out of my wing before it poisons me."

Fitzhugh shook his head. "Shouldn't we rather get you to hospital, doctor?" he asked with a concerned look.

"Fitzhugh, my brave friend," I said, "you'll think it arrogant of me, but I believe *I'm* the best doctor in Berwick today. I'd rather not catch whatever plague is going round the hospital. Find me a looking-glass and some spirits and we'll have the shot out in no time."

"Rest easy, then, while I fetch a cab!"

Fitzhugh jogged away.

The cab rolled leisurely onto the parade. I gritted my teeth and looked out the rear window. Between the dirty streaks I could see the police horses still tethered to the dark lamppost. They stood flank-to-flank, as horses do in foul weather—heads low, backs to the rain. Underneath the van the constable's crumpled body was fading into the fog.

I turned back painfully. It was a wretched old hansom. The roof leaked and I felt every cobblestone like a needle in my shoulder. Fitzhugh stared out the window and bit his lip contemplatively, like he was weighing something in his mind.

"Was that a ghost, doctor?" Fitzhugh asked presently.

"I don't know, Fitzhugh."

"But you don't seem terribly *surprised*." Fitzhugh looked at me pointedly. The wheel struck a pothole. I winced and clutched my shoulder.

"I'm sorry, Fitzhugh. I meant to say something, only just now this damned hack is shaking me apart! But to tell you the truth, I'm—well I'm delighted you saw him—*gads!* Hasn't it got any springs? Fitzhugh, I saw that ghost in broad daylight more than a week ago. He was on Old Bridge as we were coming into town. I durst not say anything for fear you'd think me a lunatic. But now you've seen him too, well, we're lunatics together, you and me."

"You and me and *Radan*," Fitzhugh chuckled. "I never saw a Lunker run so fast."

"Ye-es—" I smiled. "Radan saw him too. I wonder what he's playing at? What *was* he was raving about? A *tooth*?"

"Tooth to open the copper lady's mouth."

"Well here's Madame Copper, anyway." I put my good hand inside my valise and pulled out *John Blackjohn*, wrapped as always in the leather hunting-shirt.

"God in heaven!"

Fitzhugh drew back in surprise.

"How did—? But Radan—"

"No, no—" I chuckled. "But Radan *nothing*. Not he. I never take *Blackjohn* outside without a decoy. Radan's got two stacks of religious pamphlets wrapped in butcher paper, and I hope he enjoys them."

"*Ha ha ha!*"

Fitzhugh slapped his knee.

"Do him good, I should say!" Fitzhugh dabbed his eyes with his cuff. "Mister Radan don't have the look of a churchgoer!"

I laughed, winced, laughed again. "I'm surprised he was taken in," I said weakly. "I didn't think he would be. If he knew *Blackjohn*'s weight he couldn't possibly be fooled. It's clear he's never handled it. But," (I was serious again) "copper lady's mouth, he said? How d'you reckon he knew about *that*?" I pulled back the leather shirt. Fitzhugh studied the weathered, greenish plate.

Fitzhugh started to laugh again. Then I did too, though it hurt like the devil.

"Let's get you well, Doctor," said Fitzhugh. "We've got a bit of travelling to do."

"Travelling? Travelling to *where*?"

"Why, to Iona, of course!"

"To *Iona*?"

"Yes! To Iona!" Fitzhugh nodded emphatically. "You heard the ghost! That's your—your sacred isle, ain't it? Simply *crowded* with gods and fairies? It's plain he wants to meet us there. Show us his lonely, windswept grave—"

Fitzhugh stared dreamily out the window.

"—tell us what brought on his tragic end. Why, he might keep a summer-house there for aught *I* know! Maybe he'll invite us in; maybe—maybe oblige us insofar as a couple of pints—"

Fitzhugh trailed off. I laughed.

"I don't reckon he can drink anything," I said through my teeth. "I saw the churchyard wall where—*ouch!*—where his liver ought to be."

"Well, he's bound to tell us *something*," Fitzhugh returned. "And there'll be a lover, of course."

"There'll be a *what* now?"

"A lover!" Fitzhugh cried. "There's *always* a lover! If *she* didn't murder *him*, then *he* died for love of *her*—and if he *didn't* die for love of her, then some rival lured him out to a lonely spot and put a dagger in 'im just so he could claim her hand—"

I laughed painfully.

"I never took you for a romantic, Fitz—"

A sudden thought occurred to me.

129

I stuck my good arm out the window and banged on the roof. "Halloo!" I called to the driver, "Keep going! Take us to *The King's Arms*."

"No indeed!"

Fitzhugh was aghast.

"Doctor, you're not well!" Fitzhugh stared at me like I'd lost my mind. The driver stopped the cab and lit his pipe.

"Anywhere you gents decide," the driver observed with a philosophical air.

"No, Fitzhugh," I said earnestly, "I won't hear of home. Your good sister has had enough trouble on my account. And the trouble isn't going to end here. There'll be an inquest, of course; that's not what worries me. What worries me is Radan. He's plainly more interested in *Blackjohn* than the young duke ever was. I'd give Sir Walter the book this very moment—truly I would—but you saw Radan. He thought he had *Blackjohn* already, and he meant to kill us just the same!"

"Well—" Fitzhugh bit his lip deliberatively.

"Him waving a pistol around?" I pursued. "No! I won't stand for that! Elizabeth will be much safer if I'm not about."

"Well—"

"And we can patch me up just as proper at the *King's* as we could do in her parlour—"

Fitzhugh sighed and stuck his head out the window. "*Kings Arms*!" he called. The driver shook the reins. Fitzhugh sat back with a thoughtful look.

"Iona in the Hebrides, aye?"

"That's right."

"I wonder—"

Fitzhugh closed the window. He cleared the foggy glass with his cuff.

"You wonder *what*?" I demanded.

Fitzhugh smiled.

"I wonder if Lizzie wouldn't like a holiday."

So, Albert, I've taken to the highroad again (figuratively speaking). Fitzhugh and I managed to get all the lead out of me. My fever's on the mend, and I believe I may yet 'pull through' *per fidem meam*.[76] Why that lunatic loaded a pistol with birdshot is beyond me. (I think it's safe to say he's never brought down a buck.) When my right arm hurts, it's some comfort to imagine Mr. Radan unwrapping several dozen copies of *Six Sermons on the Nature, Occasions, Signs, Evils, and Remedy of Intemperance*, by reverends Beecher and Edgar, D.D.s.

As for an inquest, it's very strange, Albert: I've been four days recovering at *The Kings Arms*, but the brave Berwick constabulary paid me a visit only yesterday. A police inspector came up to my room wanting to know how I'd come to be shot in the arm—didn't say a word about his dead colleague; didn't say how he knew where to find me, or how he knew I'd been shot in the first place. Then without being asked he announced that 'His Honor the Magistrate' flatly denies ever having issued a warrant for my arrest, nor for the search of any property or premises of one Elizabeth McRoy, widow of the late Arthur McCroy, Ravensdowne. So, thinking it wisest not to press the issue, I simply told him there had been 'an accident involving a fowling-piece.' The inspector pretended to scribble something down in a notebook, then he said *Good day* and rushed out looking embarrassed. When Fitzhugh came around with Monday's *Advertiser* we read therein that, *unus*, a police constable had been found dead on Friday; *duo*, upon examination the cause of death was concluded to be lightning; and *tres*, the Corporation had seen the unfortunate policeman interred.

I'll post this letter along with my latest sheaf of transcription from *John Blackjohn*. Please see it's taken to Constantine's post-haste. Hereafter I'm afraid the tale of James McKenna must end, unless Fitzhugh and I should happen upon a tooth which, our solicitor informed us (at gunpoint), will open the seals on this piratical Apocalypse. It all seems terribly unlikely, but I remain—

Yours.

—*SHS*

---

[76] As promised

CHAPTER 18

Below deck I writhed about in considerable misery.

I'd been sick several times. I was half-starved, but I couldn't keep down the barley gruel Diana had kindly made for me forward in the galley. So she tried small beer, but I couldn't keep that down either, so I lay on my rolling berth[77] and I suffered and suffered while Friar Kol and Captain Blackjohn toasted each other and sang songs.

Outside the storm was subsiding by degrees.

Inside, it raged in my belly.

The sun went down. Captain Blackjohn embraced Kol for the hundredth time and said good night. He even offered Kol his own bed to sleep on, but Kol said his priestly vows forbade him to enjoy such a fine room.

"I'll sleep here in the fo'c'sle[78]," said Kol, "and keep an eye on my flock."

Blackjohn's heavy boots stumped off down the black passageway.

A squeal of rusty hinges.

The captain's door boomed shut.

Kol sat down on his bunk. He laid out his bible next to him and hunched over it, examining the pages in the intermittent light of the swinging lantern. "Could be worse," Kol muttered. "Bit of bleeding at the margin—but the center's holding—"

He turned a page.

"Without this bible," said Kol, "we can't hope to find Doonbridge in the Isles. It's the only place I know of where the Black Stag won't find us.

---

[77] Bunk
[78] Forecastle. Pronounce *FOX-ull.*

"Lily thought that was a good idea," Kol added quietly.

"Ugh—" I groaned. "What's a Doom Bridge?"

Kol gasped.

"*What?* You've never heard of *Doonbridge*? I expected you'd be amazed!"

I shook my head.

"The Brig o' Dùn?" Kol suggested. "The Vanishing Village?"

I shook my head.

 Kol folded his arms. "Well in the Isles," he scowled, "they call it *Cathair san-Adhar*—the city in the air. They say it appears out of the mist for only one day in every hundred years."

"Does it really?"

I sat up.

Kol laughed. "No, no!" he said, "that's just a fireside story for children. The real Doonbridge is nothing but a lonely little village the MacLeods forgot to levy when they marched against Donald MacDonald, Lord of the Isles. The MacLeods got soundly beaten and they acknowledged Donald king, but in the meantime they quite forgot about Doonbridge-by-the-Bay, with its little fort overlooking an ancient causeway."

Kol turned another page.

"Maybe anyone who knew how to get to Doonbridge was killed in the battle," he said, "or maybe the great fire at Dunvegan burned up all the tax ledgers. In any case, Doonbridge slipped through the chieftains' fingers, and that suited the Doonbridgers nicely. They hadn't been especially fond of paying off the MacLeods, you see, nor of sending their young men to die in the MacLeod's quarrels—"

Kol looked up at me pointedly. I knew he was thinking about Peter, and the Northumbria raid.

"The Doonbridgers weren't eager to pay tribute to Donald MacDonald either," Kol went on, "so they tore down their ancient bridge and within a generation the village was a legend. Doonbridge is nearly impossible to find. The seas outside are always rough. Vicious shoals line the coast. Only a knife-slit of an inlet leads into the bay, and the bay is ringed by towering cliffs—yes," said Kol, "Doonbridge is neatly hidden. But if, on a clear day of a spring tide, a ship (on what errand I can't guess) should chance to come inside the shoals, then a sailor up on the yards *might* just fancy he saw a peaceful harbor town appear for a moment, then vanish into the spray."

I groaned and lay back down.

"So how do *you* know so much about it?" I demanded.

"How do I— *Blackjohn* told me, of course!" Kol snorted. "John Blackjohn *lived* in Doonbridge! He told me about it when I met him in Iona all those years ago—didn't you hear anything?"

I squeezed my head between my hands.

"I heard a lot of songs."

Kol grinned. "Fair enough. Well if you'd been listening, then you'd know that back when Blackjohn was a lad of about your age he fell in with some pirates. And shortly after he fell in with some pirates, Blackjohn and the pirates had a falling-*out*. Blackjohn was sailing with a notorious cutthroat named Rudd Gallowglass, captain of the *Swift*. But Blackjohn and Gallowglass parted ways after Blackjohn spoke out against some of Rudd's, shall we say, 'crueler customs.'

"Blackjohn was no priest, mind you," Kol added. "He had his part in their crimes. But Blackjohn objected to them killing defenseless men when they might have been put ashore or held for ransom." (*Bloody noble of him!* I put in.)

"So Gallowglass—" (Kol ignored me) "—decided it would be a good joke to put *Blackjohn* ashore. And the shore he chose was a lone rock three miles off the coast of Skye.

"*I dub thee Lord of the Isle!* Rudd jeered, *though come high tide thou mayest find thy dominions reducèd somewhat.*

"True to Rudd's joke, at high tide the rock was no bigger than a sheep. The waves broke right over it. John Blackjohn was knocked off again and again—"

Kol brooded over the page. He scratched the parchment lightly with his fingernail.

"So how'd he get off it?"

"What?"

Kol looked up.

"So how—" I demanded—"did Blackjohn get off the rock? He isn't exact—"

The *Otter* lurched. I gagged.

"—he isn't exac—sitting on it—n-now—"

"Oh!" said Kol. "Well young Blackjohn clung to that rock for four nights and days. He ate sea snails and drank what rainwater he could wring out of his cap. But he knew death was coming. Freezing. Wet. Wracked with fever. Finally there came a tide when Blackjohn could cling to the rock no more. Commending his soul to God, John Blackjohn let go."

I sat up in spite of my stomach.

"And *then*?"

"And then—" Kol smiled—"two fishermen in a dinghy rowed up behind and hit him on the head so hard with an oar that it knocked his wits out and he fainted."

"They *did*? On *purpose*?"

"On purpose," Kol grinned. (I suspected Kol was coming around to forgiving me a little, now that he was warm and dry. He was telling Blackjohn's story to distract me from my stomach, and I was grateful for it.)

"You see," Kol explained, "those two fishermen came from Doonbridge. They'd been watching Blackjohn all along—him just a boy, fighting for life out there alone. They meant to bring him home with them."

"Why would they want to bring a pirate into their village?" (Diana asked this. She slipped out from the shadow between the frames[79] and sat down on the edge of my bunk.)

"Er—" Kol shot her an uneasy glance. "Erm—well—they took pity on him, I suppose. And—and also the Doonbridgers are forever in need of, of fresh *breeding stock*, if you will—"

"Of course," Diana nodded. "Fresh *WHAT*?" I squawked. Kol threw up his hands. "And you a farmer!" He shook his head incredulously. "People are like sheep, James. The flock needs new blood from time to time, otherwise the lambs come out sickly and weak. And Blackjohn—well *you've* seen him. He's a hardy sort of man, and he was a hardy sort of boy. He was precisely what the Doonbridgers needed. When Blackjohn came to himself again he was lying in

---

[79] The ribs of a ship's hull are called frames.

chains inside their fort with a considerable lump on his head. They got him healthy, and in short order they saw him—er—married.

(*After their fashion*, Kol mumbled.)

"The Doonbridgers let him off his chains?"

"They did, James."

"And they knew he was a pirate?"

"They knew."

"Then *how*," I asked in disbelief, "did they know he wasn't going to steal anything? Or, or murder anybody?"

Kol sighed. "A man is just a man, James," he said wearily. "Pirate, thief, lord, priest—names are just the clothes we give people to wear. We're all the same underneath, as like as one sheep is to another.

"At any rate," Kol pursued, "the Doonbridgers are a comparatively happy lot. No lord to bleed them. No enemy to fight. They all eat the same food and wear the same clothes, and they share freely amongst themselves. On the morning they let Blackjohn off his chains he simply strolled into a dyer's house, ate at the man's table, and commenced working his vats until the day he left Doonbridge. Blackjohn had some knowledge of the dyer's trade, you see. He learnt it from his father—"

"How did Captain Blackjohn come to leave Doonbridge?" Diana asked.

"Well—" Kol hesitated—"that was a tragedy, in my opinion. I think Captain Blackjohn would agree. But it's a story I'm afraid I can't tell," Kol said firmly. "I had it from Blackjohn in the secrecy of the confessional, and I dare not break that holy sacrament. Maybe he'll tell you himself someday. This much I *will* say—"

Kol looked at us darkly.

"—Captain John Blackjohn is every bit as eager to find Doonbridge as we are. He's been hunting it for years."

Outside the wind was getting softer. From on deck I heard the muffled *Ready about!* as the *Otter* prepared to tack.[80]

Kol cocked his ear to listen.

---

[80] A sailing vessel "tacks" when it crosses a headwind. It "jibes" when it crosses a tailwind.

Finn's voice calling. "You'll want to lie back down, James," Kol warned.
"Why—?"

—Leggo'n' haul!

"*Oo*—oh!" I clapped my hand over my mouth and gagged again. The
Otter took the first swell practically abeam.[81]

Kol laughed and patted my shoulder.

"You'll get used to it."

"S-so Blackjohn left Doonbridge," (I mumbled through my hand) "and
then—and then he went back to being a pirate again?"

Kol shifted uncomfortably. "Well—yes," he said, "that was a tragedy
too—

"Now, Blackjohn didn't return to piracy all at *once*, mind you," Kol
added hurriedly. "I only got this part of his story just today. In Iona, after I took
Blackjohn's confession, we—"

Kol paused.

"Well, let's just say Blackjohn went his way with good intentions," said
Kol. Closing his bible Kol settled back against the bulkhead[82] and crossed his
legs.

"I re—"

Kol yawned.

"I remember that day. I believe Blackjohn really meant to live honestly
from then on. He said he took a berth on the *Dionysus*; wine merchant's vessel
in the Bordeaux trade. In a few years he'd risen to Second Mate—that in spite
of how young he was. Blackjohn was a great favorite with the crew. They'd
have followed him into the very jaws of hell (he says.) Some of them are
following him still. That's his old bo'sun[83] Finn who—*ha ha!*—who pulled
you off the bowsprit, James.

---

[81] Amidship, at right angles to the keel.
[82] Inner walls of a ship are called 'bulkheads.'
[83] Boatswain

"Now the captain of the *Dionysus*—he was a hard man. Gloomy and dyspeptic.[84] Lived on nothing but oat porridge. He was a cruel master and his crew heartily loathed him. Captain Aaron was his name. Stoop-shouldered little man. Wispy red beard. Big bald forehead like an onion. Aaron would shut himself up in his quarters for days on end, leaving Blackjohn the running of the ship. If he honored his crew with an appearance it was usually to mete out some punishment—irons, half-rations, the lash. Aaron had a lackey in his sneaky little Chief Mate: Frenchman named Lapin. Lapin spied on the crew and reported back to Aaron. Of course they all hated Lapin too. They were thick as thieves, Lapin and Aaron. Blackjohn said they used to conspire for long hours together in the captain's quarters. Lapin and Aaron were afraid of Blackjohn. They'd have rejoiced to be rid of him. But Blackjohn was indispensable to the running of the ship and they dared not let him go, being poor seamen themselves.

"So at length they plotted to humiliate Blackjohn in front of the men, and by so doing (they fancied) to break his hold over the crew.

"Thus, on a particularly gusty April morning when Blackjohn had just started his watch, Captain Aaron and Chief Mate Lapin came up from the stern bent on mischief. Lapin blew assembly on his whistle and all the men formed up briskly, Blackjohn among the rest. Captain Aaron stood apart while Lapin strolled cooly down the double file of sailors.

"When he came alongside Blackjohn, Lapin stopped.

"*Zatt foresail be luffing*[85] *a' foot*—Lapin announced—*as no should be!*

"Lapin pointed at the foremast.

"*Mate Black-Jean!* he barked, *Grimpes-toi*[86] *up zem shrouds now veet! See shackles be tight!*

"*Begging your pardon, sir*—Blackjohn replies—*but I don't see the fo's'l*[87] *IS luffing, sir.*

---

[84] Prone to digestive complaints.

[85] A sail luffs—flaps—when poorly trimmed (improperly tautened; misaligned to the wind; etc.)

[86] French: *climb-you* (imperative)

[87] Foresail. Pronounce "fossil"

"*Up!* Lapin snarled. So dutifully Blackjohn climbed the shrouds, and gingerly Blackjohn sidled out onto the yard. But in the meanwhile Lapin had snuck over to the helm. Shoving the helmsman aside he took the wheel and set the *Dionysus* nosing up.[88]

"Teetering on the yard, Blackjohn reached down to try the shackle. But just then the *Dionysus* turned across the wind. The foresail bellied out backward with a terrible *crack* and Blackjohn fell straight down onto the deck. He lay there writhing in great pain while Lapin looked on and laughed.

"*Said-I sail was luffing, no?* Lapin jeered. Raising his voice, *Mon Capitaine!* Lapin called, *Mate Black-Jean be drunk at his post, in forenoon watch for shame! What chastisement,[89] sir?*

"*Eight lashes!* Captain Aaron commanded.

"*Bo'sun Feen!* Lapin barked, *Bind mate Black-Jean to mast an' strip heem!*

"But Finn never stirred.

"*So it's mutiny, is it?* Captain Aaron shrieked. *Bind him, Finn, you swine, or hang!*

"But Finn only muttered and looked down at his feet. Blackjohn picked himself up in a hellish rage.

"*I beg your pardon,* Blackjohn says quietly. *You mustn't be hard on Finn. He's never stripped a man above his station and he don't know what to make of it. But never you mind*—says Blackjohn—*I'll stand to, and Master Lapin, HE can lay on the lash.* And with that Blackjohn took off his shirt.

"Blackjohn took hold of the mainmast with both hands. He turned his broad back to the crew. Lapin looked nervous, but he took the lash out of his coat (where he'd been keeping it all along). Lapin threw back his arm—"

(Kol demonstrated, almost knocking down the lantern.)

"—and he *LASHED!*"

Diana and I jumped. Kol grinned.

"Lapin took Blackjohn square between the shoulders," Kol said. "He left a long, bloody weal down his back. Blackjohn winced, but he stood firm. Eight

---

[88] *I.e.*, up into the oncoming wind.

[89] French: *châtiment*: punishment

139

times Lapin applied the lash, drawing blood with every stroke. Eight times Blackjohn's shoulders shook, but he never made a sound.

"The eighth lash fell. Blackjohn's back was covered in blood. He let go the mast and turned himself about to face the crew. The men gasped, wondering at what they saw—"

Friar Kol stopped. He eyed Diana and me with a mischievous smile. We waited.

"Well go *on*, brother Kol!" I cried. "Tell us what the men saw!"

Kol chuckled.

"They saw Blackjohn was laughing."

"He was *laughing*?"

"Aye! He was laughing! For all eight lashes Blackjohn had been laughing so hard the tears ran down his cheeks. *Thine arm is grown feeble, Monsieur Lapin,* Blackjohn remarked, *for so much lying abed in the captain's quarters! Methinks a turn at the windlass would serve ye!*

"Well at that," said Kol, "an evil light came into Lapin's eye. Passing the lash to his other hand, Lapin drew the rapier he always wore, a gift from the captain. Slowly he circled Blackjohn; sword in one hand, lash in the other. There was murder in Lapin's face. He struck without warning, driving the point straight for Blackjohn's heart—"

Kol's shadow swung from side to side as he jabbed an invisible rapier through the air. For a moment my head stopped pounding. I perched on the edge of my berth in rapt attention.

Kol lowered his hand.

"But John Blackjohn was too much for Lapin," said Kol. "Blackjohn sailed with Rud Gallowglass, you know, and the murd'rous crew of the *Swift*. In a wink Blackjohn caught the rapier in his naked hand (though it cut him to the bone) and he *RIPPED* it out of Lapin's grasp. Over the rail it went and into the sea. Lapin screamed and came at him with the lash, but Blackjohn stuck his arm out close by the grip and the cords all spun themselves harmlessly about his wrist. Tearing the lash away Blackjohn swung it over his head.

"*THIS is how we thresh the barley in Munster, lads!* Blackjohn roared. He drew back his massive arm—"

Kol stopped.

.

Leaning forward, Kol primly spread his woolen blanket out across his knees. Then he settled back again.

"Now this lash," Kol resumed, "It had all sorts of nasty things knotted up in it—hobnails, bones, bits of glass. When Blackjohn let fly it cut straight through Lapin's coat; straight through Lapin's chest; all the way to Lapin's breastbone.

"Lapin fell backward onto the deck. Blackjohn struck him three more times, and Lapin's coat was all in tatters. Two inches of white rib lay bare over Lapin's heart."

Kol fell silent again. He cocked his head, listening to the wind above the deck. Diana and I sat without stirring. The ship's timbers creaked angrily in the stillness.

"So what happened to Lapin?" I demanded.

Kol looked up.

"Wha— oh, Lapin? He died. Blackjohn said he died."

"From four lashes?"

"From four lashes," Kol nodded. "A mad rage took over Blackjohn. At the first swing they all knew Lapin was a dead man. Everyone rushed in but they couldn't get Blackjohn's arm behind him. They carried Lapin insensible to the ship's surgeon (he a barber by trade) and the surgeon did his best to stitch Lapin back together, but it was too late. The wounds were very near his heart. Lapin died in the middle watch of the night, and they heaved his body unshrouded over the rail without so much as an *Our Father*."

Kol folded his arms and cleared his throat. "So what did Captain Aaron do?" Diana asked.

"The moment Blackjohn took the rapier," Kol replied, "Aaron ran like a rabbit for his quarters. After they'd carried Lapin away Blackjohn calmed down somewhat and he approached Aaron's door. It was four inches of oak, barred on the inside. *Captain?* Blackjohn called through the door, *Chief Mate Lapin is feeling poorly. He's taken to his bed, sir—that leaves me next in command. What bearing?*

"Aaron's quavering voice came through the keyhole. *You're to set a course for Gravesend,* Aaron cried, *to hang there for mutiny!*

"*I do wish to oblige ye,* Blackjohn returned, *but there's rope enough in Munster to hang me and I'd like to see my mother again.*

"*Oh! but you'll never see the whores of Munster more—all hands!* Aaron screamed, *Seize mate Blackjohn and fix him in irons! See him thrown in the ballast hold, or I'll see every man of you hang alongside him!*

"Blackjohn turned and faced the knot of sailors gathered behind. *I think he means to do it, lads,* he said calmly, *and I won't have anyone suffer on my account. I reckon it's the irons, then.*

"Well at that," said Kol, "the crew began to mill about in confusion. Some cried *The irons!* and some cried *Nay, he was provoked!* But all the while a strange cloud was rising in the west, like a pillar of smoke moving against the wind. Blackjohn saw it crouching low on the horizon when he first took his watch. Now the cloud arched high above the mainmast—black and boiling and edged with yellow lightning. It was closing on the *Dionysus* with unnatural speed.

"A blast of wind hit them like a fist and then the storm broke full upon them. The deck pitched and the sailors went sprawling in the scuppers.

"*Douse[90] the main!* Blackjohn bellowed. *Douse, I say!*

"Finn was loosing the mains'l halyard when he chanced to look out across the sea. Suddenly his face went gray as death. *Mother of God!* Finn wailed, and he let go the rope. Shrieks and laughter rose above the howling of the wind—"

Kol uncrossed his legs and sat up again. Taking his bible, Kol closed it reverently and wrapped it in the old leather shirt. Then he stretched out on his back, arranging the bible under his head like a pillow.

We waited.

"*Well?*"

Kol opened one eye.

"Eh?"

"Well what did Finn *see?*" I demanded.

Kol chuckled sleepily.

"Witches! He saw witches, of course."

"O-oh!" I returned wonderingly.

---

[90] Drop

"Yes," Kol nodded, "they were set on by witches riding in sieves. Well there wasn't any more talk of irons after *that*. When the storm broke it was all they could do to just to keep the *Dionysus* afloat. A few witches tried to come aboard, but they fended those off with boathooks. The real danger was from the the sea. When the storm finally lifted next day they saw the Breton coast lying in the mist to starboard and Aaron was stomping and raving like a madman below. So they dropped anchor near Brest. Aaron had a strong door, but his bulkhead was nothing uncommon. Blackjohn knocked a hole through it forthwith. Aaron greeted him with a pistol but he only managed to hit the ceiling. Blackjohn said Aaron looked terribly sick. They tied his wrists with his own lace cravat and they put him ashore with nothing but two gold sovereigns and the clothes on his back. Whether the Bretons took him in or whether he fell ill and died I can't say. Captain Aaron was never heard of more. Some of the crew went ashore at Brest and some at Plymouth. Some stayed with Blackjohn. Of course when word of it reached London the English crown pronounced Blackjohn a mutineer and set a price on his head—"

Kol yawned. The wind was quieter now. I stretched out on my back as well and Diana blew out the lantern. We lay in the utter dark, listening to the steady creak of the ship's timbers.

"This is the *Otter*, isn't it?"

"Wha—?" Kol returned drowsily.

"This boat," I said, "it's named the *Otter*, isn't it? You said Blackjohn took the *Dionysus*. How did he come by *this* boat?"

"Well Black— *ho-hum!*— Blackjohn said after the English put a price on his head, a Welsh privateer by the name of Jones was the first to come knocking. Jones happened to be captain of a fast little brigantine: the *Otter*."

Kol chuckled.

"By then Blackjohn was engaged in smuggling. It was the only work he could get, him being a known mutineer and all. He was sneaking something into England from Antwerp; he won't tell me what. Printed stuff, I'd guess. Books offensive to the Crown.[91] At any rate, Jones came upon the *Dionysus* a

---

[91] Bibles printed in English (instead of Latin) were banned in British Isles until the Great Bible of 1539. The Catholic Mary queen of Scots outlawed English bibles again in 1555. English-language bibles were printed in Holland and

little way from Calais and put a shot through her rigging with one of the new brass demi-cannons he'd mounted on his deck. Blackjohn had acquired a pair of old iron culverins[92] himself, and, as the *Otter* was fast approaching, McKee asked if they shouldn't return fire.

"Blackjohn peers through his glass. *Nay*—says he—*we might get unlucky and hit her. That's the bonniest brig I ever laid eyes on. We'll be wanting her in one piece. Drop sails! says Blackjohn. Loose the starboard main-shrouds and make ready to cut down the main!*

"Well when Jones saw the *Dionysus* drop her sails he thought she meant to surrender, so he cruises up all careless and flush with victory—*ha ha!*" Kol laughed. "Corner a badger and you'll get his teeth, my grandda' used to say. While Jones was coming near, Blackjohn and his men were sawing through their mainmast close by the deck. By the time the *Otter* drew up alongside it was only the stays keeping the main upright.

"*Yield ye, in the name of the crown!* Jones bellowed.

"*Quarter! Quarter!* cried Blackjohn and all his crew.

"*Out hooks!* Jones ordered. But the moment their keels drew even, Blackjohn let go the starboard main-shrouds and he felled his mainmast straight across the *Otter* like a tree. It lodged in her foredeck with all the yards sticking up.

"*Captain coming aboard!* Blackjohn roared, and he scrambled up onto the mast while Finn and McKee let go with both culverins at once—stone-loaded—mostly just to cause a panic.

"Jones answered with his demi-cannons and he put two holes in the *Dionysus* above the waterline, but Blackjohn didn't care a straw about *that* ship. He and his men swarmed across the mainmast while the crew of the *Otter* ran this way and that and their officers shouted contradictory things. Before the gunners had a chance to load they were fighting hand-to-hand, and it was the men of the *Otter* crying *Quarter!*

"In a moment it was won. Jones lay dead with four of his men and all the rest threw down their arms. Blackjohn kept Jones' chief mate for a hostage. He took such things off the *Dionysus* as he fancied and then he gave the survivors

smuggled into England.
[92] A primitive cannon, often loaded with stone shot.

leave to board and they cut her free, to limp back to Calais with just her foremast.

"Blackjohn's been captain of the *Otter* ever since," Kol concluded, "and the price on his head has risen considerably."

"Holy saints!" I murmured, admiringly. "And in all these years he's never—"

"Of course I don't *approve* of the things Blackjohn has done," Kol interrupted tartly. "John Blackjohn has led a reckless, ungodly life, and I doubt it will be a very long one. But these—these men of fortune—" Kol growled— "these lords and fighters; they must all take their chances, in my opinion. *Those who take the sword die by the sword*, our Savior said. He didn't say it made a diff—*ho hum!*—difference why—"

Kol yawned again.

Then he fell silent. I heard his breath getting deep, like he was about to snore.

"One last thing—"

"To sleep, James!" Kol growled. "You ought to sleep!"

"What's a 'privateer'?"

"A privateer? That's just a pirate. Only he sails for a king, or some other lord."

"What would a king want with a *pirate*?" I asked wonderingly.

Kol laughed.

"A king *is* a pirate," Kol said, "in the main."

CHAPTER 19

Doctor Scott's transcription—

Nota Bene—The previous page was bad parchment (horsehide, probably). I think an untrained hand stuck it in there after the proper leaf got torn out. All I could decipher was 'The Broch,' and 'nearly run dry.' My guess is the Otter sailed north along the coast and put in somewhere near Fraserburgh to resupply. James continues:

Captain Blackjohn was trying to teach me how to hold a sword.

We were sparring on the quarterdeck. I had Finn's rusty old falchion. After several furious attacks I had almost succeeded in cutting my own throat. Blackjohn parried with a broomstick, talking to Kol all the while (mostly about Doonbridge). The stick looked like a knitting-needle in Blackjohn's huge hand. He held it in the middle and turned my clumsy thrusts, first with one end and then with the other.

Finally I threw down the falchion. I bent over, wheezing, my hands on my knees.

"Friar Kol?"

I looked up.

"Friar Kol, will we ever see Lily again?"

I don't know why I said it.

Kol and Blackjohn stopped talking. They both turned and stared at me. Blackjohn dropped the broomstick.

"Head up!" Blackjohn shouted.

"Head up!" McKee echoed from the foredeck.

Blackjohn strode away.

Kol turned his back to me. He leaned against the rail, gazing out across the rolling swells.

"I don't know if we'll ever see her again, James," Kol said. "I rather doubt it. Lily granted you the word of her master Esus, and with his word you commanded her to leave and never to return. She was awfully relieved to be rid of you! She said she was going to miss Diana, though, and she said—"

Kol stopped.

"She said goodbye, anyway."

I hung my head. "I've tried calling her," I said sorrowfully. "I've tried all her names. She won't come."

Diana was watching us from the shadow under the mainsail.

"She *can't* come," Diana said. "Maybe I could call her, but I don't think I *should*."

Diana was different at sea. She seemed older—almost a woman. Her ragged clothes were gone and so was the starved, timid look in her face. The sailors all treated her with a sort of reverence. They called her 'my lady,' which was strange to me because I knew she was a bastard girl and no more a lady than I was a prince. Me they called 'Jamie-boy' and mostly ignored. The sailors watched Diana, but they never spoke to her unless she addressed them first. Captain Blackjohn hovered over her like a stormcloud and growled at anyone who came near.

Diana leaned on the rail next to Kol, effortless in spite of the rolling deck. Today she was wearing a fur-trimmed coat over a long embroidered dress. (*That dress was meant for lady in Cadiz*, Blackjohn once remarked. *It's worth more than your farm, Jamie-boy.*) The wind rippled in Diana's hair like it rippled on the glassy swells.

"You can call *Lily?*" I cried. "*How?*"

Diana looked down at her feet. "It's—because we're at the sea, I think. The North Sea leads to my home. If I sing, I think Lily might hear."

"So sing!" I begged. "Ask Lily to take us to Doonbridge! We'll be safe there; maybe forever! Why don't you ask her to come back?

Diana lifted her eyes. She looked me straight in the face.

"Because I don't trust you."

"*Me?*" I cried. "Why not? What harm have I ever done *you?*"

Diana curled her lip.

"You tried to give Lily over to the Black Stag."

"But that—"

"And—" Diana raised her voice—"after Lily told you what your wicked brother did, you screamed at her and called her a liar. You ordered Lady Farahain air-an-Lili off like a beggar! She an Immortal!"

I saw Diana's white knuckles. I took a step back.

"You're brave, James," Diana said, "but I think we'd all be safer without you."

"But I—

"Wait—" I blurted—"you think I'm *brave*?"

I instantly regretted it.

Diana turned red. For a moment she looked like a girl again.

"What I meant was—"

"*Ahem-HEM!*" Friar Kol coughed like he'd swallowed a herring. "I think what Diana means to say," he interrupted, "is that Lady Farahain is a powerful force—for good *or* for evil. And you, James: you still have the word of Esus. Lily could be—ah—unpredictable, in your inexperienced hands."

"Exactly!" Diana rejoined (with obvious relief).

I looked down at the boards, which I'd lately been scrubbing under bo'sun McKee's watchful eye.

"It isn't just Doonbridge," I said softly. "Of *course* I want Lily to help us like she did before. But—but mostly I just want to tell her something."

"Tell her *what*?" Diana demanded, a note of suspicion in her voice.

"Oh—nothing."

"But it must be *something*," Diana pursued. "And it could be dangerous. What might you possibly have to tell Lily?"

"No," I said, "Really. It's nothing."

"Then why did you *say* it, James? Why did you say you wanted to tell Lily something?"

I jerked my head up angrily.

"I want to tell her I'm *sorry*—" I shouted—"that's all! Are you happy now? I want to tell her I'm sorry I screamed at her, and, and I want to ask if she can she do anything to, to—"

I struggled to speak through the rising lump in my throat.

"—to help *Peter*. He's still my brother, you know. *You* know him, Friar Kol. You taught him his letters, and the *Ave Maria*. There must be something we don't know about it. Peter wouldn't just murder someone like that!"

I stalked off, wiping my eyes. I'd almost made it to the hatch when I felt a gentle hand on my shoulder.

I turned.

I was looking into Diana's strange, sapphire eyes.

"I'll call Lily," Diana said softly, "when the green fire flashes at sunset."

A day at sea, I said to myself, *is as bad as any day on the farm.*

The sun was going down. I was 'learning the ropes' from the youngest hand on board (the crew didn't consider me a sailor yet.) He was a Frisian named Ronne—barely older than me. Ronne spoke little English and, of course, no Scots. He seemed to think it was my great honor to pull on ropes until my hands bled while he pointed at things and barked their names, whether in English or in Frisian I couldn't tell.

I was starting to grasp how a ship makes way against the wind, and I confess it was a pleasure to see how the *Otter* danced across the waves. She rode the swells like a porpoise—sails tight as drumheads; white wake streaming straight back toward the bent horizon. In my whole life I'd never been past Haick, but now the coasts of all Scotland were slipping swiftly by. Friar Kol said we were sailing north around the tip of Alba, then south again through the western isles.

Somewhere in the isles, Doonbridge lay hidden.

During all the long day the clouds had been thick and lowering. Kol, Blackjohn, Diana and I were ranged along the portside rail, looking into the gloomy west. Diana leaned next to me.

"Look!" Diana pointed.

I followed her hand. A pod of dolphins were keeping up with us a little way off the port bow. Blackjohn nodded at them and tugged the ends of his beard. "Dolphins bring good luck," he observed. "Sometimes they'll escort us like this for—*Ah!*"

The sinking sun dropped out from under the clouds. Our topsails went blood-red.

"Now *that's* pretty," said Blackjohn.

The sun dipped into the sea and set it all afire. A burning crown hung over the water, then that too was swallowed up.

"Cover your ears," said Diana.

The red flame winked, and then the dying sun flashed green—as green as the water in the Lilylock. At that instant Diana sang a high crystal note, unlike any human voice. It went through me like cold water and set my hairs on end.

Blackjohn shuddered. Kol crossed himself.

I thought I heard a summons in Diana's call, though there wasn't any word in it.

"Lily will answer," Diana said, "if she wants to."

We stood and watched while the western sky faded back to gray, and not a sound did we hear save the wind in the rigging and the steady slap of waves against the hull. Near the bow a dolphin arched gracefully along with us, a sleek gray ripple in the twilight. It rolled lazily onto its side, lifting its fin out of the water and fixing us with one black eye.

"*Yes, Diana?*" squeaked the dolphin.

"*Lord* almighty!" Kol jumped half a yard. Blackjohn went gray as linen.

Diana leaned out across the rail.

"Is that you, Lily?"

The dolphin bobbed its head twice, its pink mouth flashing rows of pearly-sharp teeth.

"*Ye-ess,*" the dolphin mewed, "*this is Lily speaking. And the sea-jumper*[93] *is Mórester,*" (the dolphin waved its fin) "*High Priestess of clan Tonvacha. Mórester is lending me her voice, for I dare not approach the boy.*"

Diana nodded. "Thank you, Lady Farahain."

The dolphin rolled onto her back, keeping abreast of us with a serpentine wriggle.

Blackjohn jerked his head up like he was waking from a dream.

"Reef. The. *MAIN!*" Blackohn bellowed. "*REEF* the main! Head up! Head up!

---

[93] Scots Gaelic: *leumadhair-mara*: dolphin (literally "sea-leaper")

"And me a Captain!" he muttered angrily. The crew were scurrying around like ants. Ronne and McKee shortened the mainsail by half and lashed it off.

"Douse fore-tops'l!" Blackjohn barked.

The *Otter*'s prow dipped as she slowed.

"Gently! Gently!" cried Blackjohn, "Just way[94] enough to hold the bearing!"

Sculling the wave with her tail, Mórester rose halfway out of the water. With one black eye she scanned the knot of men clustered against the rail. "*Oh, THERE you are, Kollam!*" Mórester squeaked. "*I was worried about you!*"

Kol flushed and beamed.

"It's so good to see you again, Lil—Lady Farahain!" Kol cried. He leaned out over the rail as far as he dared.

"I mean—good to see you—as such—"

Mórester settled back into the water. "*Queen Femeen would have you know you're trespassing,*" she said with an offended puff. "*These waters belong to Clan Tonvacha; these waters and the air above them to the height of a salmon's leap. That is the law.*"

"I—I beg her pardon!" Blackjohn cried, awestruck. "I never dreamed!"

Mórester flipped her tail. "*Queen Femeen salutes Chief Blackjohn,*" she chirped. "*Queen Femeen heard how galant Chief Blackjohn drowned the ship-men who murdered the minke.*"[95]

"Aye, that'd be the whaler," Blackjohn growled. "Norse." He glared and gripped the rail. "They took a minke with a nursing calf. The sea was pink with blood and milk when we got to 'em, but I drowned their mangy captain in the brine with half his crew—HA HA!" Blackjohn roared. "*Hjelp! Hjelp!* they cried!"

Mórester dove into the swell and turned over twice. "*Yes, Mórester remembers,*" she said with a shivery laugh. "*Mórester remembers how the men struggled and kicked as their tiny lungs filled with water. Queen Femeen thanks Chief Blackjohn, and she gives him to know the murderers' bones lie mingled with the bones of the minke. They are together in death.*"

---

[94] Forward momentum
[95] Small baleen whale

Mórester turned over again. Diana leaned across the rail.

"James has something to say to you, Lily."

The dolphin swiveled her snout around to face me.

"*Speak!*" she bleated. In the fading light I could just make out the gleam of her black eyes watching me. I swallowed nervously.

"Li—Lily?" I began. "Lily, I'm sorry. I was wrong. And—and you saved us."

I waited.

The dolphin blinked.

"*Has he finished talking?*" Mórester turned to Diana. "I don't think so," said Diana.

"And, and, Lily—" I stammered—"I'd like you to come back to us again and protect us and help us find Doonbridge—"

Mórester slapped her fin on the water. "*You can't command me, mortal boy!*" she squealed. *You are speaking to Mórester, not to Farahain.*"

"I don't *want* to command you!" I cried. "Never again! Please help us, Lily, and help Peter, too! I *know* he didn't kill Kol's brother. He *couldn't*—"

The dolphin flipped her tail. With scarcely a ripple she was gone.

We waited in the dark.

Nothing stirred.

I slumped dejectedly against the rail. Friar Kol sighed and turned away. "Goodbye, Lily," he murmured. Blackjohn stuck his nose against the glass dome of the compass, squinting at the faint black markings. "Raise main!" Blackjohn called (a bit wearily). "Head down!"

Finn's watch had just ended. Ronne came grumbling up the hatch to commence his. Ronne lit a lantern and hung it from a stay, where it cast a swinging halo over the quarterdeck. Kol had put off his vespers to watch the sun set, so now he was singing *Deus In Adjutorium Meum* in a rather hurried voice.

> "*Domine, ad adjuvandum me festina,*"

The wind fell.

> "*Gloria Patri et Filio et Spiritui Sancto,*"

The wind ceased altogether.

> "*Et nunc et semper—*"

"—great heavens!" Kol broke off. "Captain? What's happening?"

All the sails had gone flat. The yards swung limp. The timbers left off creaking. In a minute the sea was silent as the grave. Ronne spun the wheel left. Then right. Then left again.

"Se begjint te driftjen!"[96] he called warningly.

Blackjohn was staring straight up into the sky.

Then I looked up too.

"Oh, *Diana*!" I breathed in wonder.

The stubborn blanket of clouds swept aside. Stars in their millions blazed down on us, and like a white tree in flower the arched bridge of the Milky Way gleamed so bright and near that for a moment I thought the *Otter* might stride out onto it and go sailing off into the heavens.

A silvery laugh trickled down from above.

It was Diana.

Diana was sitting on the topmost yard of the topsail, swaying like a bird on a reed.

"The sea leads to my home!" Diana called. "You can almost see it from here!"

Strange singing rose out of the water and the sea-girls came bubbling up, wreathed in red and brown. Some rode on dolphins and some swam with tails like fishes. Then the high priestess Mórester surfaced just off the starboard shrouds, and with a flip of her tail she sailed out of the water and up—

—Up

—Up

Up higher than the topsails,

Up over the mainmast,

—and *DOWN* she shot like a comet into a sea of mirrored stars. It was like a dream, Charlie! It was like the Black Stag's revels in the forest. Only pure this time. A taste like melting snow.

Green light gathered in a circle and then Lily strode up out of the sea. Her grass-green robes were changed for darker shades of gray. Around her neck she wore a collar of red corals. The sea rose like a staircase under her feet. In a moment she stepped out onto the quarterdeck, holding up the train of her

---

[96] *She's beginning to drift*

153

gown in one white hand. Friar Kol bowed his head. Captain Blackjohn dropped down on his knee and swept off his hat. Lily's radiance lit up their faces and made faint shadows of them both on the boards.

Lily stalked past them. She went straight up to me.

Without a word Lily clapped one hand over my mouth, closing the other around the fairy glass hanging from my neck. Her grip was not gentle.

"Say these words three times!" Lily snapped. *"Bradan-liath. Bradan-liath. Bradan-liath."*

"Br— Bradan-liath—"

My voice came muffled through her hand.

"Again!"

"Bradan-liath."

"Once more!"

"Bradan-li—"

BOOM. A big gray salmon shot out of the sea off the port shrouds. It launched high into the air. Instantly the fairy glass made a curious sucking sound. The salmon turned over once as it flew, then it came whizzing straight back down at me. I yelped and shielded my face. The fairy glass gave a blinding flash, and the fish disappeared.

Lily heaved a long sigh. The red collar crumbled off her neck and rained down onto the boards. Her shoulders lifted. Without another word she spun on her heel and strode back to Kol and Blackjohn.

"They have defiled the Lilylock, Kollam!" Lily said. Her voice trembled with outrage. "Those filthy witches came under the full moon. My oaks held them for a while, but they were too many. Then the bancorra got in, and they—"

Green teardrops shimmered on Lily's cheeks.

"My home is ruined!"

Friar Kol's face wore a curious look. For a moment he stared down intently, as if he had suddenly become interested in how the mains'l halyard was tied up.

Kol hesitated.

Then, with a resolute expression, Kol reached out his hand and gently patted Lily's arm.

154

"I am so sorry," Kol said with emotion. "Perhaps you could make another home, Lily."

I half expected Kol's hand to pass right through her, but it stopped like she was made of something solid. Kol smiled—a trifle bashfully, I thought. They stood there together a moment. Kol's hand was on Lily's arm and she was looking into his eyes, when suddenly—

Come up here!

We turned our faces to the sky.

"Come up here!" Diana shouted down at me. "It's alright! You won't fall!"

My hands and feet were in the shrouds.

My arms and legs were wrapped around the topmast, clinging on for dear life. I inched upward.

The tops'l yard was only a foot away—

Diana grabbed my arm.

"Are we getting close to your home, then?" I asked, "close to Éireann?"

Diana shook her head.

"We *are* close to Éireann," she said, "but that's not my home—not really."

"So where *is* your home?"

Diana hesitated. She looked as if she were trying hard to remember something.

"Well, it's not Éireann," she said at length. "I was only staying there awhile with the old man's sister."

"*Sowter's* sister? Your mother?"

"Méara!"

"What?"

"Méara!" Diana laughed. "*That* was her name. I'd forgotten. Sowter's sister is called Méara. I lived with her, but she's not my mother."

"Then who *is* your mother?" I asked, astonished. "And—and your father? Who *are* you, Diana?"

Diana smiled and shook her head. She pointed up at the burning sky.

"What do you see?"

"Er—stars?"

Diana shook her head. "Those aren't stars," she said. "They're islands."

"*Islands?*"

"Yes! Islands! They look like stars from here, but that's because they're in the Other World. They're really all just islands in the Deep Water."

I didn't answer. For a long time we sat there with just the slender tip of the mainmast between us. We'd each hooked an arm around it—my left; Diana's right; my arm touching hers.

Diana turned to me.

"I'm sorry," she said. "I never thanked you."

"*Thanked* me? Thanked me for *what?*"

"For saving me," Diana almost giggled. "You knocked the Black Stag off his horse!"

I grinned.

"He *did* scream so. Diana, are *you* from the Other World?"

Diana looked perplexed.

"I—I can't remember," she said. "It's so strange, crossing over. Everything changes, and yet it's all the same—like water when it turns into ice, or like thistle blossoms when they turn into wool and float away on the wind. Sometimes I can still see things as they are on the Other Side. But more often the memory fades and the Other Side gets misty. I can still reach out to it with my songs. I hope—"

She stopped. I turned to her and saw there were tears in her eyes.

"I hope I find my way back home again."

I bit my lip, thinking.

"Is Lily from the Other World too?"

Diana laughed. "Yes and no," she said. "Lily is bound to this world even more than you are. But: stars, frogs, willow-trees—they're all forged from the same fire. That fire burns bright in Lily—"

Diana leaned over and peered down at the quarterdeck below. The little black lump that was Friar Kol was standing there, bathed in Lily's glow.

"It burns bright in Kollam too."

The green halo shone beneath us. By its light we could see the dolphins and the sea-people go swirling round and round like partners in a dance. "I've seen so many strange things," I said. "I don't think I shall ever be the same."

Diana laughed.

"The strange things have seen *you*!"

"Aye, *that* they have—"

"I don't think the Black Stag knows what to make of you," Diana pursued. "You throw one rock and suddenly *plop!* Ripples in the pond. You've upset his plans—you, of all people!" She laughed. "The son of a poor farmer!"

"The son of a *dead* farmer."

Diana looked serious. "Your father followed Francis Stewart's father," she said. "And he died for it. And now Francis Stewart is following *you*. We'll see what happens to him."

I laughed. Then, not knowing what else to do, I let go the topmast and put my arm around Diana's waist instead.

Diana tilted her head toward mine. Her cheek rested ever-so-slightly on my shoulder.

CHAPTER 20

From the diary of Doctor Stewart Henry Scott—

Edinburgh – June 5, 1838

I arrived in Edinburgh on the second of June, 1838. With me were William Fitzhugh and his sister Mrs. Elizabeth McRoy, widow of the late Arthur McRoy of Berwick-upon-Tweed.

We had two strange errands: first to unlock, if we could, the rest of this mysterious book, *The Last Will and Testament of the Pirate John Blackjohn*; and, second, to reach the island of Iona in the Inner Hebrides, as Fitzhugh and I believed that was what our ghostly visitor intended for us to do. What the specter's purpose was we could not guess, but, being resolved to risk it, we must at last return to Edinburgh to meet with my associate Dr. Albert Gray, to set in order the affairs of my practice, to secure funds for our journey, etc., etc.

The post-carriage got out of Dalkeith before seven o'clock that morning. The light of the long summer day was still broad in the sky when Albert welcomed me to my neglected home: a gloomy stretch of rooms in Bread Street with my own modest home above. My housekeeper had made up the place as best she could, but I confess I was ashamed to receive Elizabeth there. An old bachelor's lair is no fit place for a woman. Going in, it struck me for the first time how shabby my furnishings were, particularly after the comforts of Elizabeth's charming home. The whole place had a rather sepulchral look (and a rather sepulchral *smell*, being shut up for weeks on end while I was out on errantry in the Borders).

Tired as she was, Elizabeth commenced fluttering about the kitchen and parlour like a fairy, and with a wave of her wand (figuratively speaking; she was in fact holding a feather-duster) she transformed the dreary place into something almost like a home. From somewhere she conjured up a tolerably clean tablecloth and tolerably clean china to put on it, and many more candles (damn the expense!) and—bless my soul—a clutch of daisies in a vase! (I haven't the faintest idea where she got them. I truly believe she *is* a fairy.)

Albert and I got the sheets off the movables and we rolled out the big hearthrug in front of a bit of a fire that Fitzhugh kindled in the grate (it was chilly after the sun went down), such that by eleven we were all in slippers, drinking my old claret and toasting a barley loaf as easy as you please.

We talked of nothing but John Blackjohn. Albert Gray is a rational man of science, so of course he thinks I've gone completely mad.

"You saw a young man in a sailor cap, I grant you," says he, "but as for spirits, I reckon you two were taking *those* from a steel flask!"

Fitzhugh said he rather wished it were so, as the experience had quite shaken him. Albert asked if he might have the pleasure of seeing the book which had nearly got me stuck in the Duke of Buckley's chimney. I fetched *Blackjohn* from the bedroom and Albert put it under the table lamp. It sat there looking like a moldy bellows: two leather covers and a half-moon of yellow parchment fanned out in between. Albert took his magnifying glass and turned *Blackjohn* over with a skeptical expression.

"I'm of the opinion your pirate book is nothing but a clever humbug," he said at last. "It's very old parchment, yes—" (Albert looked up at us over the glass, which glinted in the yellow light—) "but it's not as if *that* sort of thing never happened before. You're the historian, Stewart; tell me: haven't whole *books* been falsely attributed to famous men? Dead saints and such?"

"Oh yes," I allowed, "indeed they have been. Certainly in medieval times—you know—dusty relics get worshipped while new ideas get suppressed. That sort of thing. A canny author might be tempted to pass his work off as Augustine or Gregory or the like so as not to risk offending the Church. But 'John Blackjohn'? A *pirate*? I've racked my brains and I can't come up with any sensible reason a person would invent such a thing."

"Oh, sensible, *non*-sensible—" Albert returned. "People do all sorts of ridiculous things for their own reasons." (He glanced sideways at me.) "Why, it could have been invented by a lunatic who wants people to believe in fairies.

159

Or fancy this—" Albert laughed and wiped the magnifying glass on his sleeve. "Some rare-book dealer comes across an old blank quarto. Nothing uncommon about *that*, is there?"

I shook my head.

"Learned antiquarian—" Albert leaned forward in his chair. *He'll be about thirty-five by now*, I was thinking. His long, sallow face was starting to show age. Hard lines about the mouth. Tufts of peppery hair sticking out around his shiny temples. I imagined he had a bit of Radan's nervousness about him, though he leans more to the portly.

"—like yourself, Stewart. He says to himself, he says, *I'll spin a yarn that'll make this moldy parchment worth a fortune!* He's got an eye for making a stir in the papers, you see. A bit of Clan Scot legend come to life, aye? Put his shop front-page in the *Courant*, that would! So he mixes up some iron ink and sets to it in his finest Auld Scots—" (Albert dropped into an exaggerated brogue—) "but then his hand starts to cramp up and he loses his taste for the job, so he caches his creation in some old ruin in hopes the lairds of Buckley find it and take it for gospel."

"But who could possibly believe—"

"Maybe his books start selling again, hey? He fobs off a few old demonologies; maybe, maybe gets his little humbug cited in *Scots Peerage*—"

"And the copper seals?" I ventured.

Albert turned the book over again and studied the plate on the back cover. The green face wreathed in water lilies bulged up at him through the magnifying glass. The curious opening in her mouth made it look as if she were asking him a question, and I dimly wondered what it was.

"Catholic diary!" Albert said confidently.

"You think so?"

"Yes, from the religious wars. Guy Fawkes and all that. Take this plate off and I'll hazard ten pounds we find nothing but the meditations of a Yorkshire gent who was a bit too fond of the Pope."

"That *would* be about the right time," I admitted.

"Then it's settled," Albert said firmly. "Tomorrow we take your holy grail to a locksmith, and the quest ends. No more traipsing through bogs and neglecting our patients." He shook his magnifying glass admonishingly.

"You're a charming old fellow, Stewart, but you forget that our reputation is our rent. If the neighbors hear you've gone off chasing fairies and offending dukes they won't come to us for their pills and plasters any more. I've got my expenses too, you know."

Albert said it lightly—and I laughed—but I confess I was stung. Partly because I knew Albert was right. Partly because I was so terribly weary. But mostly because he'd said it in front of Elizabeth. I think he'd forgotten she was there, sitting in the green damask chair by the hall door, holding a book. She had a blue pencil in her hand and from time to time she would mark the page or write something in the margin. But she was looking up attentively when Albert chided me. It was his 'old fellow' that hurt most. I knew Albert thought me eccentric—I couldn't rightly blame him for that—but until that moment I'd never suspected he might think me a dotard. He'd taken a tone I'd never heard before; indulgent, like a kindly father correcting a wayward child.

"Well of course I tried that!" I retorted. I'd opened my valise and rummaged about inside. "I took it to a locksmith in Berwick. The man said that's no keyhole that *he's* ever seen. Then I was passing a wearisome time recovering at The King's Arms, so to amuse myself I melted down a lead thimble and took a cast of the lady's mouth myself—"

I took a little gray lump out of my valise and handed it to Albert.

"See? It's just as he said. There's no mechanism of any sort inside. It's nothing but a tooth-shaped hole."

Albert held the mold up beside the lamp. He squinted at it, turning it about slowly in his fingers.

"It's a premolar," Albert said musingly. "An *upper* premolar. I hope so, anyway."

"Why 'hope so'?" I looked up at him sharply.

"Oh, a lower premolar would be harder to match to a skull," Albert returned carelessly. "The jawbone is the first to wander off once its owner is dead."

"Oh, so it's a dead man's tooth, at least, not a living man's humbug?"

Albert frowned and stuck his hands in his pockets. "Well the copper plate must be ancient, at any rate," he said defensively, examining the mold again. "You certainly won't find a tooth like this walking down Queen Street. Several hundred years dead, I should say."

"And how do you know that, sir?" Fitzhugh put in.

"I know it from the wear. See the inner face? At this point the man would be about my age, but look: there isn't a trace of decay. Why, I've never seen anything like it! I'd be tempted to say this fellow never tasted bread—or precious little of it. Grains rot the teeth."

"Fascinating!" I exclaimed. "A Viking, perhaps? They pillaged the western isles centuries ago. Iona was sacked repeatedly. First came the pagan Norsemen, then came the christian MacDonalds and McLeods. The isles got pillaged just the same."

"But surely the Norsemen ate *bread*," Fitzhugh interjected.

"Yes," I replied, "but many northern strands were too rugged for farming. Imagine a little village eking out its existence at the edge of some windswept fjord. They'd rely on the cod to survive, and herring. Livestock, too."

"Well then we know whose tooth it *isn't*," said Fitzhugh.

"Whose?" I demanded.

"It isn't James McKenna's," Fitzhugh retuned. "Your writer, Doctor. *He* lived on oat porridge, from what you were telling Elizabeth. Why, I doubt a lad so poor tasted beef above once a year at Christmas."

"Ri-ight—" I mused. "Right you are, Fitzhugh."

"And it wouldn't belong to our, our ghost either," Fitzhugh pursued. "Not if, as doctor Gray says, the tooth has about thirty-odd years' wear on it. Our friend was younger than that."

"Looked about twenty-five, I should say."

Elizabeth yawned behind her handkerchief. "I've no doubt you'll raise your ghost again presently," she said, "but we the living have traveled many miles and we need rest. If you'll excuse me, Doctors—"

We stood up abruptly with much bowing and scraping of chairs and wished her goodnight. "To bed with ye, Willie," Elizabeth called to Fitzhugh, "before you die from weariness." Fitzhugh marched obediently after her. The hall door closed behind them.

Albert and I settled back down again.

"Fitzhugh's a stout friend," I said, "and it's a comfort to have him beside me on this mad adventure. Elizabeth too."

I moved my chair nearer the fire. Albert turned down the lamp.

"I can't imagine what you must think of me, Albert," I resumed. "Abandoning our practice. Ferreting about in castle drains. Running afoul of the law—"

"Larceny," Albert added wryly. "Petty or grand, depending upon whether that book of yours turns out to be a fake."

"Yes, that's what worries me most," I said. "The young duke—Sir Walter Douglas-Scott—it's *his* book, but I don't think he even wants it. It's *Radan* wants it, and I can't guess the reason why. Radan will do anything to get it. Sack Fitzhugh. Suborn[97] a magistrate. Why, he'll even show up with a scatter-gun and shoot me point-blank! I feel awful about mixing Fitzhugh and Elizabeth up in this. I'm worried about you too, Albert. Where are my dispatches, may I ask? Have you been sending them to the scrivener's?"

"Faithfully," Albert grunted. "To Constantine's."

"And the copies?"

"Constantine has them."

"And the originals?"

"In the fireproof safe."

I sighed and rubbed my eyes. "Constantine is in danger too," I said. "Radan could see him shuttered in half-an-hour."

"Oh come now!" Albert remonstrated, "He's a solicitor, not a Prince! You worry too much, Stewart."

"You think so?"

"I know so! From your letter I'd say Radan was probably out of his head when he shot you. The law attracts weak minds. Temporary insanity, I'd say. One reads about that sort of thing. He's probably run off for good."

"I hope so," I said. "Let's have a look at the safe."

The fireproof safe used to squat in my office on the ground floor. It was a broad, ugly thing like a heavy sort of coal-box, and as it was always very much in the way—and as its gray steel surface, nearly table-height, had that

---

[97] Bribe

magnetism about it which attracts office clutter for which no ready place can be found—at last I hired a man to get it onto a hand-truck and haul it to the lumber room at the end of the hall. There it sat ten years or more, acquiring first a pile of medical journals, then a stack of old newspapers tied up in twine, and finally, when the painters came to banish the ghosts of tobacco-smoke and formaldehyde from the walls, then the old safe was robed in a canvas sheet and crowned with several half-empty buckets of paint.

Albert took the lamp. We creaked down the dark corridor, past the lonesome examination rooms. The door at the end of the hall swung in, admitting the lamplight.

There sat the safe at the back of the lumber room looking just as it always had, except the canvas sheet had lately been pulled up and tucked under a paint bucket for Albert's access. I stuck the heavy key into the lock and pulled the handle.

Inside lay *John Blackjohn* in two uneven stacks. I bent down and thumbed through the pages, remarking my familiar, spidery handwriting sprawled over paper of various sorts and sizes. Branxholme castle letterhead. Inn stationery. Religious tracts. Elizabeth's own yellow note paper.

I closed the safe door and locked it. "Well, it's comforting to see," I said with a sigh. I'm no treasure-hunter, Albert. I *will* return the book. I simply— simply want to get the rest of the story, that's all."

Albert patted me on the shoulder. We turned to leave.

As we stepped out into the hall, on a sudden impulse I turned around, went back into the lumber room, and pulled the paint-spattered canvas down over the safe door, leaving it hidden.

The next morning dawned fair and almost clear. I must have been terribly worn-out, for I confess I slept much longer than I'd intended. It was past ten before I made my way up to the rooftop, there to discover Fitzhugh smoking his briar-root and gazing out on the busy scenes below. Across the rooftops the stern old fortress of Edinburgh Castle frowned down at the city from its natural rampart, as if it took a dim view of all this frivolous sun. We said 'Good morning' and I installed myself at Fitzhugh's side, elbows on the parapet. Carts rumbled in the street and passers-by came and went with all the bustle of a lively burg on a Tuesday morning.

"Fitzhugh," I said at length "I should very much like to visit that scrivener, Constantine, and see how the copying is coming along."

Fitzhugh chewed his pipe.

"So you'll come with me, then?"

Constantine the Scrivener plied his pen in Cowgate not far from Sheriff Court, where Justice sat and gorged herself upon writs and pleadings and affidavits and all the other tedious blasphemies of the law. These Constantine and his two apprentices must copy out in duplicate and triplicate from the first *Whereas* to the last *So Ordered*, while the barristers' clerks scurried in and out and the ink rained gently down from the desks until the floorboards were shiny and black as crow's feathers.

I remember Constantine's establishment as a sort of stable; dark and narrow within; wires running the length of the low ceiling where inky papers hung drying like sheets in a washhouse.

As Fitzhugh and I drew near the place I was surprised to find Constantine's two apprentices idling in the street outside the door.

"Hello, where's the master?" I asked them sharply.

"He's gone," said the boy.

"Gone? Gone where?"

"Don't know." The boy stuck his hands in his pockets and kicked idly at the curb. "Door's locked."

I put my face up to the glass and shaded my eyes. All was dark within.

Feeling dreadfully uneasy, I banged the knocker and shook the doorknob.

"Mr. Constantine!" I called.

There was a faint moan inside.

"Constantine!" I screamed, beating my palm against the dirty pane. Fitzhugh swept the startled 'prentices aside and squinted into the doorjamb. "The bolt's not drawn," he shouted. In an instant he had his penknife out and was jabbing it feelingly between the doorpost and the knob. With a deft twist he popped the latch and the door swung open. I rushed inside. Constantine lay face-down between two desks. Dry blood was caked in his hair. Blood lay in a little crusted pool beside him on the floor.

I grabbed a pair of scissors and cut feverishly up the back of his shirt. Fitzhugh swept a desk clear and stood ready to lift as I searched along Constantine's spine. Not finding any injury we hoisted him up as gently as we could and laid him on his back. Fitzhugh ordered the frightened apprentices off to fetch a constable and a street chair.[98]

Constantine's lips moved feebly. His face was ashen gray.

"There, there, my good fellow!" I said, trying to remember my old bedside manner. "You've taken a bit of a knock, but we'll get it sorted out. Fitzhugh? See if you can find anything clean for Mr. Constantine to drink."

Fitzhugh came back with a pitcher of water. Constantine took it in his shaking hand.

"Now you rest easy," I said cheerfully, "while I see to this scratch. I'll have you know you're in the care of the best doctor north or south of the Tweed."

The wound looked ugly. A heavy object had cut the top of Constantine's head all the way to his skull. I suspected he was badly concussed.

"Don't bother speaking," I warbled. "We'll get your story soon enough. We'll have the lads take it down in triplicate—"

Constantine coughed.

"The will," he said faintly.

"The what?"

"The will," Constantine repeated. "The will and testament. Wouldn't give it to him. Bastard hit me with a paperweight—"

"*Who* hit you with a paperweight?"

"M-missus Haig's son—"

I was burning with curiosity, but "Fitzhugh my friend," I called, "find the kettle and set it on to boil. And see if you can find any alcohol. I'll have this scratch cleaned before the street chair gets here." I pulled my watch out to take Constantine's pulse.

"Mrs. Haig. The old widow," Constantine resumed feebly. "She's dead, Doctor."

---

[98] Wheelchair. Public ambulances were unknown in the early 1800s.

"Oh, is she now? Well, well, it was her time. You rest eas— And here's the alcohol already! Thank you, Fitzhugh. Constantine? It'll sting, lad."

"The—*Ah!*—" Constantine winced—"the vicar gave us her will to copy. She's got that worthless son, Bruce. Brawler and a drunk. Mostly in and out of lockup in Newcastle. Never laid eyes on him before, but then he barges in here late last night—"

"You're sure it was him? Mrs. Haig's son?"

"—I'd a' had the shop locked up," (Constantine sounded a bit delirious) "only I was staying late to finish the Mayfair pleadings and the 'prentices had already gone home. Bruce must a' gotten word his ma' meant to leave her little nest-egg to the Church. He's hatched some cracked scheme, I reckon. Probably means to burn the will—"

"Probably, probably," I soothed. "The police will run him to ground in time. You just rest easy, my good man. Now, Constantine? Try to fix your eyes on the tip of my penknife. Shiny bit. That's— That's it! Now, see if you can follow it with your eyes. Left. Right. Lef—*very* good! Spot on! That knock hasn't scrambled your brains. You'll be blotting affidavits again in no time."

"Told him—" (Constantine's gaze began to wander) "Told him get out. Go see the magistrate. Lang[99] bastard. Talked like a Lunker. Rather ni-nicer coat than you'd expect. *We only have our copy*, says I, *not the original*, but *Makes no difference*, says he, so I put the paperweight on it and I said *No*."

"Stout fellow!" I interrupted. "Now here's Fitzhugh with the kettle. Let's see about washing this—this little scrape—"

Constantine cringed and shuddered.

"—so the bl-blaggard just reaches across the table and grabs the paperweight. Arm like an ape. I ran for it—"

Constantine closed his eyes.

"Then lightnings. Will's gone and about twenty deeds. Got the whole stack, he did. I lay down because my head was swimming—"

Constantine's voice trailed off.

"Now don't you trouble yourself about that," I said cheerfully. "You've earned yourself a furlough. Those laggard 'prentices will pick up the slack— serve them right! Where's that chair?"

---

[99] Tall

"—don't know what he'll do with a pile of deeds. Scatter them along the highroad—"

"Constantine, my friend?"

(I knew I shouldn't ask but I couldn't help myself.)

"Constantine, my friend? That copy you've been making for Doctor Gray—where is it?"

Constantine opened his eyes.

"Why, it's back inside my safe, Doctor, of course."

I breathed a sigh.

"Do you— Constantine, do you know what's *in* Doctor Gray's papers— the ones he sends you? Do you know what they say, that is?"

"What they—"

Constantine looked bewildered.

"Well—no, Doctor. Not specifically."

"But, if you don't mind my asking, you *have* been copying them, haven't you? You yourself, and not the lads?"

"That's right," Constantine nodded.

"And you—you don't recall what the papers say on them?"

"Well, Doctor," (Constantine's pale cheeks reddened slightly) "the fact of the matter is—I don't read so—so very quick."

"Ah!"

"I mean," Constantine added hurriedly, "if a paper says 'Deed' up top in big letters of course I know it's a deed. And if it says 'Writ' I know it's a writ. But them wee letters, so to speak—I copy *that* lot out right enough, but I don't always quite catch the meaning, you see, except for the *ands* and the *buts*—"

"Ha ha!—and what of that?" I interrupted jovially. "Who understands that legal hocus-pocus anyway? I'm sure *I* don't. Leave the Latin to the schoolboys. Poor schoolboys! So a lean, yellow man made off with a poor widow's will and a pile of property deeds—" I sniggered in spite of myself. "—something tells me he's been mistaken before."

Fitzhugh guffawed at my elbow.

Then a sobering thought occurred to me. My heart sank. "*Mister* Constantine," I said miserably, "this is all *my* fault—this terrible incident."

"Doctor?"

"Constantine, I've reason to believe I'm the cause of all—"

I stopped, considering.

"—but no matter, my brave friend. No matter."

Constantine sighed and closed his eyes again.

"You might be concussed. The less talk, the better."

"Oh?"

Constantine turned his head slightly and looked up at me.

"She was your patient, was she Doctor?"

"Er, who?"

"Mrs. Haig. She was your patient, right? For goodness' sake, don't blame your*self*, sir! Why, she lived to a great age! We should all be so lucky. Passed in her sleep like an angel, they said. Must've been happy to toddle off to—to the Sweet Hereafter and so forth—"

I smiled without answering. I hated to deceive Constantine. No rascal son of Mrs. Haig's bludgeoned him in the back of the head with his own paperweight. Somehow Radan had found the shop already, and it was only thanks to Radan's clumsiness and Constantine's illiteracy that *John Blackjohn* was still there. Looking down into the gray gash in Constantine's scalp I knew he'd had come within an inch of his life. It made me sick in inside.

I'm a menace to anyone who knows me, I said to myself.

But the more Constantine learned about it, the worse his probable danger. I resolved to end our arrangement then and there.

"Mr. Constantine," I said resolutely, "I'm happy to announce that Doctor Gray's copywork is now complete. No further installments will be coming. And so happy are we with the—the quality of your work—and with your, er, your courage in defending our private documents, that we—I'm happy to inform you we've agreed to give you a substantial gratuity plus bonus, enough for you to rest at home until this bump is healed. Those sly barristers will have to look elsewhere for their copying until August at the earliest. As your physician I hereby prescribe no fewer than eight weeks' rest! This order is not to be trifled with, Constantine. Send the 'prentices home."

"Are you in—"

Constantine got up on his elbows and raised his bushy eyebrows in wonder.

"Are you in earnest, Doctor? Or did that knock scramble my wits after all?"

"I am perfectly serious, Constantine," I said. You must take proper care of this wound. Doctor Gray and I will see your shop doesn't lose a penny for it—and here's the chair at last! That's the bell[100] coming up the lane. Is that a constable? It *is* a constable! Marvelous! Those 'prentices are good for something after all. One last thing, Constantine: I'll need to get Doctor Gray's copywork out of your safe; just whisper to Mr. Fitzhugh where you keep the key, if you'd be so kind. He's a dear and trusted friend. Quickly, if you can! There's a good man."

Fitzhugh and I bundled Constantine down into the street chair. I straitly persuaded the boy to leave off clanging the bell, and together we all trooped out into the lane. Fitzhugh ordered the 'prentices to put up the shutters and lock the shop, then he gave each of them a shilling and told them to be off home until such time as Mr. Constantine should call them to resume their employment.

Fitzhugh took the handles of the chair.

"To Bread Street," I commanded.

We set off briskly. The constable trotted alongside the chair, asking questions and scribbling things in his notebook. Constantine's head bobbed from side to side shrouded in my white handkerchief. From under the handkerchief came the occasional groan, mostly when we were obliged to bump across the cobbles. The brass bell *would* clang sometimes of its own accord, and all the passersby turned to stare at our little parade: the doctor, the butler, the constable and the groaning spectre in the chair.

It was only about a mile to Bread Street. Soon we had Constantine installed in my examination room, where an astonished Albert eyed his scalp through the magnifying glass and Constantine's terrified wife Melinda kneaded his palms and said 'Good Lord' and 'Oh my.' She'd imagined Constantine was working all through the night until Fitzhugh knocked at her door with his hat in his hands. I dressed the wound properly, then I sent Constantine home with Fitzhugh in a cab and Melinda off to the druggist's for laudanum and willow-bark[101] powder.

---

[100] The old-fashioned wheelchair was sometimes equipped with a warning bell.

The constable took his leave. Albert dazedly saw him out, then he hurried off to the lumber room to lock up Constantine's neat stack of *John Blackjohn*. Mrs. Constantine spent the better part of an hour running back and forth across Bread Street—first to me, then to the druggist's, then back to me again with a hundred fretful questions. But home she went at last with a clutch of pill-bottles clinking under her arm. Albert, Fitzhugh and I found ourselves lingering in the sudden quiet of my office.

Fitzhugh and Albert were looking at me as if they expected me to say something.

I felt the situation had become grave. Some sort of resolution was required on my part, but I didn't know how to begin.

"Ah—gentlemen?" I ventured.

Just then there came a clank and a hiss from upstairs. "Oh, thank heaven!" I breathed, "Elizabeth's just put the kettle on! Marvelous woman! Away with us!"

We had tea, and rather a lot of biscuits. I hadn't realized how hungry I was. Then Albert found a ripe cheese in the pantry, so Fitzhugh went across the lane for a fresh loaf. Albert, Elizabeth and I went up to the rooftop (as the June air was pleasant) and Fitzhugh came back with the loaf and a bag of plums and a cured sausage to boot. So we dusted off a bottle of port (we rather thought we'd earned it) and carried the lot and a whist-table up to the roof where we talked and ate and ate and talked until the evening shadows crept up the gray face of Castle Rock and the westering sun set the windows of the old fortress afire.

"I can't stay here, Albert," I said, "and that's final. Radan will be bludgeoning *you* next. How did he know you were sending things to Constantine, I wonder?"

"Aye," Fitzhugh put in, "and what good's a copy to him anyway? Copy's not a precious antique."

"What's this?" Albert smirked, "A lawyer driving a gentleman from his home without so much as a summons?" He laughed. "Bloodthirstiness is common in the profession, but I rather thought they murdered with the pen, not the paperweight. You have rights, Stewart," Albert added seriously. "I wonder:

---

[101] The earliest form of aspirin

did you happen to give Radan's description to the constable? I mean—if you're certain it was really him."

"No—" I rubbed by temples miserably. "I haven't got clean hands myself. If the police get the story then Radan gets the book—I just know he will. A constable died in Berwick just for trying to keep the thing as evidence. It was an act of homicide."

"The man was struck by lightning," Albert retorted. "I'd rather call that an act of *God*."

"True. True," I mused. "He *was* struck by lightning. And yet I thought—or rather, it really seemed that—that Radan, er, *willed* it somehow—"

"Oh come!" Albert scoffed. "He's a solicitor, not a sorcerer! It's *anno domini* 1838, Stewart! Your Merlins are all shut up in their enchanted caves these days."

"Yes, but it was all very unaccountable," Fitzhugh rejoined. "Radan said something to the constable before he died. 'There's going to be a storm.' He said it like it was a threat." Fitzhugh scowled and leaned back in his chair. "I'm not given to superstition, sir, but what are the odds of a thing like that: constable gets struck by lightning ten minutes before he can deliver a book to court? And then Radan turns up at that precise moment pointing a pistol at us."

"Rather lucky timing for *him*," I agreed.

Albert folded his arms. "Mister Radan was probably just walking behind you," he returned. "You said there was fog."

"Yes," I sighed, "well, Constantine wasn't struck by wizardry, at any rate. *He* was struck by a paperweight. And I can't have that happen to you, Albert. The more I think on it, the more I am resolved: I must be off again as soon as I can manage."

"But to where?" Albert demanded.

"To Iona."

"Oh for God's sake, Stewart! Really—"

"Yes, Albert," I said firmly, "to Iona. I hardly know what for, but I'm determined to see this thing through, and my heart tells me that Iona is where it will end."

Albert smiled, not without amusement. I supposed he wasn't accustomed to hearing me speak about matters of the heart (nor of lawyers wielding the power of Zeus).

Of course I insisted that Fitzhugh and Elizabeth shouldn't risk the journey.

Of course Fitzhugh and Elizabeth insisted that they *must*.

Elizabeth said "you're as good as dead, Doctor, if you venture out there alone, and Willie and I won't know what became of you."

Fitzhugh agreed that my going alone was out of the question (and in truth I knew it was). We went back and forth over it for some time until Elizabeth observed that if talk would transport us to Iona then we'd already be there. We all agreed with that, and (as it was now getting dark) we gathered up the vittles and carried the card table back down to the kitchen. Albert put on his coat and wished us good evening.

"Bolt the street door!" I called as he went out.

The lamps were lit. Fitzhugh and Elizabeth were sitting in the parlour. Elizabeth was knitting and Fitzhugh was reading to her from *The Faerie Queene* in a sonorous voice.

I lit the lamp in my study and unlocked the desk. *John Blackjohn* was squatting smugly inside, smelling of mutton as usual. Thinking I might while away a minute or two before bed I took up the magnifying glass and tried to tease out a few more lines. But the page was eaten away by the ink itself.

"Iron gall," I muttered.

I made out the words *Otter*, *Lily*, *chart*, *fortnight*, and *whale*, but nothing more. My head was aching from the strain. I leaned back and closed my eyes, listening to the steady toll of Fitzhugh's voice coming from the parlour. The familiar story seeped into my brain. Gloriana and her champion, the faithful red cross knight.

> *But full of fire and greedy hardiment,*
> *The youthfull knight could not for ought be staide,*

Yes, why *did* the boy need rescuing so much?

But forth unto the darksome hole he went,

What good is a knight if he doesn't know a dull allegory when he sees one?

A litle glooming light, much like a shade,
By which he saw the ugly monster plaine,

Better our heroes were barbers, or, or blacksmiths. Folk who get things done—

All suddenly about his body wound,
That hand or foot to stirre he strove in vaine:

Any fool can get himself stuck in a hole. But a fellow can't cut his own hair.

That from her body full of filthie sin
He raft her hatefull head without remorse;

Did Albert ever bolt the street door?
I was fast asleep.

When I woke the lamp was smoking badly. I jumped up and turned down the wick until it burned white again.

Outside my window Bread Street was silent and empty in a halo of gaslight. The clock on the mantle showed half-past-three. The parlour was dark. From downstairs came the steady drip-drip of a tap in the examination room.

Cold panic.

John Blackjohn was gone.

The book was gone! The desk was just as I'd left it: lamp on one side, magnifying glass on the other. But the space in between was empty.

The street door!

I pictured the unclean presence of a stranger in my home, bending over me to snatch the book. I shivered with disgust.

Then a happier thought: maybe Fitzhugh found me asleep and took the book for safekeeping. With my heart in my throat I picked up the lamp and went to his chamber.

I softly turned the knob.

Fitzhugh was snoring slightly, his shoulders rising and falling under the quilt. I tiptoed in and looked around.

No sign of *Blackjohn*.

Maybe he's stowed it under the bed, I thought. I got down on my hands and knees—

Nothing!

Just Fitzhugh's slippers. I felt sick.

I was about to shake Fitzhugh's shoulders and wake him (to what purpose I can't say) when a last, frail hope occurred to me: what if Fitzhugh had somehow thought to lock *John Blackjohn* in the fireproof safe? Had I given him the key? I couldn't remember, there'd been so much confusion. I backed out of the room and rushed to the top of the stairs.

Floorboards creaked in the corridor below.

I blew out the lamp. There was a scraping noise. I thought it came from the lumber room. I stepped out of my slippers and crept down the stairs. Ground floor. Street door wide open. At the end of the hall a light was moving inside the lumber room. I heard the whine of a man's nasally voice. A second voice answered, gruff and low.

"Why, here 'tis!" hissed the first. "Liff up that canvas there. That's the safe, hidden under that rubbish! Sneaky bastard!"

"It's locked," said the other. I heard the handle shake. "How we supposed to open it, then?"

"Wiff 'er toof, numbskull!" returned the first. (He had an accent that smacked of the East End of London and the bells of Saint Mary-le-Bow.[102])

"You've gone daft, have you?" snorted the other. "You mean to pick that lock with a *tooth*? Here, I've a bump key ought to do the trick."

---

[102] i.e., Cockney

"Naw, block'ead!" said the first, "Grim Reapah was very specific. We've got to put in the toof. It's some sor' of—some sor' of *chahm*."

Desperation gave me courage. I crept toward the lumber room, sidling along the wall where the floorboards wouldn't creak. The old hall clock barred my way. I took a long step to the other side of the corridor and went on edging down the wall. When I got close enough I leaned my head out and looked in.

There was *John Blackjohn*, safe and sound—

—only it was tucked under the elbow of the biggest man I ever laid eyes on, and I don't say it lightly. His forearm was like a ham covered in black hair. Shaggy black beard. His shapeless cap and mudstained boots bespoke the longshoreman's trade. The big man held up a lantern while the other man—a short, barrel-chested fellow in a threadbare coat and topper—crouched down and peered into the keyhole. He was holding something between his thumb and forefinger: a little round lump like a cherry-stone. He gingerly pressed it into the keyhole.

Nothing happened.

"Bloody 'ell, i' don't fit a' *tall*."

The short man dropped the lump on the floor with a snarl. The big man grinned but said nothing.

"Gimme y' bump key,[103] Murdo—"

They brooded over the lock. For a while there was rattling and quiet cursing. Then the handle dropped with a tidy little *click* and the safe door swung open.

"Them's the papers!"

"No, block'ead, them's deeds and bills! These '*ere*—these is the papers—"

The short man took off his hat and plunged headfirst into the safe, rustling about inside like a squirrel. When he came up again I could see Constantine's copy of *John Blackjohn* in his fists.

I stepped back from the door and took a deep breath, steeling myself. *I'll die heroically, at any rate*, I thought. I was just about to burst in on them (I had a vague notion of snatching *John Blackjohn* out from under the longshoreman's arm and bolting for the street door) when all at once I remembered something.

---

[103] A lock-breaker's tool.

I turned and raced back up the hall, careless of the noise. Skidding to my knees, I reached behind the big clock and pulled out the old bottle of turpentine—

I hesitated an instant, considering—

Then with a martyr's resolve I took the bottle firmly in hand and marched back down the hall. From inside the lumber room came the *clunk* of the safe door closing again.

The two men were waiting for me.

The big longshoreman loomed near the ceiling, holding up the lantern and scowling. He had a sort of shillelagh[104] in his huge hand. Its knobby black end made dull thuds as he thumped it restlessly against his leg. the Southerner, holding a long, thin dagger like an icepick, switched his blade from hand to hand with an evil grin

"And this'll be the *doke*-tah!" the Southerner sneered. Good mo'nin', doketah! *You* picked a bad time to wyke up. Now there's got to be some unpleasantness, as moughtn't have been uvverwise—"

"What we supposed to do with *him*?" the longshoreman interrupted.

"Not sure," the Southerner returned. "Not sure. So I reckon why don'cha fetch him a crack wi' that stick uv yours, 'ey? P'chance it knocks the doketah's luh-nid brines[105] out."

"And if it don't?"

"If it don't, why then we tykes woss leff uv 'im to Grim Reapah. Grim Reapah might want to ask a few questions. Or he might not."

The big man hesitated, shifting his weight from foot to foot. I put the turpentine bottle to my mouth. The rotted cork stuck out a half-inch from the spout. Their weasel eyes tracked me as I pulled it with my teeth.

"You going to offer us a drink, doctor?" the big man rumbled. He held up his lantern and studied me with amusement.

I put the bottle to my lips. Tilting back my head, I filled my mouth brimfull with the vile stuff.

"Ah!" said the Southerner, "Dram o' Scotch courage! Good on you, Doc—"

---

[104] Irish: club; also a cane or walking-stick.
[105] Learnèd brains

I lunged at the longshoreman.

He barked and drew back as I spouted the turpentine all over him. Blue flames belched out of the lantern. Fire started up his beard. He bellowed and dropped the lantern as his shirt burst into flames. Glass shattered on the floor; white fire rushed outward in all directions. The longshoreman ran about like a man possessed, beating at his beard and shirt and screaming *Put it out! Put it out!* while the Southern knave and I both scrambled to be out of his way. By chance my hand came up against the coal-shovel, and swinging it like a truncheon I brought it down on the Southerner's head, where it struck a smart clanging note against his skull. He staggered and dropped his knife. Just then the frenzied longshoreman hit his tall head against a water-pipe, and he dropped insensible on the burning floor. The Southerner found the door. He fled down the corridor like a hare, burst out into the street, and was gone.

And then—merciful heaven!—there was Fitzhugh in his nightcap and dressing-gown! Dear old Fitzhugh! He knew just what to do. With a mighty rush he swept all the treacherous old paint-cans off the safe and whipped down the canvas sheet. In a moment he'd smothered the flames on the unconscious longshoreman's clothes, and then he was beating out the fire on the floor. "Here, Willie!" called a woman's voice, and like some *dea ex machina* Elizabeth appeared and commenced flailing the fire with the braided rug from the cloakroom.

In a minute it was out.

"I feel like such an ass, Fitzhugh!"

Fitzhugh, Elizabeth and I were sitting at the kitchen table. Albert had gone back down to inspect the damage. I heard his footsteps trudging slowly up the stairs as I sat vacantly stirring a cup of tea round and round with a trembling hand.

"That'll do. Now that'll do, dear," Elizabeth put in mildly. "I fancy it's cooled by now."

I tried the tea.

I made a wry face and reached for the strainer. Fitzhugh grinned and slid me the tray. The checkered kitchen curtains bellied with the breeze as (incredibly) another clear morning flooded in. The cheerful sunlight showed the residue of oily smoke now covering the ceiling. The whole house reeked of it. Every window in the place was thrown wide open. Curious voices echoed in the street below.

Albert opened the kitchen door. He sat down heavily in the empty chair beside me. I kept my eyes on my cup.

"I'm—I'm right sorry, Stewart."

"It's alright. It's nothing."

"I forgot all about the street door."

"And I fell asleep in my chair," I returned dismally, "like a doddering old fool."

Elizabeth laid her hand gently on my mine. "Well *I* thought you were brave and clever," she said, "besting those two big rogues with nothing but a bottle of turpentine!"

"It's *my* fault," Fitzhugh interjected. "Twenty-five years in service and I didn't bother to check the door."

"Thank God they put your book in the safe!" Albert exclaimed. "It's a miracle it wasn't burnt to cinders. What did you do with the big rascal—the longshoreman?"

"Oh, we drenched his coat in gin and dumped him in the little back-lane off Spittal street. I'd rather not speak to the police just now, Albert, if you'll believe it. Though to tell you the truth I'm worried for that fellow. He might have something worse than prison to fear once 'Grim Reaper' finds out about this."

"Grim Reaper?" Albert laughed. "That'll be Radan, then?"

"I imagine so."

"He *does* look like a death's-head," Fitzhugh commented.

"Speaking of unusual heads," said Albert, "let's have a look at that green lass in your book, Stewart. I wonder if those footpads broke it open."

I waved dejectedly at *John Blackjohn*, which was lying on the table wrapped in my mackintosh. Elizabeth opened it carefully. She turned to the first copper seal. The lady's wreathed face stared up at us as before—open mouth; vacant green eyes.

"Wait!" I exclaimed.

I jumped up from my chair.

"That Londoner said something about a tooth! I'd forgotten about it in all this commotion." I charged down the smoky staircase, Albert and Fitzhugh hot on my heels.

The lumber room was dark and foul with the smell of burnt wood and lamp oil. I crunched gingerly across the broken glass. Stooping down beside the safe I squinted at the charred floor.

A little round object gleamed dully in the gloom.

We clustered breathlessly around the kitchen table. In one hand Albert held the magnifying glass; in the other, a yellowish lump that glinted in the light. Now we could plainly see it was a tooth overlaid with copper. The faint lines etched into the crown would become the green lady's lips when it was fitted into the seal.

"Ah!" said Elizabeth. "So she isn't just staring openmouthed."

"A seal upon her lips," said Fitzhugh. "Now *there's* an old saw for you."

Albert studied the inner face of the tooth, ignoring the crown altogether.

"*Well?*" I demanded impatiently, "Is that our Norseman, or a walrus with a copper crown on its tusk?"

Albert laughed.

"Yes—" he said slowly, revolving the tooth between his fingertips. "Yes, it's real, Stewart—" He looked up at us over the magnifying glass. "But I can't tell if it's your Norseman or not."

"Jove's trousers! Why not?"

Albert grinned.

"That lead cast you made? It's an upper premolar, Stewart—"

"Yes? Yes?"

"And THIS tooth," (Albert handed it back to me) "is most certainly a *lower* one."

I gnawed my fingers. "Well, top or bottom—" I said grimly—"in it goes."

My heart was racing. I confess I felt a little out of my wits, with the recent danger and with the excitement of it all. I turned *John Blackjohn* over on the table. The tooth jingled faintly as I fit it into the copper plate on the back cover. It sat loose in the lady's mouth.

Nothing happened.

"Try the other seal!" cried Fitzhugh.

I took a deep breath. Then opening the book, I turned to the copper plate between the pages.

CHAPTER 21

From the letters of Doctor Stewart Henry Scott—

In fugam[106] – June 14, 1838

Albert,

I don't dare say where we're stopping; only that after we fled Edinburgh we took a roundabout way from Queensferry, making for Dumbarton and the Clyde. You'll think I'm over-anxious: I'm afraid the very post is watched. (Did you find this letter intact? Was there any cutting around the seal?)

Accommodations have been primitive, to say the least. I'm fretful about Elizabeth. This is no errand for a lady. It was kind of you to offer to escort her back to Berwick, but you saw how determined she was to come. A most energetic woman, Elizabeth. Excess of yellow bile, probably, but I very much admire her. She packed up Fitzhugh's things and we fled by the back-ways, jostling down country lanes, and I was cursing the roads and the coach-springs and the state of things generally, but Elizabeth only observed that she could find a comfortable chair at home but she was 'thoroughly sick of knitting.'

Remarkable woman!

I am terribly sorry we rushed off like that without so much as a *goodbye* and the house in such a state—lumber room half burnt and the neighbors already beginning to ask about the smell. I thought it best we decamp before the good people of Edinburgh adjudge that our business is more interesting than *their* business, and raise a commotion. While you were looking in on Constantine (bless you!) Fitzhugh and I were down at the livery getting a

---

[106] Latin: *in flight*

carriage for our escape. The livery man wanted to know where we were going and when we intended to return, and as I hadn't the faintest idea on either point—and as the man was making us uneasy with all sorts of questions—I finally wondered aloud if we might not simply *buy* a coach and pair outright. Well, the livery man liked the sound of *that*, particularly as he was slowly beginning to grasp what a desperate hurry we were in. We went back and forth about it: I insisting upon a fair price and he (sensing his advantage) protesting he hadn't a cart nor a horse to spare. At last we settled on an old retired post-coach and two mares so aged they might have carried the mails for George the Second. The livery man demanded nearly twice what they were worth. Fitzhugh was beside himself with outrage. (I truly thought he was going to strike the man.) But I took Fitzhugh aside and whispered that time was more precious than gold if we were going to slip Edinburgh without the police or the Duke of Buckley catching us.

So round about three o'clock we quit the city at last. Fitzhugh was driving and I was sitting up on the box beside him, keeping a nervous lookout. We passed Stockbridge and got onto the Queensferry road. There we were, not three miles from the Duke of Buckley's estate at Granton, and the old mares plodding along at a snail's pace—a torment to me in my agitated state of mind. I expected every moment to see constables or armed ruffians bearing down on us. But the afternoon wore on and the spires of Edinburgh grudgingly dropped out of sight until only the castle could be seen through the trees now and again, like a black eye winking at us through the eternal coal smoke.

"He'll know how far we've come, Fitzhugh," I said with a sigh, turning about and facing forward again at last. My neck ached from so much looking over our shoulders.

"You mean Radan?" Fitzhugh asked.

"Yes, Radan."

"Aye," quoth Fitzhugh, "but he don't know where we're going. *We* don't know where we're going."

I laughed grimly. "He'll be faster than us," I said, "if he's riding backwards on a mule. If Radan doesn't find us on the Dalkeith road, then he'll look for us on the Straiton. If there's no word of us on the Straiton, well, he'll probably guess we're making for Queensferry."

Fitzhugh didn't answer, he simply reached down to the compartment under our seat and undid the latch.

I leaned over.

I caught sight of Fitzhugh's double-barrel fowling piece[107] peeking out.

At dusk we stopped at an inn, and no sooner did we walk through the door than to our horror Fitzhugh and I overheard a farrier tell a driver there was a Southern fellow about just then making inquiries.

"Lunker, you say?" asked the driver.

"Aye," returned the farrier. "Tall, yellow sort o' man says he's looking for a runaway servant and a doctor named Scott." The farrier waved the mug in his massive hand. "I says—I says, *I'm a Scotch doctor*, says I, *I'm a Scotch doctor. And here's your medicine, love. Take a pint o' this home to London with ye'. Put the bloom back in your cheek!*"

And they roared with laughter.

"Where's your patient now?" the driver panted, wiping his eyes.

"Coachyard. That's his gig."

The farrier put down his glass and wiped his mouth with his sleeve. The driver sighed and got off his stool. A little fellow in a beer-stained apron was coming up to us with a *Good evening* on his lips—

But Fitzhugh and I were already out the door and making for the old coach at a run. "Radan's here!" I said breathlessly, shoving in next to Elizabeth and drawing the tattered curtains. Fitzhugh lashed the reins like a charioteer and heroically succeeded in bringing the mares to a leisurely trot. We turned off into the first country lane and went bumping and swaying along until the inn was covered up by the trees.

So we passed Queensferry by and stopped at the village of _____ instead, just after dark. At the inn we gave them to know I was a Mr. Stewart, cousin of Mr. and Mrs. McRoy (Fitzhugh assumed the name of Elizabeth's late husband), and we were making for Glasgow in a leisurely way.

We've been obliged to lie up an entire week here in spite of their wretched rooms, in hopes of shaking off Radan. Fitzhugh manages well

---

[107] Shotgun

184

enough: he begged a rod and reel of the innkeeper and he goes splashing off through the ponds and streams hereabout as merry as a lark. Elizabeth joins him on some of these excursions, but more often she stays behind and helps me transcribe *John Blackjohn*.

There's quite a lot to be done in that regard now that we've got the middle seal open. I must say: these new pages are marvelously well-preserved, Albert; at least fifty of them before you come to that new copper plate we found. It still looks as if there are three plates in all—one on the back cover and two in the middle—dividing the book into three parts. My guess is the venerable bookbinder meant this as a sort of secretary, with a section for everyday stuff open at the front and two sections for confidential matters locked up behind.

But why it would open with a tooth instead of with a key? I tell you, it was simply miraculous, Albert! No sooner did I put the tooth in the lady's mouth than the pins just fell out like they were never attached. And they haven't got any marks on them; I can't tell how they were fixed in the plate to begin with. Utterly dumbfounding!

This last plate, Albert—the one without any device—it's pinned on tight and I haven't the faintest idea how we'll get it off (nor how we'll open the seal on the back cover either), but Elizabeth and I are determined to carry on transcribing just the same.

We're getting along faster now thanks to the improved condition of the parchment (I think pressing the pages between the plates kept out some of the damp); and thanks to Elizabeth. She is invaluable. Elizabeth writes in a clear, even hand while I read aloud from the page, and then (dear woman!) she copies out a duplicate!

Please find our latest work herein. And, Albert, you *will* keep it safe, won't you? We fugitives will hold onto the other copy ourselves for now. There's no telling what may happen.

Yours, etc.

—SHS

CHAPTER 22

Doctor Scott's transcription—

Albert: the first two pages—the ones that fell apart when we opened the seal—they are beyond repair. There was a scrap of parchment stuck between the second and third pages with a rough sketch of what looked like a snake wound about a tree, though I can't be sure. The only word I could make out was (I think) Fara—*possibly Fair Isle, the tiny haven lying midway between Scotland and the Orkneys. From what follows it would seem the* Otter *rounded the northern tip of Scotland, then made her way south again through the Outer Isles. James McKenna tells it thus:*

The gale swung around to the north-northwest, and the *Otter* went booming along with it at a great pace. Diana and I were standing on the foredeck. Boatswain Finn was taking our speed as best he could with a knotted rope that danced and curled back on itself in the waves.

"Eight knots!"[108] Finn called triumphantly.

The *Otter* drove her prow into the swell, showering us with spray.

"Seven knots dead-down!"[109]

"Seven?" I shouted over the wind. "Why would she go slower with the wind behind her?"

"Seven knots, Cap'n Plowshare!" Finn growled at me. "Boats be slower dead-down. Ask the sea witch if ye would know the reason why." He reeled off across the rolling deck. "Where's Lily?" I shouted to Diana. I hadn't seen Lily in two days.

---

[108] Roughly 14 kilometers (9 miles) per hour—an impressive rate for sustained travel in the late 16th century.
[109] Dead downwind

Diana shook out her windblown hair.

"She's in Captain Blackjohn's quarters with Friar Kollam. She wants us to come join them now."

"You talked to her?"

"No."

I was getting used to Diana's unaccountable answers. She was always right, at any rate. Diana was unaccountable in other ways, too. I could have sworn she never ate—not since the day we set foot in the *Otter*. I never saw her sleep, either. One rare night when it was clear enough to see stars I came stumbling up to take my watch, and to my great surprise there was Diana by the stern, staring up into the black sky. The wind was in her face and she was singing softly to herself in her strange tongue. Whether she noticed me or not I couldn't tell; she neither looked nor stirred. Through all the slow hours of the night Diana stood there like a stone, and when at last the sky showed gray and my watch was ended I could still hear the wild notes of her song carried faintly back on the wind.

Ronne came weaving up to us. The *Otter* was so heeled over in her jibe that Ronne was obliged to navigate the deck hand-over-hand like an ape. He shoved off the mainmast—

Made a lunge to starboard—

Swung around the fo's'l braces—

And hooked his arm around the mainstay, giving Diana a jaunty bow.

"Cap'n would see you in his quarters, *Mefrou*," Ronne said. "Also the boy."

Blackjohn's saloon[110] had an air of faded opulence. It was hung with the spoils of many ships, but the even-handed sea had been at work there and had anointed the captain's quarters with the same briny unction that bathed every inch of the Otter, from the fore-topmast to my own poor berth in the 'tween-deck. Everything on a ship must be fastened down. Blackjohn's quarters were no exception. His Turkish divan was richly embroidered with scenes from the distant East: elephants; minarets; Barbary corsairs riding on waves of faded

---

[110] French: *salon*; merely 'room.' (The American sense of *tavern* is an odd corruption. —*Ed.*)

green. But a pair of dirty ropes held these wonders tight against the bulkhead and the threadbare pillows were lashed down with black ribbon. Overhead, Blackjohn's silver lamp swung silently on a delicate chain. It moved in curious half-circles—now this way; now that—and it made me queasy to think how the lamp was really hanging motionless while the Otter turned every which way around it. I tried not to look at it, though it was hard to resist. The wick burned inside a marvelous shade of colored glass, casting golden droplets across the beams.

Under the lamp a chart was spread out on a mahogany table. Blackjohn and Friar Kol brooded over it like witches over a cauldron.

And there was Lily.

Lily stood gazing out from the wide stern windows where the Otter's wake streamed backward across the sea. She smiled and nodded to Diana. Blackjohn put his finger on the chart.

"We were making for Dunvegan on Skye," Blackjohn was saying, "We couldn't have been more than three days out."

"And that's all you remember?" Kol asked.

Blackjohn nodded. "Aye, it was strange," he said, "Like waking from a dream. I wrung my brains those first few days after I left Doonbridge. Slippery memory like water. I hadn't anyone to write it down. I'm not a lettered man—"

Ronne stepped out and closed the door behind him. Kol looked up from the chart.

"Diana! James!" Kol said brightly. "Welcome!"

"Is that a map?" I asked excitedly.

"Aye!" Blackjohn grumbled, "and a right awful one, but it's all we've got. We took it—that is—it was *given* me by a merchantman of Antwerp, (the devil take his soul!)" Blackjohn scowled and tugged the ends of his beard. "A miserable chart it is. The Belgae don't take much interest in these waters."

Friar Kol bent over the map with a troubled face. "My friends," he said, "I think we are pursued. There's something uncanny outside. This storm, I mean. Diana has been lending us her, ah, her special gift to sing these clouds away, but for three days now they're closing in behind us like a snare."

"And in front of us," Blackjohn put in.

"Aye, and in front of us, too, which is unnatural. The blackest part of the storm looks like it's coming up at us from the south. *Against* the wind."

"Witchcraft," Blackjohn grunted.

Diana reddened a little. "I can't sing the clouds away any more," she said. "I was getting on well enough at first, but now—"

Diana stopped. Her face wore a perplexed expression.

"But now *what*?"

Kol turned to her sharply.

"I've forgotten how."

Diana looked as if she were about to cry. Lily darted to her side with a silvery ripple. She took Diana by the shoulders and stared intently into her eyes.

"Another power is at work here," Lily said.

Kol shook his head gravely. "I'm worried about these young people," he sighed. "The Black Stag hates them. He's got the crook of Esus and I'm afraid—"

Kol's voice fell.

"I'm afraid this time he knows how to use it."

I wondered why Kol looked so strange and sad.

Blackjohn thumped the table with his fist. "The *Otter* can outrun any ship on the North Sea!" he said defiantly. Lily frowned and shook her head. "The Black Stag," she observed, "could catch you without raising a sail."

Kol turned to Diana and me. "I called you here," he said, "because there's something I think you ought to hear. It might help if we're ever separated by sea or by land or by the gray tide of death." Kol put his hand on my shoulder. "I've never told you this, James, but—"

He hesitated.

"Never told me *what*?" I demanded.

Kol sighed again. He was staring down at the floor, fumbling with his rosary. When Kol spoke his voice was almost a whisper.

"The church never sent me to the Borders," Kol said. "I ran there."

I shook my head, not comprehending.

Kol raised his eyes. "The church!" he said in a louder voice. "Our mother church! The Holy Roman Catholic and Apostol—"

190

"Aye. Aye," Blackjohn interrupted. "We know her by her sails. Get *on* with it, brother!"

Kol wrung his hands.

"The church never sent me to Buckley," he said. "I've been hiding there."

"*Hiding?*"

I gawked at him in disbelief.

"Yes! Hiding!" Kol sank down on a stool, elbows on the table, chin in his hands. It was unsettling, seeing him like this. "Look—" Kol pointed at the chart. "Here's Alba, James." He put his finger on the bigger of two greenish blotches. I peered over his shoulder.

"—Scots in the north, English in the south. And here's Éireann, the green isle—" (Kol pointed to the smaller blotch) "—separated from Alba by a narrow sea. That's where I was born, in Munster. My father was descended from the Northman[111] knights who took Munster when William the Bastard—"[112]

"You're a *knight*?" I gasped, all in wonder.

Kol laughed. (It was a relief to hear him laugh.) "No, no!" he said. "Nothing like that! My people are wool-merchants. My sires were granted a freehold here," he touched the parchment, "in the Laígde. My father stood at arms for the Earl of Ormond once upon a time, but he was no knight. He married a farmer's daughter of Corca and they kept sheep together. Maewyn and I—"

Kol's smile faded. Turning his back to us he bent over the table as if he were studying something.

"Maewyn and I weren't twins," Kol said presently, a catch in his voice, "but Maewyn looked so very like me—and we were born so close together—inside of the same year—that everybody thought we were. Maewyn was—he was a good boy. Tenderhearted. Especially toward animals. A little strange, maybe, but I suppose we both were."

Kol stood up, clicking his rosary.

---

[111] Norman

[112] Called "The Conqueror" in England, William duke of Normandy was known to many in his native country by a somewhat different title.

"My father always meant me for the Earl of Ormond and Maewyn for the Church," he went on, "but Maewyn didn't take to—" Kol looked thoughtful. "He didn't take to *human* society. I remember how he used to sleep for nights on end out in the fields, or amongst the sheep like young King David. And in winter when there wasn't much work on the farm, then Maewyn used to disappear for days altogether. How he didn't freeze to death I'll never know. Nobody could tame him. We all thought he was a bit mad. He used to come back with—"

Kol stared off dreamily.

"—used to come back with mistletoe in his hair—"

"Ah!" said Diana. Lily smiled.

"After I took my vows," Kol resumed; "after I was ordained, that is, and I became a monk, then the church at Corca sent me to the famous abbey on Iona, to work in the scriptorium there. I didn't know Maewayn had already gone to Alba himself on, er, on a mission of his own, so to speak."

"*What* mission?" I asked.

"We-ell—" (Kol sounded evasive) "I don't entirely know. What I *do* know is Maewyn wandered up and down the wilds, from Am Parav all the way to the Shalway and back again, as restless as the breeze. He learned the languages of animals and birds, and he came to know the Powers that still hold sway in untamed places."

Lily nodded. "I used to see him at Bealltainn,"[113] she said.

Kol coughed and his voice got thick again.

"Yes, I always loved it when Maewyn would turn up. It got lonely at the hermitage sometimes. Suddenly, without warning, there was Maewyn—always just when I needed him most. He was a bit odd. Didn't talk much. About himself least of all. But just having him there was a comfort to me. And he used to bring the most wonderful gifts. Rare stones. Healing plants. He brought that green fairy glass, James—"

Kol fell silent, smiling to himself.

"But you said you were hiding," I put in. "Who were you hiding from?"

Kol frowned and plucked at his rosary. "When we came aboard the *Otter*," Kol said, "—when Captain Blackjohn rescued us—I think I told you

---

113 Or Beltane; pre-Christian holiday roughly corresponding with May Day.

192

how, many years ago in Iona, I heard the confession of a bold young Irishman—yes?"

Blackjohn grinned. Kol steadied himself against the table as the *Otter* bucked a wave.

"I'd been at the abbey for a little more than three years," said Kol, "when young Eoin mac Diarmid found his way to us from the hidden village of Doonbridge. Captain Blackjohn is the only man alive who ever left that secret haven. We would take refuge there if we could. Doonbridge is, I think, entirely beyond the reach of the earl Francis Stewart—"

Kol looked at Blackjohn inquiringly.

"—known to you and me as the Black Stag."

Blackjohn shook his head. "That chart won't do, brother," he sighed, sinking down on the divan and taking off his hat. "That chart nor any other."

"Couldn't we—couldn't we maybe find a *better* one?" I ventured.

Blackjohn stared out the windows. "Nay," he said quietly. "I can't get back to Doonbridge. There's a curse on me."

"Oh, come, Eoin!" Kol rejoined, "You know that's not—"

"Remember that yellow afternoon?" Blackjohn interrupted. "*You* remember, don't you brother Kollam? In the abbey, when the sun lit up all those church windows like fire? Oh! that was pretty, wasn't it? I never saw the like." Blackjohn's face broke into a boyish grin.

"Yes," Kol nodded, "I remember."

"And there was that window with the ship on it, hey? How there was a man with a curse aboard, so God raised an enchanted storm and the sailors were all like to die unless they tossed the cursed lubber out." Blackjohn chuckled mirthlessly. "So over the gunnels he went, and I'd have done the same. I sat there looking up at him in the window—him in his gray dress; arms reaching out to his mates in the boat and they all looking down on him while he sinks into a wave like a featherbed. Aye, and that did the trick, didn't it? The boat was saved, whilst the cursed lubber was swallowed up by a whale and carried down, down into that freezing black emptiness—"

Blackjohn stared at the floor as if he could see through it.

"It's waiting there," he murmured. "It's waiting there for me. Just underneath this little tangle of boards and strings." (He kicked at the floor.) "I think on that from time to time."

"You misunderstand the story, my friend," Kol put in mildly. "It's a hopeful story. The prophet Jonas found redemption at the last."

"Of a sort," Kol added.

Blackjohn's shoulders sagged. He looked older and very tired.

"I think on all the men I've sent to the bottom—"

Blackjohn ran his fingers through his hair.

"And oh! but they were sorry to go, every one of them! At night I can hear their voices calling to me. They call to me out of the dark water—"

Blackjohn looked up again, and his face wore a forced smile.

"Well, it's a short life but a merry one!" he said. "I'll be joining them soon enough, and fair's fair, I reckon."

Friar Kol said nothing, but stooping underneath the table he brought up a heavy object in a leather bag. Setting it on top of the map, Kol opened up the bag and took out his precious bible, spared from the waves by Blackjohn's miraculous rescue.

Blackjohn's eyes went round. For a moment he sat staring at the bible. Then he exploded with laughter.

"HA HA HA!" Blackjohn roared. "Good on you, brother! Good on you! I'll say a *Pater Noster* for your soul tonight!"

Kol blushed furiously. "I am a sinful man," he said ruefully. "I've never pretended otherwise."

"What?" I cried. "Why?" I was wild with curiosity.

"That bible," Blackjohn coughed, "is worth more than this *boat*." He chuckled and wiped his eyes. "It belongs to the Archbishop of Armagh."

"No—" Kol returned testily—"it belongs to the Primate of all *Éireann*." (Kol put his finger on the title page.) "*Ad Archiepiscopus Arcamachenis Primas omnis Hiberniae*—I wrote that with my own pen. But on the day we fled Iona there *was* no 'Primate of all Éireann.' The bishop's seat was vacant. There was trouble with the English. Three whole years I'd spent adorning this book, and I loved it—"

Kol's voice broke.

"I loved it like—"

Blackjohn glanced up at Kol and immediately he stopped laughing. Kol wiped his sleeve across his eyes. He stood looking down at his bible, swaying slightly with the rolling of the ship.

"I never got to have a child," Kol said softly. "Nor a wife either. I gave my life to God, and I don't regret it. This book is all I have. I couldn't let it go to the English. They'd sacked the holy places of Armagh before—"

"How did you ever get it out of the abbey?" I interrupted.

Kol cleared his throat noisily.

"Well it wasn't bound," he said. "I hadn't finished illuminating it yet— not entirely. I'd only gotten as far as the seven-eyed lamb in the fifth chapter of Apocalypsis. It was meant, as I said, for the cathedral of Saint Patricius in Armagh, and my abbot decreed that no hand but mine should adorn it. My skill with the brush and pen was unrivaled, you see. Every device in the book is my own."

"Save one." Kol gave a short laugh and glanced sideways at Blackjohn. Blackjohn said nothing.

"On the morning I was to take ship for Glaschu,"[114] Kol went on, "to begin my new ministry in Alba, then the devil entered into my heart. I crept inside the scriptorium before dawn while the brothers were all singing lauds in the chapel. Inside—"

Kol shuffled gingerly over to the stern windows.

"Inside the scriptorium it was so dark I had to grope my way among the tables until I found the easel where brother Felix and I were working on the Armagh bible (for so it was called), brother Felix writing and I illuminating, one page at a time. We never had more than a few pages given to us. Each finished leaf was kept under lock and key. They belonged to our Abbot, until such time as the whole bible could be sent to Armagh with an armed guard."

Kol clasped his hands behind him and gazed out across the choppy sea. The sharp peaks huddled together under a strange yellow light. They reminded me of uncle Andrew's sheep, bunching nervously between the hurdles before a coming storm.

---

[114] Glasgow

Kol cleared his throat again. "So I fumbled about on our easel until I found a quill and the slender iron pick I'd been using to scrape the parchment. I took them and went to work on the strongbox—that's where the pages were kept. I've nimble hands, you see. I'd some experience with locks and things. The strongbox was set into the stones on the south wall and the lock was formidable. I worked at it, sweating with fright, while outside the birds started to twitter and the ghost of morning began to show between the high window bars. But I couldn't move the bolt. The old iron was heavy, and it fit tight. I heard the brothers sing their last *Amen*. Cold terror washed over me. I started muttering

Our Father who art in heaven,

—but immediately I stopped myself. For how could I pray to God in the very act of robbing God's holy church?"

Friar Kol turned to face us. The weird light cast a black outline of him against the window.

"But strange enough," Kol said, "no sooner had *Our Father* crossed my lips when suddenly—*Snap!*—the strongbox gave way. Not the lock; no, it was the iron clasp the lock was fixed on. It was all rusted through, you see? The weight of my shoulder on it was enough. The clasp broke and I raised the heavy lid. I dug inside and gathered up all the pages in my arms. Then I snatched up the last two from the easel and I stripped off my cassock. I was naked and shivering. My heart was in my mouth, but there was no turning back. I could hear the scrape and shuffle of the brothers' feet, now in the passage below, now coming up the stairs."

Kol stopped. Outside the wind was changing. I could hear a rising howl in the gale.

"So I bent my armload of parchment together," Kol resumed. "The pages were so stiff they cut me, but I wrapped them all lengthwise around my chest and I held them up with my elbows—" (He was demonstrating this in front of the window) "—while I got my cincture-rope about me."

Blackjohn had been listening to Friar Kol with an indulgent look, but now he laughed in spite of himself.

"So *that's* why you were sitting up so stiff!"

"You *saw* him?" I asked.

"Aye," Blackjohn grinned smugly, "we're old shipmates, brother Kol and me—Ah!" he laughed again, "and that's why you were in such a dreadful hurry!"

Kol nodded.

"Yes, I had the worth of Haick abbey tied around my stomach. I fled down the back stairs just as brother Felix was opening the scriptorium door. The quay was nearly half a mile away. I had to keep my hands pressed against my sides so the pages wouldn't fall out of my robe, and in that condition I stumbled all the way down to the docks. Eoin—Captain Blackjohn, that is— was waiting there, rigging out a little one-masted tub to take us to Glaschu, along with a Scottish tillerman and the tillerman's boy."

"And another monk," Blackjohn put it. "We were waiting on another monk too."

"That's right!" Kol rejoined. "A brother Marius bound for Cymru.[115] He was a good man and kind to me, but I was out of my wits with fear. *Cast off! I shouted to the tillerman. *Cast off! We can't wait!* but, *Nay*, says the tillerman, *We've another priest yet to come aboard.*

"*Never mind about that!* I cried, all in a frenzy. *You must cast off at once! Good Christian, I will say five thousand prayers for your soul if you'll weigh anchor this moment. You won't spend a fortnight in Purgatory. By the holy rood[116] I swear it!* I was on my knees in the scuppers with tears running down my face. The tillerman looked awfully perplexed, and just then the abbey bell broke out with a terrible clamor. The hunt was up! The monks had found the Armagh bible missing and they were raising the alarm.

"The tillerman just stood there gawping; first at me, then at the belfry, then at me again. I thought he was going to stand there until they carried me away in chains, so I left off begging and I sank down cross-legged on the boards, hugging my bible underneath my robe.

"*I'll be hanged*, I thought. *They won't do it here. This boat will take me to Dunvegan on Skye, and there I'll be tried and hanged—*"

"Aye, he was right miserable!" Blackjohn interrupted. "I felt sorry for him, though I didn't know what the trouble was. And I wasn't keen on that—

---

[115] Wales
[116] Cross

197

Marius, d'you say?—I wasn't keen on him coming aboard anyhow. He was big as a walrus, he was. The monks' master of—of cheeses or somesuch—"

"He *was* their master of cheeses—"

"Aye, he looked it!" Blackjohn growled. "That leaky old coracle was riding low enough as it was. To tell you the truth, brother, I was thinking on that sailor from the church window. *If we should happen on rough seas*, says I to myself, *I'll be sore tempted to pitch that fat monk overboard*—me but lately confessed and free from sin, to have a churchman's life on my conscience. So I stands up—"

(Blackjohn got off the divan.)

"—and I takes the tillerman by his two shoulders, and I shakes him 'til his teeth rattle. *See here!* says I, *I'm a lost man and a cutthroat! John Blackjohn is me name. I sail with Rudd Gallowglass and the demon crew of the Swift!*

"Well at that," Blackjohn laughed, "the tillerman's eyes get even rounder. His knees is all knocking together. *"Even now—* says I, *Even now the* Swift *is sailing south from Tiree, seeking her prize. In half-an-hour Rudd will be upon us. He'll sack this abbey from crypt to belfry. A leaky little washtub with a rich priest like Marius in it would please Gallowglass mightily. Now—* says I—*Rudd Gallowglass is a particular friend of mine—*"

Blackjohn winked at us.

"—*With just me and this poor Irish monk aboard he'll let you pass unharmed. But I wouldn't sail with Marius if you paid me his weight in gold, and may God have mercy on you!* And I sits down hard and folds me arms thus."

Blackjohn plopped back down on the divan.

"Did it work?" I asked breathlessly.

"Aye—*ha ha!* Gave him a mighty fright. He and his boy had the anchor up out of the mud quicker than brother Kol and me could cast off the lines, and we hoisted sail."

Kol stifled a guilty chuckle. "By that time," Kol said, "there were already men running down to the quay, shouting at us and waving their arms. But good luck or God's mysterious purpose was on our side. The tide had just turned and it was running out fast while a stiff westerly sprang up and filled our sail. The quay fell away softly behind us. Our little boat slipped out onto the glassy bay, all purple in the dawn with the smoky ripples playing across the surface. A man ran out onto the dock and waved at us.

"*Drop sail!* he called. *Come back!*

"*Pirates!* the tillerman shouted. His boy shivered and trimmed the sail without so much as glancing behind. We picked up speed and took the first swell.

"*Pirates!* the tillerman shouted again, but I don't know if they heard him. The abbey bell carried out across the water. Then it too faded, and all was quiet but the wind in our shrouds and the chop against our hull."

Kol fell silent. His eyes were on the floor, lost in thought.

Blackjohn cleared his throat.

"You told me you were bound for Glaschu, brother. You never told me you were in trouble."

"No," Kol said reflectively, "No, I think I must have spent all that day just praying—now for joy, now for pardon."

Blackjohn laughed. "I never saw such a wonder as all that paper coming out of your dress! *That's worse than a hair-shirt*, says I. I fancied it was some sort of—I don't know—some sort of priestly intrigue or other. A private dispatch for an archbishop."

"I *did* mean for it to reach Armagh," Kol insisted. "At first, anyway. My plan was to keep the book safe-hidden in the Borders and work at finishing the illumination until such time as the See of Armagh was peaceful again. Then I'd surrender it secretly, I imagined—at Melrose or somesuch famous church as I'd heard of. I was young; hardly more than a boy. I soothed my conscience with empty promises. My abbot meant me for another scriptorium. Dumfries, or maybe Carlisle—strange I can't remember now!—but I was a lost sheep with no place in the Lord's flock. From Glaschu I made straight for the wildest corner of the Borders, to begin life anew as a holy hermit and repent of my crime against the church. I finished the bible and bound it, and not a day went by but I looked at it—its pages all gilt and gleaming in every color of God's rainbow—such a precious thing in my rude little hut!—and I thought how my coveting it had divorced me from my Order and driven me away from the Church."

Kol looked up sadly. His eyes wandered to Diana and me. Then he smiled.

"But there were other matters to attend to," he said. "The stray lambs of Buckley needed a shepherd."

"Did you really say five thousand prayers for the tillerman's soul?" I asked.

"And more!" Kol nodded vigorously. "God has taught me a lesson today. I promised Him this bible would someday lie on Saint Patrick's pulpit. And here it lies!—on a briny table in a pirate's den. Begging your pardon, Captain."

"That's quite alright!" Blackjohn returned cheerfully. "Why, it might do more good here! We don't get a lot of bibles on the *Otter*.

"Not from the *Roman* church anyway," he added mischievously. Kol ignored this. Outside the light was fading. A blast of wind struck the stern and rattled all the panes in the latticed windows.

"Listen! The wind is rising!" said Diana.

"We're running out of time!" Kol exclaimed. He laid his hand on Blackjohn's shoulder. "My friend," he said, "It's time you explain *your* illumination in the Armagh bible."

Blackjohn's thick eyebrows shot up in surprise.

"Begg'r pardon?"

"On the way to Glaschu," Kol said insistently. "Remember? You scribbled something in the margin. Jonas chapter three verse seventeen."

Blackjohn smiled wryly. "You'll forgive me, Friar," he said. "I'm not a learned man."

"But you wrote something! And in good Latin, too. Where did it come from?"

Blackjohn laughed incredulously.

"I remember naught of the sort."

"Strange!" said Kol. He parted the heavy book. "Let's see what young Eoin mac Diarmid wrote. The third scribe, as it were." Kol turned to a page, well-thumbed and grayer than the others. He pointed to the bottommost line. "It's the story of the prophet Jonas," Kol said. "This verse tells how God prepared a great fish to swallow Jonas up and carry him into the depths of the sea. Brother Felix wrote the words—but this?"

Kol put his finger on the margin. We all clustered around the table. Even Lily, watery and serene as ever, moved a bit closer and peered over our bent heads.

At the border of the page swam a magnificent gray whale. Its monstrous jaws were gaping wide to swallow up a struggling Jonas. Curling green waves topped with white foam danced all around. It was some of Kol's finest work—but it was altogether ruined. Someone had scrawled over the top of it with a shivery, childish hand. The words were Latin.

"*Intrate per angustam portam*," Kol read. "It means 'enter by the narrow gate.' You wrote that, Eoin."

Blackjohn cocked his big head and squinted at the page. In the swinging lamplight the whale pulsed on the page as if it were swimming.

"Well I quite spoiled your fine whale if I did," Blackjohn said at length. "But no. I've no recollection of that. No man ever taught me to write so much as me own name. And yet—"

Blackjohn wrinkled his nose.

"It gives me an odd feeling, looking at it."

"There's more," Kol returned. "It's nearly rubbed out now. You drew something here." Kol put his finger on a smudge next to the whale's mouth. We all bent closer.

"I can't tell what it is," I said.

"Nor can I," said Diana.

"It's a hand," Lily observed from somewhere over our heads. "It's a hand with a pointing finger."

"That's right!" Kol rejoined. "There was a finger pointing straight into the whale's mouth."

"And you say *I* drew it?" Blackjohn asked dubiously.

"I say I couldn't *stop* you drawing it," Kol retorted. "I was horrified. We'd just gone down into that little rat-hole below deck, and I'd just got the pages out of my cassock. I was brooding over them, as it were, a bit out of my head, as you might expect. The first chapter of Jonas was lying uncovered among the heap of pages, and you, my friend—you took one look at that whale, you picked up a burnt matchstick from off the floor, and you went at it like you'd gone mad. I tried to stop you, but you threw me off. You were shouting *Sea-pig gate! Sea-pig gate!*"

Blackjohn slapped his knee and roared.

"Did I?" he gasped.

"Aye! You did! You don't remember anything?"

Blackjohn shook his head. "I remember us going below," he said. "I remember that bible spilling out of you. But I don't remember any whale." He stooped down and squinted at the page again.

"Enter by the gate, you say?"

"By the narrow gate."

"And a pointing finger?"

"Right into the whale's mouth."

Blackjohn stood up from the table. His face wore a bewildered look, but there was a hopeful light in his eyes. "Fifteen years I've searched for Doonbridge," Blackjohn said. "Fifteen years like a man possessed, and I'm sure I'll go to the depths ere I see it again, but—*ha ha*—" he laughed merrily, "what have we got to lose? You lot are chased by a sorcerer. I'm cursed to wander the sea looking for a fairy port. Doonbridge must be nigh to here, if it's anywhere on God's earth. What say ye? Shall we sail for a whale's mouth?"

"Aye!" I shouted (and Diana said *Yes*, in a more dignified voice.)

"Marvellous!" Kol exclaimed. "Lady Lily, might you look hereabout for something that suggests a whale? A cliff or a cave or something? Do you think maybe Mórester and the dolphin clan might help?"

"I think clan Tonvacha have left these waters," said Lily. "It's been two days since I heard their voices."

I realized it had suddenly grown darker outside. The colored flecks from the lamp—barely visible when I first came in—now swung bright and clear across the ceiling. The windows were dark like night had fallen. I could hear the shriek of the rising wind coming through the deck. Kol and Blackjohn didn't seem to notice, absorbed in their bible and chart.

"I remember a sea-cliff here," said Blackjohn, pointing to the map.

"With a inlet, maybe?" Kol asked.

"There's a vicious shoal before it, but we might approach to leeward—"

The windows exploded.

Flying glass blasted inside and cut my cheeks and arms. The table flipped over. Kol's bible slid under the divan. Kol dove after it. The storm howled unchecked through the shattered windows.

I could hear a voice in the wind. It was a low voice, yet it pierced the storm: a call that froze my blood.

Farahain air-an-Lili!

Lily shrieked.

I spun around.

Lily lay doubled up on the floor. For the first time it seemed as if the floor was touching her. She pressed her hands frantically over her ears and her green light wavered.

Farahain air-an-Lili!

Lily's body rose into the air. She hugged her knees tight against her chest, straining desperately.

Farahain air-an-Lili!

With a sudden jerk, Lily's legs and arms stretched wide apart. She screamed and struggled. There was a ghastly sucking noise outside the window. My ears popped and I couldn't breathe.

Farahain air-an-Lili, an ainm Esus!

Her body made a half-turn in the air, and then with a despairing cry Lily sailed out through the broken window. Her green light flashed once, a glimmer that reflected in the foam, and then she was gone.

I knew that voice.

I ran to the window and stuck out my head through the splintered grilles.

"Peter!" I screamed. "Peter!"

CHAPTER 23

When Lily came back she was taller than the mainmast.

Lily stalked deliberately toward us through the sea, threshing her arms from side to side while the yellow waves crashed around her waist. She was horrible to look at. Her eyes were dead white. Her giant head rolled to and fro and her mouth lolled open bigger than a cauldron. With an awful bellow Lily lunged for the *Otter*, snatching at us with monstrous fingers. "Come up! Come up!" Blackjohn shouted. We caught a rising swell, and the *Otter* danced out of Lily's grasp. Her hands thundered into the sea, sending up white towers of foam.

"Head down!" Blackjohn shouted.

Kol and I were tugging frantically on the t'gallant sheets, which were starting to slip. Diana was doing her best to hold onto the foot of the jib so Ronne and boatswain Finn could reef it. The slack whipped viciously in the shrieking wind, knocking her about.

BOOM.

A jet of spray shot up to starboard.

I looked back.

A two-masted yacht was closing in behind us. The emblem of the black stag pranced proudly across her mainsail. I watched as a mushroom of white smoke suddenly bloomed up from her foredeck. Another boom. The shot snarled through the air overhead.

He's amusing himself, I thought.

The giantess Lily was gaining on us faster than the yacht. She lunged, and her hands grazed the shrouds and made them whine. She floundered forward and lunged again. Her enormous bare arm scythed down. The *Otter* lurched sickeningly. Kol and I went sprawling against the rail.

I heard Diana scream.

I staggered to my feet. The jib was flapping wildly from one shackle. Diana was gone.

Something white snaked down over my head. I felt a grip around my waist like ice. For an instant I was looking down on the startled faces of the crew. Then my feet were kicking against the wind. The *Otter* was gone. I was swooping over the sea while the blood rushed to my head. I saw Lily's wet gown clinging to legs big as tree-trunks. Her grip was crushing me. I fought to breathe.

Dachaigh! said a commanding voice.

The icy grip was gone. So was Lily. I lay sprawled on the gritty boards of a ship. A raucous babble rose all around me. Cold, scaly fingers picked me up by my wrists and ankles. My head swam. I heard a rattle of chains.

Then it was dark.

At first I couldn't see anything.

I knew I was inside a ship. I could feel it rolling in a heavy sea. For a long time I sat with my back against a wet stanchion, listening to the aching drumbeat in my head. Iron fetters clanked on my hands and feet. The slimy floor pitched in the darkness while my head throbbed and the timbers kept up a squeaking chorus around me.

High overhead, a tiny beam of light found its way through a knothole. Slowly, almost imperceptibly it crept across the floor, just a faint gray circle in the blackness around it.

I clutched my head and closed my eyes.

I opened them again.

The circle was brighter now. It inched across the floor until it fell on something near me, curled-up and gray like a dead crab.

I blinked and rubbed my eyes.

It was a hand.

I yelped and shrank back, making a clatter with my chains.

The hand didn't move.

It's a corpse, I thought.

My eyes were riveted to the bright spot. Slow as eternity it crept higher, gradually disclosing a gaunt white arm, bare to the shoulder.

It crawled across a dirty furze of cloth.

Then up a shrunken neck. The neck wore an iron collar.

The circle was larger and redder. I knew outside the sun was setting, dropping toward the watery horizon. Now the circle was fading fast, but it its final gleam I saw a sunken face like a skull. Hollow black eyes stared back into mine.

The eyes blinked.

"Hullo, James."

Then the light was gone.

"Peter!" I sobbed. "Oh, Peter!"

There was a ghastly wet cough.

"Y-Yeoman James McKenna—"

He spoke in a strangled mutter.

"—the Black Stag bids you welcome to—to his guard. You have the honor of serving alongside your brother."

"Peter, what—"

Another ghastly cough.

"The Black Stag would have you know your brother John has also entered our service." (Peter's mutter took on a sardonic tone.) "His Worship regrets the cripple wasn't strong enough to attend this merry reunion, but fear not—"

The voice was Peter's, but the cadence reminded me of Lara.

"—but fear not. Cripple John McKenna is enjoying the comforts of our dungeon at Hermitage Castle."

"Peter!" I shouted at him, "stop it!"

"Ha ha—*oh?*" Peter returned. "I'm afraid I was obliged to question the cripple rather thoroughly. I assure you—" he laughed icily—"we haven't done anything to spoil his looks."

"Peter, *stop!*"

"And as for your uncle—the yeoman Andrew—regrettably he is dead."

"You're lying!"

"Alas, no," Peter answered, "You see Andrew McKenna disobeyed his lord. He hid the cripple from us. We were obliged to admonish him with a pike-thrust. In quite the same location as your father, James, I believe it was. Between the sixth and seventh ribs on the left side—ha ha!"

I was screaming and thrashing in my fetters. I tried to stand, but the chains were too short. So I lay on the sticky floor weeping and cursing. Peter had gone silent.

Finally I spoke to him.

"Where is Diana?"

There was a long silence, then:

"Who?"

"Diana!" I barked. "Where's Diana?"

Peter made a gurgling noise in his throat.

"The immortal huntress? Would to God I knew!"

"No! Idiot! Diana the—the what does your master call her? The banshee girl!"

Peter said nothing.

"The—"

I stopped short. An idea was taking root in my mind. I'd known it all along, but I was hearing myself speak it for the first time.

"The fairy girl."

Peter said nothing.

"Sowter's niece?" I ventured.

Peter coughed.

"The bastard? Was she from home? I don't remember home."

"She is *not* a bastard!" I shouted. "She's a *lady*! And you're a sorcerer's slave! You serve the witch-earl now! And after he—"

I hung my head and sobbed.

"—after he has ruined our whole *family!*"

There was a long silence. Then Peter spoke—with great effort, it seemed. They were his own words. Someone had left off commanding him.

"I'm dying, James," Peter whispered. "It's no use talking."

"No use?" I laughed mockingly. "But you talk rather a *lot*, don't you Peter? You called Lily, for one. Call her again! You've got the word of Esus now, haven't you?"

At 'word of Esus' Peter gave a strangled laugh, and then he started to drone like he was reciting a prayer:

The nymph for the boy,
The boy for the priest,
The priest for the hag,
The hag for the Stag,
I wear my lord's crest,
A chain for my chest—

"Shut up!" I screamed. "Well it's a fine word of Esus then, isn't it? How did you come by it, you and your dog-collar?"

Peter writhed and coughed.

"*Blood of this world—*"

"Shut up!"

"*Blood of the Other—*

Crook of Esus, three.
These are the Word,
And 't was Peter McKenna,
Murdered the priest of the huntress Diana,
And half a fairy was he—

My skin was crawling.

"*You* killed Friar Kol's brother?" I shrieked. "Friar Kol? Our friend?"

Peter made another strangling sound, as if his lungs were too weak to cough. He sat gasping a while in the darkness.

"The Black Stag told me to," Peter said at length. "On the Northumbria raid. Francis Stewart told me to. He wasn't in the van[117]—no, not he!" Peter

---

[117] *i.e.*, at the head of his forces.

gave another deathly laugh. "While the lads were off stealing cows and maidens, the Black Stag took me aside to a little spring in the forest—"

"Shut up!" I snarled. I tried to cover my ears, but the chains were so short they cut my wrists. So I cursed and spat at him. But Peter went on.

"I was—I was in love with him that day," Peter murmured. "In love with Francis Stewart. He spoke kindly to me. Like you would to a friend."

"*Love!*" I jeered.

"He put his hand on my shoulder, and he said he'd make me his very own lieutenant if only I'd avenge him of his enemy, the pagan priest Maewyn who used the black arts to bring about his ruin. Then he gave me a green copper blade like a sickle and he told me to hide in the willows by the spring and wait for Maewyn when he came to worship his heathen gods."

Peter stopped. I could hear the rattle in his lungs as he fought for air.

"Pr-presently Maewyn came, and so alike was he to Friar Kol that for a moment I thought it was him—only he was dressed all in green and he wore a wreath of mistletoe in his hair. Maewyn dipped his hand into the pool and he sang softly in a strange tongue, and at his touch the waterlilies opened and the birds began to sing.

"Then Maewyn turned and looked straight at me, like he knew I'd been there all along. *That thou doest, do it quickly*, he said, *But beware! I serve the Huntress, and the Huntress will pursue—*"

Peter broke off and coughed a while.

"He was trying to warn me—" Peter resumed—"you see? Maewyn wasn't the least bit afraid. I was ashamed then and I wanted to drop the copper blade and run. But then I thought of Francis and what a great man I would be forever if I would just do him this favor. So I got up and I came at Maewyn. He just stood there. He didn't move. *You're no Scot!* says I, *and you're no Christian either! And your huntress can have the same when she finds me—*

"—and then I stuck the green copper blade one time into his heart. It slid so easily between his ribs that I hardly felt it in my hand, though it came back all wet and steaming. Maewyn dropped to his knees. For a moment he knelt there in the water with his head on one side like he was listening to something. Then he pitched face-first into the pool, while his red blood spread out through the lilies.

"I turned back to the shore and I bent there, retching. It felt like—like I'd killed a songbird. Only worse. Oh, a thousand times worse! I knew I would never feel happiness again, nor the love of friends nor the light of day nor the peace of sleep nor the hope of any good thing to come. My heart died, James— my own heart died with Maewyn's.

"*Where is this Huntress?* I thought. *When in mercy will she end me?*

"Then I heard a horn in the forest and up rode Sir Francis with his captains. They all laughed when they saw me kneeling there.

"*Leave off groveling, boy!* Francis said, and he got off his horse. *You've done me a noble service, and nobly I'll repay thee.* He took the bloody copper blade out of my hand. He looked down at it, then he smiled and put it inside his coat. *An hour ago*, he said, *I commanded these my knights to hang you by your neck from an oak in this very grove—and merciful I was, thus to spare you the wrath of the Huntress.* Then he prodded Maewyn's wet body with the toe of his boot. *Of course I might have killed brother Maewyn myself*, Francis said, *only I knew he was a priest of Dana and a half-fairy by blood. Dana will avenge him—that's the curse of the priestslayer. But I fancy I'll take the crook and YOU'LL take the curse.*

"They all laughed at that," Peter said, "but he was mistaken—Francis Stewart was mistaken. He had the crook, but he didn't have the word of Esus. Fairy blood clings to the one who spills it. That's the mark of the curse."

"Murderer!" I hissed, not caring to understand.

"Francis let me go," Peter went on. "No—no, he traded me. For a prisoner. Yes. To the Northumbrians. *An exchange of hostages is agreed*, he said. *You'll make a shrewd trade. We give these English dogs a boy marked for death, and we get back a man with some life left in him—*"

"You ought to be dead already."

"They—the Northumbrians wouldn't take a foot-soldier. *A lieutenant you shall be*, Francis said, *and behold! Your lord keeps his word.* Then one of his captains put his boot on my neck and crushed me into the mud. They stripped off my coat and put the brigandine of the Branxholme Castle guard on me. Then they tied my hands behind my back and put a steel helmet on my head, and they made me run behind their horses at the end of a rope all the way back to camp."

"Ha ha!" (I was laughing and crying.) "Ha ha—Lieutenant Peter! And I was jealous of you! And proud of you! You a soldier!"

Peter hacked twice.

"They loaded me into a sheep wagon," he said. "With two others. To take us to Cartington. Francis came. He came to me just before we started off. He stuck his hand in and took me by the jaw and made me to look into his eyes. Mi-*Mind your tongue now, boy*—he said it low so the others wouldn't hear—*Mind your tongue, boy. You're a dead lad*, he said, *But your brother isn't. Nor your uncle. Nor that cripple John. Brother Lara's my swineherd and he'll be keeping watch. Speak one word of what's passed between us, and by God I'll see the lot of them roasted inside your hayrick, and your mother with them!* Then he let go of me and he was gone."

"Brave lad!" I sneered. "And after all that you go slinking back to his guard! Wanted a bunk and a quarterly—aye? Or did you miss the beef?"

Peter shuddered.

"I didn't go back," he said. "Lara sent for me the day after I reached home. I knew he would—No, let me speak, James! When I got to Cartington Castle, the sergeant-at-arms asked me some questions. Who I was. What rank. Where I came from. Well of course he knew before his porridge was cooled that I was just a poor plowboy with a dead horse. So the sergeant cursed and hit me and he said they'd been cheated and he meant to hang me. I wish he had! But then he looked on me again like something changed his mind. He spat and said I had the stench of death on me, like an evil thing that would bring bad luck. He said he didn't want me in that country, dead or alive. So they branded me with the *H* for heretic and they let me go. I slept that night in a field and I walked all the way home to Buckley. Lara kept an eye on me for—I can't remember how many days—and then the soldiers came and took me to Branxholme and the dungeon."

"Lucky for you!" I sneered. "You missed all the mowing!"

Peter said nothing.

We sat in silence a while. Then for the first time I heard what might have been a sob.

"I saw Francis in the dungeon once."

Peter sobbed again.

"He made me touch the crook. It wasn't curved anymore. It was straight like a knife. I knew it was evil and I tried not to touch it, but he only laughed and pressed it hard against my face, and then I felt the word of Esus inside me."

"So why didn't you just call Lily?" I demanded. "Why not command her to turn all the bricks into frogs or somesuch thing?"

Peter whimpered softly.

"They did—bad things. Bad things to me. In the dungeon, before he made me touch the crook. It went on for a long time. On and on and on. Oh! how I wished for the Huntress! I called and called for her in the dark, but she wouldn't come."

Peter moved slightly. I heard the faint clink his curved fingernail made as he tapped the iron band around his neck.

"This collar is enchanted," Peter said. "I say what the Stag wants me to say."

We sat in silence again.

"How can a great man like Sir Francis Stewart do these horrible things?" I asked, half to myself.

"He is noble," Peter replied. "People are like sheep to him."

"Where is our mother, Peter?"

"I don't know."

It didn't seem like I slept. I wrenched this way and that, trying to ease the fetters while weird visions paraded through my head—all the strange and sad and fearful things I'd seen since that day when first I came upon Diana in the woods. Witches and bancorra. Wolf-men and stone giants. Nymphs and gnomes and dolphins with human voices. Swirling like flames they flickered and departed while one vision was woven through it all—Peter my brother. Peter from home. Peter I used to play with. Peter who told me my freckles came from a fairy.

Peter the murderer.

Peter sitting in the dark next to me, silent and yet alive.

It must have been morning outside. I was drifting in and out of delirium. Something unbolted my fetters from the wall. Rough hands bundled me up a hatchway, and then a cold blast of salt wind struck me full against my burning face. I tried to stand but I'd lost all feeling in my feet and I promptly collapsed onto the deck.

I got up on my elbows, blinking stupidly in the light.

Diana was standing there straight and proud. Her ankles were fettered like mine and her hands were tied behind her back, but she held up her head defiantly. A rabble of witches and evil creatures clamored in a half-circle around us. Two monstrous hands seized me from behind, and a thing with the body of a man and the head of bull picked me up like a sack and set me on my feet. I staggered, but I caught myself this time and stood swaying with the rolling of the ship.

We were on the foredeck of the earl's two-masted yacht. It was a princely ship and well furnished, but it had a neglected air, even to my bleary eyes. Rope was everywhere. Loose casks bumped and rolled aimlessly. The deck was slick and treacherous. No one seemed to be on watch. At the helm I could see the neglected wheel turning idly this way and that as the rudder was left to swing free in the current. She wasn't so much as flying her topsails, and yet somehow we were booming along at a great pace, close-hauled and so nearly dead upwind that I marveled how we could be making such speed. All around a dense fog pressed in close upon us, while ragged clouds went streaming by low and fast across the sky.

A voice shrieked *Way!* and the weird congregation parted in front of us.

Up stepped Sir Francis Stewart, as fresh and fine as if he were strolling through Holyrood.[118] He looked young—a man of maybe twenty-five, but he carried himself with an unaffected boyish charm. The ostrich plume on his hat and the waves of his dark brown hair caught the breeze. He looked handsome and brave, and he smelled faintly of rosewater. The earl wore a green fairy glass like mine, only his was hanging from a fine gold chain. Brother Lara, his face all but covered by his black cassock, came slinking along deferentially behind.

---

[118] Holyrood palace, traditional seat of the Scottish monarchy.

"Good morning, my young subjects!" The earl trilled. "I trust you spent a comfortable night." He laughed pleasantly. "I bid you welcome aboard the *Raven*—fastest ship on the North Sea." He made a low bow and grandly swept off his hat. "I must confess I'm rather proud of her. That old fox Blackjohn gave us quite a chase yesterday, but he was no match for the *Raven*. Ha ha!"

Francis put his hat back on. "Oh! Right." he said. "You wouldn't have heard—Blackjohn is dead. He struck upon a shoal and foundered shortly after my servant Lady Farahain brought the two of you aboard. I'm happy to report the pirate and the hermit are lying on the cold black bottom of the sea with only the crabs to mourn them."

Francis laughed again. The bull-headed creature came stumping up the hatch. Something long and limp was swinging between his massive hands. He dropped it on the deck, and there lay Peter doubled up at our feet. He was barely moving. In the light of day he looked like a pile of white bones tied up in dirty rags that fluttered in the wind. His bright red hair had turned to gray like an old man.

"Well there's not much left of *him*," the earl observed, covering his nose with a silk handkerchief and peering down at Peter with a distasteful look. "Well, no matter. After today we shan't need him anymore. Peter lad!" he shouted as if he imagined Peter were deaf. "Summon Lady Farahain!"

Peter's lips moved. I didn't hear him speak, but in a wink there was Lily standing before us. She was ordinary size now but her face was like stone and her eyes were the same ghastly white as before. She stood uncannily still. Only her dark hair moved in the wind.

"Shiora," said the earl (apparently to Lily), "you have served me well, and now you are dismissed. A better servant has come to take your place."

He turned to Diana and tapped the fairy glass hanging from his neck.

"This will be your new home," Francis said.

Diana laughed.

"You cannot command me."

"No?" returned the earl indifferently. "Brother Lara advises me that I can."

Lara bowed meekly.

"One soul must depart, one soul must enter, my lord," he rasped.

215

"Yes—you see my young friends," the earl explained in a kindly voice, "our Lady Farahain is a *shoira*. An immortal, you might say."

He waved at Lily. Lily just stood there like a corpse.

"She is bound to her lord, Esus the Forester," said Francis. "Now, due to the—er—due to the fickle fortunes of war, it seems that at present we can only employ Lady Farahain by means of this—" (The earl heaved a weary sigh.) "—by means of this miserable boy."

He prodded Peter dejectedly with the toe of his boot. But then he brightened again.

"But Diana O'Neil!" the earl said excitedly. "Diana O'Neil is a *ban-sìthe* indeed! A fairy woman with wondrous gifts!" He looked Diana up and down with greedy delight. "I knew it from the moment you interrupted our Midsummer Sabbath. You come from the Apple Isle!"

"I don't know *where* I come from," Diana retorted. "I can't remember. And anyway, *you* can't command the fairies."

"Right you are!" the earl sniggered "I can't. But the word of Esus can. Because in these islands, Diana, Esus is lord over all the *sithichean* and *shiori*—the fairies and the immortals. To him is given charge of all the wild places. Of the forests and the desolate moors where creatures have no king.

"But *I* will be their king!" the earl exclaimed rapturously. "With you in my hand, Diana, I will rule the thrones of men, and the haunts of fairies too."

I noticed Francis Stewart was trembling all over. There was a mad light in his eye. The witches shifted about nervously and even the bull-man drew back a pace.

"Oh! We shall do the most marvelous things together!" Francis cried.

He looked down with sudden irritation.

"If that salmon doesn't die while we all stand here chattering, that is! Quick! Let's get on with it before the moment is gone. Now then," Francis said briskly, prodding Peter with his boot again. "This task falls to you, Yeoman McKenna. Brother Lara will give you the Words of Conveyance, and Diana will take Lily's station inside the fairy glass, to serve the House of Stewart forever."

"Wh-what about Lily?" I croaked, finding my voice. "Can she go back to the Lilylock, then?"

The earl laughed uproariously.

"Oh, the Lilylock isn't quite so pretty as you might remember it," he said with a wink. "My servants—the wise sisters—they left a good number of dead sheep rotting in it. After they'd fouled it in other ways." The assembled witches erupted in laughter and cheers. Sir Francis lifted his hand slightly, and instantly they were silent again.

"No, my lad," he said, "we have a fitting vessel to put Lady Farahain's soul in." Francis turned to one of the witches.

"Fetch the salmon."

The witch hurried over to the ship's rail. She plucked up a line of slender cord that hung straight and taught over the gunnel. The line twitched and danced, and then up came a big gray salmon, swinging from a metal ring that pierced through its gills on one side. Another witch held up a reed basket. Together they untied the salmon while a wolf-man, looking on, sniffed and licked his teeth.

The witches set the basket reverently at the earl's feet. Francis Stewart leaned over and surveyed the fish as it worked its jaw helplessly up and down.

"What was it again?" the earl asked. "*Ingreditur anima ad piscis*?"

"*Ingreditur anima IN piscis*, my lord," Lara humbly corrected him.

"Right! Very well. Did you catch that, boy?" he shouted down at Peter. "*Ingreditur anima in piscis*. Say it clear."

"And the banshee girl should be holding the vial," Lara advised. "Her soul is by far the readiest to enter when the nymph departs, but your lordship needs to be certain."

The bullhead creature perfunctorily untied Diana's hands. He took her wrist in a grip like stone. Francis Stewart lifted off his gold chain and put the fairy glass in Diana's palm. The bull creature closed his huge hand over hers, swallowing it up.

"Stop!" I shouted. "Don't send Lily into that fish!"

"Well why shouldn't I?" the earl asked in amazement. "The nymph's a water sprite. She has a special kinship with swimming creatures. Fish and, and eels and the like." He fluttered his fingers vaguely. "The spell is more sure to work with a salmon. One mustn't take chances with these sorts of things."

"And what do you mean to do with the salmon, then?"

"Ha ha! We're going to *eat* it! Isn't that drole?" The earl laughed so hard the tears came to his eyes, which he commenced dabbing with his silk handkerchief.

"I thought of that myself," Francis sighed, handing the handkerchief to Lara. "We'll keep Lily—"

He started to laugh again.

"We'll keep her swimming just until suppertime. Now then!" the earl coughed and cleared him throat. "*Ingreditur anima in piscis*, boy. Let's have it." And he prodded Peter with his toe.

There was a sudden hush. Even the masts and yards seemed to stop creaking. Diana, the earl, Lara, the witches, the creatures and I—we all froze there breathless, our eyes fixed on Peter where he lay unmoving on the deck.

Lily stood like a statue, her blank eyes staring at nothing.

Peter's lips moved.

Lily stirred slightly. Her hands jerked once at her sides. Then she was still.

"Again, boy!" the earl barked. "*Ingreditur anima in piscis*. Say it louder."

Peter opened his hollow eyes. He grimaced and curled back his lips, making his face ghastlier still.

"Speak!" the earl shouted.

Peter clenched his teeth as if he were fighting back the words. With a gurgling noise he drew his wasted limbs together. Then, trembling all over, Peter got up on hands and knees.

"Speak, dog!" Francis snarled. He bent down and jabbed the iron collar on Peter's bony neck. The collar squeaked and tightened itself like a noose. Peter writhed. He mouthed something in a ragged whisper but I couldn't catch the words.

"How dare you disobey me!" screamed the earl. "Irreverent cur! Oh, how your brother John will die slowly for this!" Francis snapped open his palm and held it high above his head. The collar creaked and tightened. Peter made a choking sound.

Then Peter rose up on his knees.

The witches gasped and drew back. Peter was shaking terribly, but his wasted face wore the old look of hatred and defiance that used to frighten me. He clutched the collar and gave a strangled cry.

Farahain-air-an-Lili! Leig às i!

Lily moved so fast I hardly saw her. In a blink she was beside the bull creature with her slender white finger touching his massive wrist. The bull-man dropped Diana's hand like a coal. With a bellow he jerked back his huge head, and then green seawater exploded out of his mouth and nostrils, cascading across the deck. The bull-man went rolling and thrashing over the boards, spewing water like a fountain while the witches and evil creatures shrieked and scattered. Brother Lara and the earl had to jump to avoid his flailing hooves. I dimly noticed the gray salmon was gill-deep in water now and beginning to flip its tail.

Diana sprang to Peter's side and touched his iron collar. *Bris!* she hissed. The collar snapped in two and fell from his neck. Peter dragged in a frantic breath. Diana took his bony shoulders in her hands and steadied him. For a moment they knelt there face-to-face while Peter stared into Diana's eyes.

Bradan-liath! Bradan-liath! Bradan-liath!

His voice was barely a whisper, but it resonated in the air between them. On the deck the gray salmon flopped once.

Twice.

Then it disappeared.

I heard a startled cry.

Lily was standing in front of the foremast with her hands clasped over her mouth. Tears were streaming down her cheeks. Her eyes were piercing green now and very much alive. For a moment she looked wildly about her like someone waking from a dream.

Then in one swift spring, Lily arched her slender body over the starboard rail. I listened for a splash but there was none. She was simply gone.

"Hags! Return! Return, I say!"

Francis was shouting angrily. The startled witches were gathering to him again. The bull-man lay drowned, a thin trickle of seawater running down his black tongue.

"Come! Now!" Diana cried. She was working frantically at our shackles, touching them here and there while the rusty iron crumbled and cracked.

"Where are we going?" I gasped.

"Carry him!"

I gathered Peter up, and, weak as I was, it felt like I was lifting a child. Diana already had one leg over the rail. "Throw him off!" she cried, and then she jumped.

I stumbled after her with Peter in my arms and a broken shackle clattering from my ankle. But at the rail I hesitated, peering down. The fog was so dense I could barely make out the water. The waves were rough and Diana was nowhere to be seen.

There was a vicious snarl behind me.

From the corner of my eye I saw a flash of teeth, and then the wolf-man hit me like a thunderbolt. His weight doubled me over the rail. Peter fell out of my arms.

"Peter!" I shouted, and then I pitched overboard.

The slap of icy water took my breath away. I struggled to the surface.

"Peter!" I shouted again, but all I could see were the sharp gray peaks of waves.

I struck out to starboard, fighting to swim clear of the ship. The *Raven*'s mainshrouds glided past, but I could feel the grip of her mighty draught pulling me back into her side. My head knocked against the slippery hull. I took a desperate breath, and then the current dragged me under.

I'm thinking of you as I write this, Charlie my boy. It seems strange now, but even as I rolled in the freezing dark under that ship—lungs bursting; knowing that in a moment I would suck in water and drown—even in that black horror, Charlie, it was Diana O'Neil whose image came into my mind. Not a vision, really, nor an omen of good or ill. Just a sort of picture. The ghost of her face. The weight of her hand. The echo of her voice, gentle and low like my mother's—heavy, it seemed to me, with all the quiet joy of safe and ordinary things.

Then instantly the darkness was gone and the water lit up emerald green all around. The black bulk of the *Raven's* stern surged over me, and I came up spluttering in the foam of her wake.

A gray shadow moved in the water below.

I jerked my up knees in terror.

The shadow instantly grew darker. I was flailing desperately. My hand came down on something firm.

"God save me!" I screamed.

Then with a cry of joy I flopped onto my stomach and clung on desperately as two lovely, glistening dolphins bore me up out of the sea.

They swam together, gray side pressed against gray side, each with a flipper under the other's belly. I lay astride them both and wept. The black outline of the *Raven* was fading back into the enchanted fog. Noises of wild commotion rose from her deck, but soon they faded away too and all was quiet but the wind and the waves.

Up ahead the air was clearing. To my right I could see Peter lying face-up across the backs of two more dolphins. Diana was farther off. She sat on a creature like a whale, riding confidently with her head high and her wet hair streaming backward in the wind. She was laughing. Then I was laughing too. In another moment the mist was gone and the summer sun beat down on the glassy swells. I gave a wild shout. We were coming to a ship. The black flag of a privateer flew from her mizzenmast. It was the *Otter*.

Lower away!

Blackjohn's voice was calling. I heard the creak of the windlass. A heavy cargo net came slowly down amidships. It stopped a foot or so above the water. Diana's creature came alongside, bobbing in the swells. It rolled slightly and laid a massive flipper on the surface of the water like a plank. Diana stepped off daintily and sat back into the cargo net. The shiny ridge of the creature's back sank silently into the water and was gone. Then my two dolphins drew near. They arched their two backs together and bucked me unceremoniously over their heads, leaving me to flounder for the net on my own. Diana helped me crawl in. I squirmed onto my stomach. Peter's dolphins were waiting. I gathered him up into my arms.

Hoist away! Blackjohn shouted. His round, bearded face was sticking out over the rail, grinning down at us. The sun behind his head made a fiery halo around his big Spanish hat.

We were all gathered in Captain Blackjohn's saloon again. Friar Kol laid Peter gently on the table, wrapped up in a woolen blanket. Blackjohn took off his hat and looked on gravely as Kol lit a candle, which sputtered in the draft of the broken windows. He took out his wooden rosary.

"*Pax huic dómui—*" Kol began in a calm, priestly voice. But at the first word Peter lifted his hand from beneath the blanket and laid it weakly on Kol's arm. He faintly shook his head.

"Diana," Peter whispered.

Diana came close and took Peter's hand. I looked at her curiously. There was something changed about her. A memory flashed into my mind. For a moment I saw Diana as she was on the night Lily first came aboard, swaying carelessly atop the mainmast with a crown of blazing stars above her head.

Peter looked up at her pleadingly.

"Are you going to kill me now?" he whispered.

"No," said Diana. "But you may go, if you wish."

Peter smiled longingly. He looked past Diana, and then his eyes stayed a moment, like he was seeing something far away.

"I want to go home," Peter whispered.

"Then you may depart," Diana answered. "Your crime against Maewyn was terrible, but you did a brave thing when you set me free. Be comforted, Peter McKenna. James and John will see you again."

She laid her hand on his heart. "*Rach ann an sìth,*" she whispered. "Go in peace."

Peter drew in a deep, clean breath. His bony chest swelled up and up as if a great weight had been lifted off it. A smile of deep contentment overspread his face. He closed his eyes and breathed out again in one long, peaceful sigh. His hand slipped off Diana's and fell back onto the blanket.

I noticed I was crying.

"Peter?" I called.
But he was gone.

CHAPTER 24

From the diary of Doctor Stewart Henry Scott—

In fugam – June 20, 1838

Early on the morning of the sixteenth of June, 1838, we set out from the village of Airdrie, Lanarkshire. We meant to make a forced march of it, slip through Glasgow unnoticed, and (if the roads and the rains be kind) reach Dumbarton Town before the light of the long summer day failed us.

"It'll be rough going after Dumbarton," Fitzhugh observed. He chewed the stem of his pipe with a pensive expression.

"Why?" I demanded. "How so?"

"It's either the Highlands or the Islands for us," Fitzhugh said decidedly. "Either we've got to go north up the whole length of Loch Lomond and then west through Argyle as far as Oban or thereabouts, or else we've got to find us a boat in Dumbarton Town, aye, and a pilot who knows all the trammels of the lochs and firths from here to Mull."

"It would be longer by sea," I said thoughtfully. I was sitting up on the box with Fitzhugh again. It was a rare June morning. A light rain had come with the dawn but it passed off as we were hitching up the mares and now the summer sun was turning the meadows to emeralds and the sheep to pearls as only the summer sun of Scotland can.

"Longer, yes," Fitzhugh returned, "but safer perhaps?"

Elizabeth poked her bonnet out the open window. "I've never seen Loch Lomond," she trilled. "I'd fancy having a look at it."

"Then it's settled," I said jovially. "Damn the Duke of Buckley and the whole Scots peerage with him! Begging your pardon, Madam."

"Then again," Fitzhugh said cautiously, "I don't reckon we'll get to see much of Loch Lomond with the doctor in prison."

"Oh, not to worry," I returned cheerfully. "You lot carry on—see the Loch while I'm awaiting trial."

"I suppose we *could*!" Fitzhugh guffawed.

"For shame!" cried Elizabeth. "And now you have me worried, Doctor. Do you really think it's safer if we take a boat?"

By noon the spires and smokestacks of Glasgow were shutting out the sky. I was riding inside the coach now with the curtains drawn.

"Good heavens, doctor!" Elizabeth said with irritation, "You mustn't be forever peeking out from the corner of the window! The duke of Buckley isn't watching every road in the kingdom, from last week until Doomsday."

"You're right," I sighed, letting go the edge of the curtain.

"Besides," Elizabeth pursued, "we lay up a whole week in Caldercross. Hasn't Mister Radan got something else to occupy him? Deeds or trusts or something like that?"

"I certainly hope he has," I said. "If only I can see this adventure through to the end, then I'll post *John Blackjohn* back to him and have done with it. I'd have give myself up already, only—" I pushed my spectacles up onto my forehead and rubbed my eyes wearily. "—only I keep thinking about that poor, dead constable in Berwick. Did he have a wife, I wonder? Or any children? And what did he die for, then, if we simply throw up our hands and give Radan what he wants? It's—it's positively undemo*cratic*," I ended weakly.

"Hear, hear!" Fitzhugh's muffled voice came through the roof. Cartwheels rattled on the cobbles around us. It was stifling hot inside. Elizabeth fanned herself with a pamphlet titled *Reflections Upon Gehenna*, one of my endless store of religious tracts. (They really are quite useful.)

I stuck my arm out the window and knocked on the side of the coach. "Fitzhugh," I called, "could we drive past the Royal Infirmary?

"I can't go through Glasgow without at least *seeing* it," I explained a bit sheepishly, pulling my arm back inside. "I confess I'm ancient enough to remember the ruins of the old Bishop's Castle. They tore it down to make room for the hospital. My father took me there once when I was a boy, and—"

225

"Why, doctor!" Elizabeth exclaimed. "I'd no idea you were brought up in Dunbartonshire. Why didn't you tell us? You ought to know every stone, I should think."

"No, no!" I disclaimed, reddening. "Not brought up, exactly. I—I was raised mostly in Fife, near Kirkaldy. My father—he had some sort of chicanery afoot in Glasgow. Horse-trading or the like. He was—ah—he was a man of—"

Seeing the topic made me uneasy Elizabeth was kind enough to cough into her pamphlet so loudly the horses jumped and Fitzhugh cried *Whoa!* up on the box.

"Old ruins?" Elizabeth interrupted. "Now that's interesting."

"Oh yes!" I returned warmly. "They made quite an impression on me as a boy. I never forgot it—the crumbling gothic arches all covered in moss. I made a sword out of two sticks while my father was dozing on the grass and then for an hour I was a knight of Wemyss and every shadow was an Englishma—"

I stopped, blushing furiously. Elizabeth laughed merrily.

"Oh, we're not so bad as all that.

"Not English*women*, anyway," Elizabeth added archly.

"I beg your pardon!" I exclaimed. "I was just a boy, and—"

"Stewart! Truly!" Elizabeth laughed with genuine amusement. (She'd never called me Stewart before.) "So you were a Wemyss, then?"

"Oh, of course!"

"Royal Infirmary!" Fitzhugh called down from the box.

I lifted the curtain.

"Well I must say, I liked the ruins better," I observed critically. "Look at all those Greek fripperies! I suppose they want us to think they're all wearing togas in there."

"Why? What's wrong with it?" Elizabeth demanded, craning her neck to peer over my shoulder as the grand façade rolled past.

"Oh, I don't know," I returned sullenly. "It looks out of place and so—so *modern*."

"Not much romance in it."

"No. Not much. The stonework on the Bishop's Castle—it was all black and crumbling, but it had a sort of magic. Covered in saints and birds and animals. You see with different eyes when you're a child. I remember how—"

I dropped the curtain and sat back again quickly.

"What's the matter?" Elizabeth asked sharply, seeing my look.

"There was a man staring at me."

"Doctor, for goodness' sake—"

"Yes, he was leaning against the lamppost like he was waiting for someone. Weasely little fellow. Looked me straight in the eye."

"Well I'm sure he *did*!" Elizabeth cried. "He probably wanted threepence. Stop the coach and I'll give it him."

"Wozzat?" Fitzhugh called down from the box. "Are we stopping?"

"No!" I shouted. "Drive on!

"He looked at me like he knew me somehow," I said to Elizabeth—

And then we made a sudden lurch. The right-hand mare gave a whinny and a snort. Fitzhugh shouted *Whoa!* again and there was a squeal of brakes.

"Fitzhugh?" I called.

For a moment there was muffled shouting outside, and then the door flew open so hard it hit the side of the coach with a bang. The black silhouette of a man was framed against the brightness outside. For a second his huge shoulders filled up the opening. Then he plunged his arms inside and grabbed me by the coat.

"You let go!" Elizabeth screamed. "You take your hands off!" She was slapping him about the face with her pamphlet. The man dragged me out the door like a sack and sent me sprawling onto the dirty cobblestones.

I looked up.

It was our longshoreman—the one whose clothes I'd set on fire in Edinburgh.

"Happy t' see y' again, doctor," he boomed.

"How's your head?" I returned tartly. Then, remembering myself: "And how *is* your head," I repeated, with real concern. "Not a concussion was it? I can give you—"

He wrenched my hands around behind my back with a growl. I felt cold metal on my wrists. There was a steely click. The black door of an ugly, squarish carriage loomed open in front of me. Fitzhugh was already inside, sitting on the floor with his head down and his hands behind his back. The weasely little lookout was holding the reins and sneering down at me from the box.

"Hey, what's this?" I shouted. "You can't arrest us! You're not—"

The longshoreman shoved me headlong into the carriage and slammed the door. I heard the scrape of a heavy deadbolt outside. The reins snapped and we started off.

"Fitzhugh?" I said quietly.

"Aye."

"Do you know where we're going?"

"Nay."

"Well," I said, suppressing a sob, "that's the end of John Blackjohn."

We must have creaked along for an hour or more. I tried to guess which way we were going but I lost track of all the stops and turns. It was hot and stuffy inside and it smelled of fish. I ached from sitting on the hard floor. Fitzhugh hadn't said a single word. I sensed it was best to let him alone for the present.

Gradually the rattle of cobblestones gave way to gravel, then to dirt. City noises faded. I could hear birds chirping outside. Then the burble of a brook and the hollow bump of wheels on a wooden bridge as we crossed over.

At length we stopped. We sat for some time in the stifling darkness. A few needles of sunlight found their way in through the ceiling but I couldn't see anything just the faint suggestion of blue sky overhead. Presently I heard the crunch of footsteps on gravel and the murmur of guarded voices coming near. Someone spoke up, and I knew at once it was Radan.

"Come identify them."

"Why would that be necessary?"

I sat bolt upright. The other voice was familiar too, and not what I expected to hear.

"What's to identify? Murdo knows them."

"*You* know them." I heard Radan's curt reply.

"Yes, but you can take charge of them. I'll be on my way."

"No," Radan returned icily, "I'll take charge of them and *you'll* come at once."

The deadbolt scraped back and the door swung open. I squinted out into the sunlight.

My heart sank.

I dropped my head and stared vacantly at the dirty boards under my feet.

"Hello, Albert."

"Stewart." Albert returned stiffly.

"Oh, the merry reunion!" Radan cackled. His yellow face was practically splitting with delight. "I can't *tell* you how I've been looking forward to this. I said to our friend, Mr. Murdo, not a week ago—I said: *It takes a Scot to catch a Scot*—ha ha! In very truth I did! And sure enough! We drive straight to Glasgow, lie up a week, and presto! Our runaway doctor turns up precisely where Mr. Gray said he would: outside the Royal Infirmary, *where ye once played when ye were a wee bairn* (Radan adopted a mocking Scottish brogue)—isn't that right? Albert said he heard the story from you at least a dozen times."

Albert winced and looked mortified, but he set his jaw like a man resolved to see an unpleasant matter through. "I warned you, Stewart," he said with a lecturing tone. "I told you we couldn't have you traipsing through bogs and ruining our practice. Mr. Radan paid me a visit in May, before you even returned to Edinburgh. I covered your tracks dutifully for you then, but I'll cover them no longer."

I was aghast.

"You—you saw him in *May*? And you didn't bother to bring it up?"

Albert looked truly angry.

"When did I ever lead you to believe I supported this mad escapade, Stewart?" Albert shouted. "Our regular patients neglected? People asking after you in the town? And what was I to tell them? *Oh*—" (Albert lilted) "*he's gone off chasing fairies, Mrs. McGow. Shouldn't expect him back before Midsummer. He's got a ceremony down at the henge to attend to—*"

"Albert—"

"All the work of the practice falls to me—" (Albert was pacing and gesturing in front of us.) "I cart your ravings back and forth from the scrivener's and present your cheques at the bank while you—" (he fairly choked) "—while you lot roam from inn to inn and drink away our living—"

"Gently. Gently, my friend." I broke in. "Calm yourself. You needn't go on. I'm the one in shackles, see? And you're breathing the free air. You've settled the score, I should think."

"Oh, I've more than settled it!" Albert made a proud thrust with his chin. "I perjured myself when Mr. Radan came before, but after you set fire to our offices—that was the last straw. I've taken steps to save the practice—*my* practice, anyway. Sir Walter Douglas-Scott has appointed me to be his own personal physician."

"His *personal* physician? And when did Sir Walter tell you *that*?"

"Well—" Albert hesitated. He glanced over at Radan, but Radan only smiled and looked on.

"Well—Mr. Radan told me so," Albert said defensively, "and he's Sir Walter's representative, and we're off to London soon, so it's goodbye Bread Street and goodbye fairies and goodbye—goodbye—*you*," he ended awkwardly.

I was genuinely worried. "I know you're angry, Albert," I said, "but I don't like the sound of this. Radan wants the old book like—well it's verging on madness. You can't believe a word he says. I truly think it's best you stay in Edinburgh at least for the pres—"

"You're jealous?" Albert snorted. "What, did you think *you* were getting called up to a noble house? I should think you'd leave off *burglarizing* them first." He laughed scornfully.

"Speaking of burglary," Radan interrupted, "here's the book. I took it from that crone. Would you believe she fought me for it? Does she even read?" He held up *John Blackjohn* and shook it demonstratively. I saw he'd put it in the same oilcloth satchel he was carrying in Berwick when he ran off with a bundle of my religious pamphlets. Radan noticed my look, and the gloating smile faded from his lips.

"Oh, that was a clever trick, doctor!" he said quietly. "Clever trick indeed. I've another for you. I hope you like it." He put his hand inside his coat as if he were feeling for something.

The big longshoreman (I gathered this was Murdo) pulled Fitzhugh and me out of the carriage and set us on our feet. Looking about I saw we were on a pretty little farm—one of the Duke of Buckley's crofts, I guessed, probably just north of Glasgow—with a crude cottage and a little sod barn on it.

"March!" Radan ordered. "You too, Albert. Your duties start now." Radan smiled evilly. "Somebody's going to need a doctor."

Albert looked uneasy.

"Where are they going?" he asked.

Radan turned on his heel.

"*We're* going to the pond."

It all felt rather dreamlike, there on Scotland's rarest of sunny days. The country was in full flower—birds nesting, sheep grazing on the meadow, blue smoke rising gently from the little cottage chimney—while we five marched in a sullen parade, an unclean mixture of greed and fear and cruelty.

Men are a stain upon Creation, I thought. *It's a wonder the Almighty hasn't sent another deluge to wash us off.*

Radan took the lead. Murdo brought up the rear, keeping a scowling watch on Fitzhugh and me. A little hollow opened in front of us. It was a lonely place. The furze and heather growing thick about the rim made it almost invisible from outside. We pushed through the brush and stumbled down a rocky brae to where a pond lay reedy and stagnant between outcroppings of weathered stone. The eerie silence of the place came down on us so quickly that we all paused at once and looked up at each other in surprise—all but Radan. Radan went on picking his way daintily among the rocks, one hand inside his coat.

I noticed the birds had stopped chirping.

How did it get dark so fast? I wondered.

An odd-looking cloud was boiling up in the west, curiously near at hand. It stood alone against the bright sky, looking somewhat like an angry black cauliflower with purple edges where lightning showed through.

Strange I hadn't noticed that before, I thought. *Will there be a storm?* I heard the growl of not-too-distant thunder.

We stopped because we could go no farther. The ground was already wet and marshy. We were ranged out along the rim of the pond—Murdo, the lookout, Fitzhugh and I—all looking expectantly at Radan.

Suddenly the whole situation struck me as terribly ridiculous. Here we were—two of us in chains, two of us free, all of us loitering beside a muddy hole in Dunbartonshire waiting on a deranged solicitor to tell us what we were about. I started to laugh. Fitzhugh must have sensed the absurdity too, for he smiled and then he started to laugh as well.

"So, counselor?" I said. "Here we are, by your orders. What's it going to be? Were you about to make a speech?"

"On temperance, maybe?" Fitzhugh sniggered.

Radan's face went white.

"You're a man of science, doctor," Radan snarled. "I think you might be interested in *this*." He reached inside his coat and pulled out a strange object.

"My—*word!*" I gasped.

Fitzhugh raised his eyebrows quizzically.

"Oh yes." Radan smiled like a viper. "And do you know, it has the most interesting properties."

He was holding up a pointed copper blade, about a foot and a half in length. It was tarnished and green with unguessable age, but he held it from a new-looking handle that was white and smooth like glass.

"Mister Meeks?" Radan barked.

The lookout stepped forward briskly, with a sucking sound of boots in the spongy turf. He touched the brim of his hat.

"Mister Radan, Sir?"

"You have sharp eyes, Meeks," said Radan.

The lookout bowed and touched his hat again.

"Sharp eyes," said Radan, "are precisely what we *don't* need at present. Your employment is hereby withdrawn, and the house of Buckley thanks you for your service." He held out the copper blade and pointed it at Meeks. Meeks cringed back, but quick as a fencer Radan sprang at him and touched the blade to his forehead. There was a *crack* like a pistol-shot. Meeks went stiff. He swayed for an instant, then he fell backward like a tree and landed with a slap in the mud. He lay there quivering with his eyes rolled up into his head.

We froze in horror.

"Oh, you utter fool!" I shouted, coming to life. "What have you done?" Albert and Murdo were backing away, pale and speechless. I stumbled over to Meeks and dropped down on my knees beside him. I meant to find his pulse, but as my hands were shackled behind my back I was obliged to thrust my face up against his bristly neck and feel for it with my cheek. He was filthy and he reeked of gin.

Lightning flashed, closer now. Big drops of rain began to fall.

"Steady, Mister Murdo. Steady," Radan cautioned, pointing the blade at him. "Don't take another step. I can kill you where you stand. The lightning is close by."

Murdo froze, trembling.

"Take hold of Doctor Gray."

"Why—what's this?" Albert cried. Murdo grabbed his arms and crossed them roughly behind his back.

"Doctor Gray," Radan said loftily, "your employment is hereby withdrawn also. Sir Walter is feeling quite well, and the well have no need for a physician."

Albert struggled frantically in Murdo's grip. "N—no! Stop!" he jabbered. "The jawbone, remember? I m-mean to help you find the jawbone! Just as we agreed, Mister Radan!"

Radan smiled serenely. "But I don't *need* the jawbone now, Albert," he said. "Our agreement was void from the moment Doctor Scott opened that seal."

"But that wasn't *my* fault!" Albert wailed. Radan clucked and shook his head. "I am truly sorry, Albert," he said, "but we've nothing further to discuss."

"Stop this!" I screamed, staggering up onto my feet. "Stop this at once!"

Radan levelled the blade like a pistol. He aimed at Albert's heart just as the lightning flashed again.

I felt a shock in the air like a cannon, only there was no sound. Albert shuddered once, and then his body hung limp in Murdo's arms.

"Run, Fitzhugh!" I sobbed.

233

I turned and blundered straight into the pond with no better idea than to simply get away. Radan shouted something. A light shock ran through me but I floundered on into chest-high water. Then I flopped over onto my back, bucking and squirming backward through the mud and reeds.

"It's no use, Doctor," Radan called after me. "Even if you *don't* drown, I'll only be waiting for you on the other side." He splashed excitedly into the mud. Radan was gripping the copper blade near the middle as he lifted his face toward the darkening sky.

He screamed and writhed.

Blue sparks sizzled where the muddy water touched Radan's boots. The copper blade dropped out of his hand. Radan's knees buckled, and he sat backward with a splash. Then I felt the water up around my neck. I fought to keep my head back. The mud was sucking at my legs. I sank deeper as I struggled.

"Help!" I screamed wildly. "Fitzhugh! Help!"

My hands came up against something thin and taut. I grabbed it and pushed down desperately, fighting to keep my mouth out of the water. I thought I heard a woman's voice call *Hi! Getup!* There was a gentle tug. I sucked in a breath that was half pondwater. Then I felt another tug, slightly harder. Agonizingly slow, it started to pull me back and upward. There was a vile sucking noise as I rose out of the mud. Then I was being dragged backward across the flattened reeds. My feet tripped over firm ground. Sobbing like a child, I let go what I knew was the tailboard chain of our old post carriage. The mares, with mud-smeared flanks, were heaving on the bank. I sank down on my knees.

"Oh, Elizabeth!" I gasped. "Elizabeth! Thank God!"

"What are we going to do with him?"

Elizabeth asked this. Late-afternoon sun was breaking though the clouds, turning the last drops of the uncanny rainstorm into gold. Radan lay on his back. His eyes were closed but he was still breathing in quick, shallow gasps.

"Drown the blagg'rd in the pond! That's my vote," Fitzhugh growled. He was rubbing his wrists, which were all chafed and bloody.

"Thank goodness Radan had the key and not Murdo!" I said. I looked all around. "Where *is* Murdo."

"Oh, he ran like a hare," said Fitzhugh. "I never saw a big man run so fast. He took Radan's carriage and drove off in it like he was the devil's own coachman."

I looked down at Radan. I was remembering his eager expression when he splashed into the pond behind me, like a terrier on a rat.

"We-ell—" I said slowly, considering.

"Why, what do *you* think we should do?" I asked suddenly, turning to Elizabeth.

Elizabeth frowned thoughtfully.

"I think we should go through his pockets first of all," she said decidedly. "Take whatever he's got."

"My dear Mrs. McRoy!" I gasped. "Are we thieves?"

"This is no time for scruples, Stewart," Elizabeth answered firmly. "The man tried to kill you twice. And besides: we'll need money to hire a boat. Doctor Gray isn't going to be withdrawing funds again."

"Poor Albert!" I choked, wiping my eyes. I looked at where his body lay: a lumpy shape underneath our carriage blanket, which was the only thing we could find to cover him.

"This was my doing," I said miserably. "I pushed him too far. I've known him since he was practically a boy. I never thought I'd be the death of him." I hid my face in my hands.

Elizabeth gave my arm a warm squeeze.

"You couldn't have known, Stewart," she said gently. "And you still don't know. None of us knows how this will end. But we've got to play our parts now, haven't we—Willie?" Elizabeth called.

"Aye."

"Willie, I'm afraid you've got to turn out Mister Radan's and Doctor Gray's pockets, and Meeks' pockets as well. Keep anything we can spend or pawn."

"Elizabeth! Really!"

"Well it's got to look like a proper robbery, Stewart," Elizabeth returned, "to keep the police distracted."

"But the police will think *we* robbed them."

"Well—" Elizabeth hesitated, "we *are* robbing them, I'm afraid, so that would be right, and—and who ever heard of the police getting *anything* right?" she finished (a little brightly). "This is England, Stewart."

"I think we're on the Scottish side," I said gloomily.

"They'll never make sense of this," said Elizabeth, "and while the authorities are sorting it out we'll be hidden in the Hebrides."

"So Radan gets to live?" Fitzhugh growled. He was kneeling next to Albert's body and rummaging around inside his waistcoat.

"Well he might die yet—" Elizabeth poked Radan inquisitively with her foot. "He doesn't look very— Why are you kneeling, Stewart? You aren't going to try to *revive* him, are you?"

"Oh, I suppose I must," I sighed. "Hippocratic oath and all that. Can't say my heart is in it. You might want to turn away, madam. The Amsterdam Method isn't very pretty."

"I've come up with five pounds three shillings sixpence so far," Fitzhugh called, "and—ah—"

Fitzhugh stood up with an uncomfortable expression.

"—and his watch."

Fitzhugh held up an expensive gold repeater on a chain.

"He's about your size, dear," Elizabeth advised. "We ought to get his coat and his boots as well. There isn't going to be a haberdashery in Iona."

"Oh, good Lord!" I groaned. "His boots!" I rubbed my temples despairingly. "Well I'm not seeing so much as a twitch from this one," I said, getting up from Radan. "He's comatose for sure."

"Then he won't mind me going through his coat," Fitzhugh said, coming over.

"And then what?" I asked. "Leave him to the wind and the rain? He's freezing cold already. We'd be kinder to kill him outright."

"I—I have a notion what we might do," Elizabeth said cautiously.

"And what's that?"

"Oh—never you mind about it, Stewart. You don't look well yourself, dearie. Why don't you retire to the coach and rest a bit—good heavens! The things you've been through today. To think you were nearly drowned!"

The sun was going down when we finally crossed the little wooden bridge and turned out onto the main road. The horses' legs made long, spidery shadows across the fields. The sky was all ablaze where the setting sun turned the wispy clouds to fire. Fitzhugh was back on the box. I had taken my place inside the coach, where I resumed bobbing from window to window again, furtively turning up the edges of the curtains and peeking outside. Elizabeth sighed resignedly and folded her hands in her lap.

"We must get you a wash, dearie," she commented. "It smells of bog in here."

"Smells of smoke, too."

Away behind us a thick plume was rising, dark-gray, levelled off just above the hilltops where the steady westerly breeze cut through it.

"It *does* smell of smoke," said Elizabeth. "I'm surprised. Well—" She took out a hairpin and adjusted her bonnet. "—the weather *has* been dry. The fire spread to the thatch rather quicker than we expec—"

I dropped the curtain. "The—the *fire?*" I squawked. "What fi—oh dear God! Did you set the barn on fire?"

"The barn, aye, and the cottage." Fitzhugh's voice came dimly from overhead.

"Well the hayrick was up against the barn, you see," Elizabeth explained sweetly, "and—well—once the barn took fire we thought we might as well make a thorough job of it. We want Radan discovered, now don't we?"

From across the fields there came the urgent clanging of a bell.

"Reckon they found him already," Fitzhugh remarked. The roof creaked as he shifted his weight up on the box. "Hi! Gettup!" Fitzhugh snapped the reins.

"O-oh!" I moaned, sinking my head into my hands. "Oh, I am a wanted criminal now!"

"There, there, dear." Elizabeth patted my shoulder. "You were a wanted criminal anyway. And besides: it's rather exciting, isn't it?" She giggled. "Why, it's three hundred years since a brave knight of Wemyss burned a defenseless little English farm."

"And robbed an Englishman," Fitzhugh added from the box.

I smiled ruefully.

"You're sure the cottage was empty?"

"Empty." Fitzhugh said decidedly. "Miserable little hut. Worse than the barn. No human ought to live in a kennel like that. Meant for some of the duke's lucky tenants, no doubt. Radan's gang must have gone to ground in it. There were hot ashes in the hearth. Reeked of Murdo."

"No priest-hole?" I ventured. "No trap-door under the floor?"

"No floor!" Fitzhugh returned. "Just dirt. Same as the barn."

"I can't imagine Radan was staying *there*," I mused. "He would have gotten decent lodgings for himself in town. Did you see how he kept his boots? But Albert—Albert was waiting for us. He might have spent a fortnight there with Radan's footpads, all the while thinking he was bound for London and a private situation in a great house. Poor Albert! How could he have been so gullible?"

"Some people prefer a pretty lie to an ugly truth," Fitzhugh observed.

"We won't speak ill of the dead," said Elizabeth, "but I must say, it was his choice to make a secret arrangement with Mr. Radan."

"Yes," I said sadly, "When you dance with the devil, it's the devil calls the tune, my old gran used to say."

"You remember Radan tried the same trick on me?" Fitzhugh called down. "Said the duke was ready to give me my old job back, hey? If I'd 'a' said yes, I'd probably be dead now."

I shuddered.

"Yes. Probably."

"And whatever did he mean about—was it a jawbone?" Fitzhugh pursued. "And Doctor Gray going to help him find it?"

"I couldn't hazard a guess."

Elizabeth pulled Radan's oilcloth satchel up from under the seat. She took out *John Blackjohn* and handed it to me. I felt an urge to hug it to my chest, but as Elizabeth was watching I had to forbear.

"Could be there's a jawbone somewhere with a tooth that unlocks the back seal?" Elizabeth suggested.

"Could be." I opened the book and turned to the new-found copper plate in the middle. "I can't imagine what would open this smaller one, though. It hasn't got a keyhole. Or any kind of hole whatever. And anyway, before Albert was, was gone, Radan said he didn't even need the jawbone anymore."

"Maybe Radan already found whatever he was looking for," said Elizabeth. "He had the book for more than an hour."

I thumbed the pages jealously. "Yes, and it isn't fair," I complained. "I've been so busy just making out the words that I haven't had a chance to truly read it. Radan said his arrangement with Albert was void from the moment we opened the seal, so it would have to be something we uncovered lately."

I turned the pages and studied them suspiciously in the fading light.

"Here's an *Iona* he might have read, and here's a *Doonbridge*—good heavens!" I exclaimed, glancing up. "In all this tragedy and confusion I entirely forgot!"

I took Elizabeth's hand, and, looking into her face, I kissed it with as much gallantry as I could muster considering I was wet through and covered in stinking mud.

"I thank you, madame," I said with real emotion. "You saved me from a death most horrible. How did you ever find us?"

Elizabeth laughed and ducked a little curtsey. "Ridiculous men!" she said. "You all think an old woman is daft and harmless."

Overhead Fitzhugh roared with laughter, making the ceiling creak again. "I've thought you daft from time to time, Lizzie," he called, "but I've never accused you of being harmless."

Elizabeth giggled in her girlish way. "We were raised on a good farm in Cheswick," she explained. "Willie was our father's only boy. I can plow a field as easy as bake a pie. I can certainly drive a pair of old nags like these."

"She was a terror," Fitzhugh called. "I don't think I bested her at anything before I was twelve. Ask her about the plum tree."

Elizabeth coughed and reddened (disarmingly, I thought).

"Well I tried to hold onto the book," she said hurriedly, "only that Mr. Radan jerked it away from me and he called me a—"

She stopped.

Then the coach stopped.

"Called you a *what?*" Fitzhugh thundered overhead.

239

"Ah—nothing, Willie. It's no matter. After all, Radan might be dead by now anyway."

"Ye-ess," Fitzhugh snarled. "He *might* be dead. And if we go back now, I can make certain he *is* dead."

Elizabeth opened the window and put out her head. "No, no. It's alright, Willie," she soothed. "The plan was to drive on while the day lasts. Please, Willie? I'd rather sleep in the inn at Bearsden than in the gaol at Glasgow."

We waited. Across the fields the bell clanged—now high, now low—as the sound carried on the wind. The left-hand mare puffed and jingled her traces. No sound came from the box.

At last we heard Fitzhugh say *Gettup!* in a strangled voice and the coach-wheels began to creak again.

"God *damn* him!" Fitzhugh shouted. "We're going to be sorry we didn't kill him!"

"Like as not, my friend," I answered. "Like as not.

"So Radan took the book and let you go?" I asked Elizabeth in a lower voice.

"Well he wasn't going to let me go—not at first." Elizabeth said quietly. She made a wry smile. "It was rather drole. They didn't know what to do with a woman. Radan said *Get the fetters*, and he meant for Murdo to shackle me along with you two, but— You know, I rather fancy Mr. Murdo, really," she laughed. "He blushed like a schoolboy—all sixteen stone of him. He was ashamed to touch me, so Radan said *Oh, let the*—ahem!" Elizabeth coughed. "He said, *Let her go. She's mad anyway.* So Radan got up on the box and Murdo played the footman. He's tall enough for it, isn't he? And away you all went."

"They just left you with our coach and pair?"

"Well I don't think they wanted them. The spy—did you say his name was Meeks?—he poked his head underneath for a look at the springs, and he just laughed. They left me there by the side of the road like a lady scorned."

"Then—then how did you find us?" I asked in wonder.

"I followed you, of course."

"You just climbed up and drove?"

"My goodness, Stewart, it isn't a chariot! I must say—I didn't much like this coach at first, but the disreputable look of it was a godsend. I just pulled that old shawl up over my head and people must have thought I was a gypsy or a washerwoman or something. No one stopped me or hailed me, and before long we were out of Glasgow anyway. I kept Radan's carriage just within sight, and Murdo—well I don't think he looked behind him once."

"And you came all the way to the farm? Why, whatever did you mean to do once you got there?"

"Well I'd really no idea, Stewart, but I had to do *something*. I had a notion of maybe turning Radan's horses loose or letting you two out of the carriage, but then it started pouring rain out of a clear sky, and when I came upon the hollow there was Doctor Gray lying dead and Mister Radan charging around with a rusty dagger like some sort of cutthroat."

"The blade!" I groaned. "The copper blade! I forgot about that too. We should have taken it. I didn't see it near him."

"Nor I," grunted Fitzhugh (who had evidently been listening).

"No, it would be lying in the pond," I said, "where he was before you dragged him out."

"I don't think it would have been any use looking," said Elizabeth. "That was a terrible mire. I only just spied your muddy head sticking up out of the water, Stewart. I had to run the mares down the brae, turn them, and back them straight into the pond."

"Turn them and—b-*back* them?" I gibbered. "My word! How ever did you accomplish that so quick? Why, Fitzhugh and I spent half-an-hour trying to—" (I was remembering the night in Berwick when we'd trod the dead constable's hand into the mud.) "Pshaw!" said Elizabeth airily. "That was nothing. Now, running them down the brae—*that* was a trick. I thought the coach would shake all to pieces, and the mares can't be bothered to hurry, you know."

"Aye," Fitzhugh rejoined from overhead. He snapped the reins.

"The coach was half floating," Elizabeth said. "I thought I might reach out the back window and pull you in. But when I looked behind I saw you already had hold of the tailboard, so I simply struck up the mares and out you came."

"Mrs. McRoy," I said humbly, "you're a marvel. I haven't words to thank you."

"Oh, nonsense!" Elizabeth scoffed. "Truly nothing. Good heavens, I was worried sick about you! Come sit on my side. Light the lantern and let's see if we can guess what Mr. Radan Esquire might have been reading on the way up from Glasgow."

"You don't mind the smell?"

"I *do* mind. Come across anyway. I can't read *John Blackjohn* upside-down."

I lit the little oil lantern that swung from a nail in the low ceiling. Then I squeezed in next to Elizabeth and opened *John Blackjohn* in front of us on the opposite seat. I took out my magnifying glass and squinted at the faint, blocky text in the shifting light.

"There's 'whale', I said, "clear as day."

"And here's *Intrate per angustam portam*," said Elizabeth. "A lawyer ought to read Latin, don't you think?"

I turned to her.

"I confess I'm very glad you came, Elizabeth."

(I said it low, that Fitzhugh might not hear.)

"Well," Elizabeth returned quietly, "you knights of Wemyss *do* need a lot of rescuing."

And she laid her head ever-so-slightly on my shoulder.

CHAPTER 25

Doctor Scott's transcription—

Nota Bene—I was about to commence with "My dear Doctor Gray" and then I remembered I shall not be writing to Albert again. I can't get used to the idea of him gone, nor can I stop blaming myself for his death, though Elizabeth says I must. What did they do with the body when they found him, I wonder? Will he be interred in Dalkeith, where his family lie? To think that I cannot so much as pay my last respects to the young man who came to me so eager and full of ambition, and went away the victim of such treachery, with bitterness toward me in his last breath. I confess I begin to hate John Blackjohn, *even as at times I have loved it. That I, an amateur, should stumble upon a work of such historical importance—it gave me the keenest delight at first. Yet since April nothing but misery has flowed from it. Elizabeth is right, though: the water is deep now. There's no safety in turning back. We must swim for the Other Shore.*

A few pages from a different parchment have been stuck into the book. From the handwriting it is clear they are the work of another scribe—possibly the friar Kollam Keeli. But first James McKenna continues:

We buried Peter, but a strange thing happened first.

We were all standing there, gathered around Peter's body on the table. No one was speaking and it was all very still when suddenly boatswain McKee came thundering down the hatch shouting *The dolphins are gathered! The dolphins are gathered!*

"What d'ye mean *gathered?*" Blackjohn snapped, irritated by the intrusion.

"Come and see for yourself, Captain!"

Blackjohn followed him up the hatch. Friar Kol put his arm around my shoulders. "Come, lad," he said, "I know you're grieving, but let's go find out what this means."

The dolphins *were* gathered. Thirty mated pairs of them with their little ones around. They kept a neat formation behind the stern, arching their shiny backs across the swells with hardly a ripple.

"Clan Tonvacha!" I cried, startled out of my grief. "They're here!"

A big gray dolphin came along the starboard side.

"Ah, that'd be Mórester," said Blackjohn. "I remember that scar on her back." Mórester rose straight up out of the water. She turned her head this way and that, eyeing the row of curious faces gathered along the rail.

"She looks as if she could speak!" Finn said with wonder.

"She *can* speak," Kol returned. "If only Lily were here! James, do you have any idea where Lily might have gone?"

"No," I answered. "She never said a word. She just jumped off the ship. Maybe she *is* here," I said hopefully. "Maybe Lily's words will come out of Mórester again this time."

Mórester weaved her snout from side to side as if she heard me. She flipped her tail and dove headfirst into the sea, then rising up on her tail again she opened her pearly-pink mouth and gave a chattery squeak.

"It's Mórester alone now," said Diana. "Lily is gone."

"Can you understand her?" I asked. (I was beginning to think Diana might be able to do practically anything.)

"I—I can try," said Diana. "Mórester's voice isn't meant to go through air. *Seinn còmhla!*" she called, and she sang a few notes which set my hair on end, though they were quiet and there didn't seem to be any words in them. Mórester turned over once like a wheel and then she stood high out of the water, wriggling with obvious excitement. She squeaked and chattered a while, waving her fins, while Diana put in a word here and a note there. Finally Mórester made a long leap and disappeared beneath the waves. I ran to the stern. Clan Tonvacha were gone. The sea was empty as before.

"Did she say where Lily went?" I asked eagerly.

Diana shook her head.

"I didn't understand everything, but it sounded like Mórester spoke to Lily about an hour ago. I think she's done with us, James. Forever this time."

Kol looked stricken. "And we only just got her back!" he said in an anguished voice. "Ah, well. For my sins, I suppose." He hung his head. "The Lord giveth, the Lord taketh away."

Diana looked at Kol with unmistakable sympathy.

"Mórester doesn't know where Lily went," she said quietly, "but Lily gave us a gift at parting—gave *you* a gift, Kollam. Mórester knows the way to Doonbridge and Lily asked her to lead us there. She wants you to be safe."

"Does she? God bless her!" Kol cried hoarsely, wiping his eyes on his sleeve.

"Blood and zounds!" Blackjohn exclaimed. "Am I to see Doonbridge at last?" He thumbed the fine gold chain at his neck.

"Poor Lily!" said Kol. "Who can blame her for leaving? And she hasn't got a home now. Her beautiful Lilylock is ruined. And to think she could still be living there peacefully if only—"

"If only I hadn't thrown a rock at the Black Stag," I said glumly.

"Trim the main!" (Blackjohn was flush with excitement.) "She's luffing! All hands to stations! We're following the dolphins."

"Dolphins on port!" Ronne called from the foredeck.

Clan Tonvacha surfaced ahead of us, keeping a tight V in front of our bow. Mórester was in the lead. She rose up and looked back, then she spun neatly on her tail and plunged into the sea.

"I'm sorry about your brother, lad," said Blackjohn, his hand on my shoulder. "We'll get to burying him presently, but for now we've got to fly." He stalked off shouting orders. The crew scattered to their stations. Diana, Kol and I were left by the bowsprit, watching the dolphins' silvery backs arch across the waves.

Kol turned to leave, but Diana touched him lightly on the arm.

"There was one other thing," Diana said.

Kol looked at her.

"Lily said she loves you, and she will love you forever."

We hadn't been following the dolphins long when the strange fog set in again. Sunset was still hours away but suddenly it got so dark I could barely see the foremast from the stern. Kol hung a lantern over the helm to show where it was in the gloom. He hung another near the bowsprit, and in its circle I could just make out the gleam of the nearest dolphin arching rhythmically along. Mórester and the vanguard were out of sight.

"Ready about!" shouted Blackjohn. "We're near the coast now, lad," he said to me. "I can feel it in the waves."

"*Can* you?"

"Aye. They change shape when they pile up against the land. It's a strange tide that's running. Coming in high and fast. Topsails are down and we're still racing on with it. Er-r—" Blackjohn looked at me quizzically— "And just how badly did y' offend the mermaid this time?"

"How badly did I *what*?"

"The mermaid," said Blackjohn. "Lily, I mean. You don't reckon she was so angry she might—say—tell her dolphins to run us aground, would she? Lead us onto the shoals just to get even?"

"*I* didn't offend her!" I said hotly. "Or—not *this* time, anyway. It was Peter. Well, it was Peter and I both. We might have accidentally got her enslaved to the Black Stag, but—"

Then I thought of Peter and I couldn't talk anymore. It felt like I was going to cry.

"There, there, laddie," Blackjohn said kindly. "It's a hard thing to lose a brother. I only ask because—well—because the mermaid was nigh on sixty feet tall when I watched her snatch you off the deck, and now I'm running eight knots blind into a bewitched fog with the shoals getting near. I just thought—"

He took his hat off and ran his fingers through his hair.

"—thought I might go confess to brother Kollam is all. But ah well! Won't be anyone left to say prayers for me on *this* boat." Blackjohn pushed his hat down tight and scowled resolutely into the fog. Just then a dolphin stuck its head out of the water on the port side. It gave us a blank stare as it drifted past. The reflection of Kol's lantern glinted in its shiny black eye.

"Dolphins breaking ranks!" Ronne called from the bow.

"Drop sails!" Blackjohn shouted. "Not a rag on her except the jib! Ready anchor and out sweeps. Oh-h—" he called to me—"*now* we find out if the mermaid forgives you, boy!"

A breeze sprang up astern and the fog cleared a little. It went on clearing while the crew wrestled the sweeps into the locks. We waited in tense silence. The dolphins drifted, keeping to the surface, a little thicket of fins standing black and rigid out of the water. Neither man nor creature made a sound. Everything was motionless—the sea, the *Otter*, the dolphins all around— frozen inside a little circle of gray light.

Then the dolphins disappeared.

"Rocks!" Ronne shouted.

"Back her!" Blackjohn bellowed. "Set sweeps! Back her!"

We manned the long oars that stretched from the rail all the way to the sea. Finn took the helm from Blackjohn, who went charging forward to the bow. "Hard on the port side!" Finn shouted. "Hard on port! She's turning!"

The breeze quickened and the air cleared more. Now we could see a sheer headland standing black and hard out of the fog no more than a quarter-mile away. Waves broke on the invisible shoals, casting plumes of white spray into the air. Blackjohn came rushing back, Friar Kol beside him.

"Wide inlet to port, narrow one to starboard!" Blackjohn panted, taking the wheel from Finn. "A hellish lot of spray in front of the narrow one."

"It's a test of faith, of course," Kol said matter-of-factly. "*Intrate per angustam portam.* That was what you wrote."

Blackjohn heaved a desperate sigh. "I'm not a man of faith, brother. You know that. Am but a simple sailor," (he smiled ruefully) "trying to earn his bread by piracy. Ah well! I suppose I might die alongside a priest. That ought to count for something."

"Good man!" Kol thumped him on the back. "Give the order! I tell you, we'll be through it in no time."

"Hold on, hold on!" Blackjohn growled. "God gave me a brain. I think he meant for me to use it. Let's match our speed to the waves. Sweeps in!"

"Sweeps in!" Finn shouted.

"Pull!"

We all dug in, trying our best to pull together. Ronne and I manned the sweep amidships on the port side. He was bigger than me and he seemed to know what he was doing, so I did my best not to tread on his feet.

"And pull!"

The swell picked us up and carried us forward at a great speed. Strange eddies swirled alongside the hull, evidence of the unseen rocks below. Foam shot skyward as we drew nearer the shoals.

"Aaa-nd *pull*!"

I felt the shock in my hands as our sweep hit a rock not ten feet from the port side. "Hard on starboard!" Finn shouted. "Hard on starboard! She's turning again." A towering stack of weathered rock slid by so close I thought it would catch the yards. The sea heaved around its feet and the white water ran off in torrents. The startled gulls and gannets took to the air with wild cries as our rigging swept past their nests.

"And *pull*!"

"There's a narrow opening!" Diana called back from the prow. "Catch a wave and it might carry us through!"

"Hold water!" Blackjohn bellowed. He gripped the wheel with white knuckles, watching over his shoulder for the oncoming swell. "Ho-old, I say—"

"PULL!"

The swell picked us up and we surged forward.

"Sweeps in! Sweeps in, me darlings!" Blackjohn sang. "Oh, ye're bound for the bottom now, me loves! Did brother Kollam shrive ye?"

My heart was pounding. White foam exploded all around. The Otter's keel touched bottom and she shuddered through every timber. The black wall loomed up—

Then all at once we were through. The waves burst angrily behind us, clawing at the empty gap. Through the lifting fog we could see a calm little bay opening wide on either hand. The *Otter* bobbed in glassy swells.

"HA HA!" Blackjohn roared, laughing and sobbing at the same time. "Ha ha! If ever a camel went through a needle's eye 't was the *Otter*, brother Kol. Hardly a scratch on her! Furl the jib, Ronne, me love. Drop anchor,

McKee. Man the pump, Jamie-boy. We'll lie up here and tremble a while 'til the fog clears."

BOOM.

A gray streak snarled through the air.

I turned.

Captain Blackjohn was sitting on the deck.

Blackjohn's back was against the mainmast. His eyes were calm, looking straight ahead. A big iron hook like a harpoon was buried in his stomach. Threads of blood trailed out of his mouth. From a shaft behind the hook a thin, steely cord ran straight and taut down the length of the Otter and across the stern, where it disappeared into the fog.

Blackjohn tilted his head to one side and looked down.

"A balliste," he said. "Now that's clever!"

Then he closed his eyes.

It felt like I was running underwater.

"Cut the line!" Kol screamed. The deck was all confusion. The *Otter* bucked and her prow shot up. Finn attacked the cord with his cutlass but his blade sprang off it like a bowstring. To stern the mist swirled and parted. Black sails showed through the gap in the headland. The *Raven* rode proudly behind us on the other side of the shoals. The cruel gray line ran straight to her bow, where cannon-smoke still lingered. Her sweeps were out. From her deck the evil voices rose wild above the roar of the breaking waves.

Blackjohn's arms hung at his sides, palms open to the sky. His bloody chin made a red smear across his chest as his head rolled back and forth. The hook had gone straight through his body and deep and into the mainmast. A brisk land breeze drove us backward while the Raven dug in her sweeps, pulling us toward the rocks.

"I can't cut the line!" Finn shouted. "It's bewitched!"

"Diana, do something!" Kol wailed.

Diana took the cord with both hands. She winced as if it burned her, but she held on.

"*Ta sé briste!*" Diana commanded.

249

"*Ta sé BRISTE!*" Her voice rose to a scream. Blood showed in the creases of her clenched fists. The black teeth of the shoal were hardly a sweep's-length from the stern. The *Otter* dropped with a swell. I felt the sickening shudder as her keel grazed the bottom.

"*BRISTE!*"

The seabirds rose up from the cliffs in a screaming cloud.

We were cowering where we stood, covering our ears. The cord snapped back across the stern with a vicious whine. For a moment the *Raven*'s deck was silent.

"Fend off! Fend off!" McKee came to life. "Fend off! We're running aground!"

I grabbed one of the clumsy sweeps. It was about twenty feet long and so heavy that without Ronne to help me I couldn't get it back into the lock. So I started poling it out across the rail hand-over-hand, in the stupid hope that I might lodge it against the rocks somehow.

In an instant I was doubled over the side, fighting to stay on the ship while the sweep dragged me toward the water. The rail dug into my stomach. *Ronne!* I screamed, and then the sweep slipped my grasp and disappeared into the foam.

"Filthy bastard oar!" I shouted into the swirling water. "Filthy bastard oar be damn—"

I stopped.

The water had gone black.

Huge black wings spread wide beneath us, shooting out across the bay. The wings drew in. At once a mighty surge ran through the ship. I felt it come out of the deck and push up into my feet. The *Otter* shot forward. The wind of our speed rushed against my face. I staggered back and clung onto the shrouds. Looking behind I saw a massive gray ridge break the surface, big as a jibsail. With a *boom* it crashed into the sea in a white tower of foam.

"Holy saints!" Kol shouted. "What's it—*carrying* us?"

The *Raven* and the shoals faded back into the mist. Up ahead a little rocky island was flying toward us. I could see a small lighthouse, and beside it a little stone quay. Then I felt the deck drop under my feet, and with an offended *creak* the *Otter* sank back into the bay. Like a sunrise the water all around us turned green again. The monstrous black shape vanished as suddenly as it came.

"I don't believe it!" Kol gasped. "We go through the narrow gate and we're saved by—was that a *whale*? Why, Eoin, that's precisely what—"

And then Kol started to cry.

"Eoin?" he called, lifting Blackjohn's bloody chin in his hands. "Eoin, my brother? It is I. Your old friend Kollam."

The *Otter* rode gently at anchor. We were gathered in Captain Blackjohn's saloon again, only now it was Blackjohn on the table. Peter's body was on the divan, wrapped in the woolen blanket and tied up with sail-rope. Through the broken windows I could just make out smoke rising from a little village across the water. Gray roofs and chimneys clustered up against the shore like a clump of toadstools.

"Diana?" Kol asked. He looked into her face pleadingly. Diana shook her head. She stood tall and stately over Blackjohn. She didn't seem like a girl anymore. She was beautiful. Her fierce eyes burned deep in the pale sculpture of her face. Her neck was long and slender and her high forehead was crowned with a dark waterfall of hair. It was a forbidding sort of beauty—like a queen, I thought, or an angel. I drew back from her a step and kept my eyes on the ground.

"He is slipping through, Kollam," Diana said. "His time has come. We must let him go."

"But I'd something more to say to him!"

"He knows, Kollam."

I was staring down miserably at my stomach when I noticed a familiar sparkle.

"My fairy glass!" I cried out.

Everyone turned to look at me. I reddened. "I—I just remembered I'm still wearing your fairy glass, Friar Kol," I stammered. "Lily used to be in it. She's gone now, but half the elixir of Saint John's flower was in it too, and you said—"

"Give that to me!"

Kol thrust out his hand. I took off the fairy glass and handed it to him. Kol quickly turned down the blanket covering Blackjohn's body. Blackjohn was bare from the waist up. A ragged hole defiled his left side. Blood filled it to the brim, level with his deathly white skin. Friar Kol pulled the little cork out of the green vial. He carefully poured what was left of the liquid into Blackjohn's wound.

We waited.

Blackjohn stirred. His lips moved, and then his eyelids opened. He lay still as a corpse, but his eyes roamed the circle of faces gathered around him, resting on each in turn.

"Eoin?" Friar Kol asked breathlessly. "Can you hear me, Eoin?"

"Pen and parchment."

"What?"

"Pen. And. *Parchment!*" Blackjohn snapped. His voice was faint but clear. "Fetch that parchment from the escritoire. You must take down my will before I'm gone."

Friar Kol slapped a gray roll down on the table next to Blackjohn's waist.

"Speak, my friend!"

Blackjohn closed his eyes.

"I haven't got much time."

"Do you hurt?" Kol asked anxiously, rubbing Blackjohn's limp hand.

"No. Yes. It's no matter," Blackjohn returned. "I can't move my head. Stand where I can see you. This is for my son. You must deliver this to my son."

"You have a *son?*" I blurted (forgetting the solemnity of the moment).

"Aye!"

Blackjohn closed his eyes, but tears crept out through their shuttered lids.

"Aye. I left my boy in Doonbridge and now I won't get to see him again. This will be his patrimony—my Last Will and Testament."

CHAPTER 26

Captain Blackjohn's account, being his **LAST WILL and TESTAMENT,** *as faithfully recorded by Friar Kollam Keeli aboard the brig* **Otter** *on the twenty-third day of September,* **Anno Domini** *fifteen hundred and ninety-three:*

I, EOIN mac DIARMID, being of sound mind and unsound body, do hereby set forth my LAST WILL and TESTAMENT.

WITNESSETH Brother Kollam Keeli, and master Obadias Finn, acting captain of the *Otter*.

I only have a moment, my friends.

Now don't you protest, Kollam. The fairy lady is right—my time has come. Yes, James, I heard Diana. Try not to interrupt a dying man. I have something important to say before I go. When I took that damned hook through the middle it was like a doorway opened up in my mind. I remember Doonbridge like it was yesterday. You must write my will, Kollam, and take it to my son.

Yes, and thank'ee, my old friend.

I left my son in Doonbridge. He was four years old. He ought to be about your age now, James, if he's alive. It was kind of you not to bring him up, Kollam. He's the one thing I could always remember about the place. I never forgot my boy, though I forgot all else. He was etched in my heart—his little face; his little voice. But like a fool I went off seeking treasure, and I left the treasure I had behind.

You've heard how when Rudd Gallowglass left me to die, two fisherman found me clinging to the rocks, yes? Aye, they knocked me on the head with an oar and brought me to Doonbridge. First a dyer took me in. He was a good man. He saw me married to his daughter—and right quickly, that. That's the Doonbridgers' way. New folk are very rare. Sometimes they take a man in the space of ten years, and sometimes it's twenty years go by without an Outsider joining the village. You can't reach Doonbridge by land. They only get newcomers from shipwrecks, the shoals being treacherous hereabouts. The Doonbridgers don't want to be known to the world. Once a man comes to Doonbridge, he never leaves again.

None but me.

My wife, she was a good girl. She was very young when we married. They speak strangely in Doonbridge, but I could make her understand me well enough, me knowing both the Irish and the Scots. We hadn't much to talk about anyway. She'd never seen the world outside the village—not so much as even a ship or a church. She was barren, I think, for when a year went by and still we had no child then the village Elders had me married to another woman as well. Yes, James, I had two wives. I won't spend my last moment on This Side explaining it to you. Hasn't the boy ever kept sheep, Kollam? He has? Then he ought to understand. The village needed a child, so a child they got. My second wife bore a strong, chubby, ruddy, brave little—

[*Whereupon Eoin mac Diarmid was overcome by his wounds, and required a moment to recover himself.* —KK]

As I was saying. So Meg had a boy and I named him Padraig after the holy saint, for they have neither church nor calendar and I couldn't tell on what day he was born. In the spring it was, and oh! how I loved him! Strange to think that I could ever leave him. But Doonbridge is narrow and altogether hemmed in by the bay. The fields are few. There isn't any forest or even so much as a running stream. I was still a young man. The dyer's work was tedious and I longed for the freedom of the open sea. My son was about four years old when I made myself a sealskin coracle, and of an evening I'd go out fishing on the bay, as far from the village as one might go. I'd row out to a spot where I could climb the cliffs high enough to gaze out across the sea. Night after night I perched there on the rocks like a gull, watching for a sail.

Now the odd thing is (mark me well, brother Kollam) there are three gates out of Doonbridge. There's the Narrow Gate—the *Gaeta Caol*. That's the gap that cuts through the headland, with the treacherous *Gaeta Farsaing* next to it. The *Gaeta Farsaing* is a trap, brother, like you guessed; the Wide Gate will eat any ship that tries to go through it. The Narrow Gate will too, except for when the tide is high enough for your keel to clear the bottom. That's when the Doonbridgers say the gate is open: on a spring tide, or when a storm brings a flood.

But the third gate—the Sea-Pig Gate: it's on Lighthouse Rock in the middle of the bay. I don't precisely know where it goes—only it leads away from Doonbridge somehow, even though there's deep water all around it. The Gatekeepers are Elders of great importance. The Sea-Pig Gate is only open once in every hundred years, and the Gatekeepers guard the key. Long ago the Bridge of Dùn led from the village fort to the lighthouse, where there was deep mooring for ships. That bridge is gone now, but you can still see the double file of stone arches standing broken out of the water. In ancient times the lords of MacLeod would march across the bridge in proud array to collect the yearly tribute of fighting men and silver, but these days the old Keeper rows a little skiff down the roofless corridor, where seabirds build their nests and barnacles gather. Then the Keeper climbs the lighthouse tower and stands alone beside the dead torch, watching the gates in silence.

So it chanced one evening in the cold and windy springtime that I rowed my coracle out across the bay. It was a storm tide and a mighty one, for the high-water stain on the rocks was well covered and the swells in the bay were rough. Still I labored through the waves until I came to the place where I could climb. I scaled the rocks in a stiff wind. The sky was getting dark, with ragged black clouds streaming down from the north. I clung there, shivering and looking out to sea.

Then I saw a light.

A ship was riding south! I could tell from her rigging she was a whaler, half-reefed and fighting to stay in the lee without getting too near the shoals. A kind of madness came over me. It was five years since I'd seen anything from the outside world.

She must have a chart! I said to myself. *They can mark the place. I'll come back to Doonbridge someday, and the Elders will let me in—how can they refuse? I'll take a berth,* I told myself. *I'll take a watch or two. I'll come back with silk for Meg and Gwinny and proper linen for little Paddy.* So I soothed my conscience with empty promises while I scrambled down the rocks and rowed like mad for the Narrow Gate.

The sea was rough, but the tide was running out and I had a land-breeze at my back. Between me and the *Gaeta Caol* stood the lighthouse on its rock, dark and desolate as ever.

Curse you! I shouted at it. *Curse you and your dead flame!*

But no sooner had I said the words 'dead flame' than a faint gleam shone out in the twilight.

Then I cursed again, for I remembered the old Keeper was on watch. In a moment I could see him standing on the dark quay, holding up a horn lantern and peering out across the water.

"Eoin!" he shouted. "Eoin mac Diarmid? 'T is thou, I know't. Whither goest in thy washtub, and in this dark and wind?"

"I'm going fishing, Father," I called back to him. "The lingcod come out at night. I'll be home presently."

"Art fevered, lad?" the old man replied. "Sound'st passionate and strange! Come and rest on the dock. My watch is nearly ended. We'll row back together."

Just then the setting sun dropped under the roof of grim clouds on the horizon. One last ray shone straight through the Gaeta Caol and touched the empty lighthouse, and for a moment the old stone tower shone pink as a rose. The Keeper turned and looked out to sea. Framed there in the gap rode the whaler, with the dying sun behind her.

"Nay, nay, lad!" the Keeper cried. "Surely thou'dst not be making for yonder brig?"

"Stay where you are old man!" I shouted. "I'll be a prisoner here no more." I was a stone's throw from the quay now and I could see the Keeper's craggy face in the sunset.

"Calm thyself, boy," the Keeper answered evenly. "Yon ship neither sees nor hears thee, and the sea is rough. Art a bird, hey? Canst catch her—what—in thine oyster-shell?"

Then despair welled up in my heart. You remember what it's like to be young, Kollam? Whole blessed world always hanging on a thread? I'd never wanted anything so desperately before—not even when Rudd Gallowglass left me to die out on that rock. To be free of Doonbridge. To be free of the wool-cards and the dye-vats and the oily stench of sheep. To wander green hills or sail the open seas again. I thought I was watching my one chance at happiness run out with the tide.

My coracle touched the quay. I tossed the line around the bollard and jumped out with my oar in my hand.

"True, Father," I said softly, "I can't catch her in my oyster shell. Shall we trade boats, you and me?" I pointed my oar at the Keeper's skiff, tied up against the quay. It was a good boat—light and sleek with a high seat and two long oars.

"Eoin, Eoin—" The old man shook his head gravely. "Thou know'st me. Old Hamish. Know'st I cannot do that! Come, lad," he said in a soothing voice. "I've seen this manner of madness before. 'T is common when we save a man from the rocks. Come back to Great-hall. The Elders will speak together how we may ease thy suffering, that the life in Doonbridge seem not so hard to thee."

While he spoke I watched the whaler—less than a half-mile distant—pass by the Gaeta Caol and disappear from sight.

"You saved me from the rocks," I shouted, "Why? To work me like a horse? Put me out to stud, and then—what?—d'ye mean to geld me?"

"Easy, boy," the Keeper raised his voice. "Should'st not speak to thine Elder thus. Remember, Doonbridge gave thee thy life."

"I remember Doonbridge gave me *this*," I snarled, and I swung my oar.

Kollam, I swear I never meant to hit him so hard. His legs buckled like they were broken. He just dropped onto his face and lay there with his arms at his sides. *Dear God!* I thought, *I've killed him!* I snatched up his lantern to look at him, and then I saw something gleaming on his collar. It was the beautiful gold chain he wore. All the Keepers had them. They were delicately wrought and the Keepers never took them off, though I didn't know why.

This is too fine a thing for Doonbridge! I thought. *I might need to buy my passage on the whaler, or I might need something for food and drink.* My thieving fingers were fumbling at the old man's throat. I took his gold chain and put it on. Then I untied his skiff. I stuck his lantern up near the prow and then I set to it, pulling like the devil was chasing me. It was a good skiff, I say.

Light and narrow. I was young and strong and I rowed in a sort of frenzy. The thrill of escape was humming in my head. I was only afraid the oars might break from the strain. I braced my feet against the thwart and threw in my back.

Thus I shot through the *Gaeta Caol* and took the first swell of the open sea. The shock of it went all through the skiff's slender frame. Her prow shot up and the lantern tumbled backward and went out. I watched over my shoulders right and left, fighting to keep the whaler in sight. It was nearly dark and I knew if I took a wave abeam it would roll me. Yet in the gloom I could still see the lamp swinging on the whaler's bow. She was tacking now, keeping clear of the coast as darkness came. My heart leapt within me, for I knew she'd slow when she came across the wind. I could already hear the faint ring of voices on deck. I lay back and pulled until the oars bent and the thwart creaked like it was going to break in two.

"Man overboard!" I screamed. "Ship ahoy! Man overboard!"

"*Wat de hel?*" cried someone on deck.

"Ship ahoy!"

I came up level with her stern and my oar glanced off her rudder. There was shouting on deck. The lamp unhooked itself from the bow and came swinging toward me. It stuck out across the stern rail and I saw a face squinting down.

"*Wa giêt der?*"[119]

"Lift! Lift!" I cried. "*Seeman oerboard! Fear dhan mhuir!*"

[*At that moment Eoin mac Diarmid was again overcome by his wounds. His eyes closed and we thought his spirit was fled, but presently he resumed speaking.* —KK]

The captain of the whaler, I say, was a Dutchman named van Groote, and he was happy enough to have me aboard. They'd lost three men in the Dogger Bank and they were short-handed. I told him I came from a merchantman who went down on the shoals. He didn't believe a word of it, but he gave me a berth anyway. The strange thing was, no sooner had I come aboard than the memory of Doonbridge started to fade—all but Padraig my son. I started to fancy I *had*

---

[119] Frisian: *Who goes there?*

come from a wrecked merchantman, just like I said. But suddenly the picture of little Paddy would come into my mind and I'd feel heartsick all at once. When the whaler put in at Iona I jumped ship. I was perplexed inside and I wanted to confess myself to a priest, though I hardly knew why. In those days the rumor of Rudd Gallowglass was everywhere, and Van Groote took fright and weighed anchor while I was looking after my soul at the monastery. By the time Brother Koll and I shipped off together all I could remember of Doonbridge was the name of the place and the image of my son.

So, quickly now, brother Kol. We'd best get on with it. Did you find the quills? Good. Now, then—

BY THESE PRESENTS BE IT KNOWN THAT I, Eoin Mac Diarmid, hereby bequeath to my Chief Mate, Obadias Finn, this my vessel named the *OTTER*, together with all ropes, canvas, ordnance, fixtures, and appurtenances thereof; AND

To Padraig mac Eoin, my son, I bequeath this the KEY to FAIRYLAND, which I wear, together with the gold chain to which it is affixed. Be it known that this is the key to the Apple Isle, a land undying where the soul may seek refuge and—

"That chain?" Kol interrupted. "That chain you're wearing, Eoin?"

"This chain, aye."

"And it holds— It holds the key to *Fairyland*, Eoin, you say?"

"To Avalon. Aye."

Friar Kol looked down at him, compassionately.

"I—I've got your chain out, Eoin," he said, "and it hasn't got any key on it. Just a—well it looks rather like a dried herring—yes. It's got a dried herring on it, Eoin, with thread around its tail."

Blackjohn closed his eyes.

"Aye," he said. "That's the key."

Then he too was gone.

CHAPTER 27

From the diary of Doctor Stewart Henry Scott—

Oban – July 4, 1838

It took us a whole week to get from Bearsden to Oban. We went at a leisurely pace, in keeping with our disguise as Mr. and Mrs. McRoy and their cousin Mr. Greeley, holidaymakers and sightseers (which we really were).

Elizabeth was becoming the soul of our expedition. If she'd asked me to make for Cairo by hot-air balloon I'd have obliged her, but in the event she only wanted to see Loch Lomond, so up the bonny bank we went, and bonny it was in June. We stopped often. Elizabeth had somewhere got a sketch-book and was forever wanting to sketch things (she really is quite good) and Fitzhugh had to cast a line into every little brook that fed into the Loch, so it was slow going, as Fitzhugh had predicted.

"Where did you get that rod anyway?" I demanded, looking up from *John Blackjohn*. We'd stopped for the third time that morning with a lurch that scattered my notes and pencils across the floor.

"Farrier in Balloch," Fitzhugh returned defensively, slinging his tackle-box across his shoulder. "Traded him a German tinderbox[120] for it."

"Must you angle at that muddy hole?" I complained, groping for my things. "What do you mean to catch? Leeches?"

"I recall I caught some fine perch at Arden," Fitzhugh growled. "I recall somebody ate that perch at breakfast, and he was right jolly about it."

"Right!" I sighed. "Damn good perch! Good man! Angle away."

Fitzhugh plowed through the bushes and was gone.

"How is the transcription coming?" Elizabeth asked.

---

[120] An old-fashioned firestarter.

"Fair enough," I said. "In fact I've almost finished. We've done the entire front section and most of that section we unlocked in the middle. But if we can't open the back plate somehow then I'm afraid the story has to end."

"You might just take it to a jeweler," Elizabeth ventured.

I took off my spectacles and rubbed by eyes. "Oh, I know," I said wearily. "And I *will* take it to a jeweler, if all else fails. Only—"

"Only what?"

"Oh, you'll think me a superstitious old fool. I'm not a dreamer, Elizabeth—"

I took both her hands in mine, doing my best to seem earnest. Elizabeth gave me a provoking smile.

"Not a dreamer, Stewart?"

"No! I'm a man of reason. If I weren't mixed up in this mad affair I'd be telling you right now that ghosts and fairies are nothing but a humbug concocted to frighten the simple and amuse children, but—"

"If you weren't mixed up in this 'mad affair,' " Elizabeth put in archly, "then you wouldn't be telling me anything at *all*."

"Quite true," I said, letting go her hands. "I feel uncommonly silly saying it, but I've a sort of—of premonition, if you will, that this book—well—it *wants* to be opened in its own mysterious way. My heart tells me if I simply break into it I won't find anything. It'll all be dust and leather."

"Oh, so it's your *heart* tells you?" She smiled mischievously. I reddened to the tips of my ears.

"So you *do* think me a fool!"

Elizabeth laughed merrily. "There, there, Sir Stewart." She patted my hand. "I meant no offense to your honor. Also—" she added—"I think you're right. I think we'd be fools to break into it. Like cutting open a bird because you want to hear it sing."

"Well," I smiled ironically, "my solicitor *did* mention some kind of enchanted jawbone. Just before he shot me, that is."

"Shot you for the second time."

"Quite right!" I laughed. "With lightning this time. Not to mention: met a ghost in Berwick last month advised I repair to Iona; therefore—" (I straightened my cuffs) "—as a reasonable man of science—"

"To Iona!" Elizabeth said with spirit. I confess I thought her quite charming just then. There was a youthfulness about Elizabeth which contradicted her gray hairs.

She could be a decade younger than me, I said to myself. *I wonder how long she's been a widow? I must tease it out of Fitzhugh somehow.*

We were two days waiting for the ferry in Oban, but it brought the coach and mares over to Mull and we were right glad about that. On Mull we drove southwestward thirty miles or more down the whole length of the island toward Iona. Fitzhugh had the pleasure of selling a gold watch he took off Radan. It fetched a good price, and I don't think I ever saw him so merry.

But when we reached Fionphort we could go no farther save swimming. We couldn't bring the mares across to Iona and we couldn't stable them in Mull, so we were forced to sell them to a crofter[121] at a considerable loss. The man had very little in the way of coin, so a poor farmer got a windfall and Fitzhugh was not at all merry about that. It was just as well. That old hearse was about to come apart. I'd been on tenterhooks, expecting the axles to go with every bump in the road. I rather miss the mares, though. They grew on me in an odd way. Elizabeth misses them too. She named them Lucy and Mag (I don't remember which was which) and she curry-combed them every night.

So it was that about the second week in July we finally stepped out onto the pier and found ourselves truly on Iona, the Holy Isle.

We stood on the dock for a long moment, gazing all around us.

"Well," quoth Fitzhugh at last, "it ain't much to look at."

"It *is* a bit desolate," I agreed. From the ferry I'd been watching the island getting bigger with a sinking feeling in my heart. Iona was mostly flat; rather gray and barren. I could see the ruined tower of the old abbey squatting over a few scattered houses, and that was all. Beside one or two ferrymen we were the only souls on the dock. The salty wind was cold, even in July, and the gulls were crying overhead with a lonesome sound. I shivered and thought of home—my own shabby, safe, comfortable rooms in Bread Street.

---

[121] Small-scale tenant farmer

Can I ever go back? I wondered. *Would I be arrested?* I felt uprooted and alone.

Elizabeth must have sensed this. She gave my arm a little squeeze. "Stewart?" she ventured.

"Oh, I'm alright," I replied stoutly, picking up my valise. "Here we are at last! I'm just—tired, that's all. Let's find someplace to sleep and something to eat."

"That's the spirit!" Fitzhugh thumped me on the back so hard I nearly dropped my valise again. "We'll have you sorted out in no time."

The village of Baile Mòr had only one inn, and that was just a crofter's cottage with a wooden sign that swung creaking in the wind: *Taigh-Òsta Naomh Cholmcille.*[122] I was about to trudge over and ask for rooms anyway, but "If Radan's still alive," said Elizabeth, "that's the first place he'll inquire."

That sounded wise, so I tried to ask a man with a fish cart whether he knew of anyone with spare lodgings, but the man spoke no English and I'm ashamed to say my Gallic isn't what it once was. Then at length a Presbyterian schoolteacher overheard us as he was passing by and he asked what the trouble was. I said I was Mr. Greeley, historian, come to study ruins with my dear friends Mr. and Mrs. McRoy, and did he know of anyone with a cottage to let? It happened that he *did* know of a snug, well-furnished little place just south of the village, "a bit out-of-the-way, you know, but quite nice. I'd have taken it myself," (said he) "only the lady was asking too much; holding out for summer travelers with means. You can guess how many of *those* we see out here." (He gazed mournfully off to sea.) "City of Lights *this* is! And I'm the Duc d'Orléans. She'll be happy enough to see you."

For two shillings the man with the fish cart would take us to the cottage, so Fitzhugh and I gamely scrambled up for a pungent ride back to the docks to collect the rest of our things. Elizabeth rode in front (the fishmonger trying to make conversation with her the whole way and Elizabeth politely pretending to comprehend) and thus we made our way to the cottage.

The lady was at home (where else she could have been I can't imagine): a Mrs. Campbell. She lived in a gloomy old farmhouse across the lane from a

---

[122] Scots Gaelic: *Saint Columba Inn*

brown and withered heath. She had a little cottage behind her house and she hardly spoke more English than the fishmonger, but we managed to make ourselves understood. She *was* happy enough to see us. The cottage was small, but it looked cheerier than the farmhouse. It had a little back-garden bordered with a whitewashed stone wall, and beyond that a green meadow of the kind they call *machair* running down to an inlet of the sea. A trellis and hedges and a rather blasted-looking spruce helped fend off the vast, pitiless sky.

The fishmonger lent a hand with our trunks. Mrs. Campbell dropped an old-fashioned curtsy and went back into the farmhouse. The utter silence of the place fell on us so quickly that it gave me an eerie feeling.

"Let's get inside," said Elizabeth.

"Ye gods!" I groaned. "What are we even doing here?"

It was Sunday morning, windswept and gray. Church bells were ringing in the distance. We were tramping through dense heather near the southern tip of Iona.

"Cheer up, Stewart!" said Elizabeth brightly. "It's good exercise, anyway."

"Oh, I've led you to the edge of the world! And I don't even know what we're looking for. Chasing fairies! Poor Albert was right: I *have* gone daft in my old age."

"Right, right—of course you have," Fitzhugh said soothingly. "Now what did Albert say about the tooth? That's our only clue."

"Oh, a medieval Scandinavian, possibly," I said, sitting down on a stone. Opening my valise I fished out the tooth Murdo's accomplice had dropped in the lumber-room, along with the plaster mold I cast from the back plate on *John Blackjohn*. I held up the cast.

"Albert said it showed no sign of decay."

"And the real one? The one that Southerner tried to stick in the safe?"

"Can't tell," I said, taking out my magnifying glass. "It's got this crown on it."

"Richer diet?" Fitzhugh ventured. "Yes," said Elizabeth, "Maybe our Norseman made his way south. How long ago would you reckon?"

"My goodness," I said, "it could be any time from the eighth to the eleventh century—let me see—I believe Vikings first sacked Iona abbey in the year 794."

"Imagine!" Fitzhugh chuckled. "Rich, unguarded cloister sitting out here in the waste with hardly a lock on the door and no one but flabby monks to defend it. Vikings must have thought they'd tripped on a pot of gold."

"Yes," I agreed, "they took Britain quite by surprise. The monks—and the druids before them—came to the Holy Isle for solitude and contemplation."

"Plenty o' that around here." Fitzhugh stuck his pipe in his teeth.

"But then," I went on, "the Norsemen started sailing vast distances. To Spain and even to Sicily."

"And Africa," Elizabeth put in.

"Right! Normans had short-lived outposts along the Barbary[123] coast. Sun must have killed them. Here in the north they hopped from island to island. Shetlands, Faroes, Iceland, Greenland—off into the unknown. Savages, yes, but brave ones."

Elizabeth shivered. "I'd have gone to Spain or someplace warm," she said. "They haven't got a summer here."

"Warm—right—" I mused. "In fact it *was* a bit warmer at one time. The old skaldic tales suggest the North Atlantic was much freer of sea-ice than it is today. That was one of the reasons the Norsemen got so far."

"Well," said Fitzhugh, "if that tooth's a Norseman, and if the Norsemen were looting the abbey, then maybe the abbey's where we look? He might've been killed in the fighting."

"But didn't the Vikings put their dead to sea in burning ships?" Elizabeth asked.

"Oh, they weren't particularly organized," I replied. "A rich chieftain might have had a showy funeral. But a poor lad killed in a raid on some foreign strand—I'd wager they left his bones to the crows."

"We could ask that schoolteacher if he knows of any ancient tombs about," Fitzhugh suggested.

Elizabeth tugged my sleeve.

---

[123] Northern Africa, roughly corresponding to the modern-day states of Morocco, Algeria, Tunisia and Libya.

"Or we could ask *him*, Stewart."

I looked up.

A slightly transparent young man in a bluish sailor's hat was standing about three yards off, staring at us with an icy, almost bored expression. The gorse-bush behind him was in bloom and the yellow flowers showed through his shapeless tunic.

He met my gaze.

An uamh-mara.

I rather heard him inside my head than with my ears. His lips moved but the sound came from far, far away, like a whisper in a cathedral.

I came a step nearer, hesitantly, not meaning to frighten him. (Though I don't know why I thought I might. He looked at us with all the interest of a turtle basking on a log.) It occurred to me I might try speaking to him in Gallic.

"Ahem—er—*madainn mhath*?" I ventured.

He turned slightly away from me. "Well *that* didn't work," I muttered.

His glance fell on Elizabeth, and then his eyes came alive. For an instant he seemed almost alert.

An uamh-mara.

He was speaking to Elizabeth now.

An uamh-mara. Cuidich i.

He flickered like a candle and was gone.

"Merciful heavens!" Elizabeth breathed. "You—you could see right *through* him!"

"You saw him too? Well then it's settled. I'm not completely mad." I was rummaging around inside my valise.

"What did he say?" Fitzhugh asked excitedly.

"I—I'm not entirely sure. Mrs. Campbell loaned me a vocabulary—"

I took out a copy of *McAlpine's Gaelic Dictionary*. "It's a terrible book," I said. "They give it to schoolchildren in the Islands. But it's all we've got. Let me see—"

"It sounded like *OO-ahv-MAH-duh*."

"Right you are, Elizabeth! Yes! *Uamh*—that's 'cave'—and *mara* is 'sea,' of course—" I thumbed furiously through the dictionary. "*I* is 'she,' and *cuidich*—"

I looked up.

"Help her. He said help her."

We were silent. The only sound was the eerie wailing of wind among the rocks.

"Up, boys!" Elizabeth cried suddenly. "You've got a lady to rescue after all! You were right, Stewart. That ghost led us here for a reason."

"It's simple!" said Fitzhugh. "We just walk along the beach. Or, better yet, why don't we ask about in the village? There can't be too many sea caves around here—or I'm Caliban."

"No-o—" I answered slowly. "I think we had better *not* ask in the village."

"Why not?" Fitzhugh demanded.

I stuck my hands in my pockets with a businesslike scowl. "The Duke of Buckley," I said, "or Radan, rather, was nipping at our heels for a week. Maybe he still is. Elizabeth was right: we ought to stay clear of the village if we can. I doubt it would do us any good to inquire anyway. I've never heard of a sea-cave on Iona, and also—" I kicked thoughtfully at some brownish lichen clinging to the rock, "—also the sea level was higher in Viking times."

"You don't say!"

Fitzhugh looked skeptical.

"No, it truly was!" I returned. "Like I said, it was an unusually warm period. The havens in southern Greenland were free from ice most of the year. Meaning the ice was melted. Meaning the ocean was just a wee bit—well— *deeper* than it is today. What say we tramp along the coastline a few paces in from the shore," I finished briskly, "and see if we don't happen upon our Caliban—or Canute—in some hidden grotto?"

"We're sure to find it!" Elizabeth said excitedly. "That ghost means to lead us to his lonely grave. Just like in books, Willie! That's where we'll find his jawbone."

"Not *his* jawbone," said Fitzhugh.

"Why not his jawbone?" Elizabeth demanded.

"*That* one's not missing his chops," Fitzhugh retorted. "I saw 'em clear as day right through his cheek. Saw his tongue, too."

Two days later we were still tramping, only wetter. It was early afternoon under a sullen gray sky. A fine, windy mist set in as we slowly picked our way up the northeastern flank of the isle. We were winding in and out among the high rocks, keeping to the narrow-mown turf where sheep were grazing. It was broad day and yet the fog and mist were so smothering we could hardly see ten paces in front of us. Fitzhugh's pipe had just gone out again. He looked glum as a wet dog.

"Well, Lizzie, how d'you fare? Maybe we turn back before we get any farther from home?" Fitzhugh asked, rather hopefully.

"What? Already?"

Elizabeth was wearing my mackintosh and positively glowing. Tiny droplets clung to the swirls of gray hair that escaped from under her hat. She was ruddy as a schoolgirl (and practically as slender, I thought).

"Yes already!" I panted. "I can't keep up with you, Elizabeth. My right hip aches. Fitzhugh: I wonder if we really found all the birdshot."

"All right, all right," said Elizabeth. "But let's carry on as far as that red patch up there."

"Why *that* patch?"

"Oh, I'm just curious."

"But it's rather off the path—"

Elizabeth was already gone, scrambling up the sloping front of a boulder. She went on hands and feet, digging the toes of her shoes deftly into cracks where moss and lichens were growing.

"Carefully, madam!" I shouted after her.

"Oh, it's lovely up here!" Elizabeth called down. It's almost like a table— Boys!" she cried excitedly. "Come quickly! There's something carved here. And steps! I think we've found—"

"Wait a moment!"

I came puffing up onto the flat boulder-top. The fog had grown so dense that I could only see gray outlines in the gloom.

Suddenly a black opening yawned at my feet, just big enough for a man to fit through and half hidden by a tenacious shrub. I looked around.

"Elizabeth! Where are you?"

"I'm down here, Stewart."

"Elizabeth!" I was on hands and knees, shouting into the hole. "Elizabeth! Are you alright?"

Elizabeth shrieked.

"Hold on! I'm coming!"

I plunged feet-first through the opening with Fitzhugh close behind. I felt uneven steps. There was a hiss, and then a faint glow showed the walls of a dry little cave with a dirt floor.

Elizabeth stood trembling, a burning match in her hand.

"What is it?" I gasped. "What's happened?"

"It's a skull," said Elizabeth, pointing.

"A what now?"

"There on the floor! A skull!"

"Oh, is *that* all?" I said (a touch condescending). I took a candle out of my valise and held it to Elizabeth's match-flame. "I thought you'd seen a dragon," I said. "Old skull can't hurt you."

"It. SNEEZED!"

CHAPTER 28

From the diary of Doctor Stewart Henry Scott—

Iona – Dies ignota,[124] 1838

Elizabeth, Fitzhugh and I sat in a half-circle. The light from two candles cast dancing shadows on the pebbly floor. It was a small cave—maybe ten feet across and just tall enough for Fitzhugh to stand in the middle. Eggshells of some seabird were scattered on the broken steps, but otherwise there was no sign of living occupation.

We stared at the skull.

The skull stared back.

"No skeleton—" I ventured. "No weapons. No grave goods. No ochre—"

"No gold," Fitzhugh said dejectedly.

"And no jawbone," said Elizabeth. She eyed the skull where it lay on the floor, its teeth half-sunk into the dirt.

"And you're certain it—sneezed?" I asked timidly.

"It *sneezed*, I tell you!"

"Well," I sighed, "that wouldn't be the strangest thing that's happened to us. And it's definitely missing its chops, Fitzhugh. I hope its jawbone hasn't been spirited off to the ends of the earth. We'll have to root around with our hands and see if we turn up anything."

"Like gold!" said Fitzhugh, brightening. "We could be standing on a pile of Roman coins."

We must have made for a comical sight—three old dotards grubbing about in a dirty hole on hands and knees like we'd gone mad. From wall to

---

[124] Latin: *date unknown*

wall (avoiding the skull) we went, sifting our fingers through the rubble and raising a mighty cloud of dust.

We froze.

"Oo-oh, I heard it *that* time!" Fitzhugh quavered. "It *did* sneeze!"

"I've found something!" Elizabeth called.

I half-turned to her (keeping one eye on the skull). Elizabeth was kneeling by the cave wall holding up a U-shaped bone with teeth in it.

"That could be it!" I cried. "Elizabeth, you're a wonder!"

I took the jaw from her carefully. Then I hesitated, looking down at the skull.

"Well?" Fitzhugh demanded.

"I—I guess I don't know what I ought to *do* with it," I said, feeling ridiculous. "I was so bent on finding a jawbone, I never thought what would happen if I ever *did*. Fitzhugh, maybe you ought to—"

"Oh, no!"

Fitzhugh was backing away from me, shaking his head.

"No, no! *You're* the doctor, Stewart. See if you can't—I don't know— hook it on or something."

"Alright," I sighed, "I'll try." I knelt down. It felt like I was putting my hand into a mousetrap, but I reached out and gingerly tapped the skull, expecting anything.

Nothing happened.

Emboldened, I gently picked it up. "I hope it doesn't fall to pieces," I said, though the skull felt heavy and quite solid in my hand. I tried to examine it in the flickering light. The hollow eyes were giving me a most unpleasant feeling. As I looked at *it*, I got the uncanny impression that it was looking at *me*, its dead eyes scanning my face as I turned them this way and that. So, cutting off my examination, I took the skull in my right hand and the jawbone in my left, closed my eyes, and took a deep breath.

"Well," I said, "here goes."

No noise. No click. No sensation whatsoever. It reminded me of when the copper pins fell out of the seal in *John Blackjohn*. All at once the jaw and the skull were simply joined as if a thousand years had never passed. Indeed, I found myself dimly wondering whether the two hadn't been connected all along—

And with a cowardly yelp I dropped the skull face-down on the ground like an apple core. "Oh, it moved!" I squawked. "It moved!"

"It's st-still moving!" Fitzhugh gibbered. A horrible choking sound came from the dirt. Now we could clearly see the jawbone working up and down in a ghastly way. "Merciful heavens!" I wailed—

And then Elizabeth pushed me out of the way. "Oh, for goodness' sake!" she chided. "We can't just leave it suffocating in the dirt!" She picked up the skull and gave it a gentle tap, like she was knocking the crumbs off a piece of toast. Dirt fell out of the eye sockets. There was a distant cough. The jaw twitched slightly.

Crone! Give me another shake!

"I beg your pardon?" exclaimed Elizabeth.

My head! Give it another good shake. Knock me against the wall there a bit. Ah-h! That's better!

More dirt and a couple of pebbles dropped out of the skull, and then a tooth.

Where am I? the skull demanded. *I was sleeping. Is it Ragnarök yet?*

Recovering my courage I stepped forward.

"You are in Iona, sir," I said. "*Ì Chaluim Chille*—Saint Columba's Isle."

Wozzat? The skull demanded. *Saint WHO? Izzat a druid or something? I thought this was Ì Ban Bòidheach—Isle of Pretty Gael Wenches. YOU'RE no pretty Gael wench!*

His face was only bone, and yet it seemed to wear a disdainful expression.

"No wenches here," I replied stiffly. "You're in the company of a wise steward, an honorable lady, and a skillful healer—myself."

Gods! the skull moaned. *As bad as that? I might've been in Valhalla by now! Oh, when will Ragnarök ever come?*

"If you mean the end of the world," I returned cheerfully, "I'm expecting it any day now. But if I may be so bold: who are you, sir, and how do you come to be speaking English—a man so ancient and so—er—disjointed?"

Wozzat—'English'? the skull returned. *You mean Southern? I'M not speaking Southern. You lot are speaking Norse!*

We all gasped at once, because it was entirely true. I *had* been speaking ancient Norse, and Fitzhugh and Elizabeth had been comprehending it. The words echoed curiously in our minds, as if we'd spoken them ages ago and were only just now remembering them.

I am Bran, the skull declared loftily. *THE Bran. Bran the Blessed. Don't they sing long songs about me?*

"Bran mac Llŷr?" I asked. "Well they certainly *did* sing long songs about you once. Very long songs."

Ah! the skull sighed wistfully. *I used to love those songs! So much kenning. So many heroes dying and winning renown. Oh, how I miss the renown!*

Heiðrún heitir ge-eeeit—

(He began to sing in a voice like a dog howling.)

Er stendr höllu á Herjaföðu-uuuu—

"That's truly wonderful singing," I interrupted. "Truly wonderful—but you'll forgive my curiosity: how do you know the songs of the Northmen? I heard Bran was one of the kings on the big island—the island of Prydein[125]."

Oh, my mother was from Prydein, sniffed the skull. *But my father was from Norway. Or maybe my father was Odin—how should I know?* he said testily. *YOUR father might be anyone, peasant! I grew up in Trondhjem—does that suit you?*

"Very much," I said, overlooking the insult. "That's very interesting. And how—if I may—did you come to find yoursel—er—to find *part* of yourself in this cave?"

Oh, that's a long saga, the skull said wearily. *A good three nights in the mead-hall for that one. But—what the Hel! I've been stuck in this godsforsaken*

---

[125] The largest of the British isles was known as *Alba* in some areas of the north; *Prydein* or *Prydwyn* (Britain) in some areas of the south.

hole a thousand years already. I suppose it might do to pass the time while we wait for Ragnarök. If you churls would care to roll out your goatskins—

"Oh, for Baldr's sake!" Fitzhugh growled. "Put him in your bag, Stegvard, and let's get out of here. We've still got three miles to slog."

You will NOT— Stop it, crone! the skull bellowed. *Stop it, I say! You will not stuff the head of Bran the Blessed—*

Elizabeth closed the buckle on my valise. "Home, then?" she asked cheerfully. "We'll have a listen to him after dinner."

Elizabeth started up the steps. I was on the cave floor again, hunting for the tooth that fell out of the skull.

"Here's something!" said Fitzhugh. He bent down and stuck his hand into the dirt.

"Roman coin?" I asked.

"Better! I've found me a walking-stick."

CHAPTER 29

From the diary of Doctor Stewart Henry Scott—

"Well I wasn't a *king*, strictly speaking," Bran said uneasily.

Dinner was over. Fitzhugh was in better humor now, with his feet on the hearth and his pipe in his teeth. Elizabeth had put on her artist's smock and was sitting at the little whist-table. Now and again she would glance up at Bran's skull, then down at her sketchbook.

At first we'd tried putting Bran on the table, but his jaw went up and down when he talked and it made his hollow eyes bob in a ridiculous way. After that we tried putting him on a pillow, but the pillow muffled his voice and his eyes kept bobbing just the same. So at last we simply hung him on the coat-rack, and it turned out he quite liked that. He said it felt like standing up again.

"Don't mistake me!" said Bran. "I wasn't some churl. I was a chieftain, famous and feared. From every shore the bravest and handsomest young warriors flocked to me. Everyone wanted to fight under the banner of Bran the Blessed. They were devoted to me as to a god. From sea to sea we roamed, winning fame."

"How did you win fame?" I asked.

"Oh, looting mostly," said Bran. "Some slaving. Some kidnapping for ransom. We went in as mercenaries once or twice and we did a little trading— amber, wine—rich stuff." He coughed in a self-satisfied way.

"And how did you come to find yourself in that little cave?" I asked. "Were you looting the monastery?"

"Gods no!" Bran scoffed. "The monastery is—whaddya say? A lot of fat Christians praying? No! In *my* day this place was all druids and wenches, and they didn't do much praying, if you know what I mean." Bran chuckled meaningfully. The more he spoke, the more I saw (or fancied I saw) the ghost

275

of a face covering his deathly features—like a reflection on water. A high, square forehead. Quick grey eyes. Long dark hair pulled back tight and knotted behind. Sweeping moustache. Plaited beard. A handsome man of about thirty with a restless, greedy expression.

Coal-biter, I said to myself. *Slave to adventure. Never happy at home.*

"In *my* day," Bran went on, "the Western Isles were worked by the Gaels and ruled by the Northmen. It was the Gaels who learned about the sea-pig gates."

"About the *what*?"

I'd been scribbling in my notebook, but at the words 'sea-pig gates' I inadvertently dropped my pencil.

"The sea-pig gates!" cried Bran. "You know. With the whale? *Sea-pig* is what they call a whale in Gael-speak. The *gaetaichean muc-mhara*—there's two that I know of. They open one day in every hundred years—unless you've got the key, that is. There's the one at Dùn Drochaid—good luck finding *that* one—and there's the one here, where you found me."

"And where," I asked wonderingly, "does a sea-pig gate lead to?"

"Where does a—"

Bran's empty jaw fell open in amazement.

"Oh, by the beard of Thor!" he thundered, "Can you really not know?"

We stared dumbly at him.

"The sea-pig gates lead to the Other World, peasant!" (The skull looked exasperated.) "To Avalon, among other places!"

"To *Avalon*?"

"Yes! Avalon! Sweet Baldr—have you truly never heard of the Apple Isle? Fairyland? Dana's country? Are Southerners really so stupid now? Because in my day they weren't quite."

"I—I beg your pardon," I stammered. "I confess, in these days we don't know much about the Other World. And—you'll forgive my surprise—you say the gateway to the Other World is—is in that little cave we found?"

"It isn't a *cave*," Bran said wearily. "Or—rather—it's only a cave on *this* side. On the Other Side it's—well it's rather hard to explain if you haven't been through it. But it leads to Avalon, I say."

"And you've been to Avalon?"

"Er—no," Bran said cautiously. "No, I'd no particular business in Fairyland. Strange creatures, fairies. Bit uneasy around them. No, there's an island midway between here and there: Tveirrokk. That's where I was going. It was a raid. The Seven Heroes and I, we went there to steal the Staff of Esus from the dragon—"

"The *staff* of Esus?" I interrupted, greatly excited. "We've heard tell of a *crook* of Esus, but I never knew there was a staff."

"Oh, for the love of—" Bran choked. "It's a pruning-hook, peasant! Pruning-hook's got a handle, hasn't it? Or does your master send you out to mow with—what—a scythe-blade?" He sniggered.

"Call us peasants again," Fitzhugh growled, "and you'll be waiting for Ragnarök inside a hatbox. Lizzie's got one."

Bran faked a cough (which was comical given he had no lungs). "Now, now," (he affected a diplomatic tone) "that won't be necessary, my good man. In fact I'm quite happy to explain. You see Esus is one of the Old Gods. Esus the Forester, they call him. Esus is guardian of the wilds, and of the things that live and grow there. Farmers and village-folk—they're afraid of the wild places, so they think Esus is some kind of monster. But really he's a sort of—"

Bran paused reflectively.

"He's really a sort Keeper of wild things. He keeps things in balance, as it were.

"Take foxes, for example," Bran pursued. "You can't have the foxes eating *all* the hares, can you? Foxes eat all the hares; hares don't mate; foxes starve, right? And then there's trees—you can't have the trees all strangling each other and crowding each other out. Trees have to spread their leaves, yes, but a bit of sunlight still has to reach the forest floor so the blackberries can grow, so the birds can have something to live on, and so on, and so on—"

Bran's voice trailed off and he fell silent. I fancied he was looking wistful.

"I used to pick blackberries in the forest when I was a boy," Bran said quietly, as if to himself. "I always went farther than all the other children. Farther on, and farther on. But I always—"

His voice dropped to a whisper.

"I always found my way back."

"You had a brave heart," Elizabeth said warmly. "My goodness! You've gone farther than any living man I should think. What strange and wonderful things you must have seen!"

"Oh! Yes!" Bran exclaimed, cheering up. "The Other Side is wondrous! Islands upon islands upon islands. Did you know that? Islands beyond reckoning, like stars floating in an endless sea. Or rather— No, it's like a tree, really. The Other World is a tree, and every star a blossom on it. Sometimes I have visions of it. Dreams in the darkness—"

"Ahem," I coughed politely. "So you—you say you went to the Other World seeking this staff? The handle that goes with the Crook of Esus?"

"That's right."

"And what about the blade? Where was the, the *corran ag bearradh* in your day?"

"Blade's lost," said Bran. "Dana threw it into the sea long ages ago."

"*Did* she?" I mused. "That's very interesting. Very interesting indeed. And Dana is one of the old—goddesses?"

"Dana the Huntress? No! Dana's not one of the Old Ones. Country people called her 'goddess,' but that's just ignorance. Dana comes from Avalon. She's a powerful fairy and a friend to humankind."

"To the kind she *likes*, anyway," Bran muttered. "She's no friend to *my* kind."

"Why no friend to your kind?" I demanded.

"Oh, I don't know—" Bran returned petulantly. "I'm a lord, see? A lord and a fighter. Dana doesn't like lords and fighters. She likes—I don't know— wandering druids with flowers in their hair, or—or weakling boys who are kind to the birds or somesuch thing." He sniffed disdainfully. "Dana had her people in the West. The *Tuatha dé Danann*—People of the Goddess Dana. They were mortals who followed her, but they're long gone and Dana hardly visits this world anymore. She only comes once in a very great while, when there's some terrible evil afoot or some grave injustice to avenge. There's no hiding from her when she comes. That's why they call her 'Huntress.'

"She wasn't always like that," Bran pursued. "There was a time—ages ago, in the first days of this world—when Dana was loved by the ancient fisher people of Éireann, the lesser isle. *Írland*, we call it. Dana came to Írland often, and many other fairies too. The People of Dana were many and strong then. Dana schooled them in her secret arts and together they protected the fisher folk from the Firbolg—fearsome giants who snared men and kept them for slaughter. Of war she taught her people nothing. Healing is Dana's province. It was said the Tuatha dé Danann could cure any sickness. And they had dealings with shiori—the immortal spirits that live in the wild—naiads and dryads, nymphs and fauns and all the rest. With Dana to watch over them the fisher people were poor and peaceful and long-lived and—well—rather happy, I think. There was always trouble with giants, of course, but Dana led the Tuatha and the fairies against them, and she drove them out into the waste places of Írland.

"But then came Gaels from the east—lords and fighters like me. They came with spears and helmets and horses and chariots. Iron plowshares to till the land. Gold and silver. Cattle and slaves. To the fisher people the Gaels were like a race of gods. They were bewitched by their rich ornaments and glittering swords—the young men most of all. Many of the fisher people were willing to own the Gaels their lords. Little Gaelic kingdoms sprang up across Írland, while more and more the fisher people forsook Dana and the old ways.

"Then Érimón, king of the north, came against his brother Éber Finn in battle. Érimón was a mighty warrior and deep in the secret arts. He gathered the giants out of the waste places and promised them a yearly tribute in blood if they would make him High King over all Írland. Soon the war spread to every coast. There was an awful slaughter. Gaels fought Gaels. The fisher people all became slaves and vassals. Dana tried to gather the Tuatha, but they were scattered wide. Many were killed. At last Dana and her people were driven to the far south-west of the isle.

"And it's true," said Bran, "what they say in the songs: in the last battle Esus himself took human form—a thing he had never done before—and Dana and Esus fought side-by-side."

Bran paused. I had the odd feeling he'd closed his eyes.

"I saw that battle in a vision, once," Bran murmured. "The world-tree shows me many things. Things past. Things to come. Beautiful and terrible it was! When Esus raised his staff, thunderbolts rained from the sky like the Northlights. Men— Men burned where they stood. Coals in a forge. And when

Esus opened his hand, trees and briars writhed up out of the ground. Caught their legs. Dragged them under. Earth was like water. The cliffs tore apart and the angry sea rushed in.

"Then the giants came. No fire, no briar could stop them. Living rock, coming on like a slow gray tide. I saw the people of Dana hemmed in along the cliffs with their backs to the sea.

"Finally Esus spoke, and every soul in Írland heard him.

"*If men would be masters*, Esus said, *then masters shall men be*."

Bran stopped. For a moment all we could hear was the comfortable clicking in the fire and the eerie wailing of the wind outside. When he spoke again I thought there was a tremble in his distant voice.

"It didn't make— When it broke, it didn't make a sound. There was a light came out of Esus like a star had fallen. For a moment he stood against it, brighter still, and then he was gone. When I could see again the giants had all turned back into dead stone and the pruning-hook of Esus lay in two pieces on the smoking ground.

"Dana picked up the blade and hurled it into the new-made fjord. *There let it lie*, she cried, *until this world is ended*.

"She picked up the staff and at first I thought she meant to do the same, but then she hesitated. There was doubt in her face.

"*This was cut from the sacred ash*, Dana said, turning it over in her hands. *I dare not cast it away. The dragon will know what to do with it*."

"Ahem—" I interrupted. "The dragon Níðhǫggr, yes, who gnaws at the roots of the world-tree?"

"Very good!" Bran chuckled. "Gnaws indeed! A healer, did you say? You're well-versed in lore for a healer, Stegvard."

It was the first time Bran called me by my proper name.

"So Dana picked up the staff," Bran went on. "She drew a sort of circle with it, and it was like a door opened in the air. Dana and her people all rushed through. Then the door closed and they were gone. The fairies all forsook Írland. Esus too. His grace was gone from the green isle forever."

"And the staff of Esus?" I asked. "What precisely does it do?"

"It—" Bran hesitated. "Well, take the blade," he began, "That's the cutting end, right? That's the part that gets things done. Brings rain and lightning; makes the trees bud. And the staff—that's the controlling end. The staff has the power to bend souls to the Keeper's will, and that's important when you've got a bunch of fauns to herd. Also it—it thins the ice, as it were, that separates this world from the Other. What's done in this world gets done on the Other Side—after the Other Side's own fashion, that is."

"And you went to—to this *Tveirrokk*—to get the staff?"

"*Já*—yes." Bran tried to nod, making the coat-rack jiggle. "Of course, I didn't know precisely what the Staff of Esus *was*. Only that it was a relic of mighty power and that Níðhǫggr the dragon guarded it, as the old songs tell. I was here in Iona, actually. (Is that what they call it now—Iona? I rather like that. It's shorter than the Gael name.) Anyway, I was here with my warriors. It was Midsummer's Day and we were having a rest between raids—lying close after a bit of trouble we'd stirred up in Cork. The boys and I were making merry and I confess I'd had rather a lot of mead, and then I learned from the druids that the sea-pig gate was predicted to open that very day. They open one day in every hundred years, and it just happened to be on *that* Midsummer's day. Sounds rather omen-ous, don't you think?"

"It does rather," I agreed.

"So I stood up on a mead-barrel. *Boys*, I said to the Seven—"

"Who were the Seven?" Elizabeth interrupted.

"The Seven? The Seven Heroes? Let me see if I can remember—" (Bran was being demure. He clearly had their names etched in his very heart.)

"Right," Bran said, "So there were Sven and Loki and Torsten, and Erik Jórvískmann. Odin and Leif and young Sigfried Redbeard. They were my bravest and handsomest warriors."

"And they went to the Tveirrokk with you?"

"Right you are! So I—I stood up on a mead barrel and I said *Heroes*, I said, *this day hath fortune blessed you. We are going to march right through that sea-pig gate and win fame undying! We are going to steal the Staff of Esus from Níðhǫggr the dragon and lay this world at our feet.*

"Then all the Seven cheered me (once I got off the barrel) and they shouted *skaal!* and swore they'd follow me to Hel and to Valhalla, and then we gathered up our gear and stumbled off to the sea-pig gate."

"You really went to the Other World?" Elizabeth asked breathlessly.

"*Já*," Bran nodded. "I did indeed."

"What was it like," Elizabeth asked, "crossing over?"

"Well," said Bran, "it's something like— But I don't dare say! You lot would think me insane. Everything changes, I'll say *that* much. And yet everything stays the same, like water when it turns to ice."

"And the Tveirrokk?" I asked. "What's *it* like?"

"Oh, it's beautiful!" Bran sighed. "Like a green carpet laid against a starry void. And in the middle: Yggdrasil, the world-tree. White as pearl. Glowing from within. Branches upon branches upon branches upon branches, unfolding up and up into infinity. Infinite, yes, and yet—small. Like something a boy could climb."

"Strange!" I mused. "I believe the book mentions a dragon at the beginning. Yes, in fact it does. But so far I haven't seen anything about Yggdrasil—" I had *John Blackjohn* out on the table and I was rustling gingerly through the pages.

"What's that you're doing?" Bran demanded. "Smells like a moldy boot. Turn me where I can look at it. Why—*ha ha*! Thor's beard!" he cackled. "Never thought I'd see *that* again."

"See *what* again?" I asked sharply.

"That mirror! The Christian priest's mirror!"

We stared at him.

"Well it's not a mirror on *your* side," Bran said defensively. "But *I* can't help seeing it that way. When last I saw that—that 'book,' a Christian monk was holding it."

"A Christian—"

We were all out of our chairs and talking at once. Even Fitzhugh was gesturing with his pipe-stem in a most agitated way.

"SILENCE!" bellowed the skull.

We returned to our chairs. Bran chuckled knowingly.

"Well I've stuck my snout in a beehive," he said, "that's clear. Let me tell it from the beginning—ha ha! You peasan—" He coughed. "That is—you worthy *bænumfólk* are more amusing than I'd have hoped. I haven't had this much fun in a century." He cleared his invisible throat.

"So when we came to the Tveirrokk," Bran began, "we threw ourselves down on the grass. (Such grass!) We'd had a bit of mead, I say, and we were overcome by the wonder of it all—lying there with the whole blazing cosmos reeling over our heads and the tree singing in its strange way—the voice of every creature that ever lived in Midgard or that ever will, all humming at once in a drowsy sort of murmur. Well of course in a moment I was fast asleep.

"I don't know how long I'd slept when something inside me said *Wake!* So I opened my eyes just in time to see the sea-pig gate starting to close and the Seven Heroes sneaking through it, looking back over their shoulders like they hoped I was still sleeping. Last of all went young Sigfried Redbeard with a guilty look on his face and a white staff in his hand.

"I staggered to my feet, shouting and cursing, and I ran after them, but only young Sigfried stopped. He turned him about and with a hateful look he swung the staff so hard it made the air whistle. He gave me such a knock across the face that I fell over backward and I nearly fainted.

"I got up," said Bran, "tasting blood, and there was the dragon. He had a little knot of travelers about him, all staring at me in wonder. There was a Christian monk, a fairy girl, and sailor boy in a blue hat.

"My head was altogether muddled, what with being on the Other Side and then getting clubbed in the face by my friend. *You'll wake up from this*, I said to myself. *You surely must be dreaming.*

"Well the monk had something in his hands: a mirror, and a fine one. It had a copper case with clasps on it and it was covered all over with the finest gold inlay that my dizzy eyes ever saw. It would have sold for a jarl's ransom in Jórvík,[126] but I wasn't thinking about that. My mouth was cut and there was blood running down my chin. I marched up and took the mirror right out of the monk's hands. I opened it and held it up to my face.

"*Holy Freyja!* I screamed. *Bastard lowborn villain son of a cur! He's knocked out two of my teeth!*

"I snapped the mirror shut and threw it down on the turf. *Lock that accursed thing*, I shouted. *And lock my ugly mouth along with it!* And then I— I confess—"

Bran's voice broke.

---

[126] Present-day York

283

"I confess I began to cry."

"Tell us why," Elizabeth said softly.

"Because—because I'd always been proud of my handsome teeth. Because my seven friends robbed me and left me. Because I saw something in that mirror that—that I quite didn't like. My face looked different. Unlordly and rather—rather small. Like a piggish boy who only cares about himself."

Bran coughed furiously. There was an awkward silence. At length he resumed.

"Anyway, the pilgrims all saw me crying—the boy and the monk and the fairy girl—and that made me even more angry. I looked back at the gate and the Seven were gone, but there was the white staff of Esus, just lying on the grass with my blood on it. Why Sigfried didn't take it with him I didn't know and I didn't care, such a transport of rage was on me. I ran for the gate like one possessed, though by now it was no bigger than a cod-barrel. I tossed the staff through the hole (meaning to crush Sigfried's skull with it) and I plunged my head in after. But the gate closed around my neck like water.

"I was caught fast," Bran concluded, "my head on This Side and my body on the Other."

We were silent.

"Your *b-body*?" I said at last. "I didn't know you *had* a body."

Bran took a sharp breath like he had a curt reply in mind, but then he only sighed.

"Yes. I have a body," Bran said dejectedly. "I'm—I'm still here."

"Still here? Still *where*?"

"Still here in Tveirrokk, gods damn it!" Bran shouted. "I'm lying on the greensward. I've still got my neck stuck in the accursed sea-pig gate."

"Good heavens!" Elizabeth gasped. "Bloody hell!" observed Fitzhugh.

"I can— I can just—"

Bran grunted from exertion.

"—just—get my knees under me—but—a-ah!" he breathed out. "It's no good. My neck won't budge."

"For hundreds of years?" cried Elizabeth.

"Hundreds and hundreds."

"Why, you must be terribly uncomfortable!"

"Oh, no," said Bran, "it's not as bad as all that. Time doesn't so much pass here. Time just *is*. The beginning is the end is the beginning—that's how the dragon sees it. After a while one starts to see it that way too. Funny how you mortals can only think in a straight line."

"And in all those centuries you've spoken to no one?" Elizabeth asked.

"Not quite 'no one,' " Bran replied. "I do talk to the dragon now and again. I can't see him, but I hear him through my bones."

"And on This Side?" I asked anxiously. "Has anybody besides us found the cave?"

I was thinking of Radan.

"Hmm—" Bran mused. "There *was* a boy came into the cave once. That'd be centuries ago, the way *you* reckon time. Young monk from the monastery. Pimple-faced Frankish lad—ha ha! I gave him quite a fright." Bran laughed at the memory.

"I can imagine," I said. "What did he do? Turn tail and run?"

"He tried—*ha ha!*—he tried to. He was up those steps in a twinkling, trying to wriggle out the hole, but he was fat and his robe got caught on the gorse-bush. Not a pretty sight, him with his cassock pulled up over his ears. But I was so terribly bored, you see. I hadn't spoken to a mortal in centuries.

"*Christian boy!* I called after him. *Wait! Return, I say!*

"He got his robe free and scrambled out, but then I guess his curiosity got the better of him because he came creeping back. There was just enough light coming through for him to see me there.

"*Come and have a word with me!* I pleaded. *I've been in this wretched hole for centuries and all I've seen is a rat.*

"The boy stared at me with his mouth open, and then his pimply face lit up. He rushed down the stairs and dropped straight to his knees before me with his forehead in the dirt crying *San Denee! San Denee!*[127] over and over again until I begged him to stop.

"*Carry me out of here*, I said, *Or at least come back with better company!* But the boy said No, I was *his* San Denee and he wouldn't see me shipped off to Cluny for a holy relic, and then he commenced praying to me

---

[127] French: *Saint Denis*

and confessing his sins. It was comical at first—particularly the sins—but I soon grew tired and wished him gone.

"*You might leave off praying and talk to me*, I said. *I'm right here.* But just then we heard a wild clanging of the monastery bell come faintly on the wind.

"*I must go!* cried the boy. *I'll come back again tomorrow.*

"*Could you bring some girls?* I asked. But he wasn't listening. *I must have a relic*, says the boy. He was searching frantically about. *I must have a holy relic to protect me from the Northmen.*

"*I AM a Northman*, I said. *Bring me with you! I probably know their ancestors!*

"One of my broken teeth lay on the ground. The boy snatched it up and stuffed it in his robe. Then he was gone, and I wasn't much sorry for it."

"And he never came back?" I asked.

"Never," said Bran. "Maybe the Northmen got him. I rather hope so. Though he wouldn't have sold for much. Too weak for farm work and too ugly for domestic uses."

"And the Seven?" Fitzhugh asked. "Did you ever learn what became of them?"

Bran laughed darkly.

"All that dust on the cave floor? I reckon that's them.

"Truly?"

"*Já*. You see," Bran explained, "some five hundred years had passed while I slept on the Tveirrokk—passed on *your* side. When the Seven came through the gate I think they all simply turned to dust. Yggdrasil hasn't shown me anything of them. Why *my* poor pate survived I can't say. My face turned to dust, at any rate, and in time my jaw came off too."

"Speaking of your—your jaw," I said cautiously, "I beg your pardon, but I think I now have *both* your missing teeth in my possession. How your tooth found its way from the Frankish lad to me I cannot guess, but, strange to say, we've already used it to open one of the seals on this unusual book."

"Have you really?" Bran sounded intrigued. "Let me see that mirror again. Your book, I mean—*heh heh!*" Bran chuckled, "*Holy Freyja*, did I say?

Yes, and there she is! Gazing at her own smug reflection in the sacred pool, water lilies all around. And you say my tooth was the key?"

I nodded.

"Worked like a charm."

"Ye-es—" Bran said thoughtfully—"I suppose that's how it translated on This Side. *Lock that accursed thing, and lock my ugly mouth along with it.* Somehow that 'thing' found its way back to This Side, and it came back locked with—my ugly mouth, sorry to say."

"A Norseman's tooth," I muttered. "Upper premolar."

I was remembering Albert.

"But good heavens!" cried Elizabeth. "We must get you free! Can't you pull your head back through this—this sea-pig gate? When it opens again, I mean?"

"Ha!" Bran laughed bitterly. "If only I could. It's not that simple. The Tveirrokk, you see, is like a sort of book itself. Your world is called Midgard, and everything in Midgard that ever was or ever will be is written in the World Tree—*is* the World Tree, root and branch. Yggdrasil is the living story of Midgard. And me, I've—I've jumped right off the page. I'm stuck in between the very roots of Time."

"But there must be *something* we can do," said Elizabeth. "When does the gate open again?"

"On *your* side? Not for another fifty years or so," Bran sniffed. "*You* lot will be long dead before *that* happens, from the look of you."

"We could just hang a coat on you," Fitzhugh growled, "and forget about it."

Bran snapped his jaw shut and was silent. He looked dead as a specimen, pinned up there on the coat-rack. The room grew very still except for a muffled *plumf* from the hearth as a log sent red sparks swirling up the chimney. The little clock on the mantlepiece chimed eleven in a thin, insistent voice. The skull hung motionless.

Did it ever speak? I wondered. *Did I just imagine it?*

Outside the wind made a curious wail through the chimney-pipes. *It sounds like a girl*, I thought. *Like a girl crying alone in the dark.* Then I remembered the ghost.

The sea-cave. Help her.

I stood up resolutely. Striding across the parlour, I went to the one black window and drew the curtain firmly across it.

"Now then!" I said briskly. "*Herra* Bran, I beg your pardon, but I have your other lost tooth in my pocket and it's time we tried the second lock."

The skull came alive.

"Oh, it's my *pardon* you want," Bran jeered. "Why beg? It's not like there's anything *I* can do about it. I'm just a head, after all."

"I am truly sorry about your condition," I said sincerely, "and I'm a bit embarrassed to say it, but we—well we've seen a ghost. And we have reason to believe someone might be in trouble. Some woman.

"Though I suppose you've heard stranger things," I added. (It occurred to me that, here I was, conversing in Old Norse with a talking skull.)

"A ghost?" Bran asked sharply. "What ghost? What did it look like?"

"Hard to say," I replied. "Transparent, mostly. I'd guess it was a man of about five-and-twenty. Ancient tunic. Short beard. Blank expression. Bluish homespun cap like sailors wore."

"Strange—" Bran said musingly. "Sounds a bit like the sailor boy *I* saw on the Tveirrokk. Only that boy looked younger. Fifteen or sixteen." Bran tried to shake his head. In my mind's eye I saw his handsome face wearing a thoughtful look.

"Fine!" Bran said abruptly. "You're pardoned. Open away. Just put me where I can watch."

Fitzhugh set the coatrack beside the whist-table. He took Bran's skull (a bit gingerly) and moved it to a lower hook while Elizabeth gathered up her pencils. I carefully spread *John Blackjohn* out under the lamp.

"There's three copper plates," I said, demonstrating the book to Bran, "and two keyholes. I put your top tooth in the first keyhole and the plate came off just like magic. Here it is, see? I don't know if I can put it back on again, and I don't dare try."

"And what was behind the plate?"

"Pages."

"I don't read," Bran sniffed. "What do they say?"

"It's a story."

"About what?" Bran demanded. "Speak plainly, mortal!"

"It's a story," I replied, "about a sailor boy and an Irish monk and a fairy girl."

"Thor's beard! Is it really?"

"Upon my honor. The book was all moldy and stuck together, but after we got the pages apart we came upon this next plate, see? No keyhole. The last third of the book is still locked. But *here*—" (I closed *John Blackjohn* and turned it over) "—here's another Freyja with another keyhole in her mouth, set right into the back cover." I was trying my best to sound calm and businesslike while it was all I could do to keep from dancing with excitement.

Bran was silent, looking at the cover, then—

"HA HA!" Bran laughed so suddenly that I jumped (which made Elizabeth jump too).

"Ha ha!" Bran roared. "I already know what happens! Yggdrasil just showed it to me. You're a good man, Stegvard. A very good man. I thank you. I thank you, too—heh heh," he tittered, "I thank you, too, Vilhjálmur. Why, you're as good as a jarl! Don't go hanging a coat on me yet, Vilhjálmur Húgósson.[128] And you, Elísabet! I beg your pardon a thousand times, *dama mín*![129] You're as noble as you are beautiful—oh! If only you could see yourself on the Other Side! But go on! Open it! You lot have to live this part forwards."

We clustered around the book with bated breath. Fitzhugh coughed into his fist and loosened his cravat. Elizabeth was fidgeting with the strings on her smock. My hand shook badly as I took Bran's bottom tooth out of my pocket and fit it into Freyja's serene, coppery mouth.

There was a perfect little *clink*. The tooth fit like it had grown there.

I lifted the seal off the back cover. Four copper pins came out of four holes drilled neatly through the pages. With trembling fingers I opened to the page where our transcription was cut short by the blank copper plate.

The plate slid off the page like a bookmark.

"It's ours!" I shouted, dancing around the table like I'd lost my mind. "It's all ours!"

---

[128] Norse: *William son of Hugh*

[129] Norse: *my lady*

"Wait!" cried Elizabeth. "There's a little box under that plate."

"What's that in it?" Fitzhugh demanded.

Up on the coat-rack Bran only snickered.

I tilted the lampshade and looked in. A square hole about three inches across was cut cleanly through the remaining pages. Fit cleverly inside was a wooden box, brittle as dust. Something green shone dully within.

"Hold on!" I said. "Let me get my tweezers."

I came rushing back. Gently I lifted something shiny out of the box.

Elizabeth gasped.

"A fairy glass!"

"And what's that?" cried Fitzhugh. "Is that—"

I was laughing almost as hard as Bran. Swinging from the tweezers was a little dried herring with green thread wrapped around its tail.

CHAPTER 30

"Please, brother Kol!" I pleaded. "We can't stay here!"

Kol wiped his sleeve across his forehead. "I know, James," he said wearily, "I know. You're worried about your brother John."

We were standing on a stone quay. To our backs a row of simple gray huts squatted along the bay: blue smoke rising from every chimney, green turf growing thick on every roof. Behind the cottages a narrow strip of pasture crowded up against a towering cliff where gannets wailed above their nests. Below us, the *Otter* sat in a sort of trench. She looked like a dead bird—sails gone, masts cocked to one side, naked yards swaying. She was propped up all around with spars and driftwood poles. From somewhere inside came the faint tap-tapping of a mallet.

"They might be hurting John, Brother Kol!" I wailed. "We have to go find him!"

"That could be, James," Kol said gravely. "I'm sorry. But the *Otter* isn't our boat, and she isn't seaworthy either. McKee says she touched bottom twice and she's leaking badly. We aren't sailing anywhere until she's out of dry-dock, and that could be several days. Also—" Kol lowered his voice—"the crew are scared. They've seen the power of evil and they've lost their captain. I don't think they'd sail now for all the gold in Christendom."

"So John dies in chains," (I was trying not to scream) "if he isn't dead already?"

"I'm sorry, James. I didn't—"

"The earl kills my brothers while we—" I choked—"while we do nothing?"

Kol didn't answer. He studied my face with concern. Then he sighed.

291

"Everything dies," Kol said quietly.

He came a step nearer, and then to my surprise Kol gathered me into his arms like a child and held me so tight I could hardly breath. I dropped my head onto his shoulder and cried until his cassock was wet.

"Everything dies, James," Kol repeated. "Don't let your anger poison you."

I shoved away from him.

"You smell worse than a tanner's!"

"I was just *at* the tanner's," Kol retorted.

I wiped my eyes.

"Aren't *you* worried about John?"

Kol looked thoughtful.

"God takes care of John," he said slowly. "It's *you* I'm worried about—but ho! Here's Padraig."

Padraig was Captain Blackjohn's son, and a biggish lad himself. He was so like Blackjohn in face and stature that it seemed as if the captain were still with us. But he talked strangely, like everyone in Doonbridge. Kol seemed to understand the Doonbridgers well enough, and the Doonbridgers opened their doors to Brother Kollam Keeli, the first priest the village had seen in hundreds of years. In the three nights we'd been there I hadn't seen Kol sleep. Up and down the mossy lanes he ran, baptizing and blessing and hearing confessions and marrying people two by two (and sometimes three by three) like he was Saint Columba himself.

"These lost sheep have been many years without a shepherd," Kol said. "It's not the proper way of doing things, of course, but I suppose a renegade priest is better than no priest at all."

Diana got on well enough too. She seemed to understand the Doonbridgers' speech even better than Kol. The people all treated her with something like reverence. Diana spent long hours in council with the village Elders, huddled around the fire in the gloom of a ruined church they called Great-Hall. I couldn't make sense of their deliberations—only a word here and a word there. It reminded me of the way old mother Ebber spoke back in Buckley village, she having been a girl in Skye many years ago.

Padraig touched Kol's shoulder and said something in a low voice. "Ah!" Kol exclaimed. "We've been summoned. The Elders want to speak to us."

Dr. Scott's Note:

Nota Bene: *I could not decipher what follows. The parchment would have been fairly sound, only this wretched old ink has eaten through the middle of two pages. Round about the margins the only words I can make out are* Elder, Great-Hall, key, week, *and* sea-pig gate, *as well as the phrase* "still remembered St. Michael's Mass Day." *My guess is the Elders of Doonbridge made the party wait until just past the autumnal equinox before they permitted them to attempt the whale gate. After a big crack and a stubborn mold-stain (they haven't got any oil of camphor here) James McKenna continues:*

"There isn't any gate on that bloody rock!" I scoffed.

Kol shot me an angry scowl, but I went on grumbling anyway.

"Rock's no bigger than a barn. And it's standing in water deep enough to float a man-o'-war. Where's a gate to lead to? Might be a gate for a cod—"

"That'll do James!" Kol snapped.

The Elders rowed on in silence—one Elder in front, one behind, bearded and hooded, faces like stone. Kol and I were packed together amidships. Kol's bible—rolled in a sealskin sack with pitched seams—was digging into my back.

Diana was sitting on the bow. The dawn had come with an icy northwesterly and the Elders' little dinghy was overburdened, riding low through swells that licked the gunnels. But Diana—perched up on the prow like a gull—sat tall and easy. Her eyes were toward the sea and the wind was in her hair.

"The Elders are right," Kol said in a reasoning tone. "That key found its way back to Doonbridge for a reason. The time has come to open the gate. *And* an unwed youth must open it. *And* Padraig is twice married. Therefore this honor falls to you," he concluded.

"It's a moment of grave importance," Kol added reflectively. "It might be two centuries since they last opened the sea-pig gate. They only resort to the *Gaeta Muc-Mhara* in times of the utmost distress."

"They don't *look* distressed," I returned pettishly. "They look like they're getting fat on mutton. *I'm* the one's distressed."

Kol gave an exasperated sigh. "How *can* you be so dense, James?" he said. "Do you really think Francis Stewart, fifth Earl of Bothwell, wants—what?—the three dirty McKenna boys from Buckley? Pah! The Black Stag wants the whole of *Scotland*! And the whole of England, too. And Éireann, probably. Who among us is safe? While you talk about yoursel—ah!—" Kol broke off hastily, "I'm— Forgive me, James. I'm sorry. For a moment I forgot poor Peter has left us, God rest his brave soul!" Kol rubbed his eyes with a drawn look. He pulled his robe up against the biting wind.

"Can't remember when I last slept," Kol murmured, staring about vacantly. "Venus rising in Aries. Mad sorcerer on our heels. Blessed world gone insane. Feels like I've got the fate of Doonbridge and the fate of Scotland and the fate of all green Albyn[130] on my hands. Those hands stained with sins of their own. A runaway priest with a stolen bible—ha ha!" Kol laughed bleakly.

I looked down at the gold chain in my hands, then up at the gold chain around the sternmost Elder's neck. They seemed the same, only the Elder's chain didn't have a dried herring on it. I pulled my hood up and squirmed miserably.

"Still ought to be Padraig here, not I," I muttered. "Blackjohn gave Padraig the key. Padraig can ride a dried herring to Fairyland. *I'll* sail with the *Otter*. To look for John's body, probably."

Diana turned around and pinned me with her piercing blue eyes. I winced. I hadn't thought she was listening.

"You've been wrong before, James," Diana said sternly.

Then she smiled, not like a queen but like a girl.

"The straight path isn't always the safe path. Sometimes you need to have faith."

---

[130] Alba (or Albion)

I looked down again at the little brown herring with green thread wrapped around its forked tail. Then with a sigh I took off my hood and put on the gold chain. The roofless pillars of the ruined bridge glided leisurely past while the oars beat a monotonous *slap slap* and Kol's bible dug into my back.

At last the pillars ended and the lighthouse loomed dark above us. I expected we'd make for the stone quay, but to my surprise the Elders rowed steadily until we'd rounded the rock and come up against the western side. It was low tide. The waves breaking over the naked shoals sent mighty fountains of spray into the air. I shivered.

"I don't remember the shoals being so rough!

"Bad as they were," I added.

"Ah-*hah!*" Friar Kol exclaimed. "Of course! It's the neap tide. Lowest tide of the season, and look: here's a sea-cave in the rock. It would have been under water when we came through."

A little black arch stared out at us from the waterline like a sleepy eye that blinked when the swells brushed over it. The Elders dropped oar. We bobbed steady, drifting toward the cave.

"Diana, my dear?" said Friar Kol, "I'm afraid you'll have to shove in beside us now as best you can. It looks as if we can barely clear the ceiling."

The Elders backed the oars, working to keep us straight in the current. Diana edged past the Elder in the bow seat. Stepping deftly over his arm she squeezed in beside me. The sternmost Elder crouched low, watching the cave's mouth like a cat.

We dropped heavily in the swell.

"*So-ocair!*" called the Elder in the bow with a warning voice. They dipped their oars. We edged forward.

"*So-ocair!*" called the Elder, and they dipped their oars again.

"*Rach!*" shouted the Elder. They both dug in and the skiff lurched forward. The cave swallowed us. Diana bent low. Her forehead was on my shoulder and I could feel her hair against my cheek. The skiff stopped rocking. We sat motionless. Not a glimmer of light could be seen. There was a sudden deathly calm.

"You're blushing!"

It was Diana who spoke.

"You're blushing, aren't you? Your ear feels like it's on fire!"

I coughed.

"I—I could use a wash," I said miserably. "I've been sleeping at the tanner's."

Kol and Diana broke out laughing. The noise echoed off unseen walls.

"Don't fret yourself," Kol chuckled. "Diana won't be presenting us at court."

Then I started laughing too.

"Maybe we can get a wash in Fairyland."

"Yes, well, at any rate you can sit up now," said Kol, "The roof is high enough." One Elder was scraping about in the bow. He uncovered a lamp carved from a ram's horn (for they had no glass) and hung it from a shepherd's crook. Then he stuck the crook through a hole carved in the prow. The lamp cast a dull glow over us. We were lumped together like wool-sacks in the boat. The ceiling was so low the Elder's head almost touched it, but the walls and the water were all blackness. The Elder looked at me—a weathered face barely visible in the gloom.

"*Faigh amach an bád.*"

"What?" I answered dully.

"*Faigh amach an bád,*" the old man repeated. He jerked his hood toward the unseen water.

I turned to Kol questioningly.

"He says get out of the boat, lad," Kol said softly.

"Out of—out of the *boat*?" I wailed. The Elder said something to Kol in a muffled voice. Then both Elders stood up carefully. Raising their arms they braced themselves against the dripping ceiling. Then Kol stood up and he braced himself against the ceiling too.

"Quick, James!" Kol hissed. "The tide's coming in! These good men are risking death for you. In a moment we shall all be trapped. D'you want to drown in here? No? So get in the water, and don't tip the boat. And see that chain stays on!"

I glanced back across the stern. A faint gray light showed where the mouth of the cave—smaller now—rose above the water. It winked as a wave passed over.

"We could still row back!" I said timorously. I looked down at the black, frigid water.

Then I felt something move against my cheek.

"I think you're brave," Diana whispered in my ear. "I forgive you for killing the bullfinch." Then she kissed me, and her lips were soft and warm.

I sucked in a breath.

"Looks like I'm getting a wash!"

The water closed over my head.

I came up gasping and struggling. The icy shock took my breath away. My wool coat was dragging me down like an anchor. I grabbed for the skiff, but there was nothing there. It was utterly dark. I let myself go under and tried to wriggle out of my coat. I got one arm free, and then I sucked in seawater.

I choked. Came up. Swallowed seawater again. Cold salt was burning in my lungs. I knew I was going to die. I stopped struggling, bracing myself to inhale and drown. Mingled with the panic a thought flickered through my mind:

Did Diana really kiss me?

I felt a shock so powerful it blasted the brine out of my lungs.

I inhaled nothing.

The sea, the cave, the air itself—gone. I was drifting in a black void while—brighter than diamonds, clearer than lighting—the stars in their millions burned around me.

Below my feet: a golden glow, getting brighter. Now it was the outline of a creature, swimming through nothing. It circled me with an unhurried grace, huge and sinuous. The gold tracings running down its immense body betrayed the outline of a whale; vast—

But also somehow small. Like something a boy could ride.

I felt a tug at my neck.

I looked down.

The little brown herring—very much alive—was swimming toward the whale with the nearest thing to a joy I ever saw in a fish.

The whale's mouth yawned open, big enough to swallow the moon. We drifted inside. Far, far below, the jaws and the little ridges on its tongue were edged in luminous gold. For one fleeting instant it seemed to pause.

Then its mouth closed over the little herring and me like a cloud covers the sky.

Charlie my boy, it is I—your loving uncle James. I write this strange tale, while my eyes fail, while the quill trembles in my hand, in the hope that you can someday free us from this weary curse: from John Blackjohn's curse. From the curse of forever searching for Doonbridge, and for what was lost there.

I can't describe crossing over, Charlie. Everything changes, and yet everything stays the same.

The whale was a woman.

Then it was a whale again.

Then the whale was a cave (and the herring was a daisy, I think). I was a baby. Then I was an old man, and then I was *two* old men and a sort of stunted boy, and then I think I might have been a turnip (I know I distinctly *felt* like a turnip).

Then I fell flat on my face and sucked in sweet clean air, and when I opened my eyes I was lying on the most marvelous lawn you've ever seen. A white tree was glowing in front of me. Kol and Diana were brushing themselves off, the skiff and the Elders were gone, and all the stars were blazing away in a black velvet sky so close they looked like apples you could reach out and pluck.

"Welcome to the Tveirrokk!" boomed a deep, pleasant voice behind me.

I turned.

It was a dragon.

CHAPTER 31

From the diary of Doctor Stewart Henry Scott—

"Gods! How much farther?"

Bran was back inside my valise.

Fitzhugh had tried mounting him on top of his walking-stick like a ghoulish sort of cane, but Bran complained that all the swaying made him dizzy, so back into my satchel he went.

"Steady on, Herra Bran!" I called out cheerfully. "It won't be much longer now. I'd carry you if I could, but I need two hands to scramble up these rocks."

"Sweet Baldr!" Bran coughed. "Can't you at least open this accursed bag? What do you *keep* in here? It smells like a goat—"

He coughed again.

"Like a goat—ate juniper and—died."

"Oof!" I panted. "Well, it could be the alcohol."

"The *what*-the-hel?"

"Could be the smelling salts. Laudanum. Copper sulfate. Potash. Mineral spirits. An onion—"

"Gah!" Bran choked. "Open the bag!"

"Can't—just yet—" I puffed—"We're—almost—to the top. Can't have you tumbling down a crevice, aye? Miss our only chance of pushing you back through that knothole in time."

"Aye, cheer up, *félagi*," Fitzhugh put in wryly. "You're an adventurer, what? Why, this must be the farthest you've adventured in about a thousand years!"

Muffled cursing came from the bag. "Here it is!" cried Elizabeth. (She'd just gained the top of the long smooth boulder.) "I can see the red stain on the rocks."

We gathered around the mouth of the little cave. I peered breathlessly into the gloom. The morning was gray and misty as every other.

"Pah!" Bran puffed as I took him out of my valise. "I was holding my breath!"

"Skull with lungs," Fitzhugh muttered.

I squared my shoulders and cleared my throat.

"Now then, my brave friends," I began, "we find ourselves at the last throw of this extraord—"

"Oh!" Bran interrupted. "Right. You're going to need a bucket of water."

"A—b-*bucket*," Fitzhugh spluttered. "Where the devil are we going to get a bucket from? Got one in your pockets, have you Bran? Why didn't you tell us before we tramped three miles through the heather?"

"Well it doesn't have to be any great *size*," Bran retorted, as if that solved everything. "A mere wineskin will do. Hasn't any of you got a sheep's bladder, or—or—"

"Have *you* got a bladder?" Fitzhugh snapped. "Ahem!" Elizabeth interrupted, with a quick squeeze of Fitzhugh's shoulder. "Now, now! What's done is done. No point in getting irate." She turned to Bran. "*Herra* Bran: would—say—a quart do? That's about as much as a biggish bottle."

"Hmm—" said Bran. "Yes—yes I think that might *just* do. But a bottle wouldn't work," he added quickly. "You won't be pouring it. You have to dump it out all at once."

Elizabeth looked over her shoulder.

"Oh," she said, "I think I'll manage."

"This is the last outrage!" Bran bellowed.

Fitzhugh was holding him upside-down. Water sloshed in his empty cranium and ran out of his eye sockets. We were standing in a little circle inside the cave. Fitzhugh's lantern burned on the pebbly floor. I was putting on the dried herring which Elizabeth had strung from green yarn like a sort of necklace. ("I don't know if the color makes any difference," she said, "but I *have* green.")

"How *dare* you?" Bran thundered. "I—am—a—*JARL*!"

"Hush, dear," Elizabeth soothed, "this will all be over soon. That hollow was full of rainwater, and you're the perfect size. Stewart? How are you getting on?"

"I—I don't really know how this ought to work," I replied nervously. "The herring is meant to be worn, I think, and I'll keep the fairy glass in my palm in case *that* does something. *Blackjohn* is safe at home, therefore—"

I took a deep breath.

"Hrumf!" Fitzhugh coughed. "Maybe we ought to—er—maybe we ought to—link arms? Or something?" He stuck his hands in his pockets and kicked sullenly at the floor.

"Just—you know—so we don't get—er—separated."

"I think that's a fine idea!" I said with spirit. "Who knows *what* may happen? Nothing, probably, but—"

"Just get *on* with it!" shouted Bran.

We locked arms, me in the middle. Elizabeth was trembling with excitement. Fitzhugh, one arm linked through mine, was clutching his walking-stick with one hand and trying not to spill Bran with the other.

Something moved against my cheek.

Elizabeth had darted me a kiss, quick and warm.

"Good luck, Sir Wemyss," she whispered in my ear. "I think you're brave."

Fitzhugh held the skull up over my head.

Then he froze.

A young man in an old-fashioned sailor's cap stood in front of us, just across the lantern.

He was clear and quite solid now. His clothes were an old-fashioned sort of homespun: a simple tunic reaching past his knees with shapeless felt trousers underneath. Sturdy leather boots and a leather coat, unbuttoned. He wore a short beard, and his ruddy face was all over freckles. The hair beneath his cap was wild and unkempt—reddish with flecks of gray.

His eyes—green and very alert—glinted in the lantern-light, as did the green fairy glass he wore on a gold chain.

He looked straight at me.

Then he grinned.

"Looks like you're getting a wash."

CHAPTER 32

I can't remember much of Fairyland, Charlie—just watery pictures, like my first memories of childhood. I remember there was a magnificent green dragon on the Tveirrokk, and I remember brother Kol being distraught because his beautiful bible had turned into a beautiful mirror. Then a fierce young seafarer with a bloody mouth ran up and looked in Kol's mirror, and then he picked up a stick and charged off and got his head stuck in the sky. The dragon looked at me and said *Everything dies* (he seemed quite cheerful about it), and after that the only thing I can remember is a marvelous little ship sailing up out of the stars. We all got in—Kol, Diana and me—and we set sail for Fairyland.

Whether we journeyed five minutes or five hundred years I couldn't say. Our one white sail pulled tight and full and Diana held my hand while the cosmos drifted by.

At length we came to Avalon. I remember a low, green country in the midst of an ocean like a blue sky. I remember our little ship dropping down out of the clouds and settling into waves where fish like rainbows darted. Rolling hills. Everything a garden. And apples! Millions upon millions. Apple-trees big as oaks. Long ranks receding into unguessable distance. Apples in every size and color bending from the boughs.

I don't know how long we stayed in Avalon. A few cloudy visions remain. Diana lingering in a trellised courtyard beside a silvery fountain. Towering stone walls on either side. Latticed windows climbing up into a summer sky. I see Diana's face mirrored in the water; neither young nor old, but like the sun, changeless in its beauty.

"Who are you, Diana?" I asked. I was sitting beside her. We were dressed in blue and green and Diana's hair was woven with gems.

She leaned her head on my shoulder.

"Danu, Diana—" she replied. "Mortals call me different names. I am Dana, daughter of Marabreith queen of Avalon."

"Are you the Huntress, then?"

Diana smiled.

"Sometimes."

She trailed her fingers idly in the pool, rippling her reflection.

"Mother sends me to Midgard when Esus the Forester needs our help," she said. "Esus is a dear friend, but he doesn't like to treat with mortals. So Mother sends me."

"She sent you to stop Sir Francis Stewart? Stop the Black Stag?"

"She sent me," Diana said sternly, "to stop *you* killing the bullfinch. He was our servant and we loved him. But I failed."

I hung my head.

"There, there," Diana added gently. "The bullfinch was the *reason* I came, but he was not the *purpose*. You can't always read things clearly from one side. You and I were meant to find each other. That much is plain."

"And Maewyn? Kol's brother?"

"Maewyn was our servant too. We haven't got many people left in Midgard, but Avalon still has her friends."

"But why come as a girl? And why go live with that miserable old Sowter?" I asked, remembering.

Diana laughed. "Old Sùdrach was our servant too, once, before he forgot us—and himself. There's no telling exactly what will happen when you cross over. One side fades like a dream while the other shouts in your ears with a thousand voices. But Mother doesn't worry. I always find my way back. Some parts of Midgard are closer to Fairyland than others. But come!" she stood up. "Kollam is here. It's time to go."

"Time to go where?"

Diana laughed again.

"Time to go see Mother. I'm presenting you and Kollam at Court."

I don't recall everything she said, Charlie, but I remember Marabreith, queen of Avalon, sitting on the grass in a sunlit lawn with little yellow flowers opening at her bare feet. Her dress was plain and white and she wore a crown of white apple-blossoms in her hair. Here and there the fairies passed, talking and singing together in the gardens.

"Francis Stewart is all the more deadly," said the queen, "because he is a fool. He is a child playing with his father's sword. The green blade of Esus will destroy him."

Malbreith spoke lightly, but her face was grave. There was a different shade in her unearthly beauty. Less of the Huntress, perhaps, and more of the Mother.

Diana looked down at the grass. "I wish I'd never thrown the blade into the sea," she said, almost in a whisper. "How did Francis ever come to find it?"

"Oh, that house was always dangerous!" the queen replied. "Proud. Jealous of their rich neighbors. Sir Francis found new servants when he began to play with dark magic. The bancorra have sharp eyes. Gulls and cormorants can be persuaded too."

"Can he be stopped, my lady?" Kol asked. Kol's beard was clipped short and he was barefoot. He wore a simple white robe like the queen's, only Kol's was trimmed with blue.

The queen frowned. "I do not know if he can be stopped," she said. "Avalon hasn't the power in Midgard that it did of old." The queen turned to Diana. "Esus forged that blade not for a weapon, but for a tool. He used it to bring order to the wilds. I doubt we can ever make it a pruning-hook again, now that this mad jarl has turned it into a spear."

We sat a moment in silence. I was gazing up at the queen's airy palace, tower upon tower upon gleaming tower reaching up into the perfect sky.

"There is one song—" the queen began.

She looked into Diana's eyes.

Diana met her gaze, then quickly turned away. Her hand—lying on the grass next to mine—began to tremble.

"Yes," the queen nodded, as if in answer, "it *is* perilous. I feel a warning in my heart. If you leave Avalon, my Dana, the stars will grow old before I see you again."

Diana lifted her face to the queen.

"I am going back to Midgard."

She said it stoutly, but tears like diamonds glistened on her cheeks.

The queen smiled sadly and stood up. Together we walked slowly toward the palace.

"One soul must enter," said the queen, "and one soul must depart."

I touched my chest. Kol's fairy glass was under my robe, still hanging from the plain leather string he'd given me at his cottage in Ettrick Forest.

The queen looked at me.

"A fairy glass was never meant to be a prison," she said. "It is a doorway. It leads to a waiting-place. Another Tveirrokk, if you like. Long ago Esus built a house where souls can rest while the weary ages of Midgard pass outside.

"But when one soul enters," said the queen, "another soul must leave. That has been the law ever since the slaughter of Éireann, when Esus broke his pruning-hook and the Gaels betrayed us."

"He was wise," said Diana. "Francis would trap a thousand shiori in a fairy glass if he could—each bound to him by the Word of Esus."

The queen nodded.

"The shiori keep the law," she said.

She stopped suddenly.

"I wish you would stay here with us, Dana."

A shadow of pain crossed Diana's face, but she slowly shook her head.

The queen sighed, and there were tears in her eyes.

"I will prepare a ship," she said, "if you are resolute. James is a sailor, is he not?"

I started, hearing her use my name.

"But—but I don't know the way," I said, speaking for the first time. "I can't steer through the stars."

The queen smiled.

"This was your errand from birth, James," she said. "The chart is there—" she touched me gently—"written on your arm."

I looked down at my freckles.

CHAPTER 33

From the diary of Doctor Stewart Henry Scott—

There aren't any stars, you know. Only islands.

The dragon told me that. Such a pleasant fellow! "Everything dies," he said. He's quite right, too. And I taught him the most wonderful song—No! He taught it *me*, rather. My wits are a bit muddled. It's so strange crossing over. Everything changes and yet it's all the same, like water when it becomes ice, or like thistle flowers when they turn into wool and drift away. But this was the song:

There were three brothers in bonnie Scotland
In bonnie Scotland livèd they
And they cuist kevels themsells amang
Wha sould gae rob upon the salt sea.

I don't remember the rest and it's all wrong anyway. The McKenna lads never drew straws for which would turn pirate—the notion is absurd! But I'll let James tell it. Steady on! First I must commit to paper what Bran said to us. We met Bran in Iona—met his *head*, at any rate. Let me think. How *does* one tell a story on This Side? It feels like I've been gone a thousand years.

Once upon a—

Right. So, *Looks like you're getting a wash*, says the ghost of James McKenna with a grin, at which Fitzhugh was so startled he dropped Bran right onto my head with a *clunk*. The water went all over me and in an instant I was floating in the ether with a live herring tied to my neck. Then a sort of cosmic whale swam up and swallowed me (it was a humpback, I think, only big enough to digest a battleship), and then I landed on the Tveirrokk with a thud and just sat there for a decade or so, staring up stupidly at Yggdrasil while the white tree hummed and Fitzhugh and Elizabeth brushed themselves off. Then a tall and altogether connected Bran dragged me to my feet and kissed me on both cheeks. He kissed Fitzhugh as well (I hadn't known Vikings did that), and Fitzhugh went red as a radish and was quite at a loss for words. Bran kissed Elizabeth repeatedly (she *is* beautiful on the Other Side!) and he called her *dama mín* and begged her pardon and said she had "saved [his] very soul."

"Come!" Bran cried, dancing and skipping while his funny Viking topknot bobbed on his head. "Come and meet the dragon! Níðhǫggr!" he called. "Níðhǫggr, old snake! Where are you? I want you to meet my friends!"

We walked what seemed like twenty paces and covered maybe two hundred miles while Yggdrasil towered up over us like a forest in the black sky. We rounded a trunk as big as a mountain (or it might have been smaller than a pear tree) and there we came upon a little grassy hollow sheltered between two of the World Tree's mighty roots.

A little man with an axe was chopping there. He chipped away at the root and sang to himself in a satisfied sort of way.

"Níðhǫggr!" Bran called.

The man looked up and smiled. He leaned his axe against the root and dabbed his forehead with a red handkerchief.

"Níðhǫggr! I'm free!" Bran shouted, and he jumped up and down as if to prove it. "Look! These are my new friends. From Midgard, see? Here's Elísabet—she's a lady—"

Elizabeth curtsied, looking embarrassed.

"—and here's Vilhjálmur. He's a steward. And here's Stegvard—" Bran pushed me forward eagerly. "Stegvard's a healer and a good one—ha ha! Yes I *knew* you'd like that. Just look: he's pulled my head back through Time and I've got skin on it again!" Bran patted his face and capered about with a grin that showed his missing teeth.

The little man stepped forward, wiping his hands on his neat brown apron.

"Níðhǫggr, god of death," he said, bowing and kissing Elizabeth's hand. "Charmed."

"Er—charmed as well, I'm sure," Elizabeth stammered. "I beg your pardon, but *Herra* Bran told us you were— He told us that he was acquainted with a—"

"Dragon!" said the little man. "Quite right." He wore a sandy moustache—a bit forked at the ends—and he tweaked one of the forks with a practiced air. "I try to appear to mortals in a form they like." He bobbed his head pleasantly. "I don't see so many mortals passing through the Tveirrokk anymore. As for dragon, well, that has more to do with the *Norse* than it does with me. They're simply mad about dragons."

"I love dragons!" Bran cried.

"Yes—rather," the little man sighed. "Well, here you are then."

Instantly a colossal green dragon, scaly and fierce, was wound about the foot of the World Tree. Smoke spouted from its flaring nostrils like a teakettle. Its vast wings, ribbed and veined like a bat, fanned the air and stirred the lower branches. I jumped and took a step backward.

Then he was a man again. He coughed modestly into his red handkerchief.

"Dragon. Man. Three-headed demon—" he said. "It's all the same to me. Why, I appeared as a *beaver* once. Can you imagine? They're revered in some parts, apparently. Bran sees me as Níðhǫggr the dragon, but you can call me Niles." The little man bowed again and shook my hand.

"I—I'm pleased to meet you, Niles," I said, finding my voice.

"And what brings you to the Tveirrokk?" Niles asked. "Some pressing matter, no doubt. I see you've got a whale-gate key there."

I looked down at my chest. The herring was gone. A golden key hung from my neck, strung on a golden chain.

I nodded gravely. "It's a matter of the Scots lad, James McKenna," I said. I glanced around us. "Er—he was with us a moment ago," I said, "on the Other Side. But I guess he didn't cross over."

"Ah!" said Niles. "You've got him in your pocket, actually. He's inside that little green bottle." Niles pointed at my right side. I quickly stuck my hand into my coat. I'd forgotten I'd put the fairy glass in there after I landed on the Tveirrokk. Taking it out I turned the glass over in my fingers. Emerald green.

About an inch long. Tiny cork. Small irregularities on the surface. It was unchanged.

"Yes," said Niles, "the fairy glass is the door to a sort of waiting-place, Doctor—a sanitarium, if you will, where a weary soul may rest."

"And you say James is *in* it?"

"Yes, absolutely!" Niles nodded earnestly. "I know that soul. James McKenna and an Irish monk came through here some time ago. With Dana, strange to say. *The* Dana. Crown princess of Avalon."

"This is all—very remarkable," I said in some bewilderment. "We've seen James McKenna several times. He even spoke to us!"

"He *spoke* to you?" Niles twirled his moustache thoughtfully. "And how long have you had him in your—ah—had him on your person?"

"My goodness," I said, rubbing my chin, "the bottle was in the book! If what you say is true, then I suppose I've been packing him around with me for—months!"

"And you never summoned him?" Niles asked. "You never spoke the Words of Purchase?"

"Never!" I shook my head vigorously. "He appeared on his own. Isn't that right, Fitzhugh?"

"On his own, aye, and in the nick of time."

"Strange!" said Niles. He glanced up at Yggdrasil with a suspicious look. "Souls *have* been known to cross over spontaneously," he said, "when their need is dire. Only for a moment, mind you. And they aren't very tangible. They aren't very *alert*, either. Sometimes they do more harm than good—that's why it's so rare."

"I think his need must be dire," said Elizabeth. "He led us to you."

"He said something about a woman," I added, "or perhaps a girl."

Niles thrust his hands into his apron pockets. "That's just the thing," he said, frowning and biting his lip. "Why would James McKenna be resting in the waiting-place if his need is dire?"

"Maybe he was forced?" I suggested. "Stuffed inside a fairy glass against his will?"

Niles shook his head. "That isn't possible," he said, "strictly speaking. Shiori obey the Word of Esus, true, but James is mortal. Mortals hardly ever go to the waiting-place, and only by their own free choice. And he'd have to know the Words of Purchase himself."

"But good heavens!" said Elizabeth. "Can't we go in after him? Or call him out?"

Niles shook his head.

"A fairy glass," he said, bowing slightly, "is a sort of surety. A trust, if you will. Upon entering, a soul must establish the conditions for its own release. *Until the Word of Esus calls me*—that's a common one. Or *until a thousand years of the sun are past*."

Niles picked up his axe and chopped at Yggdrasil a few times in a thoughtful sort of way. Shimmering white chips rained onto the unearthly green turf.

"No," he said presently, putting down his axe. "I'm sure of it. The only way you can get James McKenna out—get him out *permanently*—is to meet the conditions he himself has set—whatever those may be."

"And how are we to do *that*, pray?" Fitzhugh growled. "Did he mean us to pay his grocery bill?" He knocked his stick gloomily against his boots. Niles shot Fitzhugh a keen look. In the light of the tree Fitzhugh's stick shone almost as bright as Yggdrasil itself.

Bran sniggered.

"Tell me, Dragon," he said. "Why *did* young Sigfried Redbeard drop the Staff of Esus. After he tried to brain me with it, I mean?"

"What, you never noticed?" Niles chuckled. "I suppose you were stunned. Sigfried couldn't possibly bring the Staff of Esus through to the Other Side. Absurd Vikings! One simply doesn't go and raid the Tveirrokk. The white staff is part of Yggdrasil—part of Time itself. It can't be stolen. It can be *loaned*, certainly, if it serves Yggdrasil's purpose. But—ha ha!—when the staff touched the whale-gate it just stopped in midair, as I knew it would. Took him square in the stomach. And he was running, too!"

Niles laughed and wiped the corners of his eyes with his handkerchief.

"Sigfried—ha ha!—Sigfried just tumbled over it like it was a hurdle and then *poof!* he dives headfirst through the whale-gate. He probably turned to dust on the Other Side."

Niles sighed and put his handkerchief back in his pocket.

311

"Funny that in all these centuries you never asked me that, Bran."

"Funny my skull survived!"

"Well, everything dies," Niles observed, picking up his axe again. "And a good thing, too! Can you imagine? To be stuck on one island forever? Even the immortals must move on eventually. Ah!"

Niles turned and gazed out into the starry void.

"So much to see!" he murmured. "Islands upon islands upon islands."

"Will *you* ever move on, Niles?" Elizabeth asked quietly.

Niles turned back to us. He smiled (a bit sadly, I thought) and knocked a few more chips out of the World Tree.

"Yes," Niles answered, "even *I* will move on. Feels like I've been here forever, though, and the job's not half done. I wasn't *always* the god of death, you know. Had a different job once. Different island. Nowadays I keep Midgard in balance. Yggdrasil grows. I cut. Souls move on. Lucky souls!"

I studied his axe curiously. It was double-edged, with intricate tracings inlaid in the haft. Niles spun it expertly as he chopped; first one edge, then the other. Neat little chips rained onto the turf, flat and clean like they'd been cut by a razor.

"There's a lot of suffering in Midgard, of course," Niles continued. "Most of that is caused by mortals, not by me. I don't pretend to know what it all means. Tree grows. I cut."

He took another swing.

"Gets lonely here sometimes."

Fitzhugh was examining his stick, turning it over in his hands. He looked up at Bran.

"But you said *you* just tossed the Staff of Esus through the hole."

Bran chuckled knowingly. "Yes, I did," he replied, "And I reckon you ought to be thanking Herra Níðhǫggr for that. I reckon the god of death has decided to lend you his Staff of Esus, cut from the World-Tree by his own mighty hand."

Niles bowed to Fitzhugh. "Wasn't entirely certain if I'd see you here," he said briskly. "One can't always read things perfectly from This Side, not even when there's Yggdrasil to consult." He patted the World Tree.

"Thank—you—" Fitzhugh said thoughtfully, turning the staff over in his hands. It looked like an ordinary branch—about four feet long with a few knots sticking out on the surface. But the staff was flat at one end like it had been carved. It glowed faintly with an inner light.

Fitzhugh looked up at the dragon with a smile. "I'm really much obliged," he said. "From the moment I laid eyes on this stick I thought there was something—I don't know—*purposeful* about it. I'm a steward, you see. *Was*, anyway. Bit of a gardener myself." He nodded at the root where Niles had been chopping with an understanding look.

Niles grinned broadly. "Oh, I think you'll put it to *very* good use." He turned to Bran. "Speaking of moving on, my dear Bran—" he added with a catch in his voice, "Your ship is here, *ástin mín*. I shall miss you terribly, of course. Do come back sometime. And all in one piece!"

We turned to look.

A wonderful little ship, its prow carved like a dragon's head, was sailing up out of the black sky. It had a proud square sail striped red and white, and the gunnels were all hung with brightly-painted shields.

Bran gasped.

"She's beautiful!"

"I knew you'd like her," Niles chuckled. "Off with you now! Go and find the Seven. You'll be friends again. Everything's changed. A new start. A new island. A new life."

We all embraced Bran and said goodbye. Bran wept and thumped his chest in a Viking sort of way, and he swore by several gods that he would meet us all again. Then he climbed aboard (with evident delight) and the little ship floated away from the Tveirrokk. Bran was singing as he sailed. For a long time his voice came back to us, strong and clear, while his ship grew smaller and smaller:

Syndir því valda,
At vér hryggvir förum ægisheimi ór;
Engi óttask, nema illt geri;
gott er vammalausum vera

313

At last his voice faded and his ship winked out among the stars. Fitzhugh turned away, wiping his eyes and pretending to cough.

"Hrmpf! Got lungs on him *now*, hasn't he?"

"That he does." (I put my hand on Fitzhugh's shoulder.) "That he does."

"Singing hasn't improved any!"

We all laughed.

"Terrible singing!" Niles agreed. "Like a dog. I shall miss him awfully, though I mostly saw the back of him. Well—" he sighed—"to business. There was trouble afoot when James McKenna came through here, and it looks like there's trouble afoot now."

I nodded. "I can't be sure," I said, "but I think the blade of Esus is still at large—the cutting end of his Crook. We three ran afoul of a sort of—er—a sort of lunatic. He's been hurling lightning with it. Murdered three men, maybe more. We're fugitives like James."

"A lunatic, you say?" Niles twirled his moustache.

"A mad solicitor. Name of Radan. He's a sort of—er—scribe. To Sir Walter Douglas-Scott, fifth Duke of Buckley."

"Aha! *That's* the type," said Niles. "There's always a sneaky underling mixed up in this sort of thing. Buckley, you said? On Alba—the bigger island?"

"Right!" I nodded vigorously. "Our Duke of Buckley is Sir Francis Stewart's descendant. I suspect the blade was passed down through his line."

"Is it curved? Does it look like a pruning-hook?"

"I never got a chance to examine it carefully," I answered, "but no: I'm fairly certain it was straight. Yes, I'm sure it was. Straight like a knife."

Niles shook his head grimly. "That's bad," he said. "That's not the sort of thing mortals can mend."

"Ah!" Elizabeth sighed. "I was afraid of that. What shall we do?"

Niles bit his lower lip pensively.

"I can't do much in Midgard," he said at length. "Other than killing, I mean."

"Couldn't you simply kill Radan?" Fitzhugh asked hopefully. "If he isn't dead already?"

Niles shook his head. "It doesn't work in that way," he said. "I have to keep the cycle of life and death in balance. Mortals generally leave Midgard when their time is ripe. Some few—like your Radan—take matters of life and death into their own clumsy hands, and the results are always disastrous. Men like Radan cause the worst of Midgard's suffering."

Niles sighed and took off his apron, folding it carefully. "My workday's done," he announced. "I wish you'd join me for supper and a few songs. I could use the company."

We accepted in noisy chorus. Niles smiled gratefully.

"I'll do for you as much as I could do for James McKenna," he said. "I'll teach you a song or two which mortals can sing. I can't promise it will do much good. Men haven't the gifts of fairies, but—ah! Even better! Here's the lady Elísabet. I have a particular song for *you,* my dear. I think it might prove its worth, in time."

Niles beckoned us to follow, and together we climbed a well-worn path out of the little dell between the World-Tree's giant roots. At the green margin we could see a cozy little house under the starlight where the Tveirrokk met the blazing sky. Smoke rose from its stone chimney. A comfortable yellow light shone out of its windows. Niles trudged up the path, axe in hand.

"I tried to teach that song to James when he was here," Niles called back over his shoulder, "but a boy of sixteen doesn't have the head for it. I'm sure he forgot it the moment he crossed over. The Doonbridgers always sent an unwed youth to wear the herring."

"Yes, why *was* that?" I asked.

"Well they couldn't risk a married man," said Niles, "nor an old one. The whale-gate at Doonbridge is terribly dangerous. Some have drowned in the attempt. The Doonbridgers hardly ever used the key, and when they did it always came attached to some wide-eyed boy. Usually they just needed codfish or warmer weather or something—simple songs to teach. But James? James was on a quest. Pity I couldn't have done more for him."

We'd only gone what seemed a few paces but already the cottage was near at hand. The path led up to a low stone wall and through a wooden gate. I noticed the deep yellow thatch on the roof and the cheery painted carvings along the eaves. A silver lantern hung over the arched doorway. It reminded me of my old granny's farmhouse. Only better—the way Granny's farm would look on the Other Side.

"Tell me, Niles," I asked. "You didn't always live here? You said you had a different occupations once?"

"Aye."

"And what was that, if I may ask?"

Niles put his hand on the latch. There was a twinkle in his bright eyes.

"Oh, I think you already know, Stegvard."

"Aha! So you *were*, then? I knew it!"

"Yes!" said Niles, laughing all over. "I, the god of death, used to be a doctor!"

CHAPTER 34

Doctor Scott's transcription—

Nota Bene—I've almost come to the end of this strange book, The Last Will and Testament of the Pirate John Blackjohn. *What others may think of James McKenna's tale—and of my own—I cannot guess. Were I to publish it I imagine people would think me insane. If I'm arrested they'll think me the verriest fool that ever burgled the Duke of Buckley and was arraigned on suspicion of murder. But the iron's on the anvil and I must strike it. James McKenna continues:*

On a dewy morning we left Avalon. Diana said goodbye to Marabreith her mother. I will not write of their parting. The happy memories fade, while the memories that cause me deepest pain linger and linger and linger.

We boarded our little ship—Diana, Kol and me—and we sailed away from the Apple Isle. The blue sea turned to blue sky, and then the blue faded to black and we sailed among the stars. Diana held my hand. I kept the tiller, glancing now at my arm, now at the black sky, making for the constellation that would guide us home.

At length we came to the Tveirrokk. There the dragon spoke to me again, but I can't remember what he said. I saw him nip a leafy twig from off the World Tree and drop it at Diana's feet. Diana picked it up and drew a circle in the air. A doorway opened, and I could see the Other Side. It looked cold and gray. Dead grass was swaying in the wind and there was a black stone behind it. We stepped through the doorway together and crossed over.

Tall stones stood in a wide circle around us, mossy and black with rain. A cold wind blew. Diana caught my arm to steady herself. I knew the place. We were standing on Tursahan Knowe. The sun was setting under heavy clouds. The evening lights of Buckley village were just starting to come out below.

"We're home!" I shouted in astonishment. "Brother Kol! We're home again!"

I turned around.

Friar Kol was sitting on the dead grass. He was dressed in his old dirty cassock again. His bible lay open across his knees. Kol's shoulders were heaving. Tears streamed down his face.

"My bible!" Kol wept, "My bible! Gone! There's nothing— There's nothing *written* on it. It's got locks now, and—and—"

He turned the pages despairingly.

"Blank! All blank!"

Kol lay on the wet ground and buried his face in his arms.

I gasped.

"Friar Kol!" I called. "Friar Kol, look!"

Kol raised his head.

A tall lady stood before him, transcendently beautiful. Her bare white feet hardly seemed to touch the dead grass. She was dressed in green like a sunlit pond, and the folds of her gown and the shimmering cascade of her dark hair stirred with a watery ripple.

Lily stooped down and gently helped Kol to his feet. He lifted his eyes to hers.

"My—my heart got broken, Lily," he said, as if in a dream.

She nodded.

"So did mine."

Kol dropped his head and covered his face with his hands. "My bible is ruined," he sobbed. "Maewyn is dead. My home is gone."

Lily smiled tenderly.

Then in a blink she was pressed up against him. Her head lay on his ragged shoulder and her slender arms—more beautiful than an emperor's robe—were draped about his neck. Her ruby lips touched his dirty cheek, leaving teardrops where they passed.

They stood together—the queenly immortal and the little bald priest— and held each other close while the rain started to fall.

"We'll make a new home, Kollam," she said at last. She took his chin in her hand and raised his eyes to hers. "A new home, and a new heart to share."

"I love you," Kol answered. "I will always love you. What made you come back?"

She took his rough hand in hers and pressed it to her heart.

"You're going to be killed, Kollam," she replied gently, "and leave this world. But if our two hearts are one then I will leave with you, for even the immortals must depart someday."

"Can that *be*?" Kol asked in wonder.

Lily nodded.

"That power is given me," she said. "My heart is yours."

"But why—" I interrupted, aghast—"why do you say Friar Kol is going to be killed?"

Lily turned to me with a kind smile.

"You're *both* going to be killed," she said, "probably."

She pointed toward the sky.

My heart stopped.

Chilling laughter came from high overhead. I looked, but all I could see were the clouds scudding low and fast across the sky.

"I don't—"

BOOM went a canon.

A wild clamor burst over us. I stared up openmouthed. A long black shape appeared out of the clouds. It grew bigger. Soon I could see black specks buzzing around her naked masts. The *Raven* was coming down out of the sky.

A dense flock of witches and bancorra were tethered to the *Raven*'s sides. Every witch rode a broom, and every broom was tied to a rope. The *Raven* bucked and swayed madly as she dropped, while the cawing and the shrieking grew louder. At last she touched ground in the middle of the circle. Her hull creaked hideously as she rolled onto her port side and came to rest against a standing stone. The Raven's deck lay at a crazy slant. The witches and the bancorra flurried around her like flies.

All at once they loosed their tethers. A barrel rolled down the deck and bumped over the rail. It landed with a *thud* in the dead grass.

Then with a shout Sir Francis Stewart himself leaped over the rail. He looked as fine and as fresh as ever, but his handsome face was twisted with rage. In one hand he carried a silver rapier; in the other, the blade of Esus. Brother Lara crawled out awkwardly behind him.

"Ah *ha*! There's the banshee!" Francis snarled. "*Quo vadis,*[131] fairy? I beg your pardon, but I don't recall dismissing *you* when last we spoke." He flicked his rapier, making it whistle in the air.

"Avalon sends you greeting," Diana retorted. The World Tree branch was in her hand. She raised it, and at once the witches and the bancorra took to the sky in panic, shrieking as they flew.

Francis seemed not to notice. "Did you know," he asked casually, "that the green blade of Esus commands the lightning? Fascinating, isn't it?" He raised the copper blade toward the sky.

"*Dall ort!*" Francis screamed.

I staggered up off the ground. All I could hear was the ringing in my ears. Red embers of burnt grass settled through the air. Diana stood at the edge of the stone circle. The grass lay black and smoldering all around her, but she stood tall and unmoved. She lifted her branch.

"*Fàs!*" she cried.

Vines sprang up out of the ground. Lara screamed and thrashed as the grasping tendrils caught his legs. But Francis only waved the green blade in the air. "*Gearr,*" he said flippantly, and the vines disappeared. Lara took to his heels and hid behind a standing stone.

Francis smiled cruelly as he turned away from Diana.

"*Dall ort!*" he screamed again.

There was a cry of pain.

I turned around.

Friar Kol stood trembling.

Kol stumbled backward, one hand against a standing stone, the other clutching his chest. Smoke rose from his cassock. I ran to him.

"Brother Kol—" I faltered.

---

[131] Whither goest?

A round hole was burned under Kol's hand. I could see his flesh—red and blistering—directly over his heart. Kol's knees gave and he sagged backward.

Then he stopped.

Lily was holding him in her arms. Her dark hair fell across his shoulders as she tenderly laid him on the ground. Lily pressed her lips against Kol's forehead. Kol smiled. His eyes were locked with Lily's. His hand fell open on the ground.

"Goodbye, James—"

His voice was weak but cheerful: the voice of dear old Friar Kol from Buckley. Friar Kol who fed me sometimes. Friar Kol who taught me the *Gloria Patri* and my letters.

Friar Kol, my dear and holy friend.

"Goodbye, James, and God bless you, my boy. We'll see each other again."

Kol's voice dropped to a whisper.

"I am so happy."

I blinked and rubbed my eyes.

The bent grass was already springing back from the place where he had been. Kol and Lily were gone.

I thought I was dreaming.

I was running at Francis with all my strength, but my legs were like stone. I saw his lips curl back over his teeth. He thrust his rapier at me but I was already inside his reach. We collided. Cold steel touched my neck.

"*Stad!*" Francis screamed.

Something cracked inside me.

Wet ground against my neck. Francis falling back a pace, laughing and brushing off his fine coat. Something invisible pinning me to ground. Francis aimed his rapier at my side with a look of hatred and delight.

"You McKennas—" he panted—"all—die—the same way!"

I tried to move.

"Between the sixth and seventh ribs, yes?"

Francis drew back his elbow for the strike.

"The honor is *yours*, sheep, to be butchered by your lord!"

I closed my eyes.

"*STAD!*"

It was Diana's voice.

Francis hesitated. Turning, Francis lowered his rapier while his smile faded.

Diana stood on top of a broken stone. The setting sun—streaming under the boiling clouds—made a fiery halo around her shoulders and tinged her old dress blood-red. Her hands were clasped high above her head and she held the World-Tree branch between them. Out of her palms there shone a light, white and piercing like a star.

I didn't hear any words, Charlie. Her lips moved, but all I heard was a note was so high and penetrating it left me witless. Sir Francis Stewart dropped to his knees with his mouth hanging open like a corpse. The blade of Esus fell out of his senseless hand. His silver rapier rolled on the grass.

I staggered to my feet, clutching my head.

"Diana!" I screamed.

Diana's arms hung limp at her sides.

She swayed.

She collapsed sideways off the rock.

I remember sitting on the ground with Diana's head on my knees. Her dress was burned through on one side. She looked up at me as she struggled to breathe.

"I tried, James," Diana whispered. "I tried the song to bend the blade. I was too weak. The blade broke me."

She lifted her hand and touched my neck. Tears streamed down her face.

"I will miss you, dearest," Diana whispered. "I tried to save your world for you."

"No, Diana—"

I shook my head violently.

"No—"

Her hand dropped onto the grass.

"*NO!*" I shrieked. I was running, crazed, for the place where Francis Stewart lay. With my boot on his chest I tore the fairy glass off his neck, breaking the gold chain. Then I snatched up the blade of Esus from where he'd dropped it and I ran back to her.

"No, Diana—"

I worked feverishly beside her.

"Not now. Not *this* time—"

I lifted her delicate wrist. Her chest had stopped moving.

"Forgive this, Diana," I whispered.

The blade was old, Charlie—very old. Just a crude copper knife about a foot and a half long. It looked so dull, and yet it slid through her skin like a razor. Hot blood spilled out of Diana's palm, staining the blade. I was clutching Francis Stewart's fairy glass in my other hand. As I threw the copper blade away I felt a charge run through me. Lily's words. Lily's voice, speaking to me in the Lilylock in what seemed like ages past. I pressed my cheek against Diana's.

"Wait for me, Diana," I whispered. "I'm coming right back."

I sobbed and took a breath.

"*Ingreditur anima in phialum.*"

Diana flickered once.

Twice.

Then she too was gone. I was alone.

CHAPTER 35

We had a lovely evening in the little cottage on the Tveirrokk (*It's always evening here*, said Niles). I can't remember much of it. I remember rough-cut stone walls and yellow rafters and firelight. We laughed and sang songs and everything felt so safe and hidden and comfortable, like being in your mother's arms. Niles taught Elizabeth a song—just the two of them all whispery and secret beside the fire. Then we went to bed and I don't know where we slept—only that we must have slept a thousand years or more, and I never felt so smothered and peaceful with Yggdrasil singing outside. Sometimes the voice was like falling water and sometimes it was like an steady wind sighing through the trees.

At dawn (or whenever it was) we had to say goodbye. I remember standing inside the ring of light at the foot of the World Tree. I was staring up wonderingly into the endless twining branches. Niles stood beside me.

"Well," he sighed, "I do hate to see you go. But we've a job to do, haven't we? I, to bring death to Midgard. You, to extract a man from a bottle and defeat an electrostatic barrister."

"Solicitor," I corrected him glumly.

"Even worse!"

"How *do* we get back?" asked Elizabeth. "My goodness, we've been here whole ages. The Iona gate could be a volcano by now!"

"Right," said Niles. "I've thought of that." He gestured toward the tree.

Cut neatly into the trunk we saw a path of perfect stairs. Up and up the stairs climbed until, tiny in the distance, they arched over the first mighty branching of Yggdrasil and disappeared. An unbroken handrail, waist-high, was carved into the wood on the trunk side.

"Buh-*limey*!" Fitzhugh breathed, awestruck. Niles coughed modestly into his fist.

"Well I don't *just* gnaw the root," he said. "I have a bit of license to practice here and there. That stair," he tilted his head toward the tree, "is wonderfully useful. In the old days I had to transform myself into a giant snake just to get up into the branches. Norse fancied that. Hardly anyone else. Come!" he said, "I'll lead the way."

We climbed until we were so high the Tveirrok was just a little green stain below. Then it disappeared altogether and all we saw were Yggdrasil and the stars.

At the first fork we levelled off for a while. The steps got lower and longer, and then they gave way to a long, level path which shot as straight as a railway through the huge valley between the World Tree's lower limbs. Countless other paths and stairs branched off in every direction. Up ahead of us Niles stopped and looked around himself with a satisfied expression.

"Beaver," he remarked. "That's appropriate, I guess. I *have* been rather busy."

Then he trudged on again.

Another climb. Another valley. A little jaunt out onto a limb with twin galaxies orbiting underneath it. At last we came upon a thoroughly unremarkable twig with a few silvery leaves opening out of it.

The path went on, but Niles stopped.

"Here we are," he said, a bit wistfully. "This is *your* time. Won't be any turning into dust if you cross over from here. You'll have been gone about five minutes, I reckon."

Niles dabbed his eyes with his red handkerchief. Elizabeth dabbed hers with her white silk one.

"I hate all these goodbyes," Elizabeth said.

I shook Niles' hand warmly and thanked him a thousand times (it might have literally been a thousand times). Then Niles shook Fitzhugh's hand with a squeeze of his arm and said *Mind that staff now, and good luck to you.*

"It takes a gardener to know a gardener," he added.

Niles stooped down and broke off the leafy twig. "It's a good idea to link arms," he said. "Softens the landing. Farewell my friends, and don't despair! Your stars will guide you."

He waved the twig in a circle and a door opened in the air. It was entirely black beyond. I only knew it was a door because the stars winked out behind it.

With our hearts in our throats, we stepped through and crossed over.

We were back in the cave.

"Why's it dark?" Fitzhugh demanded. "Has my lantern gone out?" He fumbled around on the floor, raising dust.

"Well here's my valise," I said, "right where I left it."

Elizabeth coughed.

"Let's get out of here."

"Yes, let's!"

With our hands in front of our faces we shuffled up the stairs.

"Good morning, Doctor!"

I shielded my eyes, blinking in the sudden glare.

Radan was standing on the rock maybe twenty feet from us. He had Fitzhugh's lantern in one hand, and in the other he held a green copper blade— very old—about a foot and a half long. It looked like it was caked with dried mud.

"Welcome home from the Great Beyond!" Radan sneered. "I beg your pardon for the inconvenience, but I'm afraid I'll have to send you all back again. Master Fitzhugh? Kindly toss me that staff, will you? There's a good old gent!"

Fitzhugh went white.

"You've got my lantern."

"Come, come, Fitzhugh—" Radan said wearily.

"You've. Got. My. LANTERN!" Fitzhugh clenched the staff like he was trying to strangle it. Radan sighed and turned to me.

"Reason with him, Doctor, will you?"

I laid my hand on Fitzhugh's shoulder. I could feel him trembling with rage.

"Fitzhugh, old bloke?" I ventured.

"Aye."

"Fitzhugh, I'm sorry. You were right: I could have just opened his windpipe when I had the chance."

"Oh, for God's— Alright, then!" Radan snarled. "Just hold hands, all of you, and someone stand in that puddle." (He pointed with the blade.) "Let's get it over with.

"I was going to do this anyway," he added, half to himself.

In a flash Elizabeth's arm snaked through mine.

"*A-mach à seo!*"

There was a chime, high and penetrating.

Iona vanished.

CHAPTER 36

Doctor Scott's transcription—

Nota Bene—The manuscript resumes in a different ink here, and in a slightly different albeit similar hand. Looking back, the ink and the general tone most resemble the introductory note the author penned to his nephew at the commencement of John Blackjohn. *James McKenna concludes thus:*

There isn't much more to tell, Charlie. I knelt there in the mud in the stone circle on Tursahan Knowe while my heart broke and the rain fell. It was dark now, except for the two fairy glasses—Francis Stewart's and Friar Kol's—both glowing with a faint green light of their own. I turned Francis Stewart's over and over in my hand.

"Diana!" I sobbed. "Oh, Diana!"

I don't know how long I was there. Half the night, maybe. Francis Stewart was gone, and Lara too. Maybe the bancorra carried them away. I think Lara picked up the green blade of Esus from where I tossed it, for I never saw it again. I paid it no mind. I just sat there and hurt and hurt while the *Raven*'s yards made a ghostly creaking in the wind and the standing stones loomed over me.

At last the rain stopped and the moon came out. I found Friar Kol's old bag, and I put his bible in it (only it wasn't a bible any more). I threw it over my shoulder and stumbled off downhill, making for the road.

I walked all through the night and all the next day. There was a sickness in my heart. My only thought was to get to Hermitage Castle and ask where John was buried. But when I got to Hermitage your father John was alive, Charlie, and just being released. He was starving and feeble, but he was whole. I hugged him and cried, for John was the only brother I had in the world.

John and I made our way back to the old farm in Buckley. We found our broken mother—and you know the rest, Charlie. Francis Stewart never troubled us again. Sometimes we heard news of his mad plots against Prince James, or of his secret intrigues with the English. People said James put him on trial for witchcraft in North Berwick, and it was rumored Francis was lunatic and penniless when at last his estates were declared forfeit by the Scottish crown and he fled to France.

Father Lara never returned to Buckley either; another priest came. Some people in the village said Lara had forsaken the church and gone off fortune-telling, and others said he'd gone reiving with the lost men. But I never saw him more. I saw our farm come back to life, and in time I saw your good father wed to your mother Margaret (instead of taking orders[132]). You are the last of our line, Charlie, for I never married.

Not a day's gone by when I haven't thought of Diana.

I took up Friar Kol's book—this book you're reading now, Charlie—and I began to write about Diana in it, to soothe my aching heart. Kol's book got changed when it crossed over from the Other Side. It came back with copper plates and locks on it. All the words and all of Kol's beautiful pictures were lost. I wrote down everything I knew because my memories were beginning to fade; Fairyland, especially.

The middle part is locked with this old tooth, Charlie, which I've left you along with the book. I found the tooth set inside the lady's mouth on the first lock you come to between the pages. That lock opens and closes neatly, but the other one, Charlie—I never had a tooth for it. The lady's mouth on the back cover was empty when I found it. A blank plate lies here before me, but I dare not set it on the pins for fear it will lock itself by magic. I'll put that plate on when I'm finished, Charlie, and I'll scratch a note for you to cut through the pins if you must.

Four years went by, and I grew restless. Again and again I looked at Francis Stewart's fairy glass and thought about Diana.

Is she really inside? I wondered. *Could she still be alive? Could I use the Word of Esus to call her out?*

But I didn't dare, for fear that if I did Diana would immediately die. She was sorely wounded up on the knowe, Charlie. I don't think she was breathing

---

when I drew her blood—her immortal fairy blood—and used the Words of Conveyance to send her into the glass.

So I wore Francis Stewart's fairy glass on a string next to John Blackjohn's whale-gate key, and every day I thought of Diana and of Doonbridge.

On the day I saw your father married in Buckley Kirk I finally heard a rumor of the *Otter*. They said she was prowling the waters off Dunbar and Finn was her captain. I knew she must lie up in Berwick (to avoid Edinburgh) so I wished your father and your mother Margaret joy, and the next morning I set out before dawn.

True to my guess, I found the *Otter* lying close in shallow water. She was anchored in a cove among the rocks just south of the bay, half-hidden with her sails furled. I waded out and hailed her, and Finn (thank God!) still remembered me, though he'd lost all recollection of Doonbridge. Finn gave me a berth and I sailed as Second Mate. We shipped some wool from Aberdeen, but the *Otter* was too light for trade and we mostly made our living by smuggling.

After three years Finn was killed in a fight with English privateers. We laid him to rest at sea, and then the crew elected me Captain (for our Chief Mate was also killed). From that day forward I called myself Captain John Blackjohn, in Eoin mac Diarmid's memory.

Trade was better then. The *Otter* was the fastest brig on the Channel (with a charmed speed some said). Now we were carrying coin for merchants and letters for spies and deeds and bonds for the Crown. I came back to the farm often, Charlie, to help John buy land and to see how you were growing.

Twice—when I could afford to pay the crew—I searched the waters around Skye, looking for Doonbridge. Diana's memory haunted me. *If only I could bring her fairy glass to the Tveirrokk*, I thought, *or to Avalon. Marabreith or the dragon would know what to do.*

But we never found the secret village. On our last voyage I took ill with a burning fever and lay close to death, quaking on my bed while the *Otter* pitched and rolled in heavy seas. My heart was despairing and I did not wish to live. When we reached Dumbarton I said goodbye to the *Otter* forever. They bundled me into a cart, and thus I was carried—raving and delirious—all the way to Buckley.

I'm going to put a fairy glass *inside* a fairy glass, Charlie.

Diana's soul is in Francis Stewart's glass, and I know the Words of Conveyance. I'll hold a glass tight in each hand, and then I'll send both Diana and my own self into Friar Kol's glass. I'll wait there until such a time as Diana can be saved.

Or I'll wait there forever.

To you I leave Friar Kol's book, along with Kol's fairy glass with the whale-gate key. And this is my Last Will and Testament, Charlie: I bequeath them to you—book, glass, and key—in the hope that someday Doonbridge may be found.

It's midnight, Charlie. My candle burns low. Your mother and John are sleeping. The ice is getting thin between This Side and the Other.

Goodbye, my boy, and good luck. Take the green glass to Doonbridge, if you can. Or to Fairyland, if you dare. Save her, Charlie! Save Diana when you're grown.

And God save *you*, dear boy!

Your affectionate uncle,

—Capt. John Blackjohn

—Here ends The Last Will and Testament of the Pirate John Blackjohn—

CHAPTER 37

From the diary of Doctor Stewart Henry Scott—

At first everything was gray.

Then the light grew. Not out of any particular *place*, but everywhere, like a fog lifting. I didn't feel any ground under my feet—only Elizabeth still clutching my arm. But then solid shapes began to congeal out of the fog. Something vertical and slender—

A tree.

Then another. And another.

And then we were standing in an apple orchard under a clean blue sky— the deepest blue of autumn. Yellow leaves showed through the green. Ripe apples hung from every twig.

Among the trees a little stone fountain bubbled into a pool. Water-lilies were growing in it. A young woman—fifteen or maybe sixteen—was sitting on the rim of the pool, trailing her delicate white fingers in the water. Her clothes were threadbare and dirty and yet she was divinely beautiful. As we came nearer I could see her dress was burned through on the left side. Black ash still clung there. Her skin was deathly pale.

I nudged Elizabeth forward.

The girl looked up calmly, unafraid. "Who are you?" she asked. (Her voice was strange. Not *unkind*, no, nor challenging in any way, but frank. Oh, so frank! Like talking to a wild thing.)

Elizabeth looked a bit disconcerted but she forged ahead anyway. "Di— Diana?" she asked. "Is that your name, my dear? Diana?"

The girl nodded. I had the curious impression that, young though she looked, she was much, much older than me.

"Ah!" said Elizabeth brightly. "Good—" (She glanced around, evidently wondering what time of day it might be.) "—Good afternoon."

Diana bowed slightly.

"What brings you here?" Diana asked. Her voice was soft and low with a sort of chime in it.

"Oh, us?" Elizabeth dropped a quick curtsey. "Well I'm missus McRoy—" (she touched her bodice) "—and we're—ah—we two were just—"

Elizabeth stopped. She looked Diana over sympathetically.

"You're hurt, my dear," she said. "I've brought a doctor."

Elizabeth dragged me forward. I took off my hat.

"Doctor Scott, at your service."

Diana turned away and went back to trailing her fingers idly in the pool.

"It's too late," Diana said.

She touched her chest.

"I can't breathe. My heart has stopped beating."

"And me without any instruments!" I lamented, "or—or medicine or anything." (I was rummaging through my pockets.) "What the rotten deuce possessed me to let go my valise?"

Diana shook her head. "It doesn't matter," she said. "The shock went to my heart. It's broken."

Elizabeth clasped her hands. "*Do* lie down, love," she urged, "and let's at least have a try. Doctor Scott has come all the way from the Tveirrokk to find you."

Diana looked up sharply.

"*Did* you?"

"That I did!" I nodded vigorously. "Just got back from there. Spoke to Nile—*ahem!*—I spoke to Níðhöggr, that is. God of death, you know?"

Diana fixed me in a gaze like needles. "And what did he say?" she asked. Her voice betrayed a trace of surprise.

"Er—well—I don't entirely recall," I stammered. "I remember he taught me a little song. Silly sort of song. Can't imagine it would do any good singing—"

Diana was on her feet. She moved with an uncanny grace; not graceful like a swan, but graceful like a hummingbird. In one dart she was standing, and in another she was lying on the green turf beside the fountain. Her blue eyes stared up into the blue sky while the fallen leaves made a golden halo around her head. I knelt beside her and gently examined the burn.

"Lightning?" I asked.

Diana nodded.

"Something like lightning."

"Well now," I said in my usual bedside manner, "lightning *can* take any path through the human bod—through the *body*, that is."

"It went to my heart."

"And you say you can't breathe?"

Diana shook her head.

"Can you— I beg your pardon, my lady, but can you just *try* to breath once? Just so I can hear?"

Diana nodded. With some trepidation I gently laid my ear against her chest. It felt cold. (*Oh, to have an ear trumpet just now!* I muttered.)

Diana tried to draw a breath. Her chest rose a little, and then, *Ah!* she cried out in pain. Her chest fell again.

"Where did it hurt?"

"On the left side," Diana whispered, "and in my back."

I got up off the grass. "Collapsed lung, most likely," I said, putting on my hat. "Probably not too serious. But that stopped heart—I'm afraid we're past foxglove and I haven't got any—"

"Your song."

"I—I beg your pardon?" I stammered, not comprehending. Diana got up on her elbows and pinned me in her gaze again. "Your song," she repeated. "That song the god of death taught you. Sing it to me."

I reddened.

"I—I really haven't a voice. Maybe Elizabeth—"

Diana lay her head back on the grass and closed her eyes. "Men *don't* have a voice," she said. "That's alright. Sing it anyway."

So awkwardly I got down on my old knees, and awkwardly in my old quavering voice I sang to the beautiful immortal lady.

There were three brothers in bonnie Scotland
In bonnie Scotland livèd they—

Diana's eyes flashed open.

And they cuist kevels themsells amang—

Color rushed into her white cheeks. Her hand flew to her heart.

Wha sould gae rob—

"James!" Diana cried. She was on her feet, staring wildly around. "James! The mortal boy! Where is he?"

"He's alright, my dear." Elizabeth held her hand and patted it. "He's alright. We saw James McKenna not half an hour ago. Let's make certain you're more or less alive, and then we'll go and fetch him."

I was fluttering around Diana, frantically examining. "A pulse!" I cried. "I've found a pulse! It's faint, but it's steady. Can you breathe, Diana?"

Diana tried a breath. She winced, but her chest rose and fell.

"That's it!" I exulted. "That's the spirit! Keep at it. That lung will sort itself out by degrees. And now, Lady McCroy," (I took Elizabeth's arm) "I'm afraid we have an electrostatic solicitor to deal with."

"Yes, and I'm worried about Willie," said Elizabeth. "We must hurry back."

"Can you—how did you *get* us here, Lizzie?"

"No time for that!" said Elizabeth. "Niles taught me a song. Let's be off!"

More gray. More shapes materializing out *of* the gray (lumpy ones this time). And then Fitzhugh. He was standing on the rock with an easy air. His hat was off. His legs were crossed—

He was leaning on the pruning hook of Esus, grinning.

The *pruning hook* of Esus, I say, for the green blade was mounted on the staff now and it looked considerably smaller. As we came nearer I could see it had become curved like a sickle.

"Wh—where's Radan?" I asked in wonder.

336

Fitzhugh jerked his head toward the edge of the boulder.

I came closer and peered over.

Then I clapped my hand over my mouth, trying not retch. I waved Elizabeth back.

"You don't want to see this, Lizzie!"

Fitzhugh chuckled grimly.

"Looks like the old blade didn't fancy *him* much."

"Great—*Scott!*" I marveled, "I—I've never seen a man—seen a *creature*—so, so *burned!*"

"Aye," Fitzhugh straightened up and put his hat on, "once the blade was back on the staff it simply cut loose on him. You never saw such lightning! The blast of it knocked me over. I'm surprised there's any scrap of Mister Radan Esquire left at *all*."

"And how did the blade get back on the staff?" I demanded.

"It was Niles, he—"

"No time for that either!" Elizabeth interrupted. "Come, Stewart! We young folk still have to reunite these two ancient lovers!"

CHAPTER 38

From the diary of Doctor Stewart Henry Scott—

James McKenna (alive and breathing) and Diana, crown princess of Avalon, (equally alive and breathing) stood side-by-side with their arms clasped around each other's waists so tight you'd think each was afraid the other would suddenly take flight and vanish. Diana in the same burned dress (Elizabeth had draped her shawl over Diana for modesty's sake; *Keep it*, said Elizabeth, *as a wedding gift*)—Diana, I say, was laughing like a girl while tears streamed down her cheeks. She laughed, then she clutched her wounded side, then she laughed some more.

James was shaking my arm off and thanking me over and over again in his funny, old-fashioned Scots, and he said *Gin ye coom ta Avalon, och!—we'll mak ye sic a feste*[133](which I didn't understand at first). Diana kissed Elizabeth and Fitzhugh on each cheek and murmured blessings (I hope).

Last she came to me.

Diana stopped and looked me in the face. I simply stared at her like an idiot, transfixed by her otherworldly beauty.

"The *corran*," Diana said, reaching out her hand. Fitzhugh handed her the pruning hook.

"Kneel," Diana commanded.

I knelt.

Diana touched the blade to my shoulder. "Tho'art doubbit knycht." She touched the blade to my other shoulder. "I name thee—"

"Wemyss!" I whispered. "Sir Wemyss."

---

[133] Should you come to Avalon, oh!, we'll make you such a feast.

"I name thee Sir Wemyss." She touched the blade lightly to my forehead. "Rise, Sir Wemyss. Friend of Avalon. Foe of evil. Dana's champion."

I got up clumsily from my stiff old knees (Diana helped me) blubbering a bit and wiping my eyes.

"A knight!" Elizabeth whispered, gripping my hand. "A real knight!"

"I have no token to give you, my champion," said Diana. "Only this." She touched my heart.

"Your stars will guide you. We will all meet again on another island."

Then Diana took the pruning hook of Esus and drew a circle in the air. We all crowded around to have a look through. Beyond the door we could see a beautiful place like a garden. Apple trees were growing everywhere.

Diana gave the pruning hook back to Fitzhugh. "Return that to Lord Esus," she said, "when he comes for it."

Then with a last goodbye, James and Diana stepped through the door to Fairyland. James held Diana's hand, and Diana leaned her head ever-so-slightly on his shoulder. Their image shrank quickly, as if they had gone a great distance. Then the door closed and we stood there looking at each other.

Fitzhugh noisily cleared his throat.

"Bonny young bairns," he said with a cough. "Feels a bit lonely now, without them."

"Shall I go back for Radan's boots?" Fitzhugh asked.

I tried not to laugh, but did anyway. Fitzhugh was tramping up ahead of me. He was using the Crook of Esus for a walking-stick. The evening lights of Baile Mòr shone faintly in the distance.

"No, Fitzhugh," I returned, "I don't think it's any use going back this time. I doubt if even his shoe-leather survived. Pruning hook of Esus does a thorough job, doesn't it? How ever *did* you get the blade on the staff so quickly?"

Fitzhugh turned around and winked.

"Dragon taught me a song."

"Did he really?" I demanded. "When?"

"Ha ha—when you lot were snoring. Niles and I stayed up and had a merry old time. I don't believe he ever sleeps, truthfully."

"Death never does," I said. "Ask any doctor. But how's the song go? Let's hear it!"

"Er—" Fitzhugh hesitated—"I'm trying to remember—something like:

If men would be masters,
Then men must—master—mustard—

"—oh, I can't recall," he broke off, laughing. "Funny thing about that place. I hope you'll keep reminding me it wasn't just a dream."

"Oh, I'll be writing this all down," I said. "I wonder—how *did* Radan ever come across the blade of Esus in the first place?"

"Probably went poking around the Duke of Buckley's attic," Fitzhugh replied. "You never know what you'll find in these old houses. Ask any steward."

"Strange—" I mused. "Radan had the tooth, but *I* found the book. They must have gotten separated somehow. And yet he clearly knew *John Blackjohn* existed. Ah well!" I sighed, "Maybe Charlie McKenna left a Last Will and Testament of his own."

"Aye," Fitzhugh laughed, "that'll be your *next* holy grail, Sir Wemyss. And speaking of peers of the realm: where do you reckon we stand with the Duke of Buckley *now*, Stewart? D'you think there'll be a police inquest?"

"I—can't be sure," I said thoughtfully, "but I rather think there won *'t* be. I'd wager this whole pursuit was entirely Radan's doing. Frolic and detour."

"Well—" Fitzhugh puffed, scrambling up a rocky bank—"we won't know for sure until we get home. Unless you'd fancy living out here as an outlaw, Stewart."

I stopped and looked around.

A cold wind was blowing off the sea. Heavy clouds pressed down overhead. The wind wailed through the rocks and heather. Night had come on early.

"Is it July?" I demanded.

"Aye."

I put my head down and trudged on.

"No," I said, "no outlawry for me. Not here, anyway. I think I'd prefer the Bailey."

"If they lock you in the Bailey," Elizabeth trilled, "they'll have the Huntress to answer for it. You're her champion now."

I turned to Elizabeth and smiled.

"I rather think *you're* the true champion, Lady Wem—*ahem!*" I coughed violently.

I'd almost called Elizabeth 'Lady Wemyss.'

"And how—how did you spirit everyone in and out of those fairy glasses?" I said awkwardly. "Are you a sorceress?"

"Yes," Elizabeth returned archly. "Also, Niles taught me a song. But he hardly needed to. I'd guessed their secret already."

"What secret?" Fitzhugh and I cried at once.

Elizabeth smiled knowingly.

"Well the song goes—" She hesitated. "Well it doesn't translate very well into Souther—into *English*, I mean, but it goes something like:

One soul must enter,
One soul must depart,
But two souls knit in love may—

"—may come and go like—swallows," she finished, "Something like that."

"Swallows?"

"Yes! Like swallows! You know—swallows under the eaves. They build their nest. They raise their young. They pop in and out. That was the meaning."

"Two souls knit in love—" I said thoughtfully. "Was it really as simple as that?"

"*Simple!*" Elizabeth scoffed. "Two souls knit in love *simple*? Why, it's the rarest of things, Stewart!"

"Quite right!" I agreed. "Oh, you're entirely right."

I stopped short. Fitzhugh was out of sight over the rim of the bank. I turned to Elizabeth. She had her bonnet off and in her hand. Her long hair was done up behind, but the stray wisps caught the wind and played about her charming face. Elizabeth's eyes, I thought, were almost as bright as the immortal Dana's. There was a sort of light about her. It reminded me of the glow inside the little house on Tveirrokk: the quiet joy of safe and ordinary things.

"Elizabeth?" I asked.

She looked at me significantly. I took her hands in mine.

"Lizzie, I—"

"It's getting dark!" Fitzhugh shouted. "Are you lot ever coming?"

CHAPTER 39

From the writings of William Fitzhugh—

Branxholme – May 25, 1839

It seems patently unfair to me that I, William Fitzhugh, must take pen in hand to add my *Finis* to the strange tale of John Blackjohn. A year ago the irrepressible Doctor Scott thrust me out of a quiet life here at Branxholme and dragged me over every brae and briar in Scotland. And now, after so many dangers and discomforts, I must forsake my beloved fishing-tackle (which I've barely touched all this week) and sit in the dim library while the sun shineth merrily outside, and I must scrawl in my trembling, agèd hand (blasted pencil needs sharpening every third line), because Stewart and Lizzie are altogether preoccupied and can't be bothered—

Ergo—with a heavy heart, and with a longing glance at my fishing-rod:

There wasn't any inquest, to begin with.

The deaths of Albert Grey and of that ruffian Meeks were deemed an act of nature: an unlucky lightning-strike which cut short the lives of Doctor Grey and of his companion while the two were off fowling in the country. Lightning was said to have ignited the hayrick too, and thence the cottage, and the whole matter was quickly laid to rest.

Young Sir Walter Douglas-Scott, fifth Duke of Buckley, never pursued the matter of the old book which Stewart found at Hermitage. It seems Stewart's guess was right: the whole chase was probably Radan's from the beginning. Once the transcription was completed Stewart sent the old book (rather fanned-out and dogeared) back to the Duke in London post-haste, along with a very fine copy of his and Lizzie's manuscript in a neat leather dossier— for which offering Stewart got back a curt note from the duke's secretary saying His Lordship found the doctor's work "very interesting," and would "endeavor to read it when leisure permits."

As for Radan, his death didn't so much as make the papers. I know, because I searched every rag of a daily from John o' Groats to Penzance looking for it. I meant to take a clipping and frame it for the library, but alas!

On the fifteenth of October, 1838, Stewart Henry Scott and Elizabeth May McCroy *née* Fitzhugh were quietly married at Saint Mary's in Hawick. The little kirk is no cathedral (*I* thought Elizabeth deserved nothing short of Dalkeith), but I had already resumed my station just up the road as steward and sole gamekeeper of Branxholme Castle. In August His Lordship (*per viam* the same secretary) renewed my position on more favorable terms for an indefinite duration.

The weather was uncommonly fine that October: bright and dry and warm, and all the trees like fireworks. I "gave Lizzie away" with a light heart. She and Stewart had been mooning about like a pair of schoolchildren for weeks, and it was getting more and more preposterous pretending not to notice. They had their honeymoon in Guernsey, and I asked why they didn't just fly to Fairyland (given Stewart still had the key). He replied that maybe they *would* someday, but just then he wasn't going back to the whale gate on Iona for love nor money. Stewart said dear old Midgard was good enough for him, and then he squeezed my shoulder and said "I would miss you too much," and it was ratherish awkward for a minute or two before Lizzie breezed in.

There's only one small thing left to tell.

This very spring, when the lilacs were just blooming, a little man came crunching up the drive. I'd never laid eyes on him before. He was on foot, bareheaded and dressed all in green. His face was brown and weathered and it was hard to guess his age. His cheeks were wrinkled, but his eyes were bright as stars and his unkempt hair and bushy beard were as red as a maple in autumn.

Without so much as knocking on the door he came round the side of the old house to where I was working and he marched straight up to me. "Willie, my lad," says he, "I've come for my pruning hook." His voice was deep and pleasant (with a bit of a brogue, like my old gran-da'). I was too astonished to speak, so I simply went to the tool shed and fetched him the ancient pruning hook. (I'd been using it on the apricots. It was a right worthy hook. Slid through the limbs like they were cheese.)

So I gave it to him. "Thank'ee," says he, "and how are Lord and Lady Wemyss getting on?" I knew he meant Stewart and Lizzie.

"They're merry as swallows," says I.

He laughed a rich, earthy laugh. "Tell them I wish them joy," says he, "and mind those apricots! There's to be another frost." And then he tramps off again without another word, pruning hook in hand. I saw him go around the bend in the lane, and then he was gone.

It's nearly dusk now. The mayflies have hatched and the trout will be biting. Stewart and Lizzie are visiting from Edinburgh. There's bread baking in the kitchen. I've burnt two whole candles sitting here and I'll burn no more!

So while the day lasts, like the apostle of old—

I go a-fishing.

Made in the USA
Las Vegas, NV
08 January 2022

40849510R00204